2012 – THE SECRET OF THE CRYSTAL SKULL

Chris Morton & Ceri Louise Thomas are independent filmmakers and environmental campaigners as well as authors and screenwriters. They have each spent many years working in television, mostly for the BBC and Channel Four.

Morton and Thomas began their research into the real-life crystal skulls and the culture and prophecies of the ancient Maya over 13 years ago. Their original research led to their highly acclaimed BBC/A&E documentary on the subject, and to their best-selling factual book 'The Mystery of the Crystal Skulls'.

This book has sold more than 100,000 copies so far, been translated into over 15 languages, and recently inspired the latest Indiana Jones movie on the subject – not to mention the latest Hollywood blockbuster '2012'.

For further information about the authors please visit the website:
www.2012thesecretofthecrystalskull.com

What the critics said about the authors' last book
'The Mystery of the Crystal Skulls':

First published by O Books, 2009
O Books is an imprint of John Hunt Publishing Ltd., The Bothy, Deershot Lodge, Park Lane, Ropley, Hants,
SO24 0BE, UK
office1@o-books.net
www.o-books.net

Distribution in:

UK and Europe
Orca Book Services
orders@orcabookservices.co.uk
Tel: 01202 665432 Fax: 01202 666219
Int. code (44)

USA and Canada
NBN
custserv@nbnbooks.com
Tel: 1 800 462 6420 Fax: 1 800 338 4550

Australia and New Zealand
Brumby Books
sales@brumbybooks.com.au
Tel: 61 3 9761 5535 Fax: 61 3 9761 7095

Far East (offices in Singapore, Thailand,
Hong Kong, Taiwan)
Pansing Distribution Pte Ltd
kemal@pansing.com
Tel: 65 6319 9939 Fax: 65 6462 5761

South Africa
Stephan Phillips (pty) Ltd
Email: orders@stephanphillips.com
Tel: 27 21 4489839 Telefax: 27 21 4479879

Text copyright Chris Morton & Ceri Louise Thomas 2009

Design: Stuart Davies

ISBN: 978 1 84694 346 1

A CIP catalogue record for this book is available from
the British Library.

This novel is entirely a work of fiction. The names, characters and incidents in it are the work of the
authors' imaginations. Any resemblance to actual persons, living or dead, or to real companies,
organisations, events or localities is entirely coincidental.

Printed by Digital Book Print

O Books operates a distinctive and ethical publishing philosophy in all
areas of its business, from its global network of authors to production
and worldwide distribution.

2012
The Secret Of
The Crystal Skull

Chris Morton

&

Ceri Louise Thomas

BOOKS

Winchester, UK
Washington, USA

Author's Note

'2012 – The Secret of the Crystal Skull' is a work of fiction. However, most of the information contained within this book about the crystal skulls, and the culture and prophecies of the ancient Maya is either entirely factual, or at least based on the facts.

In particular, the Mayan prophecy for 2012 is based on the real-life Mayan prophecy for that year, as outlined in the Mayan's prophetic book, *'The Chilam Balam of Tizimin'*, and all the significant dates given in our book are based on the actual workings and predictions of the real ancient Mayan calendar.

Footnote on further background to this book

This book actually began life as a screenplay, the first draft of which was completed as long ago as 2002. Over the next few years this screenplay was widely circulated amongst some of Hollywood's top agents and producers, although 'technically' the film 'never went into production'. So we decided to re-imagine the story and adapt it into a novel – the results of which you are, hopefully, about to read.

We do hope you enjoy the results of our efforts and that this book will help you to see the world in a whole new light.

Indeed, you might also gain a greater insight along the way into precisely how Hollywood comes up with some of its biggest ideas.

So read on, enjoy, and may your life be changed by the experience!

Chris Morton & Ceri Louise Thomas.

Acknowledgements:

We would like to thank John Hunt, Catherine Harris and the rest of the team at O-Books publishing for believing in this project, together with Lizzie Hutchins our copy editor, Mike Morton and Alastair Chadwin for their sound editorial advice.

To the hundreds of people who have helped us with our research over the years, from the staff of the British Museum and the Smithsonian Institution, to the Instituto Nacional de Archaeologia y Historia (Mexico), and their counterparts in Guatemala. Also to Prof. Michael D. Coe at Yale University, and Prof. Karl Taube and Dr. John Pohl at UCLA for their expert advice on all things ancient Mayan. To the team at Hewlett-Packard for their scientific tests on the real-life crystal skull. To Nic and Khrys Nocerino, JoAnn and Karl Parks, and Anna Mitchell-Hedges for their knowledge of the crystal skulls, and to Jamie Sams and Paula Gunn-Allen for their insights into native American culture. Also to Senor Don Alejandro Cirilo Oxlaj Perez and the Confederation of Indigenous Elders and Priests of America for their practical insight into real-life shamanism and the culture of the contemporary Maya.

And last but not least, a big thank-you to our parents, friends and siblings for their vital encouragement, support and feedback throughout the long process of writing, and above all to our wonderful children, Gabriel and Noah, for allowing us the 'time out' to finish this book.

THIS BOOK IS DEDICATED TO
GABRIEL AND NOAH,
AND TO THE MEMORY OF ANGEL

Preface:

The ancient Maya of Central America prophesied that one day soon, the world will come to an end.

In fact they predicted precisely when.

But their prophecies also foretell that before that time arrives, a messenger will be sent to try to save the people of this Earth.

The question is whether humanity will heed this warning, before it is too late...

Chapter 1

Smithton Geographic Museum
New York
December 1st 2012

The clock struck midnight. Laura stared at the ancient, carved stone that lay on the old wooden desk in front of her. By the light of her study lamp, the strange figures etched deep into its worn limestone surface seemed almost to dance before her. She rubbed her eyes. It was late. She was tired and ought to be getting home.

One last time, she allowed her fingers to trace the carved outline of one of the inscriptions, when suddenly it clicked. She'd got it! She had finally figured it out. She had been puzzling over these hieroglyphs for days, and now she understood the meaning of the first glyph.

It said, *'It is written'*.

She felt a rising sense of excitement as she moved to the next inscription. This time, she got it almost immediately.

It read - *'in the cycles of time'*.

This was it. These were the moments Laura Shepherd lived for, when it all made sense. When she could understand what those who lived over a thousand years ago were trying to say. She had known this stone was important. It was the largest of its kind she had ever seen, and now she knew why. It was clearly an ancient Mayan prophecy stone carved with a prediction about the future, and she had just decoded the first of two concentric rings of glyphs.

The hieroglyphs said *'It is written... in the cycles of time... that...'*

Laura sat back in her chair and gazed at the huge semi-circular chunk of stone in deep satisfaction. It had been worth leaving Cambridge and the country of her birth just for this.

But her heart sank as she turned her attention to the remaining glyphs. Most of them were so eroded they would be difficult, perhaps even impossible, to translate. *What did the rest of the stone say? What were the ancient Maya trying to tell us about the future?* It seemed she might never know.

She reached for her coffee. It had gone cold. That's when she heard a strange noise that startled her out of her thoughts. It was an eerie sound, like someone whispering, or chanting, in some unknown foreign tongue –

'*oxlahun baktun, mi katun, mi tun, mi kin, oxlahun baktun, mi katun, mi tun, mi kin*'.

She looked up and the sound stopped. Thinking she had imagined it, she returned her attention to the stone when it started again. The sound seemed to be coming from the corridor outside her oak-panelled office.

Laura started to feel uneasy. *Who else could be in the museum at this hour of the night?* Jacob, the night porter, had told her less than an hour ago that he was settling in to watch a late night movie in his booth, so it wasn't likely to be him. Surely he couldn't have the volume up so high she could hear it in her room? So she crept over to the door and listened from behind the frosted glass, but she couldn't work it out.

Opening the door, she peered out into the corridor. It took a few moments for her eyes to adjust to the dark, but there was nobody there. All she could see was the jagged reflection of the museum security lights on the polished linoleum floor.

She called out 'Hello?'

Her voice echoed along the dark corridor.

There was no reply.

The sound seemed to be coming from the stairwell, so she ventured out carefully along the hallway and leaned over the edge of the twisted brass banisters. Down the curvilinear sweep of the grand marble staircase a pale light was shining from the corridor immediately below.

'Is there anybody there?' she shouted, and the whispering suddenly stopped.

Cautiously, Laura began to descend the stairs, when she thought she heard a muffled thud coming from the lower corridor, followed by silence. Her heart began to quicken.

Reaching the bottom of the steps, she peered around the corner. There was no sign of anyone, only a shaft of light emanating from behind one of the frosted glass doorways further along the hall.

Warily, she made her way along the dark passageway and approached the door. It stood slightly ajar. Its window was embossed with the letters 'Dr. R. Smith'.

'Hello?' she enquired, her voice filled with apprehension. There was no answer.

Laura's heart was pounding in her chest as she raised her hand and knocked. The door creaked open a few more inches, and stopped.

2

Still no reply.

So she took a deep breath, and pushed the door wide open. She reeled back in shock at what she saw inside.

There, slumped face down on top of his desk was the body of a middle-aged man. He lay ashen-faced and motionless. It was her colleague Dr. Ron Smith and he did not appear to be breathing.

'Ron!' cried Laura as she ran to his aid. She shook him by the shoulders but he did not move.

'Ron Smith!' she shouted. She was frantic now. She slapped his face and shook him as hard as she could but he was a dead weight and still he did not respond.

That's when she noticed he was clutching something, holding onto it so tightly his knuckles were white. As she shook him violently it fell from his fingers. It was a large crystalline object that rolled slowly across the desk before it came to rest right in front of her. She paused in her resuscitation attempts and gazed at it in horror.

There, staring up at her was the face of a skull. A skull of solid crystal.

She stared at it, as if mesmerized, for what seemed like an eternity.

Then, pulling herself together, she grabbed Ron's phone, and called the emergency services...

Chapter 2

Before Laura knew it, the room was bustling with police officers and forensic experts, all dusting for fingerprints, removing objects and papers, and sealing them into transparent plastic bags. Laura stood and watched as the police photographer took a series of flash photos of Ron's pale, lifeless body.

Detective Frank J. Dominguez was a big black man who had the assurance of someone who had spent many years in the force. He leaned over the body, inspecting it carefully from different angles.

'So you heard some kinda whispering' he said, eyeing Laura with suspicion, 'You went downstairs to investigate. And this is exactly the way you found him. Is that right Dr Shepherd?' he asked in his deep gravel voice, a voice that seemed to have grown rough from a lifetime working the streets.

'Y... Yes' answered Laura hesitantly, numb with shock as she gazed at Ron Smith, his body still slumped on top of his desk. She was finding it hard to reconcile that the person now lying dead in front of her was the same Ron Smith that had given her such a beaming smile in the canteen earlier that afternoon, the same Ron Smith who wore those dreadful sweaters and always went to Cape Cod on holiday every year.

A junior police officer came in to speak to the detective.

'We've searched the whole building, but there's no sign of anyone who shouldn't be here, sir.'

Detective Dominguez nodded before turning back to Laura.

'So you're telling me he's worked here ever since you started, and yet you hardly knew him?'

Laura felt the accusatory edge to his tone.

'Yes, Ron is... I mean was...' she corrected herself, 'someone who kept very much to himself'.

'Mmmm. Is that so?' Dominguez glanced at Ron's corpse with indifference. He'd seen too much of this sort of thing to get upset about it.

'Now let me get this straight...' He turned back to Laura and fixed her gaze. 'You're both... What is it?...' He flicked back through his notebook to find the right page,'...Ancient Mayan experts, and yet you have no idea what Dr Smith was working on before he died?'

He sounded as if he didn't like 'experts' in anything very much.

'That's right' replied Laura, sounding a little over-defensive, 'We all have our own very specific areas of expertise. I'm the hieroglyph specialist and Ron worked more on the anthropology side of things'.

'Is that a fact?' said Dominguez. *Huh! Eggheads in museums,* he thought to himself. He couldn't think of any other business where two people could be doing almost the same job and not know what each other was up to. But it seemed strange to him that these two Mayan specialists should be the only people in the museum after midnight, and now one of them was dead.

Laura was trying to explain 'Ron took over all the field work a few years ago when my job became more office bound.'

'Oh, really? Why was that?'

'I had... family commitments,' she replied.

Her hand rose to touch the little silver heart-shaped locket she wore around her neck.

'And you're not aware of anyone who had any kinda grudge against him, or didn't seem to like him?' asked Dominquez, casually nodding in the general direction of the body.

'No, not Ron,' she answered, 'He was a gentle, quiet soul'.

'How about anything or anyone that might have been bothering him, any strangers hanging around asking about him, or anything else out of the ordinary?' The detective rattled off his list of standard questions with palpable boredom.

Laura shook her head.

It chilled her to think Ron might have been murdered. *He can't have been,* she kept telling herself. But she *had* heard voices outside her door. *There must have been someone else in the museum. Yet why would anyone want to kill Ron?*

'And, as far as you're aware, he wasn't having any financial difficulties, health issues, family problems or anything?'

'Not as far as I know,' replied Laura, 'although his wife died a few years ago, of cancer'.

All around her Ron's things were being collected up, bagged and labelled.

'And do you have any idea what this is?' The detective was pointing at the mysterious object lying on Ron's desk.

'No. I've never seen anything like it'.

Laura stared at the strange object that had rolled out of the dead man's hands towards her just a short while before. It sent a shiver down her spine as she remembered. It was the same size and shape as a real human skull, but it was made from a transparent material that looked like solid crystal.

'But he was holding it when I found him.' she added.

'You're sure?' enquired the detective.

'Absolutely, it rolled out of his fingers when I shook him.'

'OK' said Dominguez, turning to his men, 'Exhibit A guys!'

Laura watched as the police photographer took several close-up flash photos of the skull before two surgeon-gloved forensics came forward, picked it up carefully, sealed it into a box, labelled it, and carted it off.

As a couple of paramedics arrived with a hospital stretcher, Detective Dominguez suggested gently to Laura,

'You may wish to go now. This may not be very pretty'.

'No. That's OK.' She heard herself say. She felt strangely detached, as if the whole experience were happening to someone else.

As the paramedics began to manoeuvre Ron's body back up off the desk, the detective spotted something that had been lying hidden underneath Ron's slumped torso.

'What the hell?' he exclaimed.

Laura leaned nearer to see what it was.

A hastily scrawled handwritten note was lying on the desktop. Laura recognised the handwriting. It was Ron's final note. It read simply:

'I have seen the future...'

Chapter 3

Outside, an ambulance and a row of police vehicles were parked, lights flashing, at the bottom of the museum steps. A dark haired and driven forty-year old man dashed up the steps, between the giant pillars, and into the main entrance of the grand neo-classical building.

There was only one thing on his mind as he raced across the ornate marble foyer to where a handful of police officers and a museum attendant were guarding the public turnstiles.

'I'm sorry sir, you can't go in there!' a policewoman raised her voice as she halted him. He ran his fingers through his hair in frustration. It was Laura's husband Michael. He'd got to the museum as soon as he could. All he wanted was to get to his wife, to know that she was OK.

Beyond the gates the elevator doors opened and he could see the paramedics wheeling Ron's dead body on a stretcher towards him. Behind them he glimpsed Laura, surrounded by a group of police officers, as she made her way towards the exit. Beneath her long blonde curls, her chiselled face was pale, drained with shock. She looked so frail, so vulnerable.

As she came through the turnstile he rushed over and embraced her. 'Laura, are you alright?'

She didn't answer. Her pale green eyes were transfixed on the stretcher as it was wheeled towards the doors.

'Five minutes earlier and I could have saved him.' She sounded forlorn.

'You don't know that.' He said more firmly than he intended. 'And what if he was, you know, attacked? If you had got there any earlier, where would *you* be now?'

Exiting the museum, they stood outside the enormous wooden entrance doors watching the paramedics negotiating Ron's body down the steep steps, illuminated by the flashing red and blue lights of the emergency vehicles gathered below.

'I just wish there was more I could have done,' said Laura as much to herself as to Michael.

'I'm sure you did everything you could,' he tried to reassure her, wrapping his thick coat around her shoulders.

'It doesn't feel that way.' She began the descent.

'Maybe it was suicide?' said Michael after a moment's pause. He was trying hard to think of anything that might make her feel better, something to stop her feeling so horribly responsible.

'I suppose that's possible.' Laura became preoccupied, thinking about the note Ron had left: *'I have seen the future...'* *It certainly looked like a suicide note. But what had Ron seen? What vision of the future could possibly have been so terrifying as to make him take his own life?* She shuddered to think.

A chill wind blew as the paramedics loaded Ron's stretcher into the back of the ambulance.

Michael looked at his wife, his handsome features creased with concern. He had an awful, ominous feeling. They had spent so many years trying carefully to rebuild their shattered lives, and now he feared that finding Ron's dead body was about to tear Laura's fragile world apart.

Chapter 4

December 4th 2012

Professor Lamb, Director of the Smithton Geographic Museum, was a short man with a neat beard, tweed suit and a high-pitched voice. A breakthrough on the population migrations of the late Palaeolithic era and a winning way with wealthy patrons had aided him in a seamless and apparently effortless rise to his high position in the academic world.

To be honest, Laura thought he was a bit of a creep and suspected that he might have been a serious groper in the days when professors could still get away with that sort of thing.

But even his superficial charm was absent as he and Laura entered the police precinct, a shabby grey 1960s concrete block in downtown New York, and took the lift to the fourth floor.

'I'm sure the police will have got to the bottom of it by now.' he said confidently.

'Let's hope so,' replied Laura. She didn't want to contradict her boss, but she wasn't so sure. It had been three days since Ron died, but it still felt only minutes since she had found him. Her nights had been disturbed by the memory, her dreams filled with the vision of his slumped, lifeless body ever since. There was her colleague, the quiet, diligent, Ron Smith, lying dead and alone in his room. It had been increasingly difficult for her to concentrate at work, her mind unable to stop endlessly searching for the reason why he died.

It probably was suicide. It's that time of year, she told herself as she took off her winter gloves. It was less than a month till Christmas. Laura had heard somewhere that suicide rates soar during this period. Apparently it is a time of year when the gap between the painful reality of how life is and how people would like it to be can be so overwhelming that some people see little point in going on. *Ron had lost his wife Lillian. Perhaps he couldn't face another Christmas alone? Maybe the future he saw was just too bleak without her?*

Yet something about the idea of Ron committing suicide didn't add up. It certainly didn't explain why Ron had seemed so happy the last few times she had seen him, far happier than he had been since his loss several years before.

'Take a seat!' said Detective Dominguez. His voice sounded deeper than ever, as Laura and Lamb entered his office through a glass door marked 'Homicide'. He closed the door behind them and sat down behind his desk, 'And sorry about the noise. Things are always a bit crazy around here.'

Even with the door closed, the detective's office could not be insulated from the maelstrom going on outside, its glass walls unable to protect it from the constant bustle and chatter of the busy police department all around.

Detective Dominguez had a heavy cold and was in no mood for further small talk. 'OK!' he said picking up the forensic report from the desk in front of him. Labelled 'Dr Ronald D. Smith – Deceased' he began reading straight from it, without any attempt at a gentle introduction,

'No sign of any gunshot or knife wounds, no sign of any bruising, no evidence to suggest strangulation, suffocation, or any other physical assault on the body'.

He looked up at Laura, 'So you'll be glad to hear we're ruling out murder'.

Laura was relieved. She hadn't realized quite how much that thought had been bothering her until now.

Dominguez blew his nose and continued. 'As for suicide, there's no sign of hanging or any other self-inflicted injury, no evidence of toxins, pills, alcohol, drugs of any kind. Not even a trace of anti-depressants in his blood stream.'

Just as Laura had thought, Ron's recent happiness wasn't due to medication. It was as if a grey cloud over him had been lifted. Not that Ron said much, he never had. But when he had smiled at her the other day, just before he died, it was as if he was smiling inside as well as out. No antidepressants on the market could make you smile that way.

'So if it was suicide,' continued Dominguez, 'then we have no idea how he did it, or why?'

Laura was puzzled. It didn't seem to add up. While the police couldn't rule out the possibility of suicide, she was as baffled as them as to how Ron might have done it, or for that matter why? After all, he had seemed so unusually happy just before he died.

So maybe he died of natural causes? Laura wondered, when the detective added, 'Stranger still, Dr Smith's medical records show he was in perfect physical health. I mean this guy only ever went to the doctors for his annual check up for his medical insurance. Turns out he did that only the other week and was given a totally clean bill of health. The doctors could find nothing wrong with him'.

He looked at Laura askance, before picking up another document. 'Post-mortem too... No evidence of any heart attack or other organ failure'.

So that didn't add up either.

He put down the post-mortem report and looked Laura straight in the eye.

'So what we have here is a mystery' he announced.

'What about the note he left?' inquired Laura, ''I have seen the future...'? What do you think that's about? What do you think he saw?'

Detective Dominguez just shrugged his shoulders and blew his nose, 'Who knows? Maybe it's just a coincidence?'

Laura wasn't convinced.

'And what about the skull?' asked Professor Lamb. That was the main reason he had joined Laura at the precinct.

'Now there's another mystery,' replied Dominguez. 'Our guys have been all over that thing and can find no trace of any fingerprints on it, not even Dr Smith's!' He turned back to Laura. 'You're sure he was holding it?'

'Absolutely,' she nodded.

'And you're sure you didn't just wipe down your fingerprints after you'd coshed him over the head with it?'

He put his handkerchief away in his pocket and stared at her.

Laura was taken aback. Was Dominguez seriously suggesting she had murdered Ron? But the curl of his lips soon told her this was the kind of comment that passed for humour in his world.

'Only kidding, Dr Shepherd. Cop humour,' he confirmed.

Laura was not at all amused as he continued, 'Don't worry, you're in the clear'.

He flicked his wrist.

'In fact, there's no evidence to suggest *anyone* else was involved.' He blew his nose again.

'So as far as we're concerned, it's case closed.'

Laura was dismayed that the police had reached such a rapid conclusion to their investigations. It didn't seem right. *That was Ron Smith's life*, she thought, all over and wrapped up without any real explanation. The police inquest hadn't even begun to answer the question of how Ron had died, never mind why. It seemed such an undignified, unsatisfactory end to a whole lifetime's existence.

'Surely there must be *something* else you can do to find out what happened to him?' she insisted.

'What's the point?' Dominguez shrugged his shoulders again and opened his palms 'There are no suspicious circumstances.'

That wasn't quite the way Laura saw it, but the only thing the detective appeared concerned about was getting Ron's things sent quickly back to the museum. As Ron had 'no surviving relatives to take even his most personal effects', he seemed keen simply to wash his hands of the whole affair.

Chapter 5

'Terrible business this whole thing.' muttered Professor Lamb, dusting the lapel of his tweed jacket, as he re-joined Laura at the top of the museum elevators and they marched down the corridor towards her office. His English accent was even more pronounced than Laura's.

'Yes,' she agreed, 'it's sad to think Ron's not going to be around anymore'.

'Mmm...' said Lamb, clearing his throat, 'But aren't you curious about that skull?'

Laura shuddered as she remembered the crystal skull rolling across Ron's desk, its grotesque features seeming to grin up at her as she had grappled with the realization that Ron was dead. The full horror of finding Ron was with her again, as vivid as it had been the moment she found him. She was still in shock. She would be more than happy never to set eyes on that skull again.

Lamb was still waiting for her response.

'I saw all I needed to of that thing in Ron's office,' she replied as she opened the door.

As she entered her room, Laura felt relieved to be returning to her hieroglyphs. She looked around at her office; the table with its neat row of artefacts she had been cataloguing, the academic paper she was writing, the plant Michael had given her, growing like a jungle creeper up the bookcase. It was a familiar world, a safe world, and that was where she wanted to be. She didn't want to have to deal with Ron's death. It was over. There was nothing more she could do. She wanted to put it all behind her now. Her work would help with that.

'You know something Laura? You always used to enjoy a challenge.' said Professor Lamb, with an air of contrived casualness. Laura turned round to see that he had followed her into her room and his attention was now fixed on a photograph on her office wall. It was a picture, taken ten years earlier, of Laura emerging from a cave dressed in full scuba-diving gear, triumphantly holding aloft an ancient funerary vase.

Laura wondered what he was driving at. It had been a long time since she had explored underwater passageways in search of hidden artefacts, or felt the searing heat of tropical sunshine as she sifted through the dirt to retrieve lost treasures from another time. Now her excitement came in the form of the decoding work she did.

'Well right now I've got all the challenges I need trying to translate these hieroglyphs' she said, indicating the huge slab of stone on her desk.

As she moved round behind it, her eyes fell on something else which had been placed right in the middle of her personal workspace. It was a cardboard box, labelled

'NYPD – Property of Dr. Ronald Smith – Deceased.'

She looked in the box to see stacks of folders and files, all neatly labelled by Ron Smith. It looked as if the police had sent some of his possessions back already. But what were they doing on her desk? 'Ron's things!?' she exclaimed.

'Yes, Laura,' answered Lamb, 'The Museum's Board of Trustees wants a full enquiry. They want answers. And as the police have failed so miserably in this respect, I need you to provide them.'

Laura gave him a quizzical frown.

'We just need you to go through Ron's things,' he continued smoothly, 'See what you can come up with. See if you can find out anything about that skull.'

Laura was appalled. The thought of looking any further into the skull and the circumstances surrounding Ron's death filled her with dread. Not only that, she was convinced she was close to cracking the rest of the cryptic hieroglyphs she had been translating.

'But this is the largest and most elaborate Mayan prophecy stone I have ever seen...'

She tried to explain, but Lamb interrupted her, 'Laura, we're going to need you to be a team player on this one. We're not having one of our people dying and having nothing to show for their last few years with us.'

'But Professor Lamb, I've already managed to decipher the first ring,' she pleaded, 'My job is to find and decode the rest of this.'

Lamb was losing his patience, 'With respect Laura, your job is to do whatever I and the Board of Trustees tell you to do.'

Laura fell silent as he asserted himself.

'And both the Board and I want to know what that skull is, where the hell it came from, and what on God's Earth Ron Smith was doing with it when he died'.

'But...' she tried to protest again before Lamb added,

'Besides which, I think we owe it to Ron, don't you?'

Laura was left speechless.

'I want that report, in full, on my desk, by this time next week, at the latest.' He snapped, straightened his tie, and left the room.

Chapter 6

Laura let out a deep sigh as the door closed firmly behind Professor Lamb. She resented having to investigate the crystal skull instead of getting on with her real work. It's not that Laura didn't care about Ron, she did, but she just couldn't see what *she* was supposed to be able to find out about Ron's death, if even the police couldn't get to the bottom of it.

The ancient Maya of Central America were her area of expertise, and she didn't want anything to take her away from the important task she had set herself of attempting to translate the mysterious Mayan prophecy stone.

She gazed ruefully at the huge semi-circular chunk of bone-white limestone that lay on her desk. The stone had been fascinating her for weeks, ever since it had been seized by customs and handed over to the museum. It was hard to explain, but Laura felt she was onto something with this stone. She had never before seen a Mayan carving of quite such magnitude or with quite the same level of intricacy in the design of its glyphs. Secretly, she hoped the stone might provide answers to some of the questions she still had about the ancient Maya, a civilisation about which so few of the key facts were known.

Not that Professor Lamb would appreciate any of that, she thought. *He's always been more interested in his own office politics than in the rise and fall of ancient civilisations. I don't know why he bothers working in a museum at all. He might as well work in a paper clip factory,* she found herself carping inside.

You see, to Laura, Mayan hieroglyphs were more than just writing. They were works of art that conveyed the deep philosophical understanding the Maya had of their world and their place in the universe. There was a richness to their way of seeing things that had appealed to Laura ever since she first came across their remarkable ancient culture.

Her fascination with the ancient Maya actually began when she was only a child. On holiday with her parents, in Central America, they had taken her to visit the ancient Mayan ruins of Tikal in Guatemala. There, she had gazed up at the giant pyramids that rose from the jungle floor right up above the treetops. She had been captivated by the Mayan's elaborate artworks, their mysterious gods, sombre kings, astronomer-priests, and sacred animals. Even as an eight year old child, as she looked at their hiero-glyphic writing she felt that these ancient people had knowledge that we had lost, or somehow forgotten.

So, as soon as she turned eighteen, she decided to undertake a degree in archaeology, specialising in Mayan studies. Of course her father was disappointed that she had not chosen to follow him into the legal profession, believing that Laura had all the qualities necessary to become a successful commercial lawyer like himself. But those ancient stones had spoken to her soul and she felt compelled to study them further.

By now, of course, Laura had discovered that the ancient Maya built one of the most advanced, and enigmatic civilisations the world has ever known - a civilisation that appeared as if from nowhere, already highly developed, even before the time of Christ.

They built vast cities complete with temples, palaces, and pyramids deep in the middle of the rainforest and reached extraordinary heights of artistic and scientific achievement. They built pedestrian roads, had a sophisticated mathematical system, that included inventing the concept of zero, and possessed a complex calendar even more scientifically accurate than our own. Based on the actual movements of the planets and the stars, they used this calendar to make the most stunningly accurate predictions, many of which have now come true.

And then around 890 AD the Classic Maya mysteriously disappeared, for reasons that remain unknown even to this day. All at once they abandoned their great cities leaving them to be taken over again by the rainforest. It remains a source of great controversy amongst archaeologists; where did the Maya came from, where did they get their advanced knowledge, and why did their civilisation so suddenly collapse and disappear?

This was why the prophecy stone now sitting on Laura's desk seemed so important to her. She hoped it might provide an insight into what the Maya believed the future held. For all she knew it might even answer the mystery of why their civilisation vanished.

As Laura gazed at the stone again, it struck her as strange that it was on the night Ron died she had achieved her big breakthrough. That was when she had translated the outermost of the two surviving rings of glyphs.

Her finger retraced the outline of the first inscription. It was an image of the monkey god, the ancient Mayan god of writing, and the curl of its tail meant it was in the present, impersonal tense. So the first glyph said 'It is written'.

The next glyph was a spiral symbol, a pictogram for the movement of the planets and stars as they moved through the universe, which to the ancient ones who carved it, represented *'the cycles of time'*. It was followed by a linking glyph. So the first three glyphs together read: *'It is written... in the cycles of time... that...'*

But the rest of it remained a mystery. The next ring of glyphs was so eroded she was having difficulty working out what they said.

From her knowledge of ancient Mayan texts, she could see that most of the symbols used were what are called 'head-variant' hieroglyphs, like the image of the monkey god's head. That meant this was a sacred text, particularly important to those who carved it. Those who wrote it would have been high ranking shaman priests. Only those with knowledge of the sacred realms would have been allowed to create such works. Laura wondered what secrets they had carved into this ancient surface.

If only I could translate these eroded glyphs, she thought.

But then of course there was the added enigma that even if she could translate all of the remaining glyphs, she did not have the whole piece of stone. She could see all too clearly that the stone was broken beneath the second ring of glyphs and a large chunk of it was missing completely, so there were other hieroglyphs that would remain unknown. She would not be able to translate the whole thing unless she could find the rest of the stone, and heaven only knew where it had come from. Its origins were shrouded in mystery, to say the least.

The type of glyphs used indicated it was early Mayan, dating it to sometime before 200 BC, and their ornate style was characteristic of the eastern coast of the ancient Mayan empire, what would now be the Caribbean coast of Mexico, Honduras, or Belize, but the precise origins of the piece remained unknown.

All Laura knew was that it had been seized from a Filipino-registered ship that had tried to dock in New York harbour. The ship had no papers to show where it had really come from or where it was going, or to authorize the transportation of 'an artwork of great antiquity', or for that matter any of the other mass of contraband cargo on board. It was, effectively, a modern-day pirate ship.

As apparently none of the crew could speak a word of English they had been unable to help the customs officers with their enquiries. Even with a team of translators covering a whole range of their suspected native tongues, it seems that none of the crew knew where their cargo of illicit materials had come from or who they were carrying them for.

They had clearly not intended to stop in New York but had been forced to do so after encountering terrible weather conditions just off the Eastern Atlantic seaboard. Now of course the entire crew was detained awaiting deportation.

Laura remembered being called down to the ship a few weeks earlier by the customs office in order to try to identify some of the ancient artefacts found inside the cargo hold. Amidst the ship's dripping dank interior that stank distinctly of rats' urine, the customs officers had hauled open the doors of one of the freight containers and shone in their powerful torches to reveal the beautifully ornate carvings of the prophecy stone.

After Laura had identified the stone as ancient Mayan, it was now on indefinite loan to the museum for further study until its full origins and rightful owner could be established.

This had all served to remind Laura that there was a whole black-market world out there of shadowy dealers in stolen antiquities, armaments, narcotics, endangered animal skins. You name it, whatever anyone was prepared to buy there was always someone in the world, or rather whole gangs of landless sailors and nation-less shell companies, prepared to supply.

Laura found herself wondering how much our knowledge of the world of our ancestors had been undermined by these pirates, who had profited from their illegal trade ever since the time of the ancients. Their activities were so often at the expense of our understanding of the true history of the world. Even the pirates' traditional flag, the skull and crossed bones, she remembered, they had originally stolen from the ancient Maya, to whom it had apparently been some sort of religious symbol.

If only I could find the rest of this chunk of stone, she thought. *But now all that will have to wait!* She felt deeply frustrated. But now she had been landed with the museum's own internal enquiry into the crystal skull, she decided she'd better get the investigation over with as quickly as possible.

And so it was with a sense of reluctant resignation that Laura made her way down to the museum's basement archive, not to find out where her precious prophecy stone came from but to try to find out the origins of the equally mysterious crystal skull.

Chapter 7

The museum's archive was where every single item, no matter how large or small, that had ever come into the museum's possession was carefully catalogued and itemised. Ever since the museum was established in the mid 1800's, everything from a tiny pharaoh's toothpick to a fifteen foot tall mummy's sarcophagus had been methodically listed by generations of meticulous archivists.

Whether the item was on display to the public or stored in the maze of underground storage corridors beneath the museum itself, the archive was sure to have a record of it. Usually there was a full description of the item and its original use, together with exact details of where it had been discovered.

This was the proper way of doing things, thought Laura, in contrast to what happened whenever the black market got hold of an item. Laura remembered the words of her old university lecturer; 'The only way for us to build up a proper history of our past is if meticulous records are kept of exactly what each item is and precisely where it was originally found'.

This was the job of dedicated professionals such as the museum's current archivist Mary Swinton.

Mary had worked at the Museum's archive for over 30 years, since back in the days when information was stored on index cards. Over the last twenty five years, however, she had personally overseen the transfer of all the museum's records onto computer.

If there was a record of the crystal skull anywhere in the museum's archive, Mary would soon be able to find it.

Laura watched as Mary scanned her computer screen. She smiled meekly at Laura over her glasses, which seemed to be perched on the very end of her nose, before shaking her head.

'No definitely no record of any crystal skull anywhere in the archive.' she said, much to Laura's dismay.

'...and not a single reference to it anywhere in the library either.' she added.

'How do you know that?' asked Laura, surprised.

'That's the second time I've looked' explained Mary, adjusting her glasses. 'We had poor old Dr. Smith in here asking exactly the same question only last week.'

Chapter 8

Laura's mind was racing as she made her way back through the maze of corridors towards her office. *Why had Ron Smith been asking in the archive about the origins of the crystal skull? Didn't even he know where it had come from?*

She stopped suddenly as a more disturbing thought hit her. *What am I doing following in Ron's footsteps? Ron had been studying the crystal skull, asking about it in the archive, and then...* She shuddered to think where all this might be leading.

She decided to take a short-cut through one of the underground storage corridors to get to the elevators, but as she turned the corner she realized she had forgotten how creepy this part of the museum could be. The corridor was lined up to the ceiling on either side with wooden crates from which various antique sculpted body parts were protruding.

A few yards ahead, with his back to her, a uniformed officer was slowly and deliberately wheeling an old trolley down the passageway towards the lifts. Its wheels squeaked as it went and a pale, lifeless arm hung down from beneath a white sheet that covered a very rigid looking body on top of the trolley. Suddenly, to Laura, it looked like a corpse and the whole place looked like a morgue.

Somewhat surprised at the strength of her own reaction, she decided to take to the stairwell instead, and was almost running by the time she reached her office on the top floor. The hall light didn't seem to want to work and she was still fumbling to fit her key into the lock when she heard a familiar squeaking sound.

She turned round to see that the trolley and its attendant had just emerged from the lift at the far end of the service corridor, right opposite her door. Backlit only by the elevator strip-light, she could just make out the silhouette of the body now being wheeled straight down the corridor towards her.

Laura dived into her office and took refuge behind the door. She felt strangely afraid. *What's going on?* she asked herself. She couldn't understand why the usual, once familiar sights and sounds of the museum suddenly seemed so filled with menace. But her heart hammered in her chest as the sound of squeaking wheels and the hollow echo of heavy male footsteps got nearer.

There came a knock on her door, and Laura jumped momentarily.

'Come in!' she intoned, her voice sounding shriller than she expected, and the door swung open.

There, in the doorway was a tall, thin, black museum attendant, standing over a delivery trolley.

'Professor Lamb asked me to deliver this,' he said as he pulled aside the white sheet to reveal an ancient Roman statue lying on the trolley, alongside which was a twelve inch square black leather carry-case.

'Ah, Jacob!' Laura was relieved she recognised the porter, doing his usual rounds, fetching and delivering items for the archaeologists to work on. Of course it was just a statue she had seen on his trolley earlier, her mind had simply been playing tricks on her. 'Just put it over there' she indicated.

'I'm sorry to hear about Ron,' Jacob said as he placed the black leather carry-case on the side-desk, with what Laura couldn't help thinking was an unusual degree of caution.

'Thank-you, Jacob.' Laura was grateful for his concern, but her heart sank as she realized what he was delivering.

She looked at the case. She knew only too well what was inside it. She knew it was coming but had dreaded the moment of its arrival.

Jacob appeared to sense Laura's tenseness. He paused in the doorway and turned to look at her. 'You take care now, Dr Shepherd.'

The concern in his voice left Laura wondering exactly what he had heard about the skull. She was desperate to ask him, but she thought of her reputation as a professional archaeologist, and so Jacob left unasked.

Chapter 9

Laura really didn't want to look at the skull. There were a million things she'd rather do than open that case. Instead, she logged onto her computer. She began to search the international museum database, to see if the crystal skull was listed.

Her screen flashed back:

'no match found.'

That's interesting, she thought. There was no record of any crystal skull in any museum anywhere in the world. That made it unique. She ought really to have a look at it.

Glancing back towards the dark, leather carry-case, however, she felt that strange sense of apprehension. Perhaps she should look through some of Ron's paperwork instead, she wondered, but knew that would just be putting off the inevitable moment when she would have to get the thing out of its case. The longer she left it, the harder it would be. She really had to get it out and look at it without any further delay.

So, steeling herself, Laura approached the case. With trembling fingers, she released the catch, and lifted the lid. She reached in cautiously to pick up the skull.

But no sooner had she touched its cold, glassy smooth surface, when she heard something in the corridor outside.

It was the distinct sound of heavy, almost clumsy footsteps, getting nearer and nearer.

Suddenly there was a loud thud, as if something heavy had landed on the floor right outside her door. Startled, she dropped the skull back into its case.

Cautiously Laura opened the door to see Janice, the office assistant and general gossip, scrabbling around in her startlingly short skirt and impossibly high heels, trying to jam a laptop computer back into a large cardboard box, the complete contents of which, in trying to enter without knocking, she had somehow managed to spill all over the floor.

'Sorry! Just some more of Ron's, I mean Dr Smith's, things the police sent over.' squeaked Janice, through her chewing gum.

God, how could she have dropped Ron's computer?

'Hope his laptop still works,' she said with indifference.

'Yes, so do I,' Laura answered dryly, as she bent down to help collect up all the pens, papers and other bits of office stationery now scattered across the hall.

'I hurd about what happened to him' Janice added conspiratorially, 'isn't it just awful, I mean, you poor thing. Finding him like that'n'all.'

'Thank you, Janice' said Laura rising to her feet and offering to take the box for Janice, who marched nonchalantly straight into her office and dumped the box on Laura's desk. She caught sight of the crown of the crystal skull just visible inside its case and turned to Laura.

'Gee is that the skull?' she asked, peering into the open case. Laura nodded as Janice continued; 'I hurd that thing's cursed. It got a hold over Ron. They say he looked it in the eye and it made him go totally crazy and kill himself'. She looked at Laura gleefully, waiting for her reaction.

'That's nonsense, Janice,' she said firmly, 'There's nothing to suggest this skull had anything to do with Ron's death.' Though she said it with authority, she was actually trying to convince herself as much as Janice.

'Well, all the same' Janice persisted 'I wouldn't want that thing sitting around in my office'

Laura drew a deep breath. 'Thank you Janice' she said, holding the door open for her to leave.

'I mean, you poor thing, what with all you've already been through 'n' all.' Janice quipped, chewing back over her shoulder, as she teetered off down the corridor.

Laura shut the door firmly behind her and pondered how a few words from Janice could possibly have the effect of making her feel quite so wretched.

She slammed the lid shut on the skull-case and gazed at the series of cardboard boxes now piled up in front of her.

Laura spent the rest of the day sifting through Ron's papers and searching through his files for any mention of the crystal skull. She was still poring over his correspondence as darkness fell, and the other staff finished their day at the museum.

She paused in her search to look at a photograph of Ron taken on an archaeological dig in Central America. Smiling and relaxed, surrounded by members of his team, he looked remarkably well, and happy. She turned it over. The date on the back showed it was taken less than five years ago. *He doesn't look like a man who would have chosen to kill himself,* she thought, remembering Janice's comment. *But then again, he didn't choose to kill himself did he? But just what did happen to him that fateful night? There definitely seemed to have been someone else in the museum.*

At that moment, a haunting sound brought Laura's attention back to the present: *'Oxlahun baktun, mi katun, mi tun, mi kin, oxlahun baktun, mi katun, mi tun, mi kin.'*

It sounded horribly familiar. It was the same eerie whispering she had heard the night she found Ron dead. It chilled her to the core.

Once again, the whispering seemed to be coming from the corridor outside her office.

What is that? Who is it? Laura wondered. She crept over and listened from behind the frosted glass door, but she still couldn't work it out.

So she took a deep breath, and flung the door wide open. As she did so, the whispering stopped. There was nobody there.

But a light was still on in one of the offices a few doors down. Laura ventured out carefully along the hallway and stopped just back from the door. It lay slightly ajar. She was just raising her hand to knock, when she thought she saw something like a dark shadow moving on the other side of the frosted glass. So she lowered her fist.

Suddenly, the door flew open in her face and her heart missed a beat.

'Working late again, Dr.Shepherd?' said a voice.

It was Jacob, standing in the doorway, just about to turn out the light as he exited the room.

'My God, Jacob. You scared the hell out of me!' Laura was visibly shaken.

'Sorry ma'am. Just doing my rounds,' he explained 'Making sure everything's in order. What can I do for you?'

'I just wondered… did you just hear something?'

'Like what?'

'Like a sort of whispering or chanting sound'.

Jacob looked blank. 'No ma'am. Nothing at all. Why?'

'Oh, it doesn't matter,' said Laura, thinking now that perhaps she had imagined it. 'Sorry to have bothered you'.

She felt a little stupid as she headed back to her office. *What's wrong with me?* She wondered. *Why am I getting so jumpy? And why can't I even look at that skull?*

Chapter 10

Laura was grateful that Michael had offered to give her a lift home that night. She waited for him outside the back entrance to the museum, with the grey and black reflective glass monoliths of the neighbouring office blocks looming all around. It was a side of the museum the public rarely saw, she realised as she stood there and it began to rain. But Michael would be there soon.

She looked at her watch. It was seven o'clock. Ron would have been leaving around now. He always left at seven, through the same back exit, past the bins overflowing with rubbish, with the gas cylinders and fire hydrants sitting alongside. He was such a creature of habit you could almost set your watch by his comings and goings at the museum. *But what had Ron been doing there at midnight? It wasn't like him at all.*

Just then Laura heard a noise, a rustling coming from behind one of the overflowing dumpsters. Perhaps it was a rat rummaging around looking for scraps of food amidst the rubbish bins? She hated those sneaky little creatures. In fact, she was almost phobic about them. Carefully, she turned around. That's when she saw him, slowly emerging from behind one of the giant bins. It certainly wasn't a rat, but the sight of him still made her flesh crawl.

This one she didn't recognise. She had come to know most of the vagrants that hung around outside the museum asking for spare change or unwanted sandwiches, but this one she had never seen before. This was not one of the regulars.

He couldn't have been much older than about sixteen, but his skin looked as though it had been lived in for a lifetime, his clothes as if they had just been pulled from a bog, and the stench of stale urine was enough to make Laura want to cover her nose and mouth with a handkerchief.

He opened his mouth.

'You're next!' he said, in a faraway voice.

Laura wondered what on earth he was talking about. She glanced over her shoulder to see who he was talking to, but there was nobody else there. She turned back to see that the young man's drug-crazed eyes had now narrowed, and he was gazing straight at her.

She averted her gaze, trying not to catch his eye, when he repeated, 'You're next!'

Laura was still trying to work out which he was suffering from; drug, alcohol, or substance abuse, whether perhaps he had absconded for the day from some nearby psychiatric institute, or perhaps even a mixture of all of these things, when he raised his voice and insisted.

'You're fucking next!'

She frowned, still wondering what the hell he was on about, when he started to get angry. He came right over to her now, swaggering and swaying violently from side to side as he approached.

Laura could almost taste his stinking breath, and feel the course bristles on his unshaven chin, as he pushed his face right up against hers. She raised her hands up in front of her face for protection, as he seemed to howl his verbal abuse right down her throat, through his toothless upper jaw.

'You're next, honey!' he shouted, 'You're fucking next!' he cried jabbing the air in front of Laura's face with his raised elbow and outstretched forefinger.

Then, just as inexplicably, he turned away again and staggered off down the street, leaving Laura in a state of delayed shock and fear, with the bitter taste of iron in her mouth, and the queasy rush of adrenalin coursing through her veins.

She was still feeling pretty shaky a few minutes later when Michael's sleek new silver Audi pulled up alongside the kerb.

Boy was she relieved to see him.

As she climbed in however she decided not to burden him with what had just happened. He was worried enough about her already. But as they drove home through the city streets in the pouring rain, Michael noticed she was unusually quiet.

'Ron's death's really been getting to you hasn't it?'

'Yes. I suppose it has,' Laura replied, suddenly aware of how tense she had felt, even before that evening's unpleasant encounter.

'It's not surprising. Especially after all we've been through,' Michael added sympathetically.

Laura watched the rain beating down against the car window.

'But I still don't understand why he died with that thing in his hands,' she said after a moment's pause.

They stopped at a red traffic light.

'It's just a coincidence, Laura, that's all' said Michael.

'I don't know' she sighed, 'something about it makes me feel uneasy'.

Michael looked at her and took her hand. 'You're tired and in shock. You're probably reading far too much into everything. It's just a carved stone artefact like all the others you've handled, just a plain old-fashioned object, and nothing more.' he said firmly.

Michael was right. What was she thinking? She was being ridiculous. Here she was, Dr Laura Shepherd, a noted and respected academic. She was not one to jump at shadows or be fearful of a simple representation of a human skull, however macabre or mysterious, and no matter what the circumstances of its discovery.

As she herself had just told Janice, the crystal skull had nothing to do with Ron's death. It was all just some bizarre, unfortunate coincidence, and there was bound to be some simple, rational, scientific explanation for the whole thing.

She thought about it for a moment and found herself relaxing for what felt like the first time in days, when she had an idea.

That's it! She would put the skull in for scientific tests and be done with it.

Why didn't I think of it before?'

She was buoyed by the thought that there was a way forward.

The lights changed back to green and they drove on.

Chapter 11

December 5th 2012

At work, the following day, Laura put in a call to Ian Straszewski, the museum's Chief Lab Technician, to try to book the skull in for scientific tests. Ian was renowned for being able to work out the origin of just about anything you gave him, and in return give you chapter and verse on it, but he was also notoriously difficult to get hold of. Today was no different, Laura realized as she replaced the handset once again.

So, with a disappointed sigh, she continued wading through Ron's paperwork. By late afternoon, she had put the last remaining box of his papers aside. All that remained to be checked were his computer files. She took out Ron's laptop, plugged it in and waited a few moments for it to power up. Fortunately it was still functioning after the knock it had taken from Janice the day before.

She checked Ron's emails and ran through all his documents. There were details of his field trips, applications for project funding, a paper he was writing on the ancient Mayan ballgame to be presented at a conference in Texas. Everything was in order. But there was no mention of any skull, crystal or otherwise.

Now this was odd because Ron Smith was a very systematic man. It wasn't like him not to document the skull in some way. There had to be a note in his diary on the day it was discovered, or something to acknowledge how he had come into possession of it, but there seemed to be nothing. *So what on earth was he doing with the crystal skull that night? And why didn't he mention it anywhere, not even in his paperwork?*

Laura paused for a moment and sat with her head in her hands. What was she going to do? What was she going to tell Professor Lamb? The deadline for her report on the skull was looming and she hadn't been able to find out anything at all.

With no computer or paper trail to go on, all Laura's hopes were now pinned on the scientific tests. They were now the only potential source of information she had about the damned skull.

By the end of the day, still unable to get hold of Ian on the telephone, she decided to doorstep him. She felt a sense of determination as she made her way through the warren of offices at the back of the museum in search of his laboratory. She was confident Ian would be able to come up with some answers.

Reaching the museum's scruffy-looking laboratory, she found Ian at last, in the lab-coat that appeared to be permanently glued to him. He was leaning over an unwrapped Egyptian mummy which was laid out on a table top in front of him, and he appeared to be busy taking a tissue sample from its head.

'The crystal skull eh?' said Ian raising his eyebrows.

He carried on with the delicate work he was doing

'That skull has become the talk of the museum'.

'Really?' asked Laura.

'Rumours are circulating that it's an occult object, used in deadly, secret rituals,' he said without looking up. 'Thank goodness some of us are level headed enough not to be influenced by such nonsense. Though it might make a decent *X-Files* episode I suppose.'

He looked up suddenly and gazed into Laura's face, 'I'm still petitioning *Fox* to bring the series back.'

'I was hoping you could run some tests on it?' Laura asked in a neutral voice, hoping to avoid getting dragged into one of Ian's cult TV conversations.

'I'm afraid I'm up to my eyeballs in it at the moment,' Laura wondered for a second whether he meant it literally, as he picked away at the mummy's skull, 'but leave it here and I'll try to get onto it tomorrow'.

It was after dark as Laura returned to her room frustrated at not having found the answers she was looking for. Something was wrong. She sensed it even before she got there. It might have been the ticking of her office clock, so loud she could hear it in the corridor, or the shadows along the walls that appeared darker and more elongated than usual. Whatever it was, she felt a terrible sense of foreboding. She opened her office door, and stopped dead in her tracks.

Someone was sitting in her chair. He had his back to her. She couldn't make out who it was, silhouetted against the moonlit window.

Suddenly, the intruder spun round. Now she could see who it was. He was holding the crystal skull in his lap. It was Ron Smith.

How could this be?

His greying flesh hung from the bone.

Slowly, his lips peeled back in a rictus grin.

'Ah Laura, we've been waiting for you.' His voice was hoarse, than a whisper. 'Come, I have something to show you.'

He got up and staggered towards her.

Laura tried to turn and run but got nowhere. She felt as if glued to the spot.

Ron was now holding the crystal skull up right in front of he

'Here, take a look for yourself' he croaked.

The skull was so close now she could hardly focus on it. Inste as if she could see right inside it. There she thought she could s appearing deep inside its transparent crystalline interior. They hazy at first but then they seemed to be playing almost like cinema film. She knew not what these images were but she didr look of them one little bit.

Inside the skull she swore she could see towering white cracking and splitting, and tumbling into the sea, huge tid engulfing whole cities, volcanic eruptions, the earth heaving and hurricane force winds blowing airplanes out of the sky, concrete collapsing, their vehicles bursting into flames and frying their in inside, industrial gas storage tanks and tall buildings exploding in the night, and people leaping to their deaths amid the acrid black

And then, a terrible blackness spreading quickly across the e consuming everything in its path, like the blast from some might holocaust, leaving nothing behind but blackened tree stumps, bodies and skeletal remains amidst the debris and the ashes.

Chapter 12

Laura woke up suddenly, in a cold sweat. Still struggling to emerge from the thrall of her nightmare, she looked at the bedside clock. It was 4am. She was in bed, safe at home. Michael lay beside her, sleeping soundly.

What on earth was that? she wondered. *Was it some vision of the future, perhaps the same one Ron had seen inside the crystal skull? Was that what he had meant by his final note 'I have seen the future'? Was that why he had chosen to end his life?*

Trying not to wake Michael, she got out of bed quietly and made her way to the bathroom at the far end of the hall.

By the light of the vanity mirror above the sink, she splashed her face with cold water before burying her face in the comfort of a thick white towel. Feeling better, she turned to leave. But as she glanced back up at her reflection, she stood rooted to the spot, horrified.

In the mirror she saw her face, slowly metamorphosing into the face of the crystal skull! Its jaw opened and it whispered her name,

'Laura!'

She closed her eyes and shook her head.

When she opened them, her face looked normal again.

With shaking hands, she replaced the towel and returned to the bedroom, trying hard to dismiss this disturbing vision. As she entered the room, Michael stirred and woke.

'You OK?' he asked, still groggy with sleep.

'Yes.' she replied.

Michael looked at her. Sometimes, he thought, over the last two years, it felt as if part of her had become closed off, somehow locked away from him.

'No you're not,' he said.

'You're right. I'm not really,' she confessed as she sat down on the e of the bed.

'It's that bloody skull again isn't it?'

'I don't know, I just keep thinking I'm hearing things.'

'What sort of thing?' He frowned.

'Like a strange whispering noise.' She didn't want to think about her nightmare or what she had just seer mirror. They were just too weird. *The first must have be the other just some strange trick of the light, or perhaps a*

still have been half asleep.

'It's probably just an ear infection, temporary tinnitus' Michael suggested helpfully.

'Maybe,' said Laura doubtfully. 'Only it started the night Ron died'.

She regretted saying it even as she spoke. She didn't want to think that her hearing things had any connection with the skull, or with Ron's death, and she certainly didn't want to worry Michael. These last few days he had been edgy enough about her welfare. She was relieved when he made no reference to her remark. Instead he put a protective arm round her and pulled her gently back into the bed.

'Why don't you make an appointment to get your hearing checked out?' He curled round her and fell quickly back to sleep, while Laura stared into the night, unable to rest, her thoughts still haunted by the image of the crystal skull, as it stared back at her in the bathroom mirror, whispering her name.

Chapter 13

December 6ᵗʰ 2012

The following evening, Laura found herself sitting in Dr. Willis' surgery. She liked Dr Willis. Though he was close to retirement now, she found his gentle manner reassuring. It never felt as if he was too busy to see her.

'Well, there's nothing wrong with your ears,' he said as he packed away the light pen he had used to examine her. Laura looked anxious as he sat down behind his desk.

'And tell me, how have you been sleeping?'

'Not very well. I keep having nightmares.' She paused.

'And I just have this feeling that something's not quite right, but I don't know what it is'

'These symptoms,' said Dr Willis, 'general anxiety, nightmares, hearing things, they're not uncommon. 'And tell me, how's Michael keeping?'

'You know Michael,' replied Laura, 'working harder than ever, especially since he started that new job. But I just can't explain these noises I keep hearing and I've even started seeing things too.'

'What sort of thing?' Dr Willis sounded concerned.

'Oh, I'm sure it's nothing.' She suddenly felt the need to reassure him of her sanity.

Dr Willis put his hands together 'Well, you have been under a lot of stress recently, what with your colleague's death, not to mention your own personal loss'.

Laura looked away. *There can be no escaping the forces that shape your life,* she thought to herself, *that define you, that leave you scarred and battered but still here, facing another day.* But whatever was happening to her had to be more than just stress, she decided. After all, she was an old friend to stress and loss.

'I know you're busy, but some time off might really help' said Dr Willis.

He could see from Laura's expression that wasn't an option.

'And if that isn't possible' he started writing her a prescription, 'I recommend you take one of these every night before bedtime.' He handed her the prescription for sleeping tablets. 'And do come back and see me if the problem persists'.

Perhaps Dr Willis is right, thought Laura, as she made her way home. It was stress she was suffering from, that was all. She wasn't really going mad. She simply needed to slow down a bit and get things in perspective.

The apartment was dark when she got home. Michael was working late again, as usual, and she thought little of it.

She took off her coat and hung it next to her bureau in the front hall, before settling down in the lounge, taking the opportunity to treat herself to her favourite TV programmes.

But it wasn't long before Laura felt a sudden and unexpected sense of fear and loneliness. She realised she preferred to watch these trashy programmes with Michael there, even if he did insist on talking all the way through them.

Later that evening, Laura was getting ready to go to bed, alone. She put on her nightgown and ventured out barefoot along the hallway to the bathroom. As she passed the spare bedroom door, she noticed it was slightly ajar, and a shaft of moonlight from within was shining across the hall carpet.

She pushed the door open and looked inside. The pink walls were decorated with fairies sitting on top of flowers, their smiles pale and delicate. Laura had stencilled them herself. A helium balloon globe was tethered to the bedstead, floating above the neatly folded sheets, and an orderly row of soft toys was lined up across the pillows.

A lone teddy bear was the only thing out of place, lying face down in a pool of moonlight in the middle of the floor.

Laura went in slowly and picked up the bear.

She looked at it sadly for a moment, and held it softly to her chest before putting it carefully back in its place amongst the other toys. She paused then left the room, closing the door gently behind her.

Chapter 14

December 7th 2012

The following evening Laura was on her way home from work when she got a phone call from Ian, the lab technician.

'Laura, it's about the skull.' he sounded excited. 'We've run every test we can think of, but we can't explain it'.

'Can't explain what?' Laura was crossing a busy street, struggling to hear him above the traffic noise.

'It doesn't make any sense at all.'

'What doesn't? Look, I can't hear you, but I can be with you in about ten minutes,' she suggested.

'Great!' he said, and put down the phone.

When Laura arrived at the laboratory, Ian was adjusting his spectacles as he gazed at the image of the crystal skull on the monitor of an electron microscope.

'Incredible!' he whispered to himself, scratching his balding head.

'What's so amazing?' asked Laura.

'Well, this thing's crystal, right?'

Laura looked at him as if to say 'so?'

'So it's got no carbon in it. So we can't carbon date it'.

It sounded intriguing.

'So we have no way of knowing how old this thing is. It could have been made yesterday or it could be as old as the hills – literally.' he added.

'I mean, a piece of rock crystal like this usually takes thousands if not millions of years to form, under intense heat and pressure, deep within the earth's crust. So the crystal itself is probably many millions of years old.'

Ian opened a can of Diet Coke and took a swig. 'The real question is who carved it, how, and when?' He put down his can.

'Thing is,' he continued, 'this type of crystal is incredibly difficult to carve. I mean, on the Moh's scale of hardness this stuff is only slightly softer than diamond, so it would have taken an absolute eternity to carve this thing. And not only is crystal hard but it is also very brittle, so it has a tendency to fracture.' He paused. 'Mind if I have my dinner?'

'No' said Laura as Ian opened a packet of M&M's.

'The thing is' he mumbled through his candy, 'whoever made this thing would have had to have started with an absolutely enormous piece of crystal, the likes of which I, or anyone else I suspect, have never seen – and they would have to have carved it for years and years, a whole lifetime, maybe more, and the thing with crystal is that even just as they got to finishing it, if they made even just one tiny mistake, and carved it at the wrong angle against the grain, then BOOF!'

Ian sprayed crumbled M&M's everywhere in his excitement, '...the whole thing would suddenly have shattered into a thousand little pieces! Totally disintegrated! All gone.'

He calmed himself down a little, and looked at Laura, 'So God only knows how it was done.'

Ian got up and paced around the lab in his white coat.

Laura listened intently, keeping ready to avoid another shower of half-eaten candy as he continued.

'I've had the whole team look at this and we reckon it would have been impossible to have made this thing using modern diamond-tipped power tools. The heat and friction generated by those things, especially on such a delicate area as this lower jaw here' he indicated 'would have caused the whole thing to shatter.' He sighed.

'So we reckon it must have been carved using more traditional, primitive methods, such as using sand and water alone to slowly abrade the material. Thing is, we've done the calculations, and my team estimate that would have taken at least three hundred man-years of effort!'

He spun round and gazed intently at Laura.

'That's man-years, Dr Shepherd, not hours.' He seemed to deflate again. 'In other words, it must have taken many generations of people all working around the clock for every day of their lives to finally carve it'

'Surely not!' said Laura.

'That's why we decided to look for tool-marks to see how it was done. Here, take a look for yourself.'

He turned the microscope's monitor towards her.

'I can't see anything' said Laura.

'Exactly!' replied Ian excitedly. 'No tool-marks! Either ancient or modern! Even under our newest electron microscope.' He patted the enormous piece of equipment with the pride of one who had won a great victory over the appropriations committee.

Laura looked at him with a quizzical frown. 'So what exactly does that mean?'

'It means we have absolutely no idea how this skull was made.' Ian shook his head, as if unable to believe what he heard himself saying. 'I mean, according to all logical reason, this skull shouldn't even exist!'

'Unless of course it was made using some kind of technology we've never come across' he added, almost to himself.

'But that's impossible, right?' Laura interjected.

'I guess so' he shrugged. 'Anyway, how have you been getting along? Any luck yet with Ron's paperwork?'

'No, I've been right through it all now, and still nothing.'

'In that case, it's a total mystery,' said Ian, still shaking his head in disbelief.

Chapter 15

It was after closing time, as Laura wheeled the skull-case back from the lab to her office and placed it on her desk. Intrigued now by what Ian had told her she decided to take a closer look. She undid the clasp, opened the lid, and carefully lifted the skull out from its case.

It seemed surprisingly cold to the touch and heavy, as she began to study it properly for the first time by the light of her old desk lamp.

She was struck by its pure anatomical accuracy, the way it perfectly seemed to mirror the size, dimensions and detail of a real human skull. Not only did it have a separate and moveable jawbone, but the cranium even had the zigzag pattern of 'suture marks' across the crown, just like the ones found between the separate 'plates' of a real cranium.

Gone was her initial revulsion at the sight of the skull, as Laura began to marvel at the amazing technical achievement of creating such an incredibly perfect object. As she pondered the question of what kind of tools could possibly have been used that would have left no mark upon its silky smooth surface, she was gradually taken in by its sheer beauty, and her gaze was slowly drawn deep inside its transparent crystalline interior.

There she could see literally hundreds of tiny bubbles of air that had become trapped inside the skull when the crystal itself was first formed deep inside the Earth's crust. These tiny pockets of air, that Ian had referred to as 'inclusions', seemed almost to sparkle before her eyes, like tiny stars in a distant solar system.

Laura began to roll the skull around in her hands. As she did so, she could even see tiny patterns of rainbow-coloured light being reflected off its surface and refracted around inside its multi-faceted interior. It truly was a most magnificent object, a flawless work or art. She was entranced.

As she stared into the skull, still rolling it around in her palms, an image suddenly appeared inside it. It caught her by surprise. Startled, Laura gasped. It was the image of a young child, the face of a beautiful young girl, looking out from deep within the skull's interior. It was only the briefest, most fleeting of glimpses, and then it was gone.

Recovering her breath, Laura rolled the skull back again, to try to catch a second glimpse. The image reappeared exactly as before. She lifted the skull up to try a different angle, and only then did she realise that this 'vision' was actually just the reflection of the framed photograph propped up at the front of her desk - a photograph of her own four-year old daughter Alice.

The picture had been taken a few years before when they were on holiday in Maine. How happy they had been. Michael and Alice had just finished building a huge sandcastle. The sun was shining, and the wind was blowing Alice's long blonde hair. Laura looked at the photograph with fathomless sorrow.

With a heavy heart she decided to call it a day.

She was just beginning to pack the skull away again into its case when she thought she caught sight of something, moving very swiftly, just out of the corner of her eye. She turned around to see a piece of paper floating gently to the floor, as if blown by a draught of air she had not felt, some strange, imperceptible wind.

She went over and picked it up. It was a piece of Ron's paperwork, the Police Department header page, which read: 'Property of Dr. Ron Smith – Deceased.'

She was just putting it back in its place, on top of the pile of Ron's papers on her side-desk, when she heard it again. It was very faint at first, and could almost have been mistaken for the noise of the museum's antiquated central heating system. But she knew it was not that. She felt a heavy sense of dread deep in the pit of her stomach, as the whispering began again.

It was the whispering she had heard the night Ron died. Only this time it was different. It sounded more intense and urgent than ever. And this time it seemed to be calling her name:

'Laura!... Laura!... Laura!..'

She tried to ignore it, but it would not go away. *No! Leave me alone!* She covered her ears to try to blot out the sound. But it was still there.

Trying to determine its source, to finally put an end to it, once and for all, she found herself drawn back out into the darkened corridor, down the stairs, and along the lower corridor to Ron's office, exactly as she had done only one week before.

The entrance to Ron's office was now dark, and sealed up with yellow tape which read: 'POLICE LINE – DO NOT CROSS.' But Laura entered anyway. For reasons she could not explain, she wanted to get inside that room, and before she knew it, she had torn off the prohibition tape and pushed the door wide open.

As she fumbled for the light switch she found herself momentarily transported back a week in time, half expecting to find Ron lying there dead. Instead she found his office now stripped bare of all but the most basic furniture. Only squares of pale paint remained where colourful posters and paintings once hung and an old wooden clock hung crooked on the dusty wall, its tick echoing loudly around the empty room. Though she wasn't sure quite what she had expected, or why she felt so compelled to come back down to his office, it felt strangely disturbing to see the room so stripped of Ron's identity. All the things that made it his were now gone.

Her attention was drawn to the clock. *It must have been Ron's*, she thought. It had stayed there, resolute and defiant, the only reminder that the room had once been his. But the fact that the clock was now hanging crooked seemed like an affront to his memory. So she went over to straighten it.

She clambered up onto Ron's big old desk, but she couldn't quite reach it from there, so she grabbed his office chair from between the desk and the window, rolled it over on its castors until it was up against the wall, and climbed onto it.

That's better, she thought, but it was actually only by climbing right up onto the arms of the chair that she was able to get anywhere near the clock.

She was just stretching her arms up the wall towards it when she heard a raven squawking outside, and glanced out the window.

She suddenly realised quite how precariously she was balanced, standing on the arms of an old office chair, with castors, right next to the huge floor-to-ceiling Georgian style window.

She looked down; four floors below was the little park, shadowy in the street lights, where Ron used to eat his sandwiches in the summer. It looked so small from this angle, dwarfed by the sleek skyscraper buildings that surrounded it.

The park was deserted at this hour of the night, except for one man. It made Laura quite dizzy to see him from so high up. He was weaving his way across the park when she recognised him. It was the same young man she had encountered earlier on the street at the back of the museum, the one who had shouted abuse at her, and told her she was 'next'.

Oh my God, Ron died in this chair! And maybe I'm next? Unnerved, she suddenly slipped and lost her balance. The chair spun out from beneath her as she fell and hurtled towards the window. *Oh my God, this is it!* She thought as she saw the ground looming nearer.

Then, luckily, her shoulder hit the window frame first and bounced back off it, preventing her whole body from smashing right through the glass. Instead, she fell awkwardly back into the room, her thigh accidentally colliding with the edge of Ron's heavy old wooden desk, which moved a few inches in the process, as she landed safely, but painfully on the floor.

'Ouch!' she yelped and crumpled up in pain, her hand instinctively reaching for the sore spot on her thigh to try to massage it better. Bruised and shaken, she struggled to her feet, looking down at her leg trying to inspect the damage. Fortunately none was evident, and instead her attention was drawn to something now sticking out a few inches from beneath Ron's desk. It looked like an envelope or a slip of paper.

Curious to know what it was, she reached down and picked it up. It was a Fedex-style detachable parcel label that must have fallen between the drawer panels of Ron's desk, so it had remained undetected when the police had stripped the place earlier.

The label was addressed to: 'The Mayan Specialist' at 'The Smithton Geographic Institute.' It came complete with the sender's name and address, an 'A. Crockett-Burrows' from 'The Grange, in Eastwich, upstate New York', and against its

'List of contents' it read: '1 x crystal skull'.

Instantly, Laura fumbled for her cell-phone, and called Directory Enquiries.

Chapter 16

Michael was busy packing his overnight bag on the bed when Laura got home, and burst into the bedroom.

'Guess what? I've finally got a lead on that skull.' She went over and kissed him.

'It was sent into the museum only a few weeks ago by someone who lives just upstate.' Her excitement was palpable. She passed him the Fedex parcel label so he could see for himself.

'That's great.'

He was genuinely pleased as he took a quick look at the label and passed it back to her. He would be glad when this whole business with the skull was over with. He went to get his suit out of the wardrobe,

'So have you spoken to them?'

'Not yet. No phone number listed,' explained Laura as she entered the walk-in closet and took off her coat. 'That's why I'm going up there tomorrow,' she added as she slipped off her skirt and started to change into her jeans.

'What? On your own?' Michael's brow was furrowed as he peered round the doorway at his half-naked wife.

'Why not? It's Saturday, you're off to your conference anyway, and Professor Lamb's waiting for my report. I need to get it done a.s.a.p. or I'll be out of a job,' she reminded him.

'Now hold on a minute. Think about it for a second,' said Michael. 'What kind of person keeps a crystal skull?'

Laura looked at him questioningly.

'You don't know anything about this person. They could be a psycho or something,' he explained gently but firmly.

'Oh come *on*, Michael,' said Laura, wondering whether or not to take him seriously.

'After what happened with Ron, I don't want you taking any chances,' he said as he slid his suit into its overnight carrier on the bed. As he pulled shut the zip it suddenly looked to him like a body bag. He shook the image out of his head.

'It's OK Michael. I'll be fine,' said Laura cheerily.

Although she had to admit, he did have a point.

Chapter 17

December 8th 2012

By the time Laura reached Eastwich, the pale winter light was already beginning to fade. Road conditions had been poor and, despite her normally keen sense of direction, she had temporarily lost her way. Though she had travelled less than a hundred miles, she felt as if she were a long way from home.

It was late afternoon when her car eventually wound its way up the long drive of an old Victorian mansion house, in the wintry New England countryside. Though once grand, the house now stood in a state of partial decay. It was a bleak, slightly spooky place. She could hear the sound of crows squawking as they circled above the bare branches. The heavy grey sky was threatening more snow.

Laura pulled to a halt on the crisp gravel driveway. She got out of the car, and gazed up at the house, relieved to have finally reached her destination. But all the shutters were closed and the house looked deserted. *'Damn!'* she muttered at the thought of a long, wasted journey, when she noticed a light shining above the porch.

She took the skull-case from the passenger seat beside her, and made her way up the path to the front of the house. Resting the case down on the porch, she paused for a moment in front of the dirty-brass, lion's face door-knocker. Unsure who, or what, to expect next, she took a deep breath, before rapping it firmly on the solid wooden front door.

Inside the house, she could hear the sound of large dogs barking as they rushed towards the door. The noise of them growling and scratching just on the other side filled her with panic. Suddenly she became aware of her vulnerability, standing alone on a stranger's porch, deep in the countryside, miles from home. Maybe Michael was right. Maybe she hadn't thought this through clearly enough. She had no idea what kind of person lived here. What if they set those dogs on her? Or worse?

Her fears were soon heightened by the sound of heavy bolts sliding slowly open, followed by the noise of a big old key turning in the lock. Whoever lived here kept themselves shut away. Thoughts of mad recluses whirled through Laura's head. She should never have taken the risk of coming out here alone. But it was too late to leave now, the door was creaking open. It stopped after a few inches, just the length of the door chain.

'Who is it?' a disembodied voice grunted aggressively, in a heavily tinged foreign accent. Laura couldn't even make out whether it was male or female.

'..I..I'm, Laura Shepherd from the Smithton Geographic Institute…' she began.

'What do you want?' the voice interrupted in an impatient, surprisingly surly tone.

'I..I've come to see an A. Crockett-Burrows.'

There was a long pause, during which Laura wondered if she caught a glimpse of a suspicious eye peering out at her from deep inside the darkened interior, before the voice finally replied 'Wait here!', and its owner slammed the door shut in her face and re-bolted it.

Laura glanced nervously around at the overgrown garden, dusted with snow. Stone cherubs clutched at urns overgrown with brambles, and she noticed the large, impenetrable hedge surrounding the entire property, as darkness began to close in.

The sound of the dogs still barking and scratching at the door served only to increase her sense of unease. If that was Crockett-Burrows, where had they gone? Why had they left her waiting? She reached into her pocket and touched her cell-phone, the only link she had with the outside world. It reassured her.

Suddenly the voice was back, yelling at the dogs in Spanish. A door slammed inside the house and the barking stopped. The front door was unbolted and creaked right open. Inside, on the threshold, stood a large, heavy-set, Mexican woman in her late forties. Her eyes narrowed with distrust as she looked Laura up and down. Her stern demeanour was anything but welcoming.

'Miss Anna Crockett-Burrows will see you now,' she said aggressively. 'Follow me!' She turned away and walked back into the gloomy interior. Laura assumed the woman to be some sort of housekeeper or maid.

Laura hesitated a moment before entering the dusty old, antique filled house. A grandfather clock chimed the hour, as she followed behind the maid, across the entrance hall and up the stately stairway. The walls were lined with portraits of wealthy ancestors, now long dead, who stared down at her from their gilt-edged frames. At the top of the stairs, a long hallway at the far end of which was a doorway.

'Wait here!' the maid halted her, before knocking on the door and entering.

'Dr. Laura Shepherd' she announced, before ushering Laura into a poorly lit old Victorian parlour room, illuminated only by a couple of antique table lamps on the lace-covered cabinets.

As Laura's eyes adjusted to the gloom, she took in the gold-framed mirrors and heavy wooden furniture that filled the room. Glass cases housed small stuffed animals, frozen in fake poses, harking back to the time before their death. Glancing around at the ornate furnishings and numerous antiques, Laura had the sense that she had stepped into a bygone age.

Despite the fire burning in the hearth, the room felt surprisingly chilly. And in the far corner of the room, sitting waiting for her in an old leather armchair, was a very elderly woman, who must have been in her early nineties. Elegantly dressed, with a necklace of pearls and a black wool Chanel suit hanging on her tall, thin frame, she looked almost as though she had been expecting visitors.

'Thank you Maria,' the old woman said in a distinctly British accent, before the maid turned and exited. 'Oh, and Maria,' she called after her 'How about some tea?' The elderly lady spoke with the sharp confidence of someone who had enjoyed a life of privilege. She was quite clearly accustomed to being waited on hand and foot, not just through the necessities of old age, but throughout her long life.

She motioned to Laura 'Now! Come closer so I can see you!' she ordered, finally addressing her.

Laura hesitated a moment before approaching. 'I've...' she began,

'You'll have come about the skull!' the old woman cut in.

Laura was a little taken aback.

'Yes, I was wondering...'

'Sit here, please!' the elderly lady interrupted her again, indicating an upright velvet chair uncomfortably close to her own.

Laura was suddenly aware that the old woman was staring straight ahead, not even looking at her, as she sat down on the edge of the seat. But she was obviously very aware of her.

'You'll need to come a bit closer than that!' she demanded.

As Laura leaned nearer the old woman reached out her wrinkled fingers towards her face. Instinctively, Laura flinched away, startled by the old lady's strange behaviour. But as the old woman touched her fingers together, still staring straight ahead, it gradually dawned on Laura that she was blind.

'My eyes no longer work, but I can still see,' she explained enigmatically, and Laura leaned forward again, trying to control her discomfort as she allowed the old woman to run her fingers lightly across the contours of her face.

The old woman's eyes lit up as she 'saw' Laura.

'Now I have seen you, let me see the skull again!' she ordered, and Laura found herself opening up the skull-case and offering her the crystal skull as if she were an obedient servant-girl.

The old woman took the skull and began rolling it around in her hands. She smiled to herself, as she ran her fingers gently over its features. 'Good to see you again' she said quietly to the skull as if she were greeting an old friend.

Laura looked away. She felt oddly as if she had intruded upon a private moment between the old woman and the skull.

She noticed a framed sepia photograph on the table beside the old lady. A man's face filled the frame. He looked about fifty. He wore an intense look on his face and was smoking a pipe.

Glancing back she saw that the old woman was now cradling the skull in her lap, her blind eyes beaming widely, as she gazed up to the heavens. She looked lost in another world of bizarre ecstasy. Laura had learned early on that dealing with eccentrics was part of an archaeologist's job, and she was well aware of how attached people could become to their artefacts, but she had never seen anything quite like this before. She glanced at her watch. If she was going to get back to town at a reasonable hour, she was going to have to interrupt this strange reunion. She took a deep breath.

'I was wondering if you could tell me where the skull came from?' she asked.

The old woman's hands froze on the skull and she looked up.

'That, my dear, is a long story.'

'I'd be interested to hear all the same.' offered Laura.

'Very well.' She cleared her throat. 'Do you see this photo?' Her hand moved tentatively across to touch the frame of the photograph beside her, the photo Laura had just been looking at.

'This is my father, the great British explorer Frederick Crockett-Burrows.' She paused.

'He was a great man. God rest his soul.' Her voice momentarily quavered with emotion.

'And when I was just seventeen years old he allowed me to accompany him on one of his expeditions deep into the jungles of Central America.' Laura listened enraptured.

'You see father had his own views on things.' Anna Crockett-Burrows continued. 'He was a member of the British Museum's antiquities committee, but he was by no means a conventional archaeologist. He believed that civilisation began not in the Middle East, as is commonly supposed, but somewhere in the region of Central America. In fact, father believed that Atlantis was a real civilisation that had actually existed, and that although it had sunk beneath the waves, its remnants could still be found somewhere in that part of the world.'

'And being the man he was, of course, he made it his life's work to prove it. So, to that end, he gathered together a party of explorers, including myself, although I was only young at the time, and in 1936 we set sail from Liverpool in England,' she coughed, 'bound for British Honduras. You see father had heard rumours of a lost city that some said still lay buried deep in the rainforest, and that he believed might hold vital clues to the existence of the lost civilisation of Atlantis.'

At that moment the old lady's voice grew hoarse and she was overcome with a coughing fit. Putting away her handkerchief as she gradually recovered her composure, she remarked, 'Oh dear. My voice is getting weary with the ravages of old age. Open the drawer there, would you?'

She pointed to the top drawer of the small cabinet at her side. Puzzled by her request, Laura tried the handle. The drawer had clearly not been used for some time, as it took Laura some effort to open it. When she was done, the old woman reached into the drawer, and pulled out an old handgun.

Laura flinched back as she pointed the barrel at her, before the old lady rested the gun down on top of the cabinet, reached back into the drawer and pulled out a dusty old, leather-bound album, which she offered to Laura.

'It's all here in my journal.' she said, between coughs, 'Please. Do. Take a look at your leisure.'

Laura took the album and gently blew the dust from its cover. The notion of Atlantis was something of a no-go area in conventional archaeology. It was still looked upon as nothing more than a colourful piece of mythology. She put the journal on the coffee table and began to untie its beautiful gold braid. Although she was sceptical of any talk about the lost island continent, she was also curious.

The door opened and the maid came in with a tray bearing a pot of tea and old fashioned china cups. They rattled noisily as she thumped them down onto the coffee table right in front of Laura.

Laura pulled the album out from underneath, just in time, and laid it down safely on the top of the cabinet. The maid passed her a cup of tea with all the grace and poise of a prison warden. As she left the room, Laura wondered why Anna, with all her old-world pretensions, would have chosen quite such a brusque woman as her house-keeper. But that wasn't the only question on her mind.

'So why did you send the skull to my colleague Ron Smith?' she asked.

'I simply sent it to the Mayan specialist,' replied the old woman curtly, 'Isn't that you?'

'Yes, but Ron was a Mayan specialist too,' explained Laura.

'Was?' questioned the old lady, as she began to drink her tea.

'Yes, I'm afraid he died recently.'

The old woman spluttered for a moment on her tea.

'Oh dear.' She put down her cup. 'I'm very sorry to hear that.' She coughed. Something flickered across the old woman's face, an emotion that seemed somehow out of place on hearing the news of Ron's demise. Was it shock, upset, or perhaps even guilt? Laura couldn't tell exactly what it was, but found her reaction unsettling.

'Did you ever meet my colleague Ron?' she asked, but Crockett-Burrows ignored her question, continuing instead with her own thoughts,

'..But, you know… sometimes people are drawn to death, like a moth to a flame.'

She looked lost momentarily in a trance, as she ran her fingers across the skull in her lap, her voice sounding oddly detached.

'You know, the ancient ones believed that death could sometimes be a form of healing.'

Laura wasn't feeling too happy with the way the conversation was heading, as the old woman continued,

'When an old medicine man was getting too old to carry on his work, he would lie down and put his hands on the skull, like this..' she cupped her palms gently over the skull, '..and a young apprentice would come and kneel over them and put their hands on the skull too, like so..' she said as she took Laura's hand and placed it on the skull, '..and the high priest would perform a ceremony. And during the ceremony all the knowledge and wisdom of the old would pass on into the young..'

The old woman's hand had now wandered back up again to try to feel Laura's face, but she flinched away again, '..and the old one would simply pass away quietly during the ceremony.'

Laura was beginning to feel quite uncomfortable, disconcerted by the old woman's strange behaviour and disturbed by her bizarre conversation about death. It was all starting to feel a bit creepy. She was all too aware that she was alone in the house with these two decidedly odd women, and was keen to get back to the point and out of there as soon as possible.

'But I still don't understand why you sent the skull in to the museum?' she asked, quickly finishing her tea.

'You wouldn't believe me, even if I told you,' Anna Crockett-Burrows replied.

'Why not?'

'It's difficult to explain.'

'Please, I'd like to hear, anyway.' Laura knew that most people sent possessions in to the museum either to get them valued, to sell them, or just to get rid of them, what other reason could there be? She was curious.

'Very well then,' said Anna curtly, 'The skull told me that's where it needed to be.'

'I'm sorry?' said Laura sitting up in her chair.

'The skull told me it needed to be with the Mayan specialist at the Smithton Geographic,' came Anna's matter-of-fact reply.

'Now, let me get this right,' said Laura with a puzzled frown, 'You're telling me... this thing speaks to you!?'

'See, I told you, you wouldn't believe me,' replied Anna.

Laura just looked at her in disbelief.

'But it's important. You must try to understand,' said the old woman, lifting up the skull.

'This skull is no ordinary object.'

She held the skull up above her head, her frail arms trembling as her voice boomed:

'This is the most important object ever known in the history of mankind. This skull is a doorway into another world, an entrance to another dimension.'

Laura could scarcely believe what she was hearing.

The skull shook in Anna's outstretched arms as she exclaimed, 'This skull is a doorway into the world of the dead!'

And exhausted, she dropped the skull back into her lap.

Chapter 18

Laura was speechless. From the moment she had entered the room she had thought the old lady eccentric, but this was too much, this was something else. In all her years as an archaeologist she had never heard quite such a preposterous explanation of an object.

She was beginning to have grave doubts about the old woman's sanity. But trying to be tactful, she offered in an unwittingly patronising tone, 'Well, I must say, I've never heard anything quite like that before.'

At which the old lady turned to her, her blind eyes burning with impatience, and snapped, 'Yes, but you've heard the whispering haven't you?'

Laura was shocked, as the old lady began to roll the skull around in her hands, agitated. *How does she know about that?* Laura wondered.

'That's how it begins... That's how they get your attention,' continued Anna. 'That's how they beckon to you across the veil between the worlds.' Her blind eyes were wide open and staring, her voice strangely snake-like, her throat rasping with every breath.

'They?' asked Laura.

'Someone on the other side. Someone is trying to communicate with you.'

Anna's blind eyes had now glazed over completely, as she continued rolling the skull around in her hands, her voice now sounding strangely distant and dreamy.

'I'm sorry, but I'm trying to write a serious scientific report.' said Laura, trying hard to maintain her diplomacy 'This is really not what I came here for'.

'But you must listen when they call to you.' insisted Anna.

'Look, I really don't have time for this.' snapped Laura, rising to her feet.

'No! Please!' You mustn't go.' pleaded Anna. 'She is yearning to speak to you.'

'I really need to be getting back,' said Laura, 'It's getting late. Can I have the skull back please?'

'Maria! Maria!' Anna shouted impatiently, ignoring Laura's request, and the housekeeper appeared in the doorway. 'Maria, you know what you must do.'

Laura felt alarmed. She glanced nervously after the maid as she left the room. What had Crockett-Burrows ordered her to do?

'Please. I really ought to take the skull back to the museum with me.' Laura decided to try to negotiate, although she was now beginning to contemplate leaving the skull behind in the interests of her own safety.

But the old woman ignored her, instead seeming to ask the skull in her lap, 'How can I convince her?'

Laura wondered whether she should just grab the skull from the old woman and run but thought the better of it.

'Please, I need the skull,' she begged.

'Very well then. Take it.' Anna suddenly straightened up and offered it to her.

Surprised by the old woman's swift turnaround, Laura took the skull and began hurriedly packing it away again into its case.

'..But look behind the wardrobe, you'll find it there,' added Anna, with a satisfied look on her face.

'Find what?' asked Laura, puzzled as to what the old woman was talking about.

'Wilson's ribbon!' replied the old woman with a knowing smile.

The colour drained completely from Laura's face as she stood there, frozen with shock, gazing at the old woman aghast.

'But?...' she asked in a faltering voice, 'How do you know about that?'

'I don't,' replied Anna, '...but your daughter does.'

'What!?' Laura heard herself exclaim in disbelief.

'Yes,' said the old woman, 'Alice says 'Look behind the wardrobe, you'll find it there.''.

The old woman sat there staring straight ahead, looking very pleased with herself, as Laura battled with horror, and then panic. Her mind was reeling. She couldn't think straight. All she knew was she had to get out of there, and fast.

She grabbed the skull-case and turned to flee.

But as she fled the room and dashed down the hallway towards the stairs, she saw the maid running towards her from the far end of the corridor, shouting at her in unintelligible Spanish. As she and the maid converged towards the top of the stairs, the maid started fumbling with a leather holster she wore around her waist, trying to pull something from it.

Christ! She's going for a gun. Laura could feel her heart thundering in her chest and everything seemed to go into slow motion as the maid pointed it straight at her.

This is it, thought Laura, as she froze on the spot. *This is how my life is going to end. She's going to shoot me. I'm going to die here, at the hands of these two mad women.* She felt surprisingly detached and unemotional about it - until she thought of Michael, hearing the news, and how terrible it would be for him.

She closed her eyes, and there was a flash of light.

Laura opened her eyes and there was another flash, before it dawned on her that it was not a gun the maid was holding, but an old Polaroid camera.

Laura could hardly believe it. She almost laughed out loud with relief as she realised she was still alive! The maid was simply taking flash photographs of her.

But her sense of relief didn't last long before she began to wonder what the hell the maid was up to. *Taking photographs of a distressed woman?* It was still very weird.

She turned round to see Anna Crockett-Burrows standing silently at the far end of the hall.

Who knows what they might do next? she wondered, and within moments the desire to get out of that bizarre house alive returned as Laura's only concern.

She flew down the stairs with the maid in hot pursuit trying to take more photographs. She could hear the dogs barking as she dashed across the hall to the front door.

Terrified that it might have been re-bolted, she tried the latch. Thankfully, the door opened. She slammed it behind her to delay the maid's exit, sprinted across the gravel to the safety of her car, jumped in, and drove off fast into the night.

Chapter 19

Tears streamed down Laura's cheeks as she sped down the highway. She was no longer sure what was upsetting her the most; whether she was crying with relief at having got away from those two crazy old women, or from the mention of 'Wilson's ribbon.' She looked at the blur of neon tail lights in front of her. The tears were making it difficult to see the road. She knew she should really pull over but she wanted to get as far away from that place as she could.

It was gone eleven when she got home. She closed the front door behind her and leant back against it. She felt safe at last. But the feeling didn't last long. The flat was dark and empty. Michael was still away at his conference. She had wanted so much to see him she had temporarily forgotten. He was still out dining with colleagues following the event, and wouldn't be back till later.

She still felt a bit shaky, so she went into the kitchen and poured herself a glass of wine, but it didn't seem to calm her sense of unease. *What on Earth were they doing taking photos of me like that?* she wondered, but soon realized it was something far deeper that was really troubling her.

Suddenly, Laura knew what it was. And now she knew she couldn't leave it a moment longer. She had to investigate the old woman's words, to find out if what she said about Wilson's ribbon was really true.

With her coat still on, Laura turned and raced up the stairs. She burst through the door into her child's empty bedroom. Throwing on the light, she rushed over to the heavy old wooden wardrobe behind the door, and started struggling to pull it out from its place against the wall. Unable to shift it, she opened its doors and started frantically emptying its contents across the floor.

She lifted out a large box filled with the bright pink and gold of princesses' tiaras and crowns, fairies' wings and magic wands. She dragged out a large plastic box filled with a jumble of children's toys. Dolls and games spilled into the room. She tried the wardrobe again, but it refused to budge. She lifted out a pile of children's dresses, coats and jeans and threw them onto the bed, and pulled forth a bundle of tiny shoes and boots, before she was able to heave the giant wardrobe away from the wall.

She peered down behind it at the dust-covered carpet. There, lying on the floor beneath the skirting-board was the crumpled silk fabric of a small red ribbon.

As she stared at it, she collapsed against the wall and sank to her knees. It was simply a ribbon, so everyday and innocent. Yet for Laura, the sight of that simple ribbon cut into her heart deeper than the sharpest blade.

For Laura, that ribbon symbolised a terrible change in the fortunes of her family, a change she did not want to revisit. But with the appearance of the ribbon, her mind twisted back painfully to the events of two years before.

Looking back, there had been a time when finding that ribbon would have made Laura the happiest woman in the world. She hadn't known that at the time, of course. But finding the ribbon now, two years too late, felt like a cruel joke. She reached out for it, but she couldn't do it. She just couldn't pick it up.

As she looked up from the ribbon and over at the bed it all came flooding back to her, suddenly, as vivid as the day it had happened.

It had been a bright, sunny day, a Saturday, in spring 2010. Their spirits were high, all of them. They had plans for the weekend. Michael was finishing the paper he was writing, then they were off to the zoo - a family outing, a time for them to have fun together, to laugh and relax after their busy week. Laura was back at work full-time now that Alice had started pre-school and she was anxious to spend every spare moment she could with her lively, four-year old daughter.

The sun was streaming through the window behind Alice, who was sitting on the edge of the bed holding her teddy bear, when she noticed his ribbon was missing. She called out, 'Mummy, where's Wilson's ribbon? I can't find it.'

Laura came over to her little girl and crouched down beside her. 'What's happened to your ribbon Wilson?' she asked the teddy bear, before turning back to Alice. 'I'm sure it's round here somewhere. We'll soon find it' she said, gently pushing the hair that had flopped over Alice's face back behind her ear and kissing her on the cheek.

Laura glanced round the room. She couldn't see the ribbon anywhere obvious. Tears were welling in Alice's eyes. Laura could see how important her teddy bear's ribbon was to her. 'Maybe it's got stuck somewhere. Shall I look for it under the bed?' she asked as she crouched down on the floor to begin looking.

As usual, the underside of Alice's bed was a veritable treasure trove of 'stuff'. Laura had to lie down on the floor to get a better look. The first thing she saw was the old music box that had belonged to her own mother. 'Look Alice.' she said passing the box up to her, remembering the delight she herself had experienced at the sight of the little wooden box, its cushioned red velvet lining, and the ballerina in her pink tutu and ballet shoes who spun around to the music from *Swan Lake*.

Alice reached out and took the box from Laura, a smile of delight spreading across her whole face. As she turned the little key in the slot, she remembered that Nell, her friend from nursery had given her two huge gobstoppers that she had carefully hidden from Mummy and Daddy inside the box. So she skipped off and jumped back on.top of the bed, out of Mummy's sight, while Laura disappeared again beneath the bed, looking for Wilson's ribbon.

Alice took out one of the sweets and put it in her mouth. She was happy now as she lay back on the bed sucking on the sweetie, listening to the twinkling sound of the music box as spring sunshine filled the room. She thought of a game she could play by herself; throwing the sweetie up in the air and seeing if she could catch it in her mouth. After a few goes, she succeeded. It was fun so she had another go. This time she threw the sweetie higher. Only this time, as she caught it, the candy lodged deep down into her windpipe.

Laura was still rummaging around under the bed. She really ought to have a word with Alice about tidying this up, she thought, but knew this was one of Alice's secret places where she liked to store things that she was really enjoying playing with. She looked under a stack of girls' comics and lifted up a pile of dresses from Barbie's wardrobe. But no sign of Wilson's ribbon anywhere.

'There it is', she thought, as she spotted a flash of red situated just out of reach at the far corner of the bed, next to a pile of kids' books. Struggling in the confined space, Laura pulled herself towards the ribbon on her elbows.

As she reached out towards it, Alice lay on the bed above unable to breathe. She was choking, quietly. There was a faint rasping sound as she tried desperately to get more air, but in so doing only succeeded in lodging the sweetie deeper down into her trachea. Alice started to panic, reaching out, grasping desperately for her mummy, for daddy, for anyone to help.

Unfortunately Laura could hear none of this above the soft tinkling sounds of the music box. Instead, beneath the bed she was chatting cheerily to Alice, trying to keep her spirits up.

'I bet it's that naughty cat again! He loves chasing ribbons,' she said, blissfully unaware of what was happening to her. She bumped into a toy, one of those electronic ones that sets itself off. It was a purple plastic clown that shouted, 'Hurry! Hurry! Enjoy the fun-fair!' as its lights flashed red and yellow.

Meanwhile, on the bed above, Alice lay writhing silently, the colour draining from her face, her lips turning slowly blue. 'Hurry! Hurry! Enjoy the fun-fair!' shouted the clown. Laura fumbled for the off switch. 'I've got it' she called up to Alice as she reached over to pick up the ribbon, only to find it was Barbie's sparkly red party jacket.

Only then did Laura notice that Alice had gone unusually quiet. 'Honey, are you listening to me?' There was no reply. 'Alice are you playing a game with me?' she asked as she finally emerged from beneath the bed to find Alice lying there no longer moving, her face already beginning to turn white.

'Dear God, Alice!' she whispered in horror.

In that moment, Laura's whole world stopped. Suddenly, nothing else existed except for this child of hers lying there looking dead right in front of her.

She grabbed her daughter and shook her, slapped her, turned her upside down.

'Michael!' she screamed as she tried desperately to resuscitate her before realizing that Alice had something stuck in her windpipe. 'Call an ambulance!' she shouted as she turned her on her front and winded her, attempting to dislodge the blockage in her throat. 'Michael! Michael!' she cried out, 'Call an ambulance!'

Sitting there gazing at the ribbon, Laura could still hear that scream in her mind, the desperate, searing terror of it, even though it was over two years since Alice had died. Sometimes she felt as though part of her was still screaming about what had happened and would never, ever stop.

She wasn't sure how long she had sat there, staring at the ribbon. It could have been minutes, or it could have been hours. All the while, tears were streaming down her face. When she finally did reach out and pick it up, it felt as if it was one of the hardest things she had ever done. As she did so, as she slowly and deliberately reached out and picked up the ribbon, it felt as if an invisible chord that had connected her with the past had been broken forever. She slumped onto the floor and lay there curled up like a foetus, as sobs racked through her body.

When Michael got in, that was how he found her, lying on the bedroom floor, behind the wardrobe, crying inconsolably. He put his briefcase down by the door and went over to her silently. He fell to the floor and embraced her. He knew the futility of words in this situation, the pointlessness of platitudes. There was nothing he could do or say that would make Laura feel any better. He wanted to fix things, but knew he couldn't.

'Why, Michael? Why?' she sobbed. He shook his head. It was a question he had asked himself a thousand times, a question to which he knew no answer.

'Why couldn't I save her Michael? Why couldn't I?' She burst into floods of tears on his shoulder.

'You must stop blaming yourself, Laura. It wasn't your fault' he whispered, as he rocked her back and forth in his arms.

He saw the red ribbon in her hand. It made him feel both angry and sad at the same time, and before he knew it, he felt the sting of bitter tears welling in his own eyes. He fought hard to hold them back, to be strong for Laura. He didn't want her to see his pain.

Chapter 20

December 9th 2012

It was a crisp cold morning the following day. It was Sunday and the sun was shining, but Michael was filled with a sense of dread. He knew this was what Laura would want to do even before she suggested it. They hadn't been there for a while. Not since Alice's birthday, four months ago. He hated going there, hated to be reminded. But this was what Laura wanted. Maybe it would make her feel better, and Michael was wise enough to know that helping Laura feel better might help him too.

The city skyline was visible on the horizon as they walked down the aisle of graves, row upon row, until they came to the cedar tree at the end of the line. Its branches were heavy with snow. Under the tree was Alice's grave. Alarmingly small, the way children's graves are. It still shocked him to see it. It was an affront to what he felt the natural order of things should be; parents die first, not children. That was how it was supposed to be. He felt a surge of anger at the injustice of it all.

Laura brushed the snow from the gravestone. A little angel was carved on its top.

'Alice Greenstone-Shepherd' it read,

'21st July 2005 - 27th May 2010'

'In Our Hearts Forever.'

Laura felt that part of her had died too when Alice died. Something died inside. She would never be the same again. She would always feel the ache of something missing, as if she had had a limb torn from her own body. She had never known such pain in all her life, or how to get through it in the days, months and years that followed Alice's death.

She knelt in the snow beside Alice's grave and carefully unwrapped the delicate little bunch of flowers she had brought with her. As she gently placed the soft pink frangipani blooms in the little glass vase at the foot of the grave, her breath was visible in the cruel winter air. She whispered wistfully, 'I never got a chance to say goodbye.'

Michael stood behind her, rubbing his chilled hands together in the cold. As he watched, silent and stony-faced, he noticed something standing out starkly against the whiteness of the snow. There, holding the pale pink flowers together in their delicately formed bundle, was the blood red streak of Wilson's ribbon.

Chapter 21

That afternoon, Laura kissed Michael goodbye as she climbed out of the passenger seat of his car onto the quayside.

'I'm sorry Laura, but I promised Caleb I'd get this paper finished.' Michael sounded apologetic. His new job as Head of Research at Nanon Systems micro-electronics often required him to work weekends, and his new boss, Caleb Price, seemed even more demanding than the last one, thought Laura.

'I've booked the table for six o'clock.' Michael added by way of compensation.

'OK, I'll see you then.' she said as she shut the door.

She had Christmas shopping to do. She wasn't in the mood. She wandered along the waterfront looking out across the grey expanse of water, at the ferries as they ploughed their way to and from Staten Island.

She thought of Alice, and remembered the people who had told her that her grief would probably be 'complicated' due to the guilt she would inevitably feel because her daughter had died in her care. Sometimes the loss felt almost as raw as the day it had happened, like a wound that never healed over. Like today, when the feeling of Alice's loss was palpable.

Wandering aimlessly, she found herself suddenly in the heart of a busy Sunday market. Uncomfortable at being surrounded by so many people all pushing and shoving as they scoured the stalls looking for Christmas bargains, she took refuge in a jewellery shop.

Christmas muzak played softly in the background as she gazed at some watches laid out inside a glass display cabinet. Out of the corner of her eye, she caught sight of a helium-filled balloon globe, just like the one that still hung over Alice's bed. It was sailing along on the end of a piece of string, as it floated by on the other side of the counter. She could hear the playful laughter of a small child as they pulled it along behind them, their blonde curls just visible above the cabinet top.

At the end of the counter the balloon stopped and Laura looked down to see that it was being held aloft by a beautiful young four-year old girl, accompanied by her adoring mother. Laura's heart missed a beat. For a moment, the girl looked just like Alice.

At that moment one of the sales assistants turned their attention to Laura.

'Looking for something special?' enquired the middle-aged saleswoman with a friendly smile. She held up one of the watches, 'How about this one here? It comes with a lifetime guarantee'.

But Laura wasn't paying any attention. She was still staring at the little girl holding the balloon. Some part of Laura wanted to believe it was Alice, that this was her little girl standing there and that everything else had been only a bad dream. The little girl stared back, wide-eyed, at Laura's gaze. She was beautiful, but she was not Alice.

Noticing what Laura was looking at the sales assistant smiled indulgently at the little girl and said to Laura, 'Aren't they just adorable at that age?' But Laura did not answer her. She was already heading towards the door, fighting hard to hold back the tears, and leaving the poor saleswoman wondering what she had said to offend her.

Laura had had enough. This was never really a good day for a Christmas shopping trip. Not after last night. Alice was too much on her mind. She had to get away from these crowds. Michael's new watch would just have to wait.

She pulled her coat tight against the cold, and made her way down the busy street, feeling positively shaken. The stalls were crammed high and the pavement was bustling with shoppers wrestling with too many bags of presents. Above the sea of heads Laura noticed a placard which was being held high by a down-at-heel street-preacher, who was shouting through his loud-hailer determined to be heard above the yells of street-vendors and hum of generators; 'The end of the world is nigh!'

Reaching the end of the pedestrianised street, Laura was just about to hail a taxi, when she noticed a small neon sign hanging above a basement shop. It read, 'Avril – clairvoyant, psychic, medium, tarot readings'.

Laura stood still for a moment. Usually she had no time for this sort of thing, but she was curious. She just couldn't stop thinking about Wilson's Ribbon and how that crazy old woman had somehow known where it was. Maybe this so-called 'psychic' could answer some of her outstanding questions.

Letting the taxi drive on, she crossed the road to the shop and hesitated a moment, before descending the steep steps down into the psychic's basement consulting parlour.

Letting herself in, Laura glanced around the small room. It was painted a soft, baby pink. An array of different crystals lined the bookcases. In the centre of the room was a round table, covered with a purple velvet cloth, and behind it an old armchair.

On the wall behind that was a large sign, hand written in felt-tip pen. It read 'Initial Consultation $20'

Laura found herself wondering what she was doing here. She would never have set foot in such a place had Michael been with her, and now she was here, she wasn't at all sure it would be helpful. Michael believed places like this to be run by unscrupulous people, charlatans who would make up any old thing they thought the client wanted to hear, and then charge them for the privilege.

On the wall alongside the sign there hung a neat row of framed certificates from 'The New York School of Psychic Studies' and various other training organisations for the psychic arts. It was a great surprise to Laura that there were training courses for such things. Avril must have had every qualification going in her area of expertise. Laura smiled to herself at the thought.

'Hello!' a voice greeted her from behind, 'Do take a seat.'

Laura turned round to see a smartly dressed woman in her early fifties. Her fair hair was short and tidy, and her neat attire gave her the efficient look of a well placed PA. There was no sign of the curly black hair, gold earrings, or long, flowing gypsy skirt that Laura had anticipated.

'Thank-you,' said Laura, momentarily disconcerted by the sheer ordinariness of Avril's appearance.

'Now, what can I do for you?' enquired Avril politely, as she sat down in the armchair opposite.

'I'm sorry...I've never done anything like this before,' Laura began to explain hesitantly, '...but something's happened recently and I want to know if ...if someone who has died... is trying to communicate with me'. Laura found it hard to believe what she heard herself saying.

'You mean someone on the other side?' Laura found herself nodding agreement as Avril continued, 'People don't really die, you see, they just cross over to the other side. You could say that people who have died have simply moved to another realm.'

It felt odd to be talking about the dead in this way, but Laura also found it intriguing. Her parents had been atheists. She had grown up with the belief that all you had was one short life and when it was over that was it, there was nothing more. Yet she found something strangely comforting about Avril's words, even if she wasn't sure there was any truth in them.

Avril was now placing a crystal ball in the centre of the table. It was a lot smaller than the crystal skull, cloudy and roughly hewn. She ran her long-nailed fingers across its surface and met Laura's eyes with a steady gaze.

'How does it work?' asked Laura.

'We call it 'channelling'' replied Avril. 'The crystal is like a focusing device. I go into a trance so I can receive messages from those on the other side. It is not always reliable though,' she cautioned, 'the dead do a lot of talking and sometimes all I can pick up is interference. Do you still want me to try?'

Laura thought about it for a moment. She figured she didn't really have anything to lose, apart from the $20 consulting fee, of course.

'Yes,' she confirmed, 'Why not?'

There was something strangely exhilarating about doing something so utterly against the grain, so at variance with her usual beliefs and behaviour. *Laura Shepherd visiting a psychic!* She wondered what her colleagues at the museum would have to say if they ever found out. *Funny how things sometimes turn out*, she thought. If she hadn't gone to see Anna Crockett-Burrows she would never even have considered such a thing, but now here she was sitting in a psychic's consulting room. She knew she was clutching at straws, but where else could she look for the answers she wanted?

'Very well.' said Avril as she placed her hands on the crystal ball, closed her eyes and begun humming softly to herself. It was all very strange. Laura felt as if she were attending some sort of mini-séance. All that was missing it seemed was the ouja board.

After a minute or so Avril opened her eyes and asked 'Has a colleague of yours died recently?'

'Yes!' answered Laura, amazed.

Avril closed her eyes again and resumed humming, while Laura sat there in stunned silence, wondering if she was going to have to revise her ideas about these things.

After a few minutes Avril opened her eyes and spoke again. 'But I'm afraid I don't understand the rest.' She sounded frustrated. 'All I'm getting, over and over again is, 'you need the skull for accurate communication'. Does that mean anything to you?'

'Yes!' Laura's voice was filled with excitement. 'The crystal skull. I can bring it here!'

But Avril looked doubtful. 'I don't normally work with other people's materials.'

Laura's face fell with disappointment.

The psychic hesitated, 'Alright,' she offered, 'Let me check with my cards. One moment.'

She turned her back to Laura, pulling her chair round to the small table behind her, on which lay three packs of tarot cards.

She picked up the decks, closed her eyes and concentrated hard as she shuffled each of them, and then slowly and deliberately pulled a card from each pack.

She laid them down carefully on the table in front of her, and opened her eyes. She looked down at the cards laid out in a row. Her face registered alarm as she saw that each of the cards depicted the grotesque figure of the dancing skeleton. The cards read, 'Death', 'Death', 'Death'!

'Well, what do they say?' asked Laura, craning her neck to try to see what Avril was looking at, curious to know why she appeared to have frozen stock still.

But Avril coughed and quickly cleared the cards away again back into their decks before Laura leaned over far enough to have seen them.

'I don't think that would be such a good idea.' she said, looking visibly shaken.

'Why not?' enquired Laura.

'I just don't get a good feeling about it.'

Laura looked quizzical. *Whatever is she being so secretive about?*

'It could be dangerous.' replied Avril curtly, refusing to elaborate any further.

Chapter 22

Michael was sitting alone in the crowded restaurant. He liked *Dimitri's* –
the bold, modern art that adorned its walls and the smart minimalism of its
contemporary interior. Despite being busy it had that hushed reverence
reserved for upmarket eateries. He looked around him at the other smartly-
dressed diners. Most of them were in couples.

He played with his table napkin and glanced again at his watch as he
waited anxiously for Laura. She was late and he was beginning to wonder
what might have happened to her. Ever since Alice's death he had become
more inclined to worry about her safety. Then the door opened, and in
walked Laura, indicating Michael to the eager waiter that rushed to usher
her to a table.

She came over and kissed him on the cheek, 'Hi!'

'You're late. What happened?' Michael sounded concerned.

'I'm sorry, I got held up,' she looked a little guilty as she sat down
opposite him.

'Doing what?' Michael couldn't imagine Laura getting held up doing the
Christmas shopping which he knew she had always hated, even at the best
of times.

'Have you ordered yet?' asked Laura, opening the menu.

'Not yet' he responded automatically, though he knew she was trying to
change the subject. 'Hey, tell me!' he insisted.

'Alright,' Laura took a sharp intake of breath, 'I went to see a psychic'.

She glanced at him nervously over the top of her menu.

Michael put down the piece of bread he was about to butter. He looked
stunned.

'What did you do that for?'

'I wanted to know if Alice really was trying to communicate with us.'

'Alice! How could she?' exclaimed Michael, incredulous.

Just then a waiter appeared at their table and there was a long silent
pause as Laura nodded and they waited while he poured them both a glass
of water. Laura knew Michael would not approve of her going to see a
psychic, but she was surprised by the vehemence of his reaction.

'Anna Crockett-Burrows believes that the dead can talk to us through
the crystal skull,' she explained.

'What?' said Michael, aghast.

'Even the psychic told me I needed the skull for accurate communication,' she added.

Michael glanced around the restaurant, embarrassed, hoping nobody else was listening. He lowered his voice almost to a whisper 'Laura, are you serious?' But she obviously was. 'You've been upset, but think about it rationally'.

'I know it doesn't seem to make any sense,' Laura began, 'but...'

'Too damned right it doesn't!' Michael cut in.

'...how else can you explain what the old woman knew? Alice's name! Wilson's ribbon! I mean, what if she's right, Michael?' Laura sounded excited. 'What if Alice still exists somewhere and really could talk to us through the skull? Wouldn't it be amazing? It would change everything.'

Michael's eyes were closed as he massaged his temples with his fingers. He couldn't comprehend what Laura was saying. It was too damned weird. She was beginning to sound just a little bit too irrational, it was almost frightening.

'What's happening to you Laura? Can you hear yourself?' He reached out his hands to hold hers in quiet desperation.

'But Anna said it was Alice who told her about Wilson's ribbon. ...How else could she have known?'

Michael had had enough. 'Alice is dead Laura! ...And that's the end of it!' he snapped, his elbow accidentally knocking over his wineglass. Red wine spilled across the starched white tablecloth. He grabbed his table napkin to try to mop up the mess, but his words had come out louder than he intended and the couples sat nearest to them all turned and stared, as his bright white napkin began to turn a deep blood red. Even Michael had to banish the thought that it looked a bit like Wilson's ribbon.

Michael and Laura sat there in uneasy silence as a waiter came to replace the tablecloth. Michael asked for the bill and as the waiter disappeared back into the kitchens, he added through gritted teeth, 'She's filling your mind with nonsense Laura. She knows you're vulnerable. That skull's just an ordinary object, nothing more.'

'That's what I thought,' replied Laura, 'But how can you be so sure? I mean even the lab couldn't find any tool-marks. Explain that?'

'Come on then!' he said firmly and got up from the table as more heads turned, 'I will!'

He fumbled for his wallet, slammed some cash down on the table, and headed for the door.

'But Michael, I've only just...' Laura tried to protest, then gave up, and went after him.

Chapter 23

They drove to Michael's office in silence. The new Nanon Systems building was a solid block of chrome and glass, an imposing monument to progress and profitability. As a cutting edge research facility, it had not escaped the pervasive pressure of appearance - the need to look good. Not only the results the company achieved but the building its employees worked in, were now shaped by this market requirement. Science had moved out of the domain of campus casualness and was now housed in the hi-tech offices that were favoured by the city.

As they reached the gates, a red sports car was just leaving.

'That's all I need.' muttered Michael as a man got out of the car and came over to them.

'Hello Michael!' grinned the bear-like man in his mid-forties. It was Michael's boss, company chairman, Caleb Price.

'Hi Caleb, I've just finished that report.' Michael was thinking on his feet as to why he had brought his wife out to the office on a Sunday evening. 'I was just popping by to pick up some papers for tomorrow's meeting.'

'And how is the lovely Laura?' Asked Caleb.

It was the kind of patronizing, mildly sexist comment that Laura had come to expect from Michaels' new employer.

'Fine.' she answered. Caleb was still staring at her, and she realized he was expecting her to make further pleasant conversation. Trying hard to think of something, she offered,

'You're keeping Michael busy with this new 'Z - project' of yours, what is it?

Caleb frowned, 'We could tell you Laura, but then we'd have to kill you!'

Laura was momentarily shocked, before she noticed him smirking. He stood up.

'You know the rules Michael, total confidentiality on all new projects – and that includes wives and family'.

'I know Caleb, absolutely.' Michael replied.

'See you tomorrow.' said Caleb, climbing back into his car.

'Christ Laura, you really landed me in it there.' said Michael, after he'd gone.

'I'm sorry.'

'As far as Caleb's concerned, I'm still in my probationary period'.

'Even after more than a year?'

'Yes.' He replied through gritted teeth.

He parked the car and marched towards the hi-tech office block carrying the skull case, while Laura followed close behind, trying to keep up.

'The problem is your guys down at the museum just don't have the right equipment. But we do...' he said as they entered the out-of-hours building through giant revolving glass doors.

A security guard in the foyer looked up from his bank of CCTV monitors and nodded his recognition of Michael,

''Evening, Dr Greenstone'.

Michael nodded back as he swiped his security card at the turnstiles and continued his conversation with Laura as they headed towards the elevators.

'...Right here we've got the most advanced crystal laboratory in the country, and you'll soon see there's a simple, rational explanation for this thing.' he said as he and Laura climbed into the lift and made their way to the laboratory on the second floor.

Michael swiped his ID card again to gain access to the crystal lab.

Once inside, he took out the skull and placed it under a large state-of-the-art microscope. 'Under this electron microscope here we get a magnification of a million times,' he explained as he put his eye to the viewfinder.

He looked puzzled. 'I don't get it.'

'What?' enquired Laura.

'You're right. No tool marks.' He frowned.

Laura looked gratified. Michael had come up with exactly the same result as Ian in the museum laboratory. She couldn't help feeling secretly pleased even though she knew that a more definitive result would have helped her more with her report on the skull for her boss, museum director Professor Lamb.

'It can't really be crystal,' muttered Michael, as much to himself as to Laura, 'It must be plastic or glass.' He paused another moment. 'There's only one way to tell. Here, give me a hand with this...' he said, asking Laura to help him pull a heavy sliding cabinet out from the wall to reveal a large glass tank of transparent liquid.

'What is it?'

'The acid test!' Michael replied as he dimmed the lights.

He placed the crystal skull on a small metal platform above the tank, pressed a button and the platform began to descend towards the liquid.

'What are you doing?' Laura panicked at the thought that Michael was about to submerge the skull in acid. She peered into the tank to see the crystal skull become submerged beneath the liquid, whereupon it disappeared.

'Where is it?' She was horrified.

'Don't panic' said Michael, 'It's not really acid, it's only alcohol. It's actually benzyl alcohol of the same refractive index as quartz crystal. Watch!'

He threw a switch and the skull miraculously reappeared. Laura was relieved, Michael surprised.

'Hell, it IS crystal alright – 100% silicon dioxide – pure quartz. This polarised light test proves it for sure.' He pressed another button and the skull rose back out of the tank.

'I wonder if it is piezo-electric' he pondered.

'Hey, less of the geek-speak!' teased Laura. She didn't have a clue what Michael was talking about. 'You're confusing me.'

'What do you expect' replied Michael, 'I'm a physicist. People like me have been confusing everyone else for centuries.'

Laura was encouraged to see that Michael's mood was lifting.

'But seriously, you wonder if it's what?'

'Piezo-electric,' he repeated, 'Like the type of crystal we use in all our electronics'.

Donning some surgical gloves, he wiped the skull clean and mounted it onto another piece of equipment with a large metal frame. He pressed a switch and a vice-like mechanism on the machine started to close around the skull.

'Don't damage it, Michael!'

'It's OK,' he explained, 'When you squeeze piezo-electric quartz it gives off an electric charge. Look!'

Laura was amazed to see sparks flying from the skull in the darkened room as it was squeezed between the jaws of the machine.

'Not only that,' continued Michael, 'If you apply an electric current to it, it changes its shape and density. Watch!' He attached some electrodes to the skull and flicked another switch. The skull's face started to distort.

Laura was disconcerted, 'What was that?'

'Don't worry, that's perfectly normal,' Michael reassured her, before glancing at the skull to see the image of Laura's face suddenly appearing inside it. He stared at it. The image before him was pale and lifeless. Laura's eyes were closed. She looked like a corpse.

Michael swiftly switched the machine off and the horrifying image vanished as quickly as it had appeared.

'What's wrong?' asked Laura, worried by his expression.

'Nothing.' He dismissed the disturbing apparition as nothing more than a fleeting illusion.

'But that's incredible!' said Laura.

'Not really,' replied Michael, 'That's why we use this stuff everyday in all our electronic devices,' he said as he removed the skull from the electrode machine. 'Piezo-electric quartz has all kinds of time-keeping, information storage and communications applications'.

'Communications?' Laura's ears pricked up.

'We're talking watches, computers and mobile phones here, Laura, not talking to the dead.' He smiled wryly. 'This is the kind of stuff we use to make microchips,' he continued, 'Inside those tiny silicon crystal chips is where the information inside the computer is actually stored.'

Laura shook her head, intrigued, 'That's amazing.'

'This type of crystal is like the 'brain-cells' inside the computer, the 'eyes' inside the television set or the 'ears' inside the mobile phone'.

'So where's it from?' asked Laura.

'Let's see, shall we?' Michael said as he carefully placed the skull under an imaging device linked to a computer. He typed in 'Global Geographic Search' and the device started to scan slowly around the skull from all angles. A map of the world appeared on the computer screen. Each continent was highlighted in red as it processed the information, before announcing in soft, computer-modulated tones, 'Origin unknown'.

Michael and Laura looked at one another, dumbfounded, before Michael suggested,

'OK, let's take a look at its molecular structure.'

He typed in 'Analyse Molecular Structure' and the scanner started to rotate around the skull as the computer screen built up a three-dimensional image of an octagonal crystalline matrix. The image fell apart, before the machine tried to reconfigure it, only for it to fragment again.

Michael was amazed, 'I've never seen anything like this before. Its molecular structure is octagonal instead of hexagonal like all known crystal. Even the computer doesn't seem to recognise it'. They watched as the computer kept trying to build up a stable image, but each time the matrix fell apart.

'It's like no other crystal on this Earth!'

They looked at each other.

'And it appears to be molecularly unstable.' Michael rubbed his chin, deep in thought, when he had an idea.

'Hold on! This could have applications,' he said with excitement, 'Let's check out its optical properties'.

He grabbed the skull and mounted it onto a laser machine.

He threw a switch and a stroboscopic beam of laser light fired up from beneath the skull. This beam of red light refracted back out of the skull's eyes and shined onto a nearby wall. Michael and Laura watched in awe as the pinpoint-accurate beam started to etch out digits, burning them into the paintwork.

It looked like a mysterious printed code that read:

'122120121221201212212012122120121221201212212012
122120121221201212212012122120121221201212212012
122120121221201212212012122120121221201212212012'

After a few seconds, the laser beam came to a halt and started to burn a black hole into the middle of the digits. The hole grew bigger and bigger, as smoke started to appear. It took them a moment to realise what was going on, before Michael turned off the machine, grabbed a fire extinguisher, and managed to douse the smouldering black mark just before it would have burst into flames.

'What the hell was that?' exclaimed Laura.

'I have no idea,' replied Michael, as he examined the digits freshly burnt into the wall. '...but I think it's some sort of code.'

He examined the digits more closely.

'In fact, it looks a bit like a tertiary code.'

'A what?' replied Laura.

'Our computers,' explained Michael, 'based on normal crystal, break all calculations down into ones and zeros, what we call a 'binary code'. But this, look, is a series of ones, zeros and also twos, what we would call a 'tertiary code'.

Laura was impressed.

'It looks like the crystal inside this skull is capable of far more complex calculations than all of today's computers' continued Michael.

'You really think so?'

'Think about it!' he turned to her, 'If I'm right, and this is a tertiary code, this type of octagonal-matrix crystal could offer computing power beyond even our wildest dreams.'

His eyes were shining with excitement.

'Caleb's not going to believe it. The whole company's going to want to know about this.'

He paused for a moment's thought. 'But first I need to find out where that old woman got this thing,' he whispered almost to himself.

'She said it was on an archaeological expedition to Central America.'

'There's no way this thing's ancient.' replied Michael 'This is next generation stuff. I mean, maybe a competitor's got the edge? This is like 'tomorrow's technology, today!'' he exclaimed, effectively reciting his company's slogan.

'I'm going out to see that old woman tomorrow. See where she really got this from. 'You coming?'

'I can't,' answered Laura. 'I've got to go to Ron's funeral.'

Chapter 24

December 10th 2012

Michael's silver Audi drew to a halt in front of Anna Crockett-Burrows old mansion house. He got out of the car, walked up to the porch and knocked on the front door. He was filled with an irrepressible feeling of excitement. He had a sense that he was onto something, and it looked set to be something big.

Right now, he needed a major project to come to fruition. As Head of Research at Nanon Systems he had grappled with a number of ideas over the last year and really needed one of them to take shape. His future at Nanon depended on it. Not that his boss Caleb had said anything, but Michael knew he had a reputation to maintain as Caleb's top man. He didn't want anyone usurping his position. That was always a possibility, a constant threat in the modern workplace, but if this thing worked out, this skull could help him cement his position.

He knocked again. Getting no reply, he shouted up at the shuttered windows

'Hello! Is there anybody home?' But there was still no reply. He wished Laura had got the woman's phone number.

He wandered round the side to the back of the house, hoping he might find someone there. Taking in the vast expanse of garden and the lack of neighbours, Michael was puzzled by the kind of person who would choose to live in such solitude. Without the bustle of the city, he didn't feel at ease.

'Hello!' he called out again. The deathly silence of the place made him feel on edge. He looked up at the back of the house, surveying the fading paintwork and the closed shutters. It was beginning to look pretty clear there was nobody home. He was about to call it a day and head back round to the front of the house when something caught his eye. Through a sunken window that came up to no higher than his knees, he thought he saw something in the basement. Michael moved closer to try to get a better look. The window was grey with dirt, so much so that he couldn't quite make it out, but he could have sworn he saw something in there, something that looked alarmingly like a face.

Chapter 25

Earlier that afternoon Laura had been attending Ron's funeral. As she raised her voice to sing the hymn 'Rock of Ages', it sounded as if only one other person was singing. The service was poorly attended. Only a handful of other people had arrived when Laura had filed into her seat near the front. She felt a little awkward being the only representative of the museum there. Still, she didn't suppose Ron would have minded. He would have wanted things to be low key, without any fuss.

She had arrived at the remote chapel just after three. Ron's will had specified that his funeral service take place in the countryside where he loved walking. It was where he wanted his ashes scattered too.

As Laura listened to the priest's sermon, she found her thoughts drifting back to the service she and Michael had had for Alice. The priest had commented on how joyful Alice had been. It had been part of who she was. It wasn't just the way Laura remembered her. People, sometimes strangers, had commented on how cheerful she was. Her nature had been 'sunny', there was no other word for it.

The priest at Alice's funeral had spoken of this special joyful quality of hers. He had speculated that perhaps Alice might have been so joyful because although she didn't know it, her time here was to be so short, and so God had helped her to enjoy every moment she could. At the time, Laura had found no comfort in his words, but now, she wondered. Maybe there was something in what he had said?

The priest at Ron's funeral continued, 'When I spoke with Ron at our last service together, he seemed to have found some comfort in the belief that his beloved wife Lillian was trying to communicate with him from the world beyond.' Hearing this, Laura's attention returned abruptly to the present moment.

That was it! thought Laura. *That must have been why Ron seemed so uncharacteristically happy just before he died.* He was convinced that his wife, who had died a couple of years before, was trying to communicate with him. *Could this have had something to do with the crystal skull?* she wondered. *Could the crystal skull really provide a means of communicating with the dead, just as the old lady had said? Perhaps then it really could provide a means of communicating with Alice?*

Laura wondered if the priest knew any more about Ron's newly emerged belief in the afterlife and the idea that he could somehow communicate with the dead. Of course it still wouldn't explain why Ron died or how, but she decided she needed to talk to the priest as soon as the service was over.

'Now at last they can be together, reunited in God's love' the priest continued. She looked at Ron's coffin, resting close in front of her; a life over and drawn to a close. But she was glad to think that at least Ron's final weeks had offered him some kind of comfort and hope. Believing that you could be with loved ones again made the universe seem a much kinder, more loving place. It certainly seemed a lot better than the alternative.

'We now commit Ronald Smith's body to everlasting peace.' The priest solemnly closed the ceremony, 'Ashes to ashes, dust to dust'. The sound of sombre organ music began as Ron's coffin slid slowly away on a conveyor belt behind the crematorium curtain.

Laura was glad the service was over. Getting up to leave, she was filing out of the chapel behind the handful of other guests when she was taken aback to see Anna Crockett-Burrows and her maid sitting in the back row. What was she doing there? It didn't seem to make any sense. The old woman had given Laura no indication whatsoever that she had known Ron. In fact, thinking back to her meeting with Anna, the old woman had been positively elusive when Laura had asked her about him.

Anxious to catch the priest before he left, Laura waited patiently outside the chapel door where he stood talking to the other remaining guests. But before she'd had a chance to talk to him Anna Crockett-Burrows and her maid approached.

'Hello' said Laura warily, 'I didn't know you knew Ron?'

'It is you we came for.' The old woman replied enigmatically. 'We came because we knew you would be here.'

'But why?' asked Laura, perplexed.

'You want to hear your daughter's message, don't you?'

The fact was she did want to know if Alice had a message for her. In fact, she wanted to know with an intensity she had not reckoned on. She had to know, sooner rather than later, if there was any truth in what the old woman had said to her two nights before.

'I was going to ask you about that,' Laura began hesitantly, 'How did you know...?'

'...About the ribbon?' Anna finished her sentence for her.

'I didn't. It was your daughter's way of convincing you that it was her doing the talking, not me. Your daughter says there is something else, something far more important.'

'What is it?' asked Laura.

'It is most urgent.' Anna paused. 'But she wants to tell you herself. When you are alone. Do you have the skull?'

Laura returned to her car in the chapel car park and lifted the skull case out of the boot. She tried to phone Michael on her cell-phone to tell him she was with Anna Crockett-Burrows, but he was on answer-phone so she left him a message.

She heard a car starting behind her and turned round to see the priest driving off towards the exit. She waved at him to try to catch his attention, but it was too late. He had driven off into the fading light.

She looked around the car park. It was almost empty now. Crockett-Burrows' car was the only other vehicle that remained. As she walked back to the chapel she began to feel some anxiety about her decision to stay on, alone, in this remote place.

She tried to ignore that part of her that said what she was doing wasn't safe, that it wasn't a sensible thing to do. For there was a greater part of her that wanted to believe Anna, that wanted to believe Anna really could get a message for her from Alice. She wanted, more than anything, to believe that Alice was still out there somewhere.

She paused and looked up at the clear sky. She needed to believe that out there, somewhere in the vastness of the cosmos, her child still existed. It freed her from the idea of Alice simply lying there dead in the cemetery, a thought that hung like a millstone in her mind, weighing her down with grief.

The chapel door creaked slowly open as Laura re-entered. It was now dark inside save for the flickering glow of the large, white candles which burned brightly around the altar. The chapel looked empty. Laura called out 'Hello!' before stepping past the stone pillars to see the old woman seated, staring straight ahead, with her back to her in the front row.

Laura's footsteps echoed across the hard marble floor as she made her way hesitantly down the aisle. She glanced around the room. The maid was nowhere to be seen.

'Sit here!' said Anna indicating the place beside her, hemmed in on the front pew, '...and give me the skull.'

Laura sat down next to her, took the skull carefully out of its case and passed it to the old woman. 'Perhaps you could explain...?' she began.

'There's no time for questions' said Crockett-Burrows curtly as Laura handed her the skull. 'Get yourself a pen and paper and write down everything I say,' she added, 'I shall be channelling this information and I may not remember anything I do or say afterwards'.

Anna smiled at the skull as she placed it in her lap, stroking it with her old wrinkled fingers. A shiver ran down Laura's spine at the sight of it.

But she did as she was told and began searching through her briefcase for something to write on. She took out her mobile phone and placed it on the pew, as she continued looking for a pen and paper. Just as she found them, Anna apparently accidentally knocked her phone onto the hard floor, where it landed with a 'crack!'

'Oh dear,' said Crockett-Burrows, rising to her feet. The old woman stumbled to the side, putting her full weight on top of the phone.

'My phone!' exclaimed Laura, upset by the old woman's clumsy actions.

'I am sorry,' said Anna, as she sat down again.

Laura picked up the phone and tested it, but it was broken.

'Well at least we won't be disturbed.' Anna added and Laura wondered if she caught the fleeting glimpse of a smile on the old lady's lips?

At that moment, Laura heard the door slam shut behind her and turned around to see the maid reappearing at the back of the chapel with two huge, black Great Danes. They must have been the dogs she had heard barking on her visit to Anna's house. She turned back to Anna, wondering what Alice had to tell her.

Chapter 26

Back at Anna's house, Michael was trying to work out what he had seen through her basement window. Whatever it was, he was determined to find out. He brushed away the cobwebs, wiped off the dirt, and peered in. But it was too dark for him to make out what was inside.

So he reached into his jacket pocket and pulled out a flashlight-pen. He lay flat on the ground and shone it into the darkness. What he saw lit up by his torch-beam hit him like a punch in the stomach.

There, pinned to the dirty basement wall was a collection of photographs, all of Ron Smith! There must have been about twenty of them altogether. Freeze-frame CCTV images and Polaroid photographs of Ron's face, all taken from different angles. Ron looked as though he had no idea he was being photographed. His expression was blank and emotionless. On a shelf beside the photographs was a skull.

But it didn't look like what he'd seen from outside. So he panned his torch-beam slowly across the interior. Suddenly his flashlight illuminated something much nearer to him. He pulled back in shock. His breath came in short gasps, before he dared to look again. He shone the torch now with trembling hands. It was a face he'd seen alright. Lit up in the dark before him was Ron Smith's grey lifeless head, impaled on a skewer!

Michael felt sick. The taste of bile was in his mouth. He stumbled a few feet away, and retched. He stood there for a few moments, leaning over, his hands resting on his thighs. He was in shock. That was Ron. That was his head! But how could that be? How? Had Laura gone to the funeral of a headless corpse? What was going on?

He stood up straight, and walked back towards the basement. He needed to know more. He took a deep breath and lay down again, ready to take another look. But nothing could have prepared him for what he saw next, as he picked up his torch and shone it back inside.

There, to his horror, was another set of photographs pinned to the dirty basement wall. These photographs, like Ron's, were all taken from different angles. But this time, what he saw chilled him to the core. For the likeness was unmistakeable. These photographs were all of Laura, her face a frozen mask of fear.

'Oh my God!' he whispered 'God, No!'

He wasn't sure he could bear to look any further but felt he had to. He had to know what else was in there. His arm was trembling now as his torchlight illuminated the base of another skewer. He was filled with dread. He felt a deep sinking feeling in the pit of his stomach, and his torch felt heavy in his hand as he tilted its beam upwards.

'No, it can't be!' he said to himself, 'It can't be her.' But there was no mistaking it. There, right in front of him, captured in the beam of his torch was the horrifying truth. Before him was Laura's face. It was her dead, hairless head, impaled on a skewer! There could be no denying it was her. He recognised the distinctive curve of her fine cheek bones, her wide eyes, beautiful lips, and aquiline nose; all the features of the woman he loved.

Michael suffered a moment of unimaginable horror as he looked at his dead wife. There she was, hairless, and eyes glazed, staring blankly back at him. He was caught in a moment of sheer terror that seemed to stretch for all eternity, a moment that took him straight to hell as he stared at her unable to believe his eyes. The terror reached right into him, and tore at his very soul, as if a sharp blade was being twisted around and around inside his heart. 'No!' he howled, the full force of his lungs blasting the air from him.

He drew back, numb with shock and disbelief, and vomited. How could this have happened? What evil monster could do this? He had left her only that morning, and where was the rest of her? He had to get to her. He stumbled over to the window, raised his foot up and smashed it through the glass.

He kicked off the shards and squeezed his way in.

In the semi darkness of the interior, he staggered towards her. Laura's face was blank, devoid of the animating life force that made her his lovely wife. With trembling hands he reached out to touch her face. *My Laura. My beautiful Laura*. He drew his hand back in revulsion. It was her alright. But her face was cold, clammy to the touch. Something had come away on his hands. It was damp and sticky. What had they done to her?

He reached into his pocket and pulled out his torch. His hands were shaking so much that a few tortuous seconds passed before he could turn it on. Then it was too much. He could not bear to shine the beam at her, to see what they had done.

He shone it down at his fingers. They were wet and grey.

It was clay! He pointed the beam up. His heart filled with elation. It wasn't Laura at all. It wasn't real. He wanted to leap with joy. It was only a clay model, an effigy of her!

The likeness was uncanny. He touched it again. Tears of relief ran down his cheeks. *Thank God!* he cried out inside, *Thank God it's not you!* This time he was not mistaken. It was definitely only clay. He went over and examined the effigy of Ron. Again, the likeness was incredible. It was hard to the touch. It must have been made a while ago.

He went back to Laura. Her head was fresh, newly made. The joy he had felt was beginning to disappear. Alongside the head was a table on which a selection of knives and blades lay. He presumed they had been used to make the effigies.

He picked up a blade. It was razor sharp. *What are they doing making an effigy of Ron, who is dead, and now Laura?* He scanned the cellar for more clues. But there were none. All that was there were the heads, and a clay skull.

He tried the door. It was locked. He took in the photographs lining the walls. Whatever had been going on here, it wasn't good. *This is bloody weird.* He found himself panicking at the thought. He had to tell Laura. He had to warn her she was in danger!

He dashed back over to the window and dragged himself through, as broken glass tore at his trouser legs. Stumbling to his feet, he ran as fast as he could round to the front of the house and back to his car.

He jumped in, grabbed his phone from the passenger seat and dialled her number.

Pickup Laura, pickup! he willed her, but there was no answer. A recorded announcement informed him that her number was 'Not in service'. Instead, there was 'One new message' from 'Laura' which he played back. It was the message she had left him earlier that afternoon:

'Hi Michael, you won't find Anna out there. You won't believe it but she's right here at Ron's funeral. She says she has something she wants to share with me, in private. I really want to hear what it is, so we're staying on here alone at the chapel after everyone else has gone. So I'll see you later. Love you. Bye!'

Michael had hoped Laura was safe, but now it felt as if his whole world was collapsing, all over again. Whatever that woman had done to Ron, she also had designs on Laura.

He threw down the phone, turned the key in the ignition and slammed the accelerator down hard. His car screeched out of Anna's gravel driveway, while the grotesque image of Laura he had just seen ran over and over in his mind.

Chapter 27

In the chapel, Anna Crockett-Burrows was sitting with eyes closed, her fingers resting lightly on the skull. Laura felt uneasy as she waited, poised with pen and paper in hand. She glanced at the shadows from the candles as they danced on the wall and listened to the sound of the wind as it whipped around the lonely car park and rattled in the porch outside.

'Now we can begin' said the old woman. She started slowly rolling the crystal skull around in her hands. Then unexpectedly, she lifted it up and pressed its forehead against her own. She began a tuneless low-pitched humming sound. She seemed to be willing herself into a trance-like state. Laura was finding the whole experience very strange indeed.

Suddenly, the old lady's blind eyes sprang open and she started speaking in a bizarre staccato voice, 'You must know and all must know that S K times M C squared equals minus one, not zero. I repeat, S K times M C squared equals minus one, not zero'.

Puzzled, Laura wrote down what the old woman was saying, in shorthand formula: 'sk x mc2 = -1, not O.' as Anna Crockett-Burrows repeated it again, her voice growing in pitch and intensity.

Laura looked at what she had written and up at Anna. 'That's not my daughter!' she said. But Anna ignored her 'I repeat, equals minus one, not zero'.

'I'm telling you, that's not my daughter' exclaimed Laura, putting away her pen and paper. 'She was only four years old, for God's sake! That's not her!'

'But you must listen,' the old woman insisted, her voice now strangely menacing 'You are in great danger. You must heed my warning or you will die! Heed my warning or you will die!'

The grotesque horror of Anna's words hit Laura like a punch in the chest. This isn't how it was meant to be, thought Laura. There was no way that was her beautiful little daughter's voice. She hadn't allowed her self to dare to imagine what Alice's message might be, but this certainly wasn't it. This was just too disturbing. These were not the words of a joyful, playful, innocent child. This was no message from Alice. To Laura, the whole thing suddenly seemed like a sick joke at her expense.

'That's not Alice! That is not my little girl,' she cried. She was angry now and frightened. 'You lied to me! You tricked me into staying on out here.

What are you trying to do to me?' she said, getting up quickly to leave.

But Anna just raised her voice, even more insistent now, 'But you must heed my warning or you will die, daddy will die, all will die!'

Laura felt a rising sense of panic. This was all too much for her. She stuffed her notepad back into her briefcase and turned to leave, as the old woman started shouting: **'HEED MY WARNING OR YOU WILL DIE, DADDY WILL DIE, ALL WILL DIE!'**

The old woman's voice echoed after Laura as she began to flee down the central aisle. Her brisk walk broke into a run as she felt compelled to get out of that chapel as quickly as possible. But just as she neared the back of the chapel, the two big, black dogs, upset by the commotion, blocked her exit. They barked and growled fiercely, baring their teeth as they strained against their leads. As the maid got up from her seat, Laura, terrified, dashed down one of the rows of pews and round to the side-aisle in her attempt to escape.

She could hear Anna's strange voice now shouting, 'Mummy! Please! You must listen! You are in great danger. You must stop at the sign of the cross! **MUMMY! PLEEASE! STOP AT THE SIGN OF THE CROSS!'**

These words echoed after Laura as she finally managed to exit the door at the back of the chapel. She didn't notice that above the door there hung a large wooden cross.

It was dark outside as she ran down the chapel steps and across the car park to the safety of her car. She jumped in and slammed the door. She started the engine. It turned over and cut out. Looking up, she saw the housekeeper emerging from the chapel with the dogs. She looked at Laura and released them. The dogs bounded towards Laura's car.

Laura tried the ignition and the engine cut out again. *Come on!* she said to herself, desperate to get the car started. The dogs were now jumping up at her window growling ferociously, as the housekeeper ran across the car park towards her, shouting.

Eventually the engine kicked in, and her tyres spun momentarily on the black ice, before she screeched off out of the car park.

It was snowing heavily and road visibility was poor as she drove off fast into the night. As she sped along the thickly wooded, empty country road she felt furious with herself. How could she have been so stupid? After the way the two women had behaved when she went out to their house! What was she thinking of staying on to get Alice's so called 'message'? It bothered her that she had made such an enormous error in her judgement. It frightened her that she had been so foolish as to be taken in by two people who were clearly insane. There was no other explanation for it.

She had been driving for less than two minutes when the engine spluttered and cut out, and her car slowed to a halt.

She had broken down in the middle of nowhere, not far from the chapel, surrounded by nothing but forest.

She got out her torch and looked under the bonnet. The engine ticked quietly as it cooled. There was nothing obviously wrong that she could see. 'Damn!' she said to herself, under her steaming breath. *What a place to break down - And with my phone broken!*

The wind was getting up and a blizzard looked likely. She glanced nervously back in the direction of the chapel, pulled her collar close against the cold, and set off ahead, on foot. She couldn't remember having seen any houses for miles, and wondered how long it would be before the two women caught up with her.

Lost and alone in the dark, she was wading on along the edge of the narrow snow-covered road trying to find help, when she heard a car coming quickly towards her. It was travelling at some speed and, before she knew it, it screeched round the corner right in front of her, almost blinding her in its headlights. She jumped quickly out of its way, and was just recovering from the shock, when the car ground to a halt and started slowly reversing back towards her, its red tail-lights all that were visible in the dark.

Laura held her breath in fear as the car pulled up right alongside her.

She was so relieved to see that it was Michael sitting in the driver's seat.

He jumped out of the car and rushed over to her,

'I'm so sorry Laura, are you alright?' He tried to hug her, but she shied away.

'What the hell d'you think you were doing?' Though unhurt, she was trembling.

'I know I was driving too fast, but I had to warn you'.

'Warn me!? You nearly killed me!' exclaimed Laura.

'But the old woman, she's up to something.' said Michael. 'Your life could be in danger...'

Chapter 28

Michael looked at his wife. She looked tense and distraught. What had been a day at a colleague's funeral, never an easy thing at the best of times, had taken such a surreal and unexpected twist. It was one neither of them could have foreseen. They certainly hadn't expected to have to get back in touch with Detective Dominguez, the Homicide detective in charge of Ron's case.

Michael was now on his mobile phone to him, but he wasn't at all sure he was actually getting through to him. He could just picture the detective on the other end of the phone and he sounded as if he was lying back in his chair with his feet up on the desk in front of him.

'So what you're saying is, you think this old lady might have had something to do with Ron's death?'

The detective sounded sceptical and Michael was getting impatient, 'How else can you explain what I saw in her basement?'

He could almost hear the detective shrug and lazily roll a pen across his desk. 'So what do you want us to do about it?'

'Arrest her, of course!' Nothing could have been more obvious, thought Michael.

'Now hold on a minute,' retorted Dominquez, taking his feet off the desk and sitting forward, 'What for?' He paused, waiting for Michael's answer, 'Voodoo?' He paused again, 'Witchcraft?' before giving his own answer. 'Officially they don't even exist.' He raised his voice, 'And in any case, maybe this maid just fancies herself as a bit of an artist, a sculptor, and there's certainly no law against that!'

Now it was the detective's turn to be sounding impatient.

'But surely there must be *something* you can do?' The incomprehension was written all over Michael's face.

Dominguez shrugged again. 'Problem is, there's no forensic evidence to suggest anyone else was involved in Ron's death, and what you're giving me here ain't exactly concrete. It's hardly even circumstantial.' He paused. 'I'm afraid it's no grounds for arrest'.

Michael was outraged. 'But you have to do something!' He looked at his wife. 'Next time it could be Laura!'

Dominguez had to admit that maybe Michael did have a point. 'Granted, it does look a little strange from where I'm sitting,' he was beginning to sound a little more reconciliatory, '...and if it makes you feel any happier, we'll have one of our guys drop by and ask them a few questions. Now if you don't mind...?'

The detective made it clear that he had other business to attend to and rang off.

'What was a waste of space!' muttered Michael as he turned back to watch the emergency mechanic who had arrived to fix Laura's car.

Lit by the flashing amber light of his road-recovery vehicle, they sat in Michael's car and sipped some flask-made coffee from polystyrene cups the mechanic had provided while they waited for him to finish.

Laura's mind was grappling with the weird events of the day, trying to make some sense of them. She hadn't said anything to Michael about the events at the chapel. After Michael had told her about the heads he had seen in Anna's basement, she had been in too much of a state of shock. She felt embarrassed by her naivety. She didn't know how she had been so easily taken in by the old woman. She had wanted so much to believe that Anna had a message from Alice that it had clouded her judgement. She had not been able to see what Crockett-Burrows was really up to. She had been completely unaware that the old lady had some other, much more sinister, agenda.

'So what exactly did happen at the chapel?' asked Michael, but before Laura had had a chance to respond, the mechanic appeared outside the window waving the keys to Laura's car.

'Ah Good!' said Michael 'Now let's get home.'

An icy wind was blowing as they headed back to the city. Michael raced along the empty country road while Laura's car followed some distance behind as she tried to keep up. *Slow down, Michael. Slow down!* she said to herself. It bothered her that Michael drove too fast. He was someone always in a hurry. Sometimes it seemed that he had got so used to living at a fast pace that he was in danger of becoming incapable of slowing down. It was one of the hazards of modern life, thought Laura, one that she had found slightly easier to escape in the museum.

Laura heard a rattling sound. It was the distinctive sound of one of her hubcaps. *It must have come loose again. That's all I need.* It was a regular problem she'd had with her old vehicle ever since she'd bought it from a second-hand dealer.

Michael was tearing on ahead and she was still trying to keep up, when she noticed a crossroads sign by the side of the road and some traffic lights ahead. The lights were changing to green and Michael drove straight on across the junction.

Just then, Laura heard the old woman's voice in her head; 'You must stop at the sign of the cross! MUMMY! PLEEASE! STOP AT THE SIGN OF THE CROSS!'

Suddenly she slammed on her brakes, and her car began to skid towards the crossroads, throwing her forwards against her seatbelt.

At that moment, a huge oil tanker appeared as if from nowhere and careered across the blind junction right in front of her. The tanker had been travelling far too fast when the lights had changed against it. Although its giant wheels were now locked, as the driver slammed on his brakes, it was too late. The speeding juggernaut skidded out of control on the black ice, and was now hurtling straight towards Laura's skidding vehicle.

The huge ton of metal flew forward, horn blaring only at the last moment, as the driver tried in vain to prevent disaster.

Laura felt as if everything had gone into slow-motion, as its great bulking weight slid, wheels screeching towards her. She watched, helpless, as the giant tanker loomed ever closer. She closed her eyes, and waited for the impact.

It never came. The enormous vehicle slid right past, missing her car only by inches.

The tanker drove on, horn still blaring, and disappeared into the night.

Laura was overwhelmed with relief.

She looked at the loose hubcap that had rolled forward from her car when she had stopped so suddenly. It lay on the road, on the very spot she would have been had she not slammed on the brakes the moment she did. It had been crushed entirely flat under the merciless wheels of the giant vehicle.

Michael, hearing the driver's horn, had watched all this, horrified, in his rear view mirror. He pulled to a halt, got out of his car, and ran back to check that Laura was alright.

He found her still sitting in her car. She looked stunned, but not hurt.

'Dear God, Laura! Are you OK?' He opened the car door and hugged her, drinking in her familiar scent, overwhelmed that she was unharmed.

She turned slowly towards him.

'She saved me, Michael, she saved me!'

Michael was crouching down beside the car next to her. He couldn't understand her calmness, or what she was talking about.

'Who?' he asked.

'Anna' answered Laura '...I mean, the skull ...or,' her face lit up '...maybe it was Alice after all?' She looked at Michael, her eyes shining with hope.

Michael's heart sank. She was back there again, talking about Alice as if she were still alive. 'You're not making any sense, honey. What happened?' He wasn't sure he really wanted to know the answer.

'I didn't get a chance to tell you earlier,' began Laura, 'and I know you're not going to like this but... Anna did a 'channelling' session for me at the chapel.'

'What?' He was horrified.

'She tuned into the skull. She said it was Alice. She told me I had to stop at the sign of the cross, and if I hadn't...' Laura looked at the flattened hubcap lying on the icy crossroads. 'She saved me, Michael' Laura whispered, 'Alice saved me!'

'No, Laura!' said Michael firmly 'You're in a state of shock. This has nothing to do with Anna, or Alice, or anyone else.' He stood up straight and rubbed his hands together against the cold.

Laura gripped her steering wheel, 'But there was more' she paused, trying to take it all in. 'She said, 'You will die, Daddy will die' ..Oh my God! I didn't find out what's going to happen to you! I've got to go back out there!' She closed her door and started the engine.

'No, Laura. Listen to me. You can't go out there, it isn't safe!' Michael protested loudly, but Laura ignored him and started to pull away.

'No Laura, please!'

She turned the car and wound down the window, 'Michael can't you see? I'm trying to save you!' She shouted as she drove off.

'Damn!' Michael cursed, as he ran back to his car. He had no choice but to follow Laura back out to the old woman's house.

Chapter 29

As Laura pulled into Anna's drive, she saw Anna's car parked near the front door. Something didn't look right. The headlights were still on and the maid was struggling to lift something out of the car. It was Anna's slumped body. She was trying to manoeuvre Anna out of the passenger seat. She dragged her body onto the lawn and collapsed onto her knees on the snow-covered grass.

Laura jumped out of her car and ran over to help. Anna Crockett-Burrows lay on the snow. Her body looked stiff and awkward, her face pale and lifeless. Her eyes were wide open, and her expression frozen in a half smile. She was clutching the crystal skull. Laura reached for her wrist to check her pulse, but there was none. She was stone cold. The old lady was dead.

'I'm sorry' said Laura softly.

The housekeeper let out a penetrating wail of sorrow, then turned on Laura, 'Look what you've done! You killed her!'

Laura was bewildered.

'It's all your fault!' the maid snapped. 'She was trying to get your daughter's message. She knew it was dangerous, but she did it for you. I knew you would be trouble from the start' the maid was glaring at Laura, 'I said that to Anna, she just smile. And now look what you've done to her.' She tried to release the skull from Anna's grip. 'You wouldn't listen, you stupid woman!' she wailed.

'What happened?' asked Laura.

'When you went out the church she started shaking all over. She said '*If you won't listen, the future is set in stone!*' She said it over and over, all the time she was shaking. '*If you won't listen, the future is set in stone!*' I tried to get her out of it, *Wake up, Anna!* I said *Wake up!* But then she went into a coma and I couldn't get her back. Now she's dead and it's all your fault.'

The maid leaned over Anna's body and, with some force, prized the crystal skull free from Anna's dead fingers and hurled it onto the snow.

'My poor Anna, she is gone.'

She looked at Laura, her eyes filled with tears. 'Oh my God! What am I going to do? Thirty years, and now this! My Anna, dead and gone...Oh my God! What am I going to do?' She broke down sobbing uncontrollably. Laura tried to put an arm around her to comfort her, but she shunned

Laura, pushing her arm away.

Michael appeared solemnly at Laura's side. 'The ambulance is on its way' he said quietly, putting away his mobile phone.

When the paramedics arrived, they wrapped a blanket round the house-keeper's shoulders and led her away. They closed Anna's wild, staring eyes, pulled a sheet over her whitened face, and loaded her dead body into the back of the ambulance, its blue light flashing overhead. They took a brief statement from Michael and Laura, before helping the maid climb into the back, where she sat down alongside the stretcher.

Laura was still desperate to understand Anna's final words, so she asked the maid gently,

'What do you think she meant, *the future is set in stone*'?'

To which the maid snapped, bitterly,

'Now she's dead, you'll never know!'

The doors slammed shut in Laura's face. The crew climbed into the front, and the ambulance drove off into the dark.

As Michael and Laura headed back to their vehicles they noticed the lights were still on in Anna's car. The crystal skull lay half-buried in the snow, illuminated by the blaze of headlights, alongside the icy outline of deeply compacted snow where Anna had lain dead.

Laura knelt down to pick up the skull, while Michael went over to turn off the headlights. As he did so, he noticed the skull-case sat on the back seat and opened the rear door to retrieve it. He lifted it out to discover an old leather bound album, lying underneath it. Its cover was tied up with a golden ribbon. Curious to know what was inside it, he undid the bow and opened the cover.

At that moment, a gust of wind whipped up and blew through the car, lifting some of the fine loose-leaf pages right out of the album. Michael cursed and slammed the door shut as quick as he could, but some of the pages had already blown right out of the vehicle.

Laura looked up from the face of the skull to see a piece of paper fluttering by, as several pages of the album were carried past on the icy breeze. She caught one of the pages and held it up to the light, still shining from inside the car. She could just make out the words of a delicate text, hand-written in black ink. She scanned the page. It was dated '19th

February 1936'. The first line read, 'It was a cold winter morning when we set sail from Liverpool on board the banana steamer, *The Ocean Princess*, bound for British Honduras.'

As Laura stood there admiring the loops and swirls of the elegant text, it gradually dawned on her that what she was looking at was Anna Crockett-Burrows' handwriting. This was clearly a page from Anna's personal journal, the one the old woman had tried to give to her when she first visited her, but which Laura had left behind in her panic to get away.

'Oh No!' Laura cried, as she watched the other pages spiralling off on the wind as it whipped around the garden. She realised she was watching the old woman's life story about to disappear before her very eyes. 'Michael! Help' she shouted as she ran after them, trying desperately to grab them as they flew around the lawn.

Michael pulled out his torch and bounded over to help. They reached the hedge and were grateful for its height. Several pages had become trapped in its branches. Michael reached up to retrieve them, before flashing his torch along the bottom of the hedge. There they discovered several more pages, but they were no longer legible. They had become smeared and sodden in the snow. How many others had been lost, they could not tell. It seemed they had watched many simply disappear upon the breeze.

Laura realised that these words, this journal Anna had written, was now the only link she had with the skull's past. It was the only hope she had of answering her questions; the only way of knowing what the skull was and where it had come from, her only hope of ever knowing what the old woman meant by her cryptic final words, "*if you won't listen, the future is set in stone*", and more than anything else, her only hope of ever being able to find out how to reconnect with her beautiful daughter Alice, through the skull.

They retrieved the leather binding and remaining pages from the back seat of the car, and headed for home.

When they got back, Laura went straight upstairs to the study. It was 3 am. She set about drying off the pages of the journal that might still be legible on the radiator, and ordering all the other ones that had survived intact. There was no denying some of Anna's story was missing, but it looked as though the bulk of it remained.

It seemed uncertain whether a document written as long ago as the

1930's could help her, but the truth is, she needed to know as much as she could about the skull. However tenuous some of that information might be, she needed to know now more than ever. Maybe, just maybe, the journal might help. Right now it was all she had to go on.

She made herself a cup of coffee, picked up all she had managed to piece together of the journal, and began reading as much as she could of what Anna had written. She hoped she might find the answers she so desperately needed to all her burning questions about the crystal skull.

Chapter 30

Anna's journal was divided into sub-headings, each section of which had obviously been written-up some time after the events described had actually taken place, but as Laura read on the full vividness of the young woman's story leapt off the page at her:

The Adventure Begins:

19th February 1936

We set sail from Liverpool on board The Ocean Princess... *I was beside myself with excitement. I had heard so many tales about Daddy's wonderful adventures in the rainforest on his expeditions of overseas discovery, and now I was finally getting my chance to join him.*

My great aunt, Lady Bess had been dead set against it. According to her the jungle was no place for a young girl. I was quite offended. After all, I was nearly eighteen. In the end Daddy persuaded her that it would be educational and she warned me that if I came back a little savage, she would send me off to finishing school in Switzerland!

There were five of us Brits on the expedition altogether; Gus Arnold from the British Museum, Bunny Jones, Richard Forbes, my father and I. Bunny was a close friend of Daddy's and had put up a lot of the money for the trip. Richard was a recent archaeology graduate from Cambridge, keen to get some experience in the field.

The journey to Central America was arduous. After weeks of gazing out on nothing but sea, we finally reached the port of Punta Gorda on the Caribbean coast of British Honduras on the 9th April 1936. It was nothing like I had expected. The town was made up of a run-down assortment of wooden houses, and the whole place was filled with the stench of rotting fish.

Now I have always thought of myself as a bit of a tom-boy, perfectly capable of standing my own ground, but there seemed to be swarthy men; fishermen, sailors, and others that looked just like pirates, on every corner leering at me threateningly. I didn't like it one little bit and I was greatly relieved when we finally set off into the steaming rainforest in the back of a banana lorry. Not perhaps the most elegant way to travel, but it got us as far as it could inland before we were to leave the luxury of road travel behind.

The next leg of the journey, by boat up the Rio Grande, proved to be a bit of a disaster. Dug-out canoe was the only way to get around. Richard, who thought himself a bit of a dab hand with the punt at Cambridge, soon ended up with all our provisions in the river. Tents and mosquito nets were soaked through leading to a most uncomfortable night. In fact, it was to be the first uncomfortable night of many as we made our way slowly up the course of the river, but with no roads to speak of, it was the only way to get into the jungle interior.

You see, Daddy had heard rumours in the port of a lost city still said to be buried somewhere deep in the rainforest, and he was determined to find it. It was believed to lie around ten miles north of Chilam Balam. This was a minor Mayan city that had been discovered about five years previously by people who had been collecting rubber from the trees in the area. It was here that a beautiful green jade mask had been discovered.

Daddy had been fascinated by tales of its discovery. Apparently the mask had been discovered in a tomb, on the face of a strange skeleton that was over seven feet tall. Now this was particularly puzzling because the local Mayan people rarely grew any taller than about five feet.

So the discovery of this skeleton had lead to all kinds of speculation. As far as my father was concerned this was further evidence for his view that the ancient Mayan civilisation had not been founded by the Maya at all, but by survivors of some earlier, even more advanced civilisation, perhaps even the survivors of the lost civilisation of Atlantis!

Laura was already engrossed as she read on:

The Lost Civilisation of Atlantis:

I had heard a lot about Atlantis when I was growing up. By the age of ten I knew off by heart what the ancient Greek philosopher Plato, writing around 300 B.C., had said about the lost island continent; information which he said had originally come from the priests of ancient Egypt. Plato said Atlantis was 'situated in the Atlantic Ocean beyond the Pillars of Hercules', in other words west of Spain, and that 'from it one could reach the other islands and whole opposite continent which surrounds the ocean.'

My father wondered whether Plato's words might be a reference to the islands of the mid-Atlantic or Caribbean from which one could reach the 'whole opposite continent' of America.

He never really did accept that Christopher Columbus was the first to discover the American continent, as he knew the ancient Egyptians and Phoenicians were perfectly capable of doing so.

Whenever he was at home, Daddy was to be found in his library poring over books and maps, looking for clues as to the whereabouts of the lost continent. 'Take a look at this Annie,' he would say, map stretched out in front of him, pointing to some obscure underwater mountain range, 'Perhaps Atlantis is buried there?'

You see, although father believed that the island of Atlantis itself had vanished beneath the waves when sea levels rose at the end of the last Ice Age, he thought that some survivors of the lost continent might have made it to Central America and taken some evidence of their own civilisation with them. In fact, it was Daddy's one over-riding passion, his dream as an explorer, to find such evidence of the lost civilisation, wherever it might be. But he couldn't always talk to other people about it as it seemed to be a controversial subject.

Secretly, I knew that the whole purpose of our trip, as far as Daddy was concerned, was to see if we could find any evidence in Central America that might finally prove that Atlantis had really existed. In fact, the reason my father was so interested in this rumoured lost city we were now searching for wasn't just that it was said to cover an extensive area, but that the local Mayan people said that their 'once great city had been founded by a great leader who came from over the seas to the east' - and thus, in Father's opinion, from Atlantis.

This was why he had spent so many years planning the trip and why he had put nearly all of his life savings into it. As British Honduras came under UK government jurisdiction, father needed the British Museum in order to get the permissions necessary for exploration and excavation, but he knew better than to make his hopes for the expedition known to Gus Arnold of the British Museum prior to departure.

We finally reached the tiny settlement of Santa Cruz after four gruelling weeks of travel. We had been living on a diet of stale biscuits and water that tasted disgusting with the tablets added. We had blisters on our feet and leeches on our ankles. I had been longing for a decent wash and some clean clothes, but on closer inspection it looked as if we would be lucky to get a roof over our heads at night.

The settlement was made up of traditional Maya houses, constructed from wooden sticks with thatched branch roofs. The main route through the place was a muddy track. One ropy-looking building made of wooden planks, with a rusting corrugated iron roof, served as a kind of 'shop' with nothing in it, and that was it.

It was here that we were supposed to collect the mules already pre-purchased from Senor Giorgio Gomez, a Spanish trader who had recently moved into the area. Senor Gomez, who was in the process of building a fine hacienda on the south side of the settlement, had singularly failed to organise anything in the way of our trip.

In fact he had already lent the mules to a farmer who lived some distance away. We moved into a wooden hut and hung up our hammocks, to wait further until Snr. Gomez got back from his trip to collect our mules.

But we really were in the jungle now and I soon found myself absorbed by our new surroundings. I loved hearing the monkeys chattering in the trees and watching the humming birds as they drank nectar from brightly coloured flowers the size of trumpets. Snr. Gomez' daughter even taught me a few sentences of the local Mayan dialect, which I practised with the villagers - much to everyone's amusement!

Daddy was surprisingly philosophical about our delay, seeing it as an opportunity to research more thoroughly the suspected whereabouts of his lost city. While Gus and Richard went off to see if they could find Snr Gomez, Bunny and Daddy decided to crack open the case of Scotch whisky they had brought with us, to have what Bunny called 'a wee dram' in the evening.

When Gus and Richard got back, Gus had a very heated debate with Daddy about the skeleton found at Chilam Balam. I don't think the whisky helped matters. As far as Gus Arnold of the British Museum was concerened, the bones discovered at Chilam Balam proved absolutely nothing and had nothing whatsoever to do with Atlantis, or any other ancient civilisation other than the Maya! For Gus, the whole concept of Atlantis was nothing more than an elaborate fantasy.

The argument about the existence of Atlantis seemed to go on for hours, even days and although it helped pass the time while we waited for our transportation, it seemed to make both Daddy and Gus more and more certain that they were right!

Everyone was getting pretty fed up now. We had no idea what had happened to Mr Gomez. Daddy began to contemplate finishing the expedition on foot, but we needed the mules not only for ourselves, but for all our equipment. It must have been days later when we heard a male voice singing loudly to himself. We went outside and were amazed to see Snr. Gomez riding into town singing Spanish love songs, a string of mules following behind him. We were so happy to see him we could have hugged him, which in fact I did. Richard complained we could have walked to the coast and back in the time it took him to fetch the wretched animals, but I was just glad we could get on with the real purpose of our trip.

Our Quest for the Lost City:

We rose at sunrise the next morning and set off on our quest for the lost city. We made our way, on mule-back now, into the dense jungle. After a few days of trekking we found a spot right next to a beautiful jungle waterfall. We were about ten miles north of Chilam Balam. There we set up a base from which to begin our investigations.

We divided into teams. Gus worked with Bunny, whilst Daddy joined Richard and I. We were restricted by the heat of midsummer to working only in the early mornings and in the later part of the afternoon. It was backbreaking. Working with machetes and spades we spent every day clearing tracks through the dense undergrowth in search of any evidence of ancient settlement.

Two months later, the case of whisky long finished, morale had sunk to an all-time low, as we began to suspect that we might be on a fruitless search. We were only days away from abandoning the area completely in favour of a location further inland, when we finally made a breakthrough.

We were tired and frustrated after another long and difficult day clearing foliage. We were just about to return to camp when Daddy accidentally tripped over Richard's spade. He landed awkwardly, just missing a large rock. Luckily he was unharmed, apart from a twisted ankle. While Richard, apologising profusely for having forgotten the first aid kit, began tying his neck-scarf round Daddy's ankle, Daddy's attention turned to the rock against which he had almost knocked himself unconscious.

The rock looked unusually angular so Daddy tore away some of the vegetation from around it. He could have been mistaken, but it looked as though it might be made from cut stone and so possibly, just possibly, the remnants of some ancient building. Though in the half light, he could not be sure. Father began to get quite excited and began scrabbling around trying to find more. But the light was fading fast and we had no torches with us. The darkness of the jungle would soon be upon us, so we had no choice but to return to base camp and wait till the next morning to continue our investigations.

That night I don't think any of us slept much. I sat outside my tent looking at the stars twinkling in the night sky above as I waited for the dawn. The next day we all went back to the spot where we had found the strangely shaped stone and everyone took turns carefully clearing the foliage from around it until, by late morning, it looked as though what we had found might have been man-made. But if so, it was extremely eroded, and it could just as easily have been some strange quirk of nature. We certainly couldn't be sure without further excavation, so we began slowly clearing the soil from beneath it.

Meanwhile, Richard had another idea. He began digging the soil about fifteen feet away. Not even he seemed sure why. Two hours later, he shouted for us to come and see. He had uncovered what looked like a neat limestone paving block. The question was of course whether this was just another isolated stone, or one of many that made up a man-made structure.

We could hardly contain our excitement as Richard loosened the soil around it to reveal another similar stone immediately next to it. Gus explained that if there were any more adjacent stones, then it was a sure sign we were onto a 'Sac Be' or 'White Road', traditionally used to link one Mayan city with another.

This was the moment of truth. As Richard scraped further with his tiny pick-axe, under Gus's expert eye, we all watched with baited breath, as another flat, limestone slab came into view.

'We've found it!' Daddy shouted with excitement. He hugged me close. Bunny let out a whoop of joy and threw his hat into the air. Daddy then joined Bunny throwing his hat skyward as they both began dancing about with joy. It was kind of infectious and soon all of us joined in, even Gus. We were all making a hell of a racket, cheering, shouting and hugging each other.

It might have seemed an awful lot of a fuss about a few stones but these stones indicated that in all likelihood there was an ancient Mayan settlement of some considerable size further along the road, and the base of the pillar suggested it shouldn't be too far away.

Sure enough, as we cleared more of the Sac Be, we discovered another unusual mound of stone. We cut away the roots and branches and scraped away the moss to reveal what looked distinctly like the fallen crest of a carved stone archway or entrance gate, that had once sat proud astride the road, held aloft upon two giant stone pillars. Beyond the arch we were able to discern a visible trace of the 'White Road' stretching on up the steep hill.

Bunny, a keen geographer, speculated that this hill, rising up from a generally flat area of land might be the rim of a volcanic caldera, the hollowed out crater of an extinct volcano, or even the edge of a crater created by an ancient asteroid or meteorite impact. Either way, Gus thought it a highly unusual location for an ancient Mayan city, but it would certainly have helped keep it secret from the outside world, possibly for centuries.

Daddy, Richard, Gus and Bunny redoubled their efforts. They took turns with the machetes, hacking through the dense undergrowth trying to clear the limestone pathway up the hill, stopping only to wipe the sweat pouring from their brows or drink from their water containers. They worked in silence with a concentration I had never seen before. They worked right through the mid-day heat, steadily clearing the jungle as best they could until, by mid-afternoon, it became clear that the time had come to enlist more help. So Bunny and Richard set off for the nearest

Mayan village to try to find some more men to assist with the clearing work.

By the following morning we had ten men helping us. They used their machetes to slice quickly through the dense foliage, speaking only occasionally to each other in Mayan. They worked tirelessly. Slowly but surely the road was cleared of soil and vegetation revealing the smooth limestone slabs on which the ancient Maya had once walked. Though it felt like an eternity, by the end of that day we had cleared a path all the way to the top of the hill. The moment we reached its prow was unforgettable. For what we saw there took our breath away...

The Lost City of Luvantum:

There, in front of us, encircled on all sides by steep jungle-clad hills, was a vast, overgrown, ancient city. It had temples, palaces, monuments and plazas, even huge pyramids rising right up above the treetops. The whole city was swathed in roots, branches, creepers and vines. It looked magnificent.

Father was speechless. We all were. We were simply lost for words as we tried to take it all in, amazed by the immensity and beauty of the ruins that lay before us, bathed in the golden evening sunlight. Then, one by one, and in silence, we wandered on entranced into the heart of the lost city, admiring the majestic buildings, elaborate art works, intricate stone carvings and delicate hieroglyphs that seemed to decorate almost every visible façade.

The next day the local Mayan chief showed up, complete with his entourage. He was dressed in his finery of jaguar-skin cloak and feathered head-dress. He had heard about our discovery from the workmen we had hired. He watched silently as we went about our work clearing the site. Daddy tried to engage him in conversation but he seemed to be a man of few words. He gave the impression that he was not over happy about what we were doing, though he did not intervene in any way.

Our helpers on the dig told us that this city had been spoken about in their ancient legends. It was known to them as 'Luvantum', a Mayan word which meant 'the city of the sacred stone'.

Chapter 31

'Morning Laura' said Michael, bringing her back to the present with a jolt. He came in and kissed her, 'Would you like a coffee?' She hadn't noticed the time passing. It was still dark outside, but the city was already buzzing with life as people set about their day. The 'big apple' always woke up early and Michael was already getting ready for work.

He returned from the kitchen and handed Laura a mug of steaming coffee. 'How you getting on?'

'It's absolutely fascinating but no mention of the crystal skull so far.' She stretched and realised how tired she felt. 'And I've just reached a point where there seem to be some pages missing.'

'Let's see if I can get some answers,' Michael picked up the skull case, 'Mind if I take this?' Laura had all but forgotten the skull was there. But now she had been reminded she felt she wanted it with her

'What do you want it for?' she asked.

'I thought I might run some more tests on it in the lab' Michael explained.

Laura thought about it. She only had till the end of that week to finish her report on the skull. Perhaps Michael's tests might throw up some more information.

'OK, but I'll need it back by Friday', she said before returning her attention to Anna's journal.

The next legible entry caught her eye:

My Big Adventure:

Nothing could have prepared me for what happened next. Never, in my wildest dreams could I have imagined it. For a day came that was to change the course of my life. It seems it was my destiny, and it ignited in me a purpose to my life that no one could have foretold.

By now we had cleared the Great Plaza at the centre of the city and discovered that the steep jungle-covered hill at the far end of the plaza was actually a huge stepped pyramid. We had begun clearing it, but I was under strict instructions never to climb it. Daddy said it was too steep and dangerous. It must have been nearly two hundred feet high.

It annoyed me that Daddy wouldn't let me climb it. I wasn't a child any more, although sometimes he acted as if I still was. I was dying to get to the top of that

pyramid. I longed to climb to the platform and little temple at its summit and be able to look out across the rainforest. It seemed every one else had been up there and it seemed jolly unfair on me.

Then, one day, I got my chance. It was lunchtime. Everyone was having a siesta in the midday heat and I decided to take my chances and get to the top while they were resting. I planned to be back before they ever noticed I was gone. I waited until I could hear snoring coming from the tents and then I set off. The workers had strung their hammocks under the trees and they didn't see me go either.

I entered the plaza and began to climb carefully up the steep steps of the pyramid. The noon sun blazed down on me and I was glad for the protection of my hat. Insects buzzed noisily in the trees around me. I needed to pay careful attention to my footing as I made my way up the side of the pyramid. It was more difficult than I had imagined.

Though it was what is known as a 'stepped pyramid' in overall design, it was actually only on one side that a flight of steps were provided small enough for a person to climb up, but they were jolly big and steep too. It was made all the harder by the fact that some of them were missing, so I had to pick my way around them or even pull myself up a few steps at a time. Over a hundred feet up, I looked down to see how small the plaza now looked, but the top still seemed some way off.

I must have been about forty feet from the top when one of the steps I put my foot on suddenly gave way beneath me and I started to fall. I reached out and grabbed a creeper that had mercifully not yet been cleared from the pyramid. It was the only thing that stopped me from falling to my death in the plaza below. I could see now why Daddy had been so against me making the climb, but now I was so near to the top, I couldn't possibly go back. Besides which it looked as though it would be even harder to get back down the steep steps than it was to get up them!

Finally I scrambled onto the platform at the top. I was tired and out of breath. I looked around me and what I saw was magnificent: wild untamed jungle all around, stretching on for miles in every direction, as far as the eye could see. It formed a vast ocean of green, above which colourful birds soared freely in what seemed like an endless blue sky. I drank in the deep sense of spaciousness all around me. After all, it had been worth the difficult climb.

There was a little temple in the centre of the platform at the pyramid's summit. I was keen to explore it before I returned. I would have to make it brief as the team would soon be waking from their siesta.

The temple was a fairly solid limestone structure not much bigger than a large drawing room, or a small house. It was adorned with the remains of an ornate roof-

comb that would once have resembled a plume of feathers. Its walls were decorated with delicate stucco carvings that were now very eroded, and its single entrance was surrounded by thick jungle creepers which seemed to arch aside like curtains around the open doorway. Once, only the holiest of shaman-priests would have been allowed to enter this sacred building, where they would have performed prayers and rituals to appease the gods and ancestors.

I crept through the doorway into the cold, damp, darkness of the interior. As my eyes were still adjusting to the gloom I thought I could discern a beautifully carved image of Cimi, the great Mayan God of Death on the far wall. I took a step forward to take a closer look, when I heard an almighty crack. Suddenly, the ground gave way beneath my feet and I began to fall. It had to be an earth-quake, I remember thinking as I fell, certain in the knowledge that I was going to die.

Inside the Pyramid:

How long I lay there in the darkness, I do not know. The pale light shining from the temple doorway above me looked hazy and out of focus. I was relieved to find that I was alive and, miraculously, as I reached to feel my limbs, I appeared to be unharmed, apart from what felt like bruising. My head felt cloudy as I tried to work out what had happened to me.

Slowly, I pieced it together. The wooden floor on which I had stood had given way and I had fallen into a hidden chamber underneath the temple floor. I could see the rotten timbers I had fallen through lying all around me. Though they had been unable to bear my weight, fortunately, they had also broken my fall onto what would otherwise have been a hard stone surface. I was now lying on the floor of the bare chamber with what remained of the temple floor high above me.

But I was confident I would soon be out of there. Since the other night when we had been lost without our torches, I now came well prepared. I had packed a cigarette lighter and some paraffin in my backpack. I tore off the bottom of my jodhpurs and tied them round one of the timbers that had splintered under me, fumbled around inside my rucksack for the paraffin, poured it over the material and turned the branch into a torch which I held up to look at my surroundings.

I had fallen further than I thought. The false floor of the temple was at least fifteen feet above my head. I scanned the walls for foot-holes, or some other way of being able to pull myself up out of there. There was none. I looked at the assortment of broken timbers, wondering if I could construct something to climb up, but none were of a suitable size or strength. I realized I was trapped.

I started to feel panicked. How was I going to get out? I shouted 'Help!' at the top of my lungs, hoping that one of our small party would hear me, but the enclosed nature of the temple prevented the sound from carrying far. I shouted again and again. There was no response. Perhaps they had chosen this afternoon to clear the undergrowth from around the main water well, or 'cenote', as it was called. If so, they would not necessarily expect me to join them and would not even begin to notice I wasn't there until nightfall.

I sat down. My voice had gone hoarse. I began to wonder how long it would take for them to find me. The site was so huge it could take days. I could die of thirst in that time. The small amount of light that reached me through the doorway was fading. Night was beginning to close in. I shouted again. There was no response above the busy drone of the cicadas in the surrounding jungle.

For several hours I stared at the four chamber walls in the flickering light of my torch, trying to ignore the hunger I felt. There was nothing else I could do. I knew I ought to conserve the paraffin I had and put the torch out. I got up to see if I could move some of the branches that had fallen into the chamber together to make some sort of a bed, when I realised I could light a fire. The timbers seemed dry enough.

I felt an incredible sense of relief, as I used my naked torch to ignite the pile of timbers I had gathered together in the middle of the chamber floor. At last I had found a way of getting everyone's attention. The fire would surely burn like a beacon in the night and I would be out of there in no time.

I was right, the ancient timbers caught quickly and the fire raged fast and hot. Too hot.

I was hit by a wall of heat as if from the doors of a mighty blast furnace. I staggered back against the wall, trying to get as far from the flames as I could. The searing heat scorched my face and thick smoke choked my lungs. I feared I had inadvertently lit my own funeral pyre. My skin began to blister and my lungs felt like they were about to burst, when thankfully the flames began slowly to subside. Coughing and spluttering, I watched the fire die away, leaving only a pile of smouldering embers on the floor.

I stood there and waited for the rescue party to arrive. I shouted as loud as I could and I waited, for what seemed like an eternity. It must have been several hours. It must have been gone midnight. My lips were cracked, my tongue was swollen and I hadn't had a drop to drink in almost a day. And still I waited. But nobody came.

Nobody had seen my beacon of fire. They hadn't even smelt its smoke. Then I remembered, the temple door faced the opposite way from our encampment so no-one had seen my flames, and the wind must have been blowing in the wrong direction and carried the smoke away. I was horrified at the thought that nobody knew I was there. What terrified me most was the idea of remaining trapped there, alone in the dark, waiting for help that never arrived, dying slowly on my own.

I slumped to the floor in despair. As I did so my torn trouser leg accidentally brushed aside some of the ash from the fire, exposing a small area of the bare stone floor. Something caught my eye. It looked as though there were two small circles carved on one of the paving stones. I took out my pen-knife and scraped away the remaining ash and dirt from one of the circles, and it appeared to move. So I eased the knife in around it and pulled. I managed to lever it out completely. It turned out to be a stone stopper, or pin, that came away in my hand.

So I set to work quickly to remove the other pin. One large piece of timber had survived the fire almost intact and I was able to slide its splintered end under a corner of the flagstone. Then I pulled with all my might. I really didn't think I would be able to move it on my own but, to my amazement, after some considerable effort, the stone shifted and I was able to lever it aside. And I found myself staring into a deep, dark hole inside the pyramid.

I reached for my torch and held it over the opening and was surprised to discover that it was not just a drop into an abyss. Instead there were stone steps leading down inside it. I had discovered the entrance to a hidden passageway, a secret stairway that led deep down inside the pyramid.

The Secret Stairway:
I felt the pull of the unknown and terror in equal measure. Though I was frightened, I wanted to know what was down there. I wondered if perhaps it might lead to a way out, an escape from the prison in which I had found myself entombed.

I looked down at those steps. I was scared, but I knew this could be my only chance. Of course, I could stay and wait in the hope that one day someone might find me before I died of thirst. But right now the chances of that seemed slim. Odds were that staying there and doing nothing would cost me my life. I had no choice. I had to go down.

There was also something incredibly exhilarating about finding something like this all by myself and, despite the gravity of my situation, I could not repress this burning desire to be the first to walk this ancient path that had not been trod for over a thousand years.

As I began my descent, by flickering torchlight, I could feel myself trembling all over.

Heaven only knew what I might find down there. Perhaps some buried *treasure, like the jade mask found in the tomb at Chilam Balam, or perhaps some festering human remains. I shivered at the thought.*

The steep steps led deep down into the heart of the pyramid. Down and down they went, before changing direction and leading down still further. They seemed to lead back down even below ground level, before they flattened out into a short, narrow corridor.

At the end of the corridor a huge slab of stone was blocking the passageway. In keeping with the contours of the corbelled-arch corridor, the stone slab was shaped like a giant coffin. I half expected to find human skeletons lying in the passageway, but there were none. As I walked along the corridor towards it, my torch flickered and went out.

I fumbled around inside my rucksack in the dark. I found my flask of paraffin and shook it but there wasn't a single drop left. The only way I could see now was with the aid of the solid brass cigarette lighter I had borrowed from my father. I pulled it from my pocket and flicked it on to find myself face to face with the enormous slab of stone.

By the light of my flickering flame, I could just make out that it was carved with elaborate hieroglyphic inscriptions that looked vaguely like heads, arranged in three concentric rings. At its centre was the carved stone image of a human skull. I was trapped. There was no way out.

I realised I was going to die.

Chapter 32

The Great Slab of Stone:

In desperation I pushed against the huge slab. It did not move. I tried again, this time pressing my whole body weight against it. But the stone would not budge. I tried again and again. For what seemed like ages I pushed and shoved against that stone, but all my efforts were in vain. I didn't have much time. Now even my cigarette lighter was beginning to burn low.

I broke down in tears. I was totally defeated. I couldn't bear any more. I turned around and leaned back against the stone, exhausted. That's when I heard a deep scraping sound and felt something move behind me.

I spun round and flicked my lighter back on to see that one of the concentric rings of carved stone heads appeared to have moved slightly, in an anti-clockwise direction.

Excited, I gathered all my strength and, pushing hard, I managed to move the stone ring further round in the same direction, until it made a loud clunking sound and would move no further.

I pushed at the second ring, and it moved in the opposite direction, until it too sounded as though it had clunked into place.

The third and final ring moved, counter-clockwise again, just like the first one, until finally each of the rings of hieroglyphs appeared to be properly aligned with each of the other concentric rings of carved heads, like the dials of some giant stone combination lock.

I was amazed. It seemed I had stumbled upon some sort of carved stone doorway. Perhaps this was a way out after all. I pushed my whole body weight against the slab again, but try as I might, it would not move. What was I to do?

I studied the stone skull at its centre for some time. There was something about it that made me want to touch it. I put my fingers inside its eye sockets, and pushed against its open jaw, but nothing happened. Eventually I got so frustrated I started hitting the giant slab as hard as I could. As I did so I accidentally struck the stone skull at its centre.

I looked at the skull. It appeared to have moved. So I pressed on it hard, leaning all my weight against its forehead. Suddenly, the skull depressed back into the stone and the whole slab began to move away from me, like some ancient bank-vault door creaking slowly open on its hinges.

A felt a shiver ran down the back of my spine. What had I done? What had I opened? What dark secrets lay hidden behind that door?

I held up my little lighter and stared into the void.

The Secret Chamber:

I called out. My voice echoed around a cavernous space. I stood there a moment not knowing what to do. I was just about to step through the doorway when I remembered what had happened in the temple upstairs. For all I knew behind that doorway might be a sheer drop. Or perhaps there might be snakes and scorpions in there? I held my lighter down to the ground to check what was underfoot. The floor looked solid enough. I stepped slowly forward to find myself inside a large chamber.

I could just make out that its walls were adorned with carved stone skulls, row upon row of them. They stretched on ahead of me. It seemed to be some kind of tomb. Perhaps I was about to find the remains of bodies that had lain here undisturbed for thousands of years?

I looked to see if there were any sign of bones or sarcophagi, when my lighter flickered and went out. I shook it and lit it again. The flame was so low it was hard to see.

Then something extraordinary happened, and my eye was drawn to the far end of the chamber, where something seemed to be shining in the darkness. I thought I was imagining it. I closed my eyes and opened them again. But I was not mistaken. Somehow, a pale, thin, beam of light was beginning to penetrate the darkness of the tomb.

That made sense, thought Laura. The ancient Maya often built a tiny, straight and narrow shaft of air into the structure of their pyramids, to link the burial chamber with the outside world. It was a feature of their pyramids which was remarkably similar to those of ancient Egypt. Like the ancient Egyptians, the Maya believed that, after death, the souls of the deceased could travel through this shaft to take up their rightful place for all eternity in the heavens beyond. This 'spirit shaft' inside the pyramid at Luvantum must have been at such an angle that it was allowing the dawn sunlight to shine into the tomb.

Anna's journal continued…

This shaft of morning sunlight was illuminating a large stone structure at the far end of the chamber. At first I thought it was a sarcophagus, but it was circular, not the shape normally used to house the bodies of the dead. It was in fact an elaborately carved altar.

I watched as the shaft grew in brightness and intensity. Then suddenly an explosion of light filled the entire chamber as the ray of sunlight touched upon a strange object sat on top of the altar. I couldn't make out quite what it was, but it appeared to be glowing in the darkness, as if it were illuminated by some immense inner flame. It shone as though it were made from liquid gold, radiating light in every direction.

Everywhere I looked arced patterns of rainbow-coloured light were being refracted around the chamber and bouncing back off the walls, as if the whole place were suddenly filled with thousands of tiny rainbows. I fell to my knees, awestruck.

Never before had I been in the presence of quite such radiant beauty. Even now words fail me as I try to describe the simple majesty of what I saw, as if I were witnessing the rays of the very first dawn. And I swear, senseless though it may seem that I heard the wondrous sound of voices chanting then singing in blissful unison, as if they were emanating from inside the object itself. Tears streamed down my cheeks and my heart soared with joy as I gazed upon this magical scene.

Laura noticed that the ink was becoming smudged and hard to read.

Then gradually, as the sun outside moved up into the sky, the fantastic spectacle I was witnessing began to fade. The rainbows disappeared. The chamber walls began to recede into shadowy darkness, and the golden glow began slowly to disappear. My moment of reverie had passed and I became gripped by the thought that whatever it was on that altar, I wanted it.

But as I made my way trance-like across the chamber towards it, I wasn't watching my footing, and managed to trip over a slab of stone in the middle of the chamber floor. For a moment, as I fell, I imagined I had stumbled upon some ancient trapdoor that had flown open and I was about to plunge to my doom into a deep pit full of sharp spears, designed to impale unwanted intruders. Or perhaps I had fallen over a trip-wire that would cause a bamboo portcullis to descend and skewer me from above. Fortunately neither of these were the case, and I landed face down on the floor.

But as I scrambled to my feet and staggered across the room I imagined I might be confronted by a deadly white scorpion its tail poised and at the ready, or perhaps a giant snake might suddenly swing down from one of the ceiling beams, hissing loudly, its head dangling right in front of me, and its tongue flicking backwards and forwards in its mouth, only inches from my face. I would have to dodge my way past it and wave it away with what remained of my naked flame. Luckily however, each of these hazards was only in my mind.

And so shaken, but unhurt, I finally made it to the altar. The altar was huge and came up to above the height of my head. I climbed onto the large step at its base and, as I pulled myself up, I came face to face with the object. It really was magnificent, truly horrifying and yet devastatingly beautiful. It appeared to shimmer and glow before me.

I reached out for it, as if mesmerized…

But beyond that the ink had become blurred and illegible. Laura could just make out the last few lines which read, '…I came face to face with the object. It really was magnificent, truly horrifying and yet devastatingly beautiful. It appeared to shimmer and glow before me…' But that was it. That was all Laura was able to read.

She looked at the remaining pages, the ink was smudged, the words that had been so neatly written, no longer remained. They were no more than dirty blotches on the dried out paper.

So she flicked back a few pages and looked again at Anna's words, 'I couldn't make out quite what it was, but it appeared to be glowing in the darkness'.

Was it the crystal skull Anna had found on that altar deep inside the pyramid at Luvantum? Laura wondered. It certainly sounded a bit like it. But if so it would have been quite incredible. Finding an object like that was something most archaeologists could only dream of. The excitement of walking down a secret stairway, entering a hidden chamber and finding something that had lain undisturbed for millennia was more than most could ever hope for.

But it wasn't clear from what was left of Anna's diary whether or not it was in fact the crystal skull that Anna had found there, and Laura needed to know for sure, for her report.

And that wasn't the only question Laura needed answering for Professor Lamb and his Board of Trustees. For even if that was where Anna had found the crystal skull, her journal still didn't explain what on earth the skull really was, or for that matter what Ron Smith was doing with it when he died?

Nor had Anna's journal shed any light on Laura's own more personal questions, like how the crystal skull might be used to communicate with the dead, what Ron had meant when he said he had 'seen the future', or what Anna herself had meant by her final words 'the future is set in stone'?

Laura simply had to find out more.

She logged onto the internet and entered the name of the city Anna and her father had discovered; 'Luvantum'. She searched through the entries. The best she could find was: 'Ancient Mayan city in Belize (formerly British Honduras). Built around 600 B.C. Excavated in 1936. Party led by Gus Arnold of the British Museum. Architecture representative of the period: temple-pyramids, palaces, ball-court, and plazas. Many ornate stone carvings and hieroglyphs. 'Secret' stairway and chamber inside central pyramid. Elaborate detail on chamber door and main altar. No other finds of any note.'

It was this last bit that bothered Laura, 'No other finds of any note'! If the crystal skull had been discovered at Luvantum, why did there appear to be no record of it even on the British Museum's own website?

She looked under the entry for Gus Arnold. He had died 35 years ago. The website brought up a list of items, books and journals, he had written, but nothing about Luvantum.

If Anna had discovered the skull at Luvantum then why didn't it show up in any of the official records? Why had Gus Arnold, the British Museum's Mayan specialist at the time, never written about it or made any reference to it? It was all very mysterious.

Laura's experience also told her that the skull did not remotely resemble any other Mayan artefact she had ever seen. Neither did it look like an object that had been produced by any of the other ancient civilisations that had flourished in the area, like the Aztecs, or Toltecs. Their style was much more abstract and stylised than this. None of their artworks or artefacts looked quite so anatomically accurate, quite so 'real' as the crystal skull.

Laura wondered whether Anna had maybe even made the whole thing up, writing a journal to add authenticity to her claim that the skull was ancient. Maybe she was simply planning to sell the skull to the museum, and had invented the story of its discovery, and faked up an old journal, simply to increase its value. That was certainly a possibility. After all, some aspects of Anna's story did sound a little far-fetched.

And yet Anna had never even hinted at the idea of trying to sell the skull to the museum or anyone else for that matter, so that theory didn't seem to add up. Had she perhaps discovered it somewhere else?

There was more to this than met the eye, Laura was sure of it. The question was how was she going to find out now that Anna was dead and gone and the maid was unwilling to talk to her.

She looked again at Anna's hand written note of the names of the others who had accompanied her to Luvantum. She scanned their names; Frederick Crockett-Burrows, Gus Arnold, Bunny Jones and Richard Forbes. *They must all be long dead.*

She showered and began getting ready for work. She was just about to leave when she found herself drawn back to Anna's journal. There was something she wanted to check. 'Richard was a recent archaeology graduate from Cambridge keen to get experience in the field'. There was something about his name that sounded vaguely familiar. Richard Forbes.

Laura 'Google-searched' his name on the internet. There were hundreds of Richard Forbes, the most famous of which was a breeder of Labrador dogs based in Kentucky!

She refined her search by adding the category of 'archaeologist'. That reduced it to only three. One was a PhD student at the University of Maryland, another was an expert in aboriginal culture, from Brisbane, Australia.

Under the third entry, a prolific record of work popped up, academic writings, published mostly between the 1950s and 70s.

Laura thought for a moment. If Richard Forbes had been 'a recent graduate' back in 1936, that would have made him around 21 at the time, just the right age to be at the peak of his career from about the 50s. So maybe it was him? But the articles listed were nearly all about early European history, the Bronze Age in particular. There was however one early article listed about early Mayan pottery but that was all.

Could this possibly be the same Richard Forbes that had accompanied Anna Crockett-Burrows to Luvantum? Laura was intrigued by the idea that it was certainly possible.

Extraordinary though, she thought, if this was the same Richard Forbes, that he too had never written about the skull's discovery. Anna's story was beginning to sound a little suspicious. But how could she find out more?

Was it possible this Richard Forbes might still be alive? She looked at his entry. The last of his articles had been published back in the 1990s, by a small academic publisher in Cambridge, England named Crestwell Hall. They had published all his most recent articles and were based in the same town where Anna's journal said Richard had graduated way back in the 1930s, so maybe she was on the right trail. But there were no further details given for their contact address.

Laura looked at her watch, calculating the time difference with Great Britain. Though it was still early for her, the UK was about five hours ahead, so it would be nearing midday for them. They would all be in their offices by now. So she picked up the phone and called International Directory Enquiries. 'I'm afraid there's no address or phone number listed' came the curt response. 'Assuming you have the right name, they must either have gone out of business or been taken over by another firm.'

Disappointed, Laura put down the phone and sat thinking for a moment. All the other articles were so old and their publishers even more obscure, so probably not even worth trying. However, there was a possibility, a slim one but worth checking. She logged back on to the internet. She looked up The British Museum's Society of Fellows. She scanned for Richard's name. Nothing there.

She yawned, feeling the effects of the lack of sleep, when she had another idea. She logged on to the website for The Royal Society of Arts and Sciences of Great Britain.

It was worth a try. Access to members' details was denied. 'Damn it' she said. She should really have left for work.

She got up and left for the museum.

Chapter 33

December 11th 2012

Laura wasn't about to give up. At work that morning, Laura phoned the Royal Society and explained that she wanted to find out if a Richard Forbes was a member.

'Actually, we do have a Richard Forbes listed.' the membership secretary informed her.

'That's wonderful. Could you give me his number?'

'I'm afraid I am not authorised to give you any further information than that. All members' contact details are strictly confidential.' the secretary replied.

'But I'm calling from the Smithton Geographic Institute, and I'd very much like to talk to him in connection with an urgent report I'm writing,' Laura explained

'I'm afraid the only way you can access members' personal details is by written request to the Society's Director outlining the purpose of your enquiry. He can then pass on your request to the member concerned, and they can then decide whether or not they want to contact you.'

Laura sighed. Who knew how long that might take for her to get a response and she was fast running out of time to finish her report on the skull. What was she going to do?

'How long will that take?' she asked.

"Difficult to say. Depends how long he takes to get back to us. Usually at least a few weeks.'

Frustrated, Laura asked to speak to the Director.

'I'm afraid they are out of town. You need to send in a written request.'

'When will the Director be back?' she asked.

'Not for another two weeks.' the secretary replied, 'But you're calling from the United States, aren't you?'

'Yes. Why?'

'Well, you might be interested to hear he's in your neck of the woods at the moment. He's in Boston for the Society's International Award Ceremony, tonight, and then he's off for a family holiday.'

'Where's it taking place?' asked Laura.

'The Boston Hilton' came the reply.

That was it. Laura decided she was going to have to pursue the Director herself, while he was still on her side of the Atlantic.

She called the Boston Hilton and asked to be put through to the Society's Director, but there was no reply from his room extension. She tried again several times, but still no luck. It seemed he was going to be tied up all afternoon preparing for the evening's event before he was due to check out the following morning. If Laura was going to speak to the Director it seemed she was going to have to do it in person.

'What time is the ceremony this evening?'

'Seven thirty.' The receptionist replied.

Laura looked at her watch. It was gone noon. If she was to get to Boston before the award ceremony began, she was getting short of time. She phoned Michael, who was on answer-phone, to let him know she wouldn't be back till late, then set off for the airport.

She was relieved to reach the Boston Hilton without delay. The hotel was bustling with people getting ready for the award ceremony. She dodged her way across the red-carpeted foyer to the reception desk, where one of the Society's administrative assistants offered to try to find the Director for her.

As she waited patiently by the entrance to the Ballroom she cast a curious eye over the evening's Order of Proceedings and Schedule of Awards. The Royal Society had many different categories of award: the Arts in general, Science as a whole, and specialist categories for Archaeology, Engineering, Medicine, Philosophy and so on. She did a double take, her eye suddenly skipping back to the entry for 'Archaeology'.

There, included in the short list of nominees was the very name she had been looking for. A 'Richard Forbes' had been nominated for an award for his 'outstanding lifelong contribution to the field of archaeology'. She could scarcely believe it but there it was, right in front of her as plain as day.

The question was, of course, whether this was the same Richard Forbes she had been looking for. Could it possibly be the same person who had accompanied Anna Crockett-Burrows and her party to Luvantum way back in the 1930's, or was this perhaps someone else, some other completely unrelated Richard Forbes entirely? She was burning with curiosity to know. She checked with reception. 'Yes' there was a Richard Forbes staying at the hotel this evening, and 'Yes', he had already arrived.

Laura was hardly able to contain her excitement as she asked to be put through to his room. This was the moment of truth as she waited for someone to answer. After a few moments an elderly man picked up the phone.

'Good afternoon, Richard Forbes speaking.' He answered in an old school English accent.

'Hello, I'm Dr. Laura Shepherd, an archaeologist from the Smithton Geographic Institute. I would very much like to speak to you about an excavation you might have been involved in many years ago.'

'Yes,' said Richard 'Which one?'

'Luvantum.' There was a pause.

'Where?' asked Richard.

Oh no, he's going to say he never heard of it.

'Luvantum in British Honduras, now Belize.' she explained.

There was a long silence on the end of the phone.

'Lu-van-tum' Richard said slowly, giving the word great emphasis, 'The city of the sacred stone.' He was silent again, then sighed heavily. 'Now that was a long, long time ago,' he paused, 'a time in many ways I would rather forget.'

'Please!' Laura pleaded, 'It's important.'...

After the call, Laura cancelled her request to meet the Society's Director, having now found the person she was really looking for. She was surprised at how nervous she felt as she checked her face in the ladies restroom mirror, before making her way across the lobby to the bar, where she had arranged to meet Richard Forbes. The sound of soft piano music filled the air as she entered.

She spotted an elderly man, seated on a velvet chair at a small table. He was already dressed for the evening in a tuxedo and bow tie. He was shorter than Laura had imagined. He had round glasses and a moustache. A wooden stick leant against the table. He gazed absentmindedly up at Laura from his copy of 'The Times' crossword.

'Hello, Richard Forbes?' asked Laura. Richard rose stiffly to his feet and held out his hand to Laura. She shook it and they both sat down.

He looked younger than his 97 years. Laura ordered a pot of tea as Richard packed his newspaper away. 'I am here to receive an award for my longstanding contribution to the archaeological profession.' he informed her.

'You must be very pleased.' said Laura.

Richard smiled weakly, smoothing creases from the table cloth.

'Thank you so much for agreeing to see me' she added, 'particularly at such short notice.'

'Yes' he said glancing at his watch, 'I've only an hour to go before the ceremony starts. I'm not sure what I can really tell you in that time.'

'I wanted to know what happened while you were in Luvantum.' explained Laura.

'Luvantum,' Richard said again, as if he were chewing over troubled thoughts, 'It's ironic that it should have come back to haunt me, now, of all times.' he said almost to himself.

'Why, is it a problem now?' asked Laura.

'It's a long story.' He looked away. 'Look I'm not sure about this.' he added, reaching for his stick and beginning to rise, 'Maybe we should talk about this some other time.'

At that moment the tea arrived.

'But I've an urgent report to write.' Laura pleaded. Richard was standing now. 'And I understood you have to fly back to England tomorrow. Please, you're the only person I can speak to who was there, in Luvantum. Anna Crockett-Burrows has given me her account of what happened and it's very important I get the facts right.'

'Ah, Anna.' he said, and sat down again.

Laura poured him a cup of tea. 'I was wondering whether you remember anything you found at Luvantum?'

'I think you know,' replied Richard, a wry expression on his face, 'That is why you are here.' His voice now reduced to a whisper. 'You want to know about the discovery, don't you?' Laura nodded.

Richard stirred his tea and took a sip. 'You know, I have not spoken about it to anyone for over 70 years. Not even my wife knew about it when she was alive, before she had her stroke.'

'I'm sorry.' said Laura.

'Anna Crockett-Burrows... She's dead, isn't she?' asked Richard.

'Yes' answered Laura. 'Only two days ago.'

Richard's eyes looked watery. He took a handkerchief from his pocket and began dabbing the corner of his eye. 'It's ridiculous,' he said, 'I haven't seen her since she was 17 years old.'

Laura put her hand gently on his arm.

'Our profession is about unearthing what has been buried, looking at what lies hidden and forgotten - but on a personal level, digging up the past can be painful.' said Richard. 'Sometimes, it brings to the surface what we would rather forget.'

'Yes.' said Laura softly. 'I know.'

'Though this may sound hard to believe, the thing is, in many ways, Luvantum was the finest moment of my career.' reflected Richard, drying his eyes and putting the handkerchief away. 'I have to say that it was astoundingly good luck that Anna discovered it. What a thing to find! It was truly amazing - exquisite, really. I think we were all a little jealous. We all wanted to have been the one, the first on the scene, to bring it out into the open. I was young, I suppose I took it for granted. I assumed that the crystal skull was only one of many such objects that I would find throughout my life, although I have to say, that I have never seen anything quite like it before or since. It was truly unique.'

'So Anna Crockett-Burrows did find the crystal skull in Luvantum?' Laura wondered for a moment whether Richard was talking about some other discovery and felt the need to double-check what she had just heard.

'Oh, she found it there alright.' confirmed Richard.

'So why is there no mention of the skull in any of the official records of the dig?'

'Now therein lies a long story.' replied Richard, before noticing the quizzical expression on Laura's face. 'I can see it must look somewhat extraordinary from where you are sitting. I think I had better explain'.

'I will start with the day she found the crystal skull on that secret altar, deep inside the Mayan pyramid.'

Chapter 34

As the old man spoke Laura found her mind drifting back to what she had already learned from Anna's journal:

'I'll never forget that day, when we finally found her. We were all so worried about her. She had disappeared you see. We hadn't seen hide nor hair of her in almost a day. Had no idea where she was. We were calling her name, looking for her everywhere, but she appeared to have vanished without a trace. Poor Frederick was beside himself with worry, when one of the Mayan helpers who had shinned up the main pyramid heard her shouting with what sounded like joy!'

'I must say we were all a little surprised by her cheerful state, when we pulled her up on that rope from beneath the broken floor of that temple. We could see she was clutching something inside her little rucksack. As she emerged from the temple into the sunshine, she stopped and took it out of her rucksack. She held it in her arms, cradling it like a baby. Her face was radiant, more beautiful than I had ever seen it. She looked so peaceful. Then I noticed what it was that she was holding.'

'It was the crystal skull.'

'There was a moment of stunned silence as we gazed at what she had found, mesmerized. Anna's father, Frederick, took the skull from her and stood in front of the temple at the top of the pyramid steps holding the skull up high for all to see. It captured the morning sunshine, reflecting it all around, in a myriad of rainbow colours. Then all at once everyone seemed to go wild with joy. All the Mayan helpers on the dig seemed to recognise the skull. They started laughing and crying, and hugging and kissing one another. It was a truly magical moment.'

'I remember as evening fell and the first stars appeared in the sky, Frederick Crockett-Burrows placed the skull on a makeshift wooden altar the Mayan helpers had built. Fires were lit all around it and in the light of the blaze we watched as the Mayan people knelt before the skull. They chanted and kissed the ground in front of it.'

'I remember that night. There was drumming you know and these amazing dancers who appeared out of the jungle shadows as if from nowhere decorated with the plumes of tropical birds and the skins of the jaguar. We could hardly believe it, these poverty-stricken people decorated so finely. They moved around the skull to the rhythm of the drum. The skull looked magnificent, sat amidst the dancers, reflecting the light of the fires. As we sat and watched that night of feasting and celebration I think we all felt as if some ancient and powerful force had returned to the lives of those present.'

'Of course, Gus Arnold didn't see the skull until the following day. He had been laid up with a dose of the 'Delhi belly' and so had missed our first encounter with the strange object Anna had found. When he saw it, I could not have been more surprised by his reaction. You have to remember he was a highly respected archaeologist, a leading authority in his field. Gus stared at the skull for ages, he kept touching it then he burst into tears! He wept and wept! I didn't know what to say! When he finally wiped his eyes dry, his only words were, 'This changes history you know. It changes everything!'

'You see, Gus could see that the crystal skull was not like anything the Maya had ever made before. As you yourself know, their artwork was highly stylised. They depicted the faces of gods and kings, not real people. There was nothing realistic or naturalistic about the images they created. That was not the purpose of their art. And yet here was an object which displayed a stunning degree of anatomical accuracy - a perfect, scientifically precise, representation of a human skull. It was an object entirely at variance with anything that had ever been found on any ancient Mayan archaeological dig, an object that did not fit with what we knew about the creative expression of the Maya, an object clearly way in advance of anything they had ever produced before.'

'Gus could see that the implications of this find for modern archaeology were astounding. The history books would have to be rewritten! There was no other way. There was a recognised chronology, as you know; Mesopotamians and Egyptians, followed by ancient Greeks and Romans, all advanced European civilisations, leading right up to the Western civilisation of the present day. We, in the modern Western world are of course at the pinnacle of mankind's evolution. A bunch of blood thirsty savages in Central America couldn't possibly have been more advanced than our ancestors were at the time.'

'But the discovery of the crystal skull raised the possibility of the existence of a previous civilisation that had technical skills way in advance even of the Maya. And then of course, there was the even more horrifying possibility that these early ancestors might be in some way related to Frederick Crockett-Burrows' dreaded Atlanteans. Many would argue this could be the only explanation. This was all very exciting territory, archaeo-logically speaking, and it was obvious that Frederick at the very least was convinced that the skull provided evidence of the existence of Atlantis.'

'Obviously Gus Arnold would never use the expression 'Atlantis' as it was something of a taboo in archaeological circles, but nonetheless even he talked about the skull 'pointing to the possibility of a pre-Mayan civili-sation with an unusual degree of technical proficiency' which was as near as he could bring himself to utter the 'A' word. Don't get me wrong, Gus was as excited about the skull as the rest of us.'

'I don't understand.' said Laura, 'You were all amazed by the skull, overwhelmed by its archaeological implications. You say it could even have changed the accepted history of the world, and yet you never got it to a museum? None of you even mentioned ever having found it. I don't understand how that could have happened?'

Richard sighed deeply. 'I've asked myself that many times. But I could never have foreseen how things would work out.'

Laura looked quizzical.

'I suppose the real problem was that the local Maya considered that the skull had been returned to them. They seemed in some way rejuvenated by the skull's discovery. There was talk that the return of the skull had been prophesied. The Maya believed that they lived in an era known to them as 'the veil of tears' and that the appearance of the crystal skull heralded the end of that terrible age and the beginning of a new era known as 'the time of the awakening' which represented a new and much more hopeful time for their people.'

'You see, what people often forget is that the arrival of the Spanish Conquistadors around five hundred years ago destroyed much of what was left of the ancient Mayan culture. The Spanish thirst for gold left many sites such as Luvantum desecrated, ransacked by men hungry for gold, jewels and riches. When you think that the ancient Maya also had a fantastic written heritage of hieroglyphic 'codices' - books that had been painstakingly painted onto parchment. These were all destroyed by the church. Of course, you know all this already, but Luvantum was my first trip to Central America and it took me by surprise to find that the Spanish invasion some five hundred years before was still having an impact on these people.'

'When I went out there, I had no awareness of how the destruction of the Mayan peoples' culture so many centuries before had left such ongoing devastation in its wake. With their social and religious life destroyed, these once-noble people now lived on the margins of the Spanish empire. No wonder when the crystal skull appeared, they wanted to celebrate this powerful symbol of the change in their fortunes.'

'Believe me, those Mayan people wanted to see that skull. Word was out and our quiet archaeological dig became a magnet for people from all over the region. It became a place of pilgrimage. Older people mostly. They knelt in front of the skull. Chanted incantations, prayed and lit incense. For the Maya, it was a very serious business. They seemed to think that the skull had something to do with their great 'cycles of time''

'Apparently they believed it to be a vital part of the birth of a new era. According to them, every now and then time itself has to be re-born, and as the Maya themselves knew all too well, the time of birth can be a tumultuous one. They said it is a time during which we cannot know whether or not a new era will be successfully born or not. Apparently it can be no more assured than the successful birth of a child.'

'Anyway, they took it all very seriously and I dreaded to think how the Maya would respond the day we had to tell them that the skull was coming back with us to England. I rather think Frederick was hoping that interest in the skull would eventually die down and the Maya would return to their usual activities. But unfortunately that wasn't to be the case.'

Chapter 35

'It must have been about ten days after the skull was discovered when Anna began to get ill. She became deathly pale, started vomiting, had diarrhoea and was running a fever. At first we thought she had contracted a particularly bad case of Delhi belly, but it just didn't stop. I had been nominated as honorary medic for the trip, with all of two day's training behind me. I took on the nursing duties, mopping her fevered brow, finding blankets for her when she complained of the cold, a sure sign of an extremely high temperature. I went through the supplies we had brought with us and gave Anna the quinine tablets we had left. She was unable to keep them down.'

'I was very worried about her. Anna became increasingly delirious muttering, raging, chanting and whispering about the skull. Despite my scientific training as an archaeologist I began to fear that somehow chancing upon the skull had brought bad luck on her, although I refused to use the word 'cursed'. It was then that Gus Arnold identified the yellowing of her complexion as a sure sign that she had picked up malaria.'

'By then Anna was too weak to travel. There was no way she would have made it to the port where we could have found a doctor for her. Even if we sent for medical help, assuming we could get some, it would be weeks before anyone arrived. I was watching Anna weaken by the day. It was awful. She was vomiting water and had reached a very critical condition indeed. Frederick was consumed with anxiety. In the end, out of desperation, he saw but one course of action remained.'

'He had heard that there was a local medicine man, a shaman, or witch-doctor, call him what you will, and he believed the only chance Anna now had of recovery lay in this fellow's hands. So he set off to see the local chief and explained to him that Anna was very sick. They sat together a long time in silence as the chief contemplated what to do. Eventually he said to Frederick that he would allow the medicine man to treat his daughter but only on condition that the crystal skull was left there forever with the Mayan people of Luvantum.'

'You can imagine how poor Frederick must have felt. He had spent his whole adult life searching for evidence of Atlantis. He'd put everything into it, even his life savings. Now he had found, as near as anyone had, proof of the existence of some truly ancient and technically advanced civilisation, and he was being asked to give it up! He was devastated. Yet his daughter lay dying, he had to save her, whatever the cost.'

'He agreed to the terms without hesitation, though how they would later be enforced, remained to be seen. Right then, Crockett-Burrows had but one priority and that was doing what he could to save his daughter's life.'

'Amidst the tall trees, right at the edge of the plaza, the Maya had made a small circular lodge of sticks and branches in which to house the skull. They called it *'Ichla Mon'*, the womb of the great mother.'

'The medicine man duly arrived, a small wiry chap with penetrating eyes. Anna's limp, thin body was carried into the dark interior of the lodge and laid in front of the skull, which sat on a small raised platform at the back. The medicine man lit a fire in the centre and then pulled shut the door. Dogs were muzzled so as not to disturb the proceedings and children were kept away.'

'In the stillness, a strange, haunting chant rose from the lodge and seemed almost to echo through the trees around the plaza. It was a whole, long three nights we waited, as Anna hovered on the brink of death. It seemed as if time itself stood still, as we waited outside that hut for news of Anna's fate.'

'We were scarcely reassured when the Maya told us that death could sometimes be a form of healing, that sometimes what was needed was for the soul to escape the confines of the body so that it could be joined again with the ancestors. I didn't want Anna to go. I didn't want her to leave us. I realised then just how much she mattered to me.'

'The truth was I had fallen in love with her. I enjoyed her company and wanted to be with her. I wanted this feisty, strong-minded young girl to live more than I had ever wanted anything in my life before. I was not a religious man, but I prayed for that girl. I joined Frederick and the others in shifts, keeping silent vigil outside that lodge, turning away those who had come to pay homage to the skull, until we knew for certain either way.'

'On the fourth day, the medicine man emerged from the lodge. He had changed out of his jaguar skins and wore his simple cotton bag over his shoulder, indicating his work was done. I ran after him and asked in my clumsy Mayan how she was. He simply looked at me, his face impassive as he walked off into the forest in silence. I was terrified that Anna had died. With a heavy heart, I ducked my head and entered the lodge. Frederick was kneeling beside Anna's bed. I was greatly relieved to find Anna, very weak but alive. It felt as if by some miracle she had been spared. I could have jumped with joy. At last, all seemed right with the world. I had Anna back.'

'Of course, what I didn't know then was that I was about to lose her all over again.'

Richard's eyes had filled with tears.

'Can I get you anything?' asked Laura.

'I could do with a glass of water' said Richard, struggling to regain his composure.

Laura called the waiter over and he brought them both a glass. Richard stared down into his.

'It was after that, things began to change' he continued.

'After her illness Anna was strangely withdrawn. Perhaps it came about because she was too weak to join us on the dig, but she seemed to spend more and more time in the presence of the local Maya. Often I would see her entering or leaving the skull lodge. I felt that I was losing her even though she had not died – she was changed. No one else seemed to notice, they were busy with the site excavations, but I could feel her slipping away from me in some subtle, indefinable way.'

'Around this time Bunny became increasingly restless. He said that it was more than time we send word to the British Museum that we had made a discovery of some considerable import. Frederick told him that the time was not yet right. Exactly how he intended to explain to Bunny and the rest of our small party that he had promised the Maya they could keep the crystal skull, I really do not know. I suspect he wasn't sure either, as he certainly seemed keen to postpone that moment.'

'What happened next took us all by surprise. The local chief called Frederick to his hut, along with Anna. Later Frederick came to discuss with us what had happened. I remember it was close to dusk, we were sat under the canopy we had rigged up to protect us from the sun during mealtimes. We had just finished eating a meal of tortillas and beans when Frederick approached. 'I have something to discuss with you all' he announced. His face showed an anxiety he was trying to mask. 'When Anna was ill' he began 'I asked the Maya to help. You all know how desperate it was. Well they agreed, on one condition. The condition was that they keep the crystal skull here in Luvantum.'

'Not a chance in hell, and I hope you told them that' said Bunny light-heartedly.'

"Well,' said Crockett-Burrows, his eyes darting nervously between the team members, 'At the time, I had only one concern, my daughter's life and how I could save it' he said. 'I did what any parent would have done, I gave the chief my word that the skull could stay.' There was a stunned silence amongst the group. 'I know what you are thinking, I should have lied to him. I thought of it, but I felt certain that if I had, Anna would not have stood a chance."

"Christ almighty!' said Bunny 'I don't believe it!'

'Now hold on a minute,' said Crockett-Burrows, 'it's not as bad as it seems. The good news is that the chief has now agreed that we can keep the skull...'

'Whoopee!' I can remember yelling, before I saw their stony faces, balking at my immature response. '...on one condition' continued Frederick, 'That you all agree to maintain a vow of silence about the skull forevermore. The chief believes this is necessary to protect the skull. He says we don't know what we are dealing with here. These are the only conditions on which he would agree to the skull leaving Luvantum."

'Well, of course, Bunny hit the roof. He jumped up from the table, sending metal plates clattering to the floor. He spun round to face Crockett-Burrows 'We've made the most impressive discovery of the century and you're asking us to keep quiet about it! I can't believe my ears!' He was furious, said it was 'preposterous'. 'I've never heard anything like it' he yelled, 'I'm not having some chap in a mud hut telling me what to do, least of all when it comes to the crystal skull. We found it, Frederick, not them!' he said as he jabbed his finger in the direction of the Mayan village.'

"It's not that simple' said Crockett-Burrows trying to appease him, 'The Maya say they already knew about the skull, but they didn't want to disturb it until the time was right.'

'What nonsense!' shouted Bunny, even more agitated now. 'I'm not going to stay and listen to this claptrap' and with that he marched off to his hut. I could see then that there was no way that Bunny was going to go along with this.'

'Gus Arnold had sat silently listening to the whole argument. Crockett-Burrows was shaken by Bunny's response. He turned to Gus. 'What do you think?' Gus's hands were still folded around the cup of coffee he had been drinking when Frederick arrived. He looked deep in thought. 'I've been doing a lot of thinking about the whole business with this skull' he answered. 'The thing is, I don't think the world is ready for a discovery of this magnitude' he said, 'It's just too controversial, too challenging.''

'Gus sighed, his eyes cast down. 'I've reached a point in my career when it is not worth the upset of introducing something that will be met with fury or ridicule. There will come a time when we in the archaeological world will be ready for such a challenge but I fear that the time is not now'. Reaching forward, he put down his coffee cup. 'You have my word, I will not be speaking to anyone about it.' And so he agreed to the vow of silence.'

'Well I was bitterly disappointed by Gus's response. I had hoped that he would champion the skull, make it the centrepiece of his research findings for the trip.'

'Then I realized that all eyes were upon me. Crockett-Burrows was awaiting my answer. I didn't know what to say. I scrabbled onto the floor to pick up the plates that Bunny had knocked over.'

'I was completely torn. I knew that Gus needed a research assistant to help with his next project and I was ideally situated to take on the job. Gus and I had already worked well together. Yet if I broke the vow and spoke out about the skull my employment prospects would be ruined as far as the British Museum were concerned.'

'In my heart of hearts I was with Bunny, he was absolutely right, this was too good to sit on. But if I spoke out I would jeopardise my chances with one of the most prestigious archaeological institutions in the world.'

''Can I sleep on it?' I asked, returning the plates to the table.'

'We disbanded for the evening, an uneasy tension weighing heavily on the air.'

'I lay awake all night long, my thoughts interrupted by night animals in the jungle as I considered what I should do. The skull and the circumstances of its discovery were quite incredible in archaeological terms. An object like that, any archaeologist could see that it had not been made by the Maya. The question was who had made it and why? It would be a fascinating area to research. But who in the orthodox world of archaeology would want to touch it? It was just too different. It challenged everything that had gone before.'

'Perhaps I was the one to rise to that challenge? I would take them all on and say 'Yes, it is time for us to revise our narrow notions of the past, time for us to consider the possibility of a civilisation existing in the distant past that was way in advance of our own'. I would do as Galileo had done when he challenged those who continued to think the earth was flat. I would be the bold Galileo of the archaeological world, challenging the old order of things. Every generation needed its pioneers, those who were prepared to lead the way and challenge the status quo.'

'But as dawn broke, it became clearer to me. I wanted to work. Gus Arnold was my best chance of the coveted job of archaeological assistant. As for the crystal skull, well, I reasoned Gus Arnold knew what was best. If he said the archaeological world wasn't ready for the skull, who was I to challenge him? I went to Frederick and gave him my answer.'

Laura looked at Richard.

'What you have to remember is that all this was happening in a very different academic climate than we have today. This was back in the 1930s and of course people are more open-minded now, but back then archaeology was not about rocking the boat.'

'I sometimes wonder what would have happened if I had 'gone public' about the skull, if I had not been afraid to risk my career and challenge conventional orthodoxy. But you have to remember that this was in the days before TV archaeologists, I was fearful that there would be no career for me in archaeology if I challenged the way things were.'

'In many ways it seemed a dishonest course of action, one that was not in the best interests of the profession. I was abandoning truth in favour of convenience. I was choosing expediency above the expansion of knowledge, opting for a job rather than working to further our awareness of our origins, where we as a species really came from and how we have developed.'

An elderly gentleman appeared at the entrance to the bar, wearing a red velvet tuxedo.

'Ladies and Gentlemen, can I have your attention please? The award ceremony will begin in twenty minutes' he announced.

'We are running short of time my dear, I had better press on.' said Richard.

'But what puzzled me,' he continued, 'was why the Mayan chief changed his mind about the skull. One minute he couldn't countenance it leaving and the next he agreed that so long as his conditions were met it could go. It struck me as very odd.'

'I remember asking Frederick why the chief had changed his mind. Frederick looked guilty. I will never forget his response.'

''It is thanks to Anna' he replied casually, heading off to the well to wash. I was perplexed.' 'Why?' I called out.'

''She wants to train as a Mayan priestess.' came Frederick's reply. Just like that, completely matter of fact. 'She wants to train as a Mayan priestess.' He said it as if she had just announced she was going to get her hair cut!'

'I was stunned.'

Chapter 36

Richard still looked devastated, even now, decades later.

'Did you ever find out what the training involved?' asked Laura.

'Not the specifics, no' answered Richard. 'She refused to go into detail. What she did tell me was worse than I had imagined. She informed me that she would spend the next ten years in Luvantum immersing herself in the culture, language and ways of the Maya. The worst of it I found out later from Bunny.'

'Bunny told me that the priestess training meant Anna would swear to a life of celibacy and that she would devote her entire life to serving the crystal skull. She would also learn what he referred to disparagingly as 'the black arts', the unsavoury practices involved in discovering the 'secrets of the skull'. What these were, he didn't say. I have a suspicion that he didn't actually know, as Bunny wasn't known for his reticence in bringing forward information of this nature.'

'Whether Frederick knew the specific practices of Anna's training I do not know. What I do know is that he did try to talk her out of it, but she wasn't having it. We all tried. I was horrified at the prospect of her embracing this impoverished monastic life, but she had made up her mind that is what she wanted. I couldn't for the life of me understand it. I wondered whether perhaps she felt indebted to the Maya for saving her life. Frederick, who was more inclined to believe in supernatural explanations, thought that perhaps Anna's decision was a result of the time she had spent in the skull's presence in the skull lodge. Whatever the reason, none of us could change her mind.'

'Bunny was particularly insistent in his attempts to dissuade her. He berated Crockett-Burrows for allowing her to even consider such a thing. Frederick took the view that she would tire of it in due course. He also knew that it was a way of securing the skull without any trouble. Better to have the skull and not speak of it than not have it at all, is probably what he thought. Bunny was unconvinced. He remained restless and unhappy, smouldering quietly at all the goings on.'

'Anna had now moved into the Mayan settlement and was spending a large amount of time with the medicine man. I was heartbroken. How I missed her energetic presence and strong views. I missed the gentle way she had of teasing me when I tried too hard to impress her. Working at the site lost its magic for me.'

'Anna had been gone only about a month when she suddenly appeared at the site one morning. I was busy unearthing one of those carved Mayan stones that look like grave stones. It's on the tip of my tongue...

'A stella,' volunteered Laura.

'Of course' replied Richard. 'My heart leapt at the sight of her and for a moment I thought that she had come back to join us. I noticed that she was now wearing a blouse embroidered with the same birds and flowers favoured in the designs of the local Maya. We put down our tools and went to greet her. 'I have come to invite you all' she said 'to a special ceremony that will mark the beginning of my new life as a priestess. It will take place in three weeks' time at the top of the central pyramid, by the light of the full moon.' Then she walked off again without another word.

'It sounded intriguing. But it was also disturbing to think that the competition for the affections of the woman I loved came not from another man, but from a crystal skull! I was most unhappy about it, but what could I do?'

'Bunny came to see me soon afterwards. I was down near the river, taking a rare opportunity to shave. He strolled towards me, his face pinched, his look purposeful. 'I wanted to speak to you in private' he said in a low voice. 'Look old chap,' he added, 'I know that you have grown rather fond of Anna.''

'This embarrassed me. I was not aware that anyone else knew. 'The others, they don't know, do they?' I asked. Bunny's wry expression told me that my feelings were no secret. 'What about Anna?' I blurted. 'No idea' he said. 'Although it's probably about time you made your feelings known to her.' I was thrilled to think that Bunny thought this was a good idea. Only later did it occur to me that he might have been taking advantage of me for his own ends.'

'Bunny went on to tell me that he couldn't stand it any longer. He had had enough of the Maya wanting to control the crystal skull and now they were in the process of taking Anna away from us too. They needed to be stopped. He said he had a plan and he wanted my help.'

Richard took a sip of water from his glass.

'At first, what Bunny suggested rather shocked me,' he continued. 'Bunny was proposing to steal the skull. His plan was to take it back to Britain and make it public. I cautioned him that taking the skull could lead to a great deal of trouble with the local Maya, but he was convinced that it was the right thing to do. He said not only did we owe it to Anna but we owed it to the world, which deserved to know the truth about the history of its own civilisation.'

"Crockett-Burrows might have forgotten the purpose of this expedition,' he said, but he had not. Besides which, he had also put up much of the money to fund the trip. It was both his right and his duty to tell everyone about what we had found.'

'Not only that, but he would get the recognition he deserved for all his searching and he would be remembered for bringing the skull out into the light of public awareness. He also thought that once the fanfare of publicity got going, Frederick and Anna would soon forgive him and join him. He really believed that Crockett-Burrows would 'soon come on board, and all that stuff about priestess training and promises to the Maya would be quickly forgotten about."

'Instantly, I saw the possibility of having Anna back working alongside me again on the dig. It would be just like it had been before the skull was discovered. If that were to happen, I would finally get a chance to let her know how I felt. It might be that she had feelings for me too.'

'It also struck me that it might be extremely useful to have the skull made public without me personally risking the career damage that might have come from taking on that responsibility myself. I began to see that stealing the skull was in fact an excellent idea and I agreed to help Bunny in whatever way I could.'

'Bunny knew that every night the Maya would come and light the fire at the centre of the skull lodge and they would sit in the lodge praying and keeping vigil over the skull overnight. During the day, the skull was not guarded, but Mayan people liked to be able to pray in front of the skull at any time during the day. Daytime seemed the best time to try to take the skull although the risk of being caught seemed considerable.'

'The next day I set off for Santa Cruz, ostensibly to pick up more supplies, but what I was actually doing was arranging for Senor Gomez to bring the mules ready for Bunny's escape. I was gone a week. I made all the necessary arrangements for Bunny's getaway.'

'Bunny planned to pretend to make a trip to Santa Cruz the day before Anna's skull priestess initiation ceremony. Everyone would understand that Bunny was staying away because he didn't approve of Anna's decision. It would appear to be a very diplomatic solution that he should suddenly remember to collect urgent supplies that involved him being away whilst the ceremony was taking place.'

'Of course, what he would actually do was hide away in the jungle overnight. The following morning, when he knew the skull was unattended, he would steal it from the skull lodge. Nobody would suspect him, at least not at first. Bunny gave me a letter to give to Crockett-Burrows explaining that he had acted as he had to protect Anna from her fate languishing in the lands of the Maya and asking that Frederick forgive him and come on board to help promote and publicise the skull. He asked me not to give Frederick the letter until a month after he had stolen the skull to allow him time to make good progress towards the port. *The Ocean Princess* would be docking around then before her return to Britain.'

'The morning of the ceremony soon came. The medicine man had spent the night before in the skull lodge, fasting and chanting. Anna had been kept elsewhere, in isolation. That morning I stayed in my hut, skipping breakfast. I began moaning and complaining of chest pains. Frederick Crockett-Burrows came in, saw the condition I was in, and straightaway went to find the medicine man, to tell him that I was sick. He asked him if he could come immediately to my hut.'

'The medicine man came straight to my aid. Bunny's plan was to slip into the lodge and take the skull whilst I was being treated. Much to his surprise however, the medicine man asked Frederick to stay and keep watch over the skull until he got back. It was bizarre because the skull had previously always been left unattended during the day.'

'The medicine man came into the hut where I was lying in my hammock, feigning illness. He rummaged in his bag, lit some herbs and passed them over my body chanting. He then put his hands on my chest. He only stood there for about two minutes before muttering something in Mayan and leaving. Frederick came in. 'The man said you will live' explained Frederick, 'You suffer only from love that does not return to you. Unrequited love would be another way of putting it.' I felt very foolish as I scrambled out of my hammock, wondering whether Frederick suspected who might be the object of my affections. I said nothing.'

'I had arranged to meet Bunny by the river and went to our rendezvous point once again. Bunny was in a state of agitation at his failed attempt to steal the skull. He said that he would have to revert to 'plan B'. He said he didn't want to do it this way, but he could not see Anna go through with the initiation ceremony, she had to be stopped before that.'

'I agreed, but then he told me his plan. I tried my best to dissuade him but his mind was made up and he was determined to carry it through.'

Chapter 37

'The night of the ceremony was soon upon us and I felt a deep sense of dread about what lay in store.'

'It was a clear sky and as the sun slipped down beneath the horizon I climbed to the top of the great pyramid alongside Gus, Bunny and Frederick, to take up our places at the back of the small platform, behind the assembled priests.'

'Once the moon began to rise, flaming torches were lit, illuminating the pyramid steps. A steady drumming began and Anna appeared in the Plaza below, two Maya girls at her side. She looked fabulous. Gone were her torn shirt and riding breeches. She wore flowers in her hair, like a bride. She was dressed in a snugly fitting white Mayan tunic, adorned with ornate gold and jade jewellery. She looked a little apprehensive. Her hands were tied behind her back, as she was marched up the pyramid steps. I felt Bunny slip from my side, unnoticed to the rear of the pyramid, behind the little stone temple that housed the ancestor shrine.'

'The Priests were chanting now in Mayan, their voices growing louder and louder, as Anna arrived at the top of the central stairway. The air was heavy with the rich, sweet smell of copal incense that swirled in a dense cloud around her head. I watched as she knelt before something. I could not see what it was. The medicine man raised an obsidian blade high into the air and brought it down behind Anna's back, slicing through the rope that held her hands tied. She fell forward raising her hands at exactly the moment a jaguar pelt was pulled aside to reveal the crystal skull. She placed her hands on the skull and lowered her forehead against it.'

'At that moment an earth-shattering noise came from behind us. The chanting stopped. I turned round to see Bunny stood there by the ancestor shrine, a 12 bore shotgun in his hand. He cocked the trigger and fired again. A bullet ricocheted off the altar stone. Everyone froze. The drumming ceased. Anna looked up. 'That's enough' shouted Bunny, staggering forward to the centre of the pyramid platform, waving his gun menacingly.

'The skull is too precious for this. It needs to be investigated and examined scientifically, not used for some backward, primitive, voodoo ceremony. It belongs in a proper museum, back in England, not languishing here amongst superstitious savages.''

''Frederick' he said, turning to his friend, 'and you too Anna, one day you will thank me for this'. He knelt down beside Anna and lifted the skull from the granite stone upon which it had been placed. The blood on the skull, fresh from the jaguar pelt, covered his hands as he hurriedly packed the skull away into his shoulder bag.'

'A young Mayan man was about to step forward and confront Bunny, but a priest grabbed him by the arm to restrain him. Bunny fixed him within the sight of his shotgun. He turned to Anna. His voice softened 'What I'm doing - it will set you free.' Anna looked at him, her face full of incomprehension and fear.'

'Bunny rose and made his way to the top of the pyramid steps, his gun at the ready, pointing menacingly along the line of priests. He pointed the gun upwards and fired again.

The sound echoed round the whole complex, sending monkeys chattering and birds flying from the trees. He ran down the pyramid steps, brandishing his gun, dashed across the plaza, and disappeared into the darkness of the dense jungle.'

'Anna ran crying to her father. The priests began shouting, their voices filled with anger. It was chaos. Bunny had done it. He had stolen the crystal skull. The plan had worked. I should have been pleased. Instead I felt an intense paralysis of guilt. This bizarre ceremony, this whole business with the skull, it was what Anna wanted, it was what the Maya wanted and I had allowed Bunny to destroy it all. I returned to my hut, crestfallen.'

'Over the next few days it seemed that the whole community was consumed with grief. Though they had sent out various search parties to try to track down Bunny, nobody had found him. I lay in my hammock, unable to face anyone. Bunny had got away with the skull. He would be out beyond Santa Cruz by now, well on his way to change history. Anna was catatonic with grief. She shut herself away and refused to speak to me. What had I done?'

'Three days later I saw them pass, Mayan women, clothes piled high upon their heads, children at their heels as they made their way down to the river to do their washing. They're the ones who found him. They found Bunny's body. They came to get us, to pull him out. Frederick, Gus and I went. Poor Bunny. He was floating face down. His body bloated, his flesh grey. As we heaved his body up the riverbank, we saw it hanging in a jute bag around his neck. It was the crystal skull, hung like an evil talisman.'

'It was strange that Bunny should end up in the river, why it was that he came to drown. There was some speculation that he had tried to escape the pyramid complex using the underground river system. Those underground rivers are notoriously dangerous, subject to unexpected currents. It would be a foolhardy enterprise even at the best of times. I listened to all the speculation. I was the only one who knew that travelling through the river system had never been part of Bunny's plan. No, he had arranged for Senor Gomez and his mules to be waiting just beyond the Plaza ready to carry him away, so who knows what went wrong? His death was a mystery, and remains so to this day.'

'If there was any foul play involved, we shall never know. Frederick was convinced that Bunny's death was an accident. Frederick believed that Bunny had taken the skull because he was unhappy with the idea that Anna was about to become a skull priestess. He thought Bunny had been drunk on the whisky I had brought back from Santa Cruz the week before.'

'Frederick was convinced that Bunny had removed the skull during the ceremony simply to make his point and that he would show up a few days later. He never suspected that Bunny actually planned to take ownership of the skull. He trusted Bunny too much for that. In fact, that's why I didn't give him the letter. It was hard enough for him to live with his best friend's death, I didn't want to burden him further with the knowledge that his best friend died in the process of betraying him.'

'Bunny's body was placed in a makeshift coffin made from the wood of rubber trees. It was held together with jungle vines. Frederick had inscribed 'R.I.P. B.J.' on top, in red letters. We carried his coffin deep into the forest, in silence. We found a spot under the shade of a majestic ceiba tree. That's where we buried him. It was a solemn occasion. I'd like to say we accompanied his body back to the port, boarded *The Ocean Princess*, as he himself had intended, and held his funeral back in Great Britain as he would have wished, but no. In those days it simply wasn't possible to transport a dead body across such distances, given the heat and humidity of the rainforest. Decomposition was already beginning to set in within hours. No, I made that last leg of the journey alone.'

'I never again returned to Luvantum. Neither did Gus Arnold. As for the others, I have no idea. Sadly, we lost touch after that. At first I missed Anna tremendously. All I had to remind me of her was a photograph Gus had taken. I wrote to her almost a dozen times but I never heard anything back. Unless she never received any of my letters, I could only assume that if there had ever been anything between us, now it was over.'

'Where was I?' Richard asked himself. 'Ah yes. After Bunny died, Gus offered me the job of research assistant on his next project, excavating a Mayan tomb in Mexico. I thought I could make up for it, make up for not revealing the crystal skull, by making other fascinating discoveries, finding other ways to expand and challenge our level of understanding of the past.'

'But each shard of pottery, each piece of broken jewellery, everything we painstakingly removed from the earth in Mexico seemed somehow diminished alongside what we had found in Luvantum. Bearing the knowledge about the skull that I did, exploring the domain of the ancient Maya became joyless and mechanical. I knew that the Maya had been connected to something far greater, but I was not at liberty to share that knowledge with others. That project in Mexico was to be the last project on the ancient Maya that I ever did.'

'After that I switched to ancient British history, hoping to find something to redeem myself for my silence on the skull, some wonderful challenge, but I found nothing of note. I took the path of the coward, I see that now.'

Richard looked Laura in the eye.

'I did not have the strength of my convictions - to stand up and argue my case against others. I turned my back on the greater good because I wasn't prepared to do that. I thought only of myself and my own career prospects. I realise now that was a mistake.'

'That is why I feel such a fraud here,' Richard gestured to his hotel surroundings. 'Here I am, about to receive an award this very night for my outstanding contribution to the profession. If only they knew! I could have made a truly outstanding contribution if I had spoken up about the discovery of the skull, but instead I chose silence, a silence I now bitterly regret.'

'Of course' said Richard 'I could stand up there tonight, use it as a platform. I could tell them, 'by the way I wanted to let you know, that I found something over seventy years ago that could change everything you know about human history!' They would all simply assume that I have dementia. No, it is too late for all of that now.'

Laura remained silent for a moment in acknowledgment of the old man's memories and sorrow.

'I can see it has not been easy for you.' she said. 'Thank you for going through it all with me.'

'I'm glad I finally had the chance to talk to someone about it. Thought I would carry it with me to the grave.'

Laura felt a momentary stab of disappointment. She had hoped that what Richard told her would illuminate in some way some of the stranger things Anna Crockett-Burrows had told her about the crystal skull. She was desperate to know whether Anna's final words might really have been from Alice, as the old woman claimed, but nothing Richard had said appeared to answer that question, so she asked tentatively,

'I know this might sound a little strange, but did Anna ever make any suggestion that the crystal skull might somehow be used as a means of talking with, or communicating with the dead?'

'Nothing about that skull would surprise me' said Richard, 'especially if it had anything to do with death, but no, Anna was strictly forbidden by the Mayan priest from telling us anything more about it. And we in turn had all vowed to keep everything to do with the skull secret in any case.'

Laura was still burning to know what Anna had meant by her final words, *'the future is set in stone'*. She really wanted to ask him directly but knew she would have to put it delicately. These were after all the final words spoken by the woman he had once loved.

'I hope you wouldn't find it too upsetting if I were to ask you if you knew what Anna meant by her final words?'

Richard's eyes moistened as he nodded his agreement to be asked.

'She said 'If you won't listen, the future is set in stone'

Richard listened thoughtfully, and shook his head gently before responding,

'I'm afraid I have no idea what she could have meant. No.' He sounded perplexed, before adding apologetically 'I'm sorry not to be of any more help.'

'On the contrary,' Laura reassured him, 'everything you've told me has been very helpful.'

Although she was a little disappointed on a personal level, everything he said had corroborated Anna's words and there was no denying it would be useful for her report.

Richard reached for his stick. 'I have one other question, myself' he said, rising to his feet. 'Did she ever marry anyone else?'

'Not as far as I'm aware,' answered Laura, 'She referred to herself as Miss Crockett-Burrows. And you might be interested to know she kept the skull with her almost till the very end'.

Richard smiled softly. 'So she really did become a skull priestess after all.' He shook his head. 'Wed to the skull. Incredible! I wonder why?'

'I'd like to know the answer to that question myself' said Laura. Why Anna, an attractive and vivacious young woman should have chosen a life of celibacy and secrecy, caretaking an inanimate object such as the crystal skull was truly puzzling.

'Oh, I almost forgot' said Richard. He began busying himself with the contents of his ancient, battered briefcase. 'The Royal Society asked me to dig out some photos of myself when I was still a young man, just starting out on my career, for their magazine article about the awardees.' he explained, as he pulled out a large envelope full of old photos which he rummaged through until he found the right one.

'Ah, here it is.' he said as he passed an old sepia photograph to Laura.

'I'm afraid the quality isn't good. But you might be interested in it for your report'.

Laura looked at the photograph. It was a photo of the young Anna, standing inside the Mayan pyramid, smiling from cheek to cheek as she held the crystal skull up triumphantly towards the camera. A young Richard Forbes stood grinning by her side.

'I found it the other day when I was going through my old album. I must say, it brought an awful lot of old memories flooding back.'

'You keep it.' he said.

'But I couldn't possibly...' protested Laura.

He looked down at the clutch of photos in his hand. 'I went through them all with the magazine's editors this afternoon, and they preferred one of me on my own anyway. Please.' Richard insisted. 'That time is past.'

'Thank-you very much' Laura put the photo away in her bag.

'But before you go,' added Richard, 'I would like to ask you just one small favour.'

'Yes, what is it?'

'I want you to know that the reason I agreed to stay and talk to you tonight was I thought, maybe you could do what I didn't have the courage to do. Maybe you could let people know about the skull and its history'.

'I'll do my best.' said Laura. They shook hands and Richard picked up his stick and walked slowly off to the award ceremony.

Chapter 38

Laura caught the last flight back to New York. As she boarded the plane, her mind was buzzing with everything Richard had told her.

She felt a little disturbed by some of what he had said. She wondered why Bunny, just like Ron, and for that matter Anna, had all died with the crystal skull in their possession, and she was frustrated she still hadn't got to the bottom of what Anna had meant by her final words *'the future is set in stone'*.

But as she sat down she tried to calm her thoughts. She needed to take stock of where she had got to in her investigation of the skull, for her report.

Whilst Richard had been unable to answer some of the burning questions she still had about the crystal skull, he had certainly answered the question of where Anna Crockett-Burrows had originally found it, and he had even raised the intriguing possibility that perhaps the Maya themselves had actually inherited the crystal skull from some other even more advanced civilisation that had existed prior to their own.

Laura had always been fascinated by the fact that the ancient Mayan civilisation appeared as if from nowhere, already highly developed, even before the time of Christ. Their elaborate artworks, buildings, sciences and hieroglyphs appeared already beautiful and technically proficient, without any sign of the usual trial and error, the gradual improvement of style and evolution of technique that was evident in the culture of every other ancient civilisation she could think of.

Could the crystal skull have had something to do with why the Maya were so highly developed? Was it because it was left behind by a civilisation even more advanced than theirs? Could the crystal skull really have been left behind by the survivors of Atlantis, as Frederick Crockett-Burrows believed, or perhaps by some other highly advanced and technically sophisticated civilisation we have yet to discover?

Laura thought back to the scientific tests which had shown that the skull bore no tool marks. Could this be because the skull had been made by a civilisation which possessed some kind of technology we do not yet have? She thought of all the properties of the skull Michael had discovered in the crystal laboratory. Michael was certainly of the opinion that the crystal skull had been made by those who had technical knowledge far superior to our own.

As Laura began writing up her findings on her laptop, she wondered how Professor Lamb would respond to her suggestion that the crystal skull might be the missing link with some advanced civilisation. She suspected he was not going to be amused.

She looked out of the window as the moon appeared over the horizon. She had given her word to Richard Forbes that she would 'do her best' to let people know about the skull and its history. It was now more than 75 years since the crystal skull had been unearthed inside a Mayan pyramid. Maybe now was the time for the crystal skull to be made public.

But what on Earth was she, Laura Shepherd, 'the expert', going to tell everyone? That she still had no idea what the crystal skull really was, or where it had originally come from. So much of what Richard said had raised more questions than answers.

She sat back in her chair and sighed. Then she remembered that while she had been away, Michael had taken the skull off for further tests in his crystal laboratory. She hoped that maybe now, *he* might have found some more of the answers.

Chapter 39

December 12th 2012

All the while Laura had been away at the award ceremony in Boston, Michael had been carrying out further tests on the crystal skull in Nanon Systems' Crystal Laboratory. Though he had been working on the skull for little more than twenty four hours, he looked as though he hadn't slept for days.

Now he was busy checking the calibration of his measuring equipment in the darkened laboratory, as he waited anxiously for his boss to arrive.

Suddenly Caleb appeared in the doorway. He barked an order at one of his underlings, who scurried off to carry out his bidding before the great bear of a man, marched into the lab.

'OK Michael, so what have you got?' He noticed the crystal skull mounted on the laser machine and did a double-take. 'What the hell is that!?'

'It's that next generation computer I was telling you about.' replied Michael.

'Well it doesn't look much like a computer to me' said Caleb as he eyed the skull suspiciously. 'Look, I don't have much time, so this better be good.'

'It won't take a minute. Just watch this!' said Michael as he dimmed the lights and flicked a switch on the machine.

A razor-sharp beam of red light penetrated the base of the skull, refracted around inside it, and shot out of its eyes. It shone onto a piece of paper mounted on a metal clipboard Michael had placed in front of the skull, where it began to burn in the digits:

'122120121221201212212012

'122120121221201212212012

Just as it had done before when Laura was in the lab.

Though he found it hard to admit it, Caleb was impressed. He stood gazing at the skull, amazed. He just couldn't help admiring it. He had never seen anything quite like it. He didn't want Michael to know, but there was something about this object that really grabbed him.

The laser beam finished etching out its digits and started to burn a black hole into the middle of the piece of paper in front of the skull's face. The paper started to smoulder and burst into flames.

'What the hell!?' exclaimed Caleb as Michael switched off the machine and rushed to blow it out.

He passed the piece of paper to Caleb, who looked at it, puzzled.

'At first I thought it was a tertiary code' explained Michael, 'but I've been running these tests for days and all I'm getting is this same printout over and over again. I just can't seem to get past this basic operating code'.

Caleb was a man who liked solutions, not problems. 'So why are you wasting my time?' he snapped.

'Well...' Michael was applying some electrodes to the skull, 'then I tried blasting it with power, and look what happens!'

Michael made some final adjustments to the electrodes and turned the voltage up to full power. 'Only now look inside the skull, instead of what it's printing out'.

Caleb stared into the skull's transparent crystalline interior, where he thought could see some movement going on deep inside it.

'You see that?' asked Michael, 'It's like its internal density changes, as if the core of the crystal is kind of plasmalyzing, almost like it's turning into liquid and its centre is moving towards the outside'.

Caleb was deeply intrigued as he watched a small dark area appear inside the centre of the skull. 'It's like there's a *hole* beginning to open up inside it!'

The two men watched in awe as a small dark hole began to appear inside the skull. They stood mesmerised as they witnessed the density changes occurring inside it, as what had previously been solid matter, shifted and moved before them.

Caleb looked at Michael whose face was filled with the excitement of treading new ground, of moving into the unknown. He should have guessed. Michael wasn't one to waste his time. Michael was a rare breed, a man of uncanny vision. When he was onto something, it had to be good.

Caleb was about to congratulate him when Michael spoke.

'That's not all. I've noticed an even stranger effect when I add the laser light. Watch this!'

Michael flicked a switch on the machine and a short, sharp pulse of laser light shot up through the base of the skull, where it was refracted back out of its eyes, and shone onto the metal clipboard in front of the skull's face, as before.

'Do you see the time on that clock?' Michael asked pointing to a digital clock on the laser machine, situated beneath the skull, alongside the source of the laser beam.

'Yeah.'

'What time does it say?'

'9am, 1 minute, and 100 nanoseconds' responded Caleb blankly. 'Why?'

'Well, that clock records the exact time when the laser beam was fired from the machine. Now do you see the time on *that* clock' Michael pointed to another similar digital clock he had attached to the metal sheet mounted in front of the skull.

'Sure,' Caleb sauntered over to the clock, 'It says 9am, 1 minute, and 99 nanoseconds'.

'Well,' began Michael, '*that* clock records the exact moment when that laser beam of light, having travelled through the skull and been refracted back out of its eyes, finally arrived at its destination. It records the precise nanosecond when the laser beam first hit that metal clipboard'.

'But it's one nanosecond *earlier*!' exclaimed Caleb, 'That's impossible!'

He looked at Michael who simply raised his eyebrows and opened his palms.

'You gotta be kidding me, right?' said Caleb.

'Impossible I know,' said Michael as he walked over and took a look at the clock, 'but I've tested it dozens of times. I've even tried using all these different clocks'

He opened a drawer to show Caleb all the clocks he had previously wired up and now discarded, 'but it's always the same effect - the light always arrives at its destination at least one nanosecond BEFORE it was sent!'

'That's unbelievable!' Caleb scratched his head, before he began to sound almost angry. 'Einstein said nothing in the universe can travel faster than the speed of light and so nothing can go backwards in time!'

'I know' said Michael quietly 'That's what *I* thought.' He paused. 'But maybe Einstein was wrong?'

They looked at each other.

Michael was the first to speak. 'I know it's only a tiny fraction of a second, but if we were to apply massive amounts of electricity and laser power...'

Caleb clicked his fingers. 'Michael! Hold it right there! Forget the tertiary code.' He began to get very excited. 'Check this effect! Multiply it! I want to know how much we can amplify this effect and how much pressure this thing can take even when fully plasmalyzed'.

'No problem.' said Michael, grinning from ear to ear.

'We're onto something here' enthused Caleb 'If this thing works out I've got an application in mind you would not believe, an application that could change our whole future.'

'You think so?' asked Michael.

'I know so!' answered Caleb, his voice filled with excitement 'I can see it now, you and me, we'll be up for the Nobel Prize'.

Michael looked hesitant, before Caleb added 'I want total confidentiality in this, understand?'

'Of course,' said Michael, thinking for a moment, 'The only problem is the skull actually belongs to the museum'.

'I don't see why that should be a problem' Caleb gave Michael a knowing smile.

Chapter 40

December 13th 2012

The following morning Laura arrived for work much earlier than usual but even at this hour, there were already workmen perched on scaffolding all over the front of the Smithton Geographic Museum. It was a crisp, clear winter day, and what breeze there was tugged at the brightly coloured banner the men were unfurling over the grand neo-classical façade of the proud old building.

'Sponsoring the Smithton Geographic Museum'
The banner yelled, in letters six foot high.
'Nanon Systems – Creating the Future - today!'

'Gee, that Caleb of yours must be quite a guy!' A voice said in an almost lecherous southern drawl and Laura spun round to see Janice standing beside her wearing a thigh-high designer fur coat but still no sign of any skirt worth speaking of underneath. *Even in this weather? She must be freezing!* Laura couldn't help thinking to herself.

'He's not *my* Caleb,' She felt the need to explain, 'He's Michael's Caleb, and he's only sponsoring the museum because he wants something.'

'So what does he want? Maybe I can give it to him?' Janice quipped, wiggling her hips, she believed seductively.

'He wants the crystal skull.' replied Laura.

'Why on Earth would he want that creepy thang?' Janice faked a shudder.

'He and Michael have some kind of theory about its 'potential scientific applications', but don't ask. It's all highly confidential. In any case, that's the cost of it', she nodded towards the banner, 'A new library for us and Caleb gets the crystal skull to do whatever the hell he likes with.'

'Well maybe he can do whatever the hell he likes with me sometime?' Janice wiggled her hips again. "You got his number?'

'Thank God, No!' replied Laura as they made their way inside the museum and rode the elevator to the third floor.

Janice went off to fetch some coffee from the kitchens while Laura unlocked her office and placed the crystal skull she had just got back from

Michael in its case on the side-desk.

She was just settling in behind her desk and powering up her computer when Janice came in with a scalding hot cup of black coffee and plonked it down in front of her.

'Professor Lamb says you've only got until six o'clock this evening to finish that report on the crystal skull, before he hands it over to the lovely Caleb at Nanon Systems.'

'I know!' Laura felt under pressure 'I'm just trying to finish it now.'

'Meaning, leave me to get on with it?'

'Meaning just that!'

'Oh, and don't forget.'

Laura looked up.

'Don't Look it in the eye!' Janice quipped, as she nodded towards the crystal skull.

Trust Janice thought Laura. Rumours about the 'curse of the skull' were obviously still circulating.

Janice was just about to leave when she stopped and turned back, 'Oh, and don't forget to let me know when that Caleb of yours arrives.' Laura frowned.

'So I can arrange to run into him of course!' Janice grinned and teetered off down the corridor.

Laura took a gulp of the hot black coffee. Whatever Janice's warning she decided she'd better take one final look at the crystal skull to see if it helped her think of anything else she could add to her report, for Professor Lamb.

She went over to the side desk and opened up the skull-case. She lifted the crystal skull out carefully and held it in her hands. As she sat down again behind her desk she rolled it around in her palms studying it carefully by the light of her old desk-lamp.

It seemed strange now to think how frightened she had been of this thing when she had first come across it. She wondered whether she'd still have had a bad feeling about it even if it hadn't rolled out of the fingers of a dead man. She found herself staring at it.

Richard's story had really got her thinking. The idea that the skull might have been linked to an earlier, even more advanced civilisation was fascinating. She looked again at the way the skull caught and refracted the light. When she held it at a particular angle, a myriad of rainbow colours seemed to dance upon its surface, just as Anna had described in her journal.

She noticed that her feelings towards the skull were softening. The fear and revulsion she had once felt in its presence were now gone. She realised that in many ways the crystal skull really was quite beautiful.

As she sat looking at the skull, she found herself becoming totally absorbed by it. She couldn't take her eyes off it now. All outside distractions faded away as she observed the way the crystal had been carved to lead the eye inwards, spiralling round towards the centre, towards its eye sockets. And despite Janice's warning, Laura was aware that she kept wanting to look down into those eyes, that were not eyes, into those dark spaces where the eyes would have been.

How deeply she was drawn into those crystal orbs. She was mesmerised, lost in a place beyond thought. And before she knew it, she had lost track of time. Several minutes, maybe more, had passed during which she had been gazing deep into those hollow crystalline sockets.

It took an enormous effort of will to break free. She had to drag herself back into her office, back into the here and now. She pushed the skull away and knuckled her eyes with screwed up fists.

As she opened her eyes and looked at her surroundings, she felt as though she had been in some kind of trance. She shook her head, trying to shake off its effects, and sat quietly for a moment, trying to allow herself to return to normal. She took another sip of the coffee and was surprised to find that it was now cold. *Had that much time really slipped by?*

She turned her attention back to finishing her report.

Before Laura knew it, darkness had fallen, and it was 6 0'clock in the evening.

She noticed that she had put the crystal skull down on her desk just in front of the photo of Anna Crockett-Burrows that Richard Forbes had given her the night before. She looked at the photograph, now propped up at the front of her desk, beside her own framed photograph of Alice.

She realised that this picture of Anna Crockett-Burrows was the nearest she had to any kind of photographic evidence of the skull's discovery, but it was so out of focus, she wondered whether it was really worth including in her report. She decided to put it in anyway, it all added to what she had heard.

She picked it up, intending to drop it into the folder she would deliver to Lamb, and as she did so, she glanced at the photograph of Alice. Her little face was beaming with joy. She remembered what Anna had said about Alice somehow trying to communicate with her through the crystal skull. Unbelievable, she knew, but deep down she wished it were true.

Laura ran her hand across the surface of the photo. She really wanted to believe that Alice was still out there somewhere and that she could somehow communicate with her. But nothing she had read in Anna' journal or heard from Richard Forbes had shed any more light on how such a thing might be possible. No, this was the real world. She sighed. The idea of talking to her dead daughter was nothing more than a hopeless dream, a fantasy, and nothing more than that.

She knew she would never see Alice again. Never speak to her, whisper comfort to her in the night, hold her small, warm hand in her own. She stifled a tear. It saddened her to accept it but she knew she'd have to let go of the unrealistic idea of having any kind of contact with Alice ever again.

Perhaps the idea of trying to communicate with the dead was best left alone. Her dealings with the crystal skull would soon be over in any case. *Enough is enough*, she told herself. In some ways she would be glad to be seeing the back of it.

She clicked on her laptop and waited for her document to attach. Then, with a sense of relief, she emailed her report to Professor Lamb.

She was just about to pack the crystal skull away again into its case, when something caught her eye. She looked at the skull. Through its transparent crystalline interior she could see the photograph of the young Anna Crockett-Burrows, standing holding the crystal skull, and something incredible was happening.

Chapter 41

To Laura's amazement, seen now, through the prism of the crystal skull, the out of focus photograph of Anna Crockett-Burrows suddenly appeared to become sharply focused and she could see everything in it clearly for the first time.

The last time she had looked at the photo of the young Anna, it looked as if Anna had been standing in front of some sort of rock or stone, but the photo was too blurred to make out any proper detail. But now that Laura was looking at the photograph through the crystal skull, she could see what she had not seen before.

Anna was not standing in front of any old piece of rock, seen now through the prism of the crystal skull, Laura could see that Anna was in fact, standing in front of a hieroglyph encrusted stone!

Moreover, it looked like a stone doorway. And whilst some of the hiero-glyphs remained hidden behind Anna's body, those that were visible suddenly came sharply into focus, now magnified, and startlingly clear.

Laura's eye scanned the inscriptions, which were now eminently readable, and she instinctively began to translate them. Something about these hieroglyphs looked vaguely familiar. She recognised the wording from somewhere:

The outermost ring of hieroglyphs said.

'It is written… in the cycles of time… that…'

Her jaw dropped as she had a sudden realization.

It can't be, she thought to herself. It was almost unbelievable.

She grabbed the photo and the skull off her desk and took them over to her work-table on the other side of the room. The prophecy stone that she had been puzzling over for the last few weeks was lying there, surrounded by her notes.

She looked at the photo through the skull again, and looked at the huge semi-circular chunk of hieroglyph stone that had been sat on the table in her office all along.

'It's part of the same stone!' she whispered to herself in amazement. 'Dear God! It's part of the same stone!'

She drew in a quick, excited breath. She could hardly believe it. The chunk of hieroglyph stone that had been sat there in her office for weeks, ever since it had been seized by Customs and handed over to the museum, the one that she had been trying so hard to translate and work out where it had come from, was in fact from Luvantum, from the same ancient Mayan city where Anna Crockett-Burrows said she had found the crystal skull.

She could see all this quite clearly now when she looked at Anna Crockett-Burrows photograph through the crystal skull.

She could see that the chunk of broken stone on her table had in fact originally formed part of the massive hieroglyph-encrusted stone doorway at the entrance to the skull chamber inside the temple-pyramid at Luvantum. It had originally been part of the stone doorway that protected the entrance to the chamber where Anna Crockett-Burrows had found the crystal skull.

She could scarcely believe it.

After weeks' of effort and speculation she had finally stumbled upon the answer to the mystery of where the stone fragment had come from.

If only she could figure out what the rest of the stone said, but most of the remaining hieroglyphs were so badly eroded she had still not been able to translate them, and the innermost ring of hieroglyphs were still missing completely.

Laura was about to put the crystal skull down again and give up on any further translation attempts when she accidentally caught sight of one of the eroded hieroglyphs through the skull. She closed her eyes and opened them again, but she had not imagined it. Like the hieroglyphs in the photo, when looked at through the transparent crystal of the skull, the hieroglyphs on her work-table too now came into view, magnified and no longer eroded, but instead looking as crisp and clear as the day they were carved.

She knew it shouldn't be possible but there they were right in front of her, as plain as day.

Her hands were trembling as she held the skull in front of them and started to translate them.

She already knew that the first three glyphs said, 'It is written in the cycles of time that...' But now she was able to recognise the next inscription. It was the elegant pictogram that represented 'sunset'. She also recognised the distinctive configuration of hieroglyphs the Maya used to convey a date; a certain number of dots and lines to convey the number, combined with a 'head-variant glyph' to convey the day name. So the next series of glyphs meant 'on the day named...'

She started to translate the numbers and day names she knew from her studies of the ancient Mayan calendar, which gave her the date, in Mayan: '13 Baktun... 0 Katun... 0 Tun... and 0 Kin...'

In other words, the whole sequence of hieroglyphs she had spent so long puzzling over actually said, 'It is written... in the cycles of time... that... at sunset... on the day named... 13 Baktun... 0 Katun... 0 Tun... and 0 Kin...'

But the innermost glyphs were still missing, and even in the photograph they were obscured behind the young Anna Crockett-Burrows. Laura had translated every glyph she could, but she had now reached the edge of the broken chunk of stone and could not translate any more.

Puzzled, she sped over to her bookshelves and began pulling down books, leafing through them, scanning the indices until she found what she was looking for; a conversion table to enable her to translate the date. She ran her finger across the matrix of dates as she calculated.

She gazed at the date for a long time. There was something extremely odd about it. *It couldn't be!* She grabbed another book, found its conversion table, and translated the date again. She shook her head. She had to double-check the conversion... It came out as before.

Laura flopped onto her chair holding her scribbled notes in front of her. Her hunch that the stone contained information about the future was right. That, in itself, was not unusual. The ancient Maya made many predictions, sometimes way into the future. Usually the focus of these predictions was astrological events such as eclipses and the arrival of comets. They were able to predict eclipses they could not even see that were happening on the other side of the world, or eclipses that were to happen over a thousand years after their own civilisation so mysteriously collapsed and disappeared. One carved stone found in Guatemala even appeared to predict the collapse of their own empire.

But Laura had never before seen a prophecy stone carved with a prediction quite so far into the future. The only other one that came close was a stone in Mexico that had predicted the solar eclipse that happened over Mexico City in 1992, but that was over twenty years previously. This was something else entirely. This stone appeared to be predicting something that was going to happen not just in the Mayan's future, but in our near future. The stone was predicting something that was about to happen this century.

'Surely not!' she whispered to herself. She could hardly believe her own thoughts. But it struck her then, like a bolt form the blue. Anna's final words, which she said were from Alice.

'The future is set in stone'.

So this is what Alice meant, she realised. This is what Anna was referring to in her final message. This is what Alice wanted her to know when she said 'If you won't listen, the future is set in stone'.

Laura was filled with emotion. She felt an overwhelming sense of awe, and sadness. For this is what she had given up hoping for. This is what she had decided was not possible. But now it had happened. Her beautiful little girl had effectively communicated with her through the skull. This was Alice's message. This is what Alice had been trying to tell her about.

What was she thinking! Alice was dead. Her little girl was gone. There couldn't possibly be messages from beyond the grave, could there?

At that moment Michael entered the office. He took one look at Laura and knew something was wrong.

"What is it?"

"I've got it, Michael!" Her voice was filled with excitement.

"Got what?"

"Alice's message. Now I understand it!"

She saw his face and decided to rephrase it for him.

"Now I understand what Anna meant."

He stared at her. He'd thought Laura had got over this business about communicating with Alice, thought it was only a passing phase, a comforting fantasy, and nothing more, especially now that Anna Crockett-Burrows was gone. He assumed she had put such irrational ideas behind her and moved on, but now he wasn't so sure.

"What are you talking about?" He sounded uneasy.

Laura came over to him and took his hands in hers. She led him over to the hieroglyph stone, sat him down in front of it, and stared him in the face.

"*'The future is set in stone'*, Michael. This is it! This is what she meant!" Her eyes were shining with joy.

Michael looked at her - confused, concerned.

"This stone, it's carved with a prediction about the future! It says that something's going to happen on the day 13 Baktun, 0 Katun, 0 Tun, and 0 Kin."

"Which means, in English...?" Michael was struggling to work out where Laura was going with all of this.

"It's a date, in the ancient Mayan calendar," she explained.

"So when was it?" Michael was expecting to hear of some event that had happened hundreds of years before

"That's just it." replied Laura, struggling to comprehend it herself, "It translates into our calendar as..."

She scanned the conversion table with her finger again just to be absolutely sure she had got it right. Michael was waiting for her reply.

"...It translates as... December 21st 2012!"

Chapter 42

After a moment's pause, as he tried to take it all in, Michael protested, "But that's next week! That's impossible."

Laura looked at her husband and spoke slowly.

"No it's not Michael. The ancient Maya made predictions way into the future. And everything they ever predicted on one of these prophecy stones has come true, exactly on the day they said it would."

He stared at her, still struggling to comprehend the significance of what she was saying.

Laura started rummaging through her briefcase for her address book. She flicked through it till she found what she was looking for, picked up her phone, and dialled.

"Hello, Dr Brown? This is Dr Shepherd from the Smithton Geographic Institute. I need you to take me to Luvantum... as soon as possible."

There was a pause while Dr Brown spoke on the other end of the phone.

"Is that the only flight?"

"What are you doing?" Michael sounded perturbed.

"OK, I'll see you there at 2 o'clock tomorrow." She put down the phone and turned back to him.

"Look" she said. "I'm going to have to go to Luvantum..."

"Laura, are you out of your mind"

"No, Michael. This is important. I have to go...for all kinds of reasons."

He stared at her, started to protest, but she raised a finger and pressed it to his lips.

"Can't you see? This is what Alice was trying to warn us about."

He looked at her, appalled.

"Something's going to happen in one week's time." She said. "It's right here, 'set in stone', but some of these hieroglyphs are still missing. I can see from Anna's photo that there's another inner ring of hieroglyphs, but I can't translate them because Anna is standing in the way.' She held up Anna's photo.

'I need to find the rest of this stone, Michael. I've got to go to Central America and I'm going to have to take the skull with me to decode the other glyphs."

Michael couldn't believe what he was hearing. It was bad enough that she thought she had got a message from Alice. Now she was planning a dangerous trip to Central America. It was utter madness, totally incomprehensible to him. But he knew just how stubborn she could be once she had made up her mind.

He was about to protest again, when Laura's office door swung open and in walked Professor Lamb, accompanied by Caleb and two security guards from Nanon Systems.

Professor Lamb was in a jocular mood, all smiles, no doubt filled with the milk of human kindness now that the Smithton Geographic's coffers had been so amply filled by Nanon Systems.

He greeted Michael with a warm handshake before turning his beaming smile on Laura.

"OK Laura, your time's up with the skull." He smiled.

She frowned.

"Professor Lamb, I'm afraid something's come up that needs further investigation, so I'll need to hang onto it, just for a few more days."

Lamb shot her an angry look. This hadn't figured in his plans for a smooth handover. He had been more than happy at the thought of the skull going. He didn't want the skull, that sorry reminder of Ron's demise, hanging around the museum any longer. The fact that he had gained the museum a lucrative sponsorship deal in return for its effective sale - a long-term loan to Nanon Systems for them to 'carry out further research'- was an added and unexpected bonus that he had no intention of jeopardising.

"I'm afraid that's out of the question," he replied. "Officially, the skull now belongs to Nanon Systems."

"It became ours as of six o'clock this evening," added Caleb, looking at his watch, "and that's nearly half an hour ago."

He sat down on the corner of Laura's desk.

"I signed over a hell of a lot of money for this thing and we've got a pressing deadline on this project...So...If you don't mind..."

He held out a hand.

"I'm sorry, Caleb" Laura began, "but the skull is absolutely vital to our hieroglyph research program."

"It is?" said Lamb. It was certainly the first he'd heard of it.

"Yes." Laura looked around at their blank faces. "Look at these hieroglyphs. They're totally unreadable, right?" Laura ran her hand across the eroded glyphs, "Now look at them through the skull!"

She offered the skull to Lamb. He deferred to Caleb, who looked through it instead.

"See how they're transformed by it?" said Laura, "The skull makes it possible to read them even though they're so badly eroded."

There was a long pause while Caleb peered at the stone through the skull, moving it a little to left and right.

"I can't see anything!" said Caleb bluntly. "Is this a joke?"

He put down the skull.

Laura picked it up to check again herself.

"But look! Professor Lamb! They show a date in the ancient Mayan calendar, clear as day."

Lamb raised an eyebrow and she offered the skull to him.

"Just hold the skull steady and you'll see what I mean."

Lamb took hold of the skull and positioned himself elbows on the desktop, legs apart, as if he were about to take a shot on the golf course. He stared hard into the skull at the hieroglyphs.

"Those glyphs you can see there translate into our calendar as December 21st 2012 - exactly a week today!" She explained.

Lamb looked uncertain.

"Are you sure about this, Laura?"

"Absolutely!"

"I'm sorry, Laura... I can't see them."

He put the skull down.

Laura stared at him. She was starting to feel nervous now. It worried her that they couldn't see what she could through the skull.

"Michael, show them I'm not going crazy!" she joked, handing the skull to Michael.

Nobody else was smiling. Michael didn't want to take the skull. She could see that. His posture became tense and awkward. He didn't really want to be a part of it, didn't really want to be put in this position. All eyes were upon him as he lifted the skull and looked at the hieroglyphs through it.

There was a silence as Michael adjusted and readjusted the position of the skull, his brow furrowed with concentration.

"Well?" asked Laura.

"Just a minute!" He squinted his eyes. He changed the angle of the skull again. Then he turned to her.

"No, Laura. I can't see anything either."

"But, Michael, you must be able to see them!" There was desperation in her voice.

Michael looked again and shook his head. "I'm sorry, Laura. There's just nothing there."

He put down the skull and looked at his wife, concern etched in his face.

They all stared at her in silence.

She put her hand to her brow.

"I don't understand why you can't see them."

Her face was full of pain.

"It's important. You have to understand," she implored, "Something's going to happen in a week's time, and I need the skull to find out what."

There was an awkward silence before Caleb cleared his throat and spoke.

"I'm afraid you won't be having any further contact with the skull, Laura. It's been given high-security status. Access will be limited only to key scientific and military personnel."

"What!?" Laura was horrified.

Caleb nodded to his Head of Security, a former police officer of Russian descent. Keeping a wary eye on Laura, he came forward and started packing the skull into its case.

"No! Please! Wait!"

She stepped forward to try to stop the security guard, but Michael took her arm firmly in his hand.

"Let it go, Laura." He said quietly.

"No!"

She broke free from his grasp, lunged forward and tried to grab the skull from the security guard, but within an instant the other officer restrained her, holding her in a vice-like grip.

"Please!" She begged, trying to break free, "I need to find out what she was trying to warn us about!"

She struggled helplessly against the security guard. The first officer finished packing the skull away, as Lamb ushered he and Caleb out of the door.

"I'm terribly sorry about all this, Caleb. I've never seen Dr Shepherd like this before." Lamb was deeply apologetic as he guided his guests towards the lifts.

They were well on their way down in the elevator before Laura gave up and relaxed in the grip of the guard.

"Have you calmed down now, ma'am?" asked the security guard. She nodded. He gave her an uncertain look, then let her go and left the room to follow the others.

Laura stood there deflated, crushed, devastation on her face. Michael went over to her, almost afraid. He didn't know what was going on inside her head. He felt like he didn't know her anymore. Something had happened to her, something he couldn't understand.

"Laura, what's got into you?" he asked. He didn't mean it to sound that way but he couldn't stop the fear and anger he felt inside from registering in his voice.

But instead of answering the question, Laura made a dash for the door.

Stunned, Michael shouted, 'Laura!' and ran after her, but she slammed the door shut in his face.

She had only one thought, and that was how to get the skull back. She had, at best, minutes to work it out, before it left the building for good and she would never see it again.

She scanned the corridor. The second security guard had just gone down in the lift. She ran along the hallway, dodging past an open-mouthed Janice.

"Wait!" She heard Michael shouting behind her, but she ignored him and pushed open the door to the emergency stairs.

She threw herself down the steps, almost injuring herself in the process, but she had little regard for her own safety.

At the bottom of the stairs, she found herself in the underground service corridor, at the far end of which she could see through the fire door into the underground car park. Through the window she saw Lamb shaking hands with and bidding goodbye to Caleb and his men.

Caleb was about to leave, with the skull. Her heart stood still.

She could hear Michael crashing down the stairs behind her. She looked round for somewhere to hide and dived into the 'Ladies' rest room, letting the door close quietly. She leant back against it, thinking he would hear the sound of her heart, it was beating so loudly. She heard Michael run past. She heard the fire door open as Professor Lamb returned from the car park and she overheard Michael ask him if he'd seen her.

'No, I haven't seen her down here.' answered Lamb.

She heard them retracing Michael's steps back upstairs to the next level, before she breathed for what felt like the first time in minutes.

When she was sure they were out of earshot, she pulled out her mobile phone and dialled, while cautiously re-emerging into the corridor.

Through the fire door window, she could see Caleb climbing into his car and fastening his seat belt. *Shit*. They were about to leave.

She whispered quietly into her phone, "Jacob, we've been robbed! Someone just stole the crystal skull from my office. It's a big guy in a navy suit with two fake security guards. They're in a black 4x4 just about to leave the car park."

The line went dead almost at once.

She turned back to the window. Caleb's vehicle began to pull out of its parking space.

Come on, Jacob. Why are you taking so long?

Caleb's car approached the exit gates.

Another fifteen seconds and they'll be out of here.

She watched as the security barrier was raised.

No, they mustn't leave.

In a panic, she pushed through the fire door and started to run across the car park towards them. She could see Micron's Head of Security in the driving seat. He raised his hand in a farewell gesture to the guys in the museum security booth.

Oh no, it's too late.

Suddenly the car park was shattered by the wail of the museum's alarm system, the exit barrier slammed down in front of Caleb's departing vehicle, and three uniformed museum officers emerged from their security booth and pulled a shocked looking Caleb and his colleagues out of their car, at gunpoint.

Laura ducked down out of sight behind a dumpster. She saw one of the museum officers retrieve the skull-case from inside Caleb's car and place it on the hood of the vehicle. They forced Caleb and his men up against the wall, legs splayed and arms behind their heads, as they removed their guns from them.

Laura needed to get nearer. Keeping her head low, she made her way across the car park, dodging and weaving amongst the parked cars, trying to remain down out of sight, until she reached the end of a row of vehicles. There she paused, hidden behind Professor Lamb's brown Volkswagen. Between there and Caleb's car, parked by the exit, there was nowhere left to hide.

She eyed the skull-case on the bonnet of Caleb's vehicle. It was less than twenty yards away now.

She heard Michael and Lamb emerging from the fire door behind her, coming to see what was going on.

She hesitated. Once she came out from behind Lamb's car, somebody would be sure to spot her. She looked at the unattended skull-case on the hood of Caleb's vehicle. Beyond it were three armed officers, and the museum exit gates. Across the outer doorway, an automatic security grille was slowly but surely descending.

This is it! She thought. *It's now or never.*

She had only seconds to decide, and then, under the flashing red glare of the museum's emergency alarm system, she made a dash for it. She threw herself across the hood of Caleb's car, grabbed the skull-case, and ran for the exit gates.

Lamb spotted her first.

'Stop her!' He yelled and everyone turned round to see what he was shouting about.

Still held back by one of the guards, Caleb watched in horror as Laura flew through the museum exit gates, shinned underneath the descending security grille, and vanished into the night, with his precious crystal skull...

Chapter 43

Laura's heart was pounding in her chest as she turned the corner onto Broad Street. Luckily, the rush-hour was nearly over and she managed to hail a taxi almost immediately. She climbed in, and as the cab began to wind its way through the city streets, her mind began reeling at the thought of what she had just done.

The journey to the airport seemed to take forever. All the while Laura was glancing back to see if the others were following. She knew that Caleb would be after her. He would not have taken what had just happened at the museum at all well.

In fact, Laura's taxi was making good progress, despite the evening traffic, and she was soon leaping onto the kerbside at Newark International airport.

Laura was quite out of breath as she raced towards the solitary check-in desk for Condora Airlines. She knew from her telephone conversation with Dr Brown that she was cutting it fine. She had known that when she first grabbed the skull and jumped into the taxi, but she was hoping, beyond hope, that she could still make it.

As she neared the desk, she watched in dismay as a young Hispanic air stewardess put up a sign saying that the check-in was now closed. Her male colleague was switching off the luggage conveyor belt. Laura scanned the faces of the airline staff, praying they might still somehow be able to let her through.

'I'm sorry I'm late...' she began, between breaths.

'I'm afraid we are closed,' said the young stewardess.

'But I have to catch this flight! There's no connecting flight to Santa Cruz for another week!' cried Laura.

'I'm very sorry,' Came the reply again.

'Please! It's urgent,' she begged.

'Wait here a moment,' said the older Mexican man behind the stewardess, and he disappeared behind the screen. He returned a few moments later, his expression uncertain, 'You have luggage, no?'

'Only hand luggage.' Laura indicated the skull-case. His expression eased.

'Then it is OK. You are lucky we have had a cancellation. But you have to be quick. Do you have your passport and credit card?'

Laura thanked the man profusely as she purchased her ticket, and he wished her well in his part of the world, before she ran to join the long queue waiting to go through to Departures.

Outside the airport, the big, black 4 x 4 pulled up alongside the terminal building. Michael, Caleb, and one of the Nanon guards leapt onto the kerb and waded through the hoard of Christmas travellers towards the airport entrance doors. They squeezed past suitcases piled high with skis, surfboards and Christmas gifts of all shapes and sizes, as they hurried towards the check-in desks.

As Michael scanned the list of flight departures, his anxiety about Laura grew. He worried that she might be in the throes of some kind of mental breakdown. Who knew what she might do next, after having taken off with the skull? He knew she could be impulsive, on occasion, but what worried him most about what he had just seen was that Laura's behaviour seemed so completely irrational. She appeared to have abandoned all reason in favour of the utterly crazy notion that Alice was somehow trying to communicate with her.

And it was one thing to be cracking up at home, he pondered, but it would be quite another to have a nervous breakdown in some remote and dangerous region of Central America. Michael couldn't swear to it of course. In fact, he couldn't be sure exactly where Laura was or where she might be going, but his best guess was that, now she had secured possession of the crystal skull, she would be trying to get to Luvantum as quickly as possible.

But maybe they were at the wrong airport? Maybe her flight was leaving from JFK? Or maybe they'd already missed her?

Michael scanned the departure monitors. The only flight that appeared to be going anywhere near Luvuntum that evening was Condora Airlines Flight 101 to Guatemala City.

They headed for the Condora check-in desk.

'Did a blonde woman in her late thirties just buy a ticket to Guatemala City?' Michael asked the airline steward who was packing away his briefcase, about to leave the empty counter.

The steward eyed Caleb and his colleague with suspicion.

'I am not allowed to reveal such information for security reasons.'

'Please, I'm her husband' pleaded Michael, 'She's having... some problems. She needs help. She shouldn't be travelling alone. You must let me travel with her'

'I'm sorry, we are closed. And in any case that flight is full.'

'Then let me travel on another flight.'

'There are no other seats available to Guatemala now till after Christmas.'

'Then sell me a ticket on any other flight you've got seats for this evening.' Michael was thinking on his toes.

The steward looked puzzled. 'The only other flight we have is to Panama, over a thousand miles from Guatemala City.' He waved his hand dismissively.

'That's fine. Just sell me a ticket.' Michael pulled his passport from his jacket pocket and slapped it on the counter.

'But it leaves around the same time as the other flight,' he glanced at his watch, 'in less than 20 minutes. You won't make it.' He nodded towards the queue waiting to get through security to the departure gates.

'Just give me a ticket!' Michael insisted, offering his credit card.

He had no intention of travelling to Panama. But he had to get through to the departure area, even if that involved buying a ticket he would never use. He needed to get to the departure gate for the flight to Guatemala. He had to stop Laura getting on that flight.

'Very well.' The steward shrugged his shoulders, opened his briefcase and began to issue Michael with a ticket to Panama.

He turned to Caleb and his escort. 'Can I see your passports please?'

The Nanon guard just shook his head.

'We don't have them here' replied Caleb.

'Then I'm afraid I can't help you.'

Caleb just stood there, rooted to the spot, silently seething with anger. Then, after a few moments, his chest puffed up and he exploded.

'This is an outrage!' he stormed, banging his fist on the check in desk. 'Do you know who I am?'

The steward looked up from his papers, his eyebrows raised.

'I am Caleb Price, Chairman of Nanon Systems, and I demand to speak to your Head of Security.'

'Very well, sir,' said the steward trying not to get flustered, 'I'll give him a call right away.'

Chapter 44

It seemed to take Michael an eternity to get through security and into the Departures area. Begging his way to the front of the queue, he almost got himself arrested for acting in a suspicious manner, before finally explaining his way through, as the x-ray scanner attendant and body searcher could each find no technical grounds on which to detain him.

As soon as he was released, he dashed across the departures lounge, dodging through the crowds of people most of whom were on their way to spend Christmas with family and friends. Michael ran as fast as he could. He ran as if his very life depended on it. He had to catch Laura before she got on that plane. All that mattered was that he got to Gate 12 before it closed, before the doors to the waiting aircraft were bolted shut, and it was too late.

He skimmed round the suitcase that toppled from a young man's trolley right in front of him, before boarding the first of a series of moving pavements that led to the departure gate. He leapt over a pile of shopping bags that belonged to two Indian women who were trying to restrain a screaming toddler, as he sprinted toward the next moving pavement.

Laura finally reached Departure Gate 12. This was it. She was stepping into the unknown. Once she boarded that flight there could be no going back. She would not be able to go back to her boss, Professor Lamb, and say 'sorry', that she had suffered a temporary loss of sanity, that through her grief reason had escaped her and she had behaved in a way that, in retrospect, shocked even herself.

She hesitated. If she turned back now there might still be a chance, however remote, that she could redeem herself. She had been a loyal and diligent member of the museum staff, reliable and hardworking. If she turned around now, it might still be alright. She might still be able to undo some of the damage she had done. She could appeal to Professor Lamb to forgive her and allow her to continue in her post at the museum. She could argue it had all been a passing blip, a singular blemish on an otherwise successful career.

If only he would see it that way, then it wouldn't be too late. Perhaps she should call him right now and explain all that without further ado. Her hand touched her mobile phone. She looked around the departure gate lounge. It was almost empty now as the final passengers were filing through and boarding the aircraft.

What she wanted was some sign, some sense that going to Central America was the right thing to do. Back in her office, she had been so certain. There had been no doubt in her mind that the information she received had been a message from Alice. It had been so clear to her. But now, as she stared at the airport departure gate, she wasn't quite so sure. How could she possibly tell whether or not it really was a message from her little girl?

Over the airport p.a. system she heard the announcement: *"Final call for all passengers on flight CO101 to Guatemala City."* She watched the digits on the departure lounge clock ticking away the final minutes towards departure time. It would soon be too late to change her mind either way.

As Departure gate 12 finally came into view, Michael could see that the woman hovering by the gate in the distance was Laura. He would recognise the swing of her neat blonde ponytail anywhere. He could make out the contours of her crisp, linen work suit and the distinctive outline of the skull-case in her hand. He had been right about her course of action. Now she had the skull, she was on her way to Central America, to try to prove her bizarre theory about the Mayan prophecy stone.

He stifled the urge to yell her name, to get her attention. He had to get to her before she boarded that plane. If she saw him coming, there was a chance she would run straight on and he didn't want that to happen.

Then it struck him. She was standing there alone at the departure gate staring at the clock above the door. He was puzzled as to why she was still standing there, why she had not yet boarded the plane?

Michael wondered if perhaps Laura was beginning to see sense after all. Perhaps she had decided not to jeopardise her whole career, and his, on this crazy notion that Alice was somehow trying to communicate with her. Perhaps she had decided not to risk so much based on the strange and befuddled notion that she could see something through the crystal skull that he, and Professor Lamb, and Caleb could not.

But then again, maybe her behaviour was not the result of any carefully thought out reason, but simply the outward manifestation, the symptom of a deeply disturbed state of mind. Perhaps she was staring at the clock because she no longer knew what she had originally intended to do?

Perhaps she was so confused that she simply no longer knew what she was doing or where she was supposed to be going?

An air stewardess was standing at the desk in front of the departure doors checking through the final flight paperwork. In less than a minute's time, the gate would be closed.

Within him, Michael found a renewed energy. He was only moments away from her now. He was going to get to her in time. He was going to get his Laura back. He would keep her safe and, in time, they would learn to put this madness, this crazy episode behind them. It might take something more than he alone could give, counselling, therapy, possibly even medication. But he was pretty sure it was probably just an isolated moment of madness, a bursting out of all the left-over feeling that Laura still had for Alice, erupting and pouring out of her. He hoped it was simply a last outpouring of grief, in all its destructive, pointless, painful rage, but soon to be dissipated, diffused and gone.

Laura glanced down at the passport and boarding card in her hand. Looking up, she caught sight of something she didn't like in the distance. It was the disturbing vision of Caleb and his guard, accompanied by two armed members of airport security, emerging from a double doorway at the far end of the long concourse, and marching straight towards her.

Her mind was made up.

Michael was nearly there now. He saw Laura approach the air stewardess behind the desk. Oh no, she was offering her passport and boarding pass.

'Laura!' he shouted, then louder, 'Laura! ...Laura Shepherd!'

But it was too late. If she had heard him, she didn't turn back. The next moment, just before he reached the gate, she disappeared through the doorway.

She scurried along the air-bridge towards the waiting aircraft. The cabin crew bolted the doors behind her, and the walkway began to retract towards the terminal building.

Finally reaching the gate, Michael pulled his passport and boarding pass from his jacket pocket.

'I'm sorry sir, the flight is now closed,' said the stewardess, 'We held it as long as we could.'

'Call the pilot! Don't let the plane leave!' Michael gasped between breaths.

The stewardess just looked at him coolly, 'I'm sorry sir, I am not autho-rised to do that.' She glanced down at his papers, 'And this is the wrong ticket sir!' she raised her voice as he attempted to run past her, but he could see that the far end of the air-bridge was closed.

So he ran over to the glass wall of the lounge through which he could see the aircraft as it began to pull away from the terminal building. Laura was all he had left, and now she was slipping through his fingers like sand. Filled with rage, he banged his fists on the glass 'Goddamit Laura!' he whispered in desperation, when Caleb and his cohorts arrived at his side.

'Thank God you're here,' said the air stewardess, 'This man has been causing a disturbance,' and the airport security men grabbed Michael's arms and tackled him to the ground.

'You idiots!' shouted Caleb, 'You're arresting the wrong person,' he said as he looked out through the glass at Laura's plane now taxiing towards the runway for take-off.

Chapter 45

As Laura had descended the walkway onto the aircraft, she thought she had heard Michael calling her name, but she had not looked back, even though she had wanted to. Her heart was being torn in two. Part of her wanted to rush back and hug him, to apologise for borrowing the skull and explain to him why she was going. Face to face she might have been able to reassure him that she would be OK and would be back in a couple of days. She wanted to say goodbye properly.

'Laura Shepherd!' she heard him shout again. It took all her willpower to keep going. It felt so awful to be running away from her husband like some sort of fugitive. But she could not let herself look back. Seeing Michael would have broken the fragile resolve she had made, to do her best to find the rest of that prophecy stone.

But how could she even begin to explain to Michael that if she didn't even try to find the stone she would not be honouring what she was now convinced her daughter wanted? She just couldn't ignore what her heart told her was a message from her little girl. But Michael would not understand.

She took a seat and gazed out of the window. Through the falling snow she could see a figure looking through the departure lounge window at the plane. It was a man banging his fists against the glass, shouting. In silhouette, she could not be entirely sure, but it looked like Michael. What had she done to him?

She wasn't sure whether he would ever find it in himself to forgive her for this. Abandoning him like that, not to mention the damage she had undoubtedly done to his career. Tears stung her eyes and she was filled with remorse. It could well be the end of their marriage.

Her fingers flew instinctively to the heart shaped locket she wore around her neck. She fought back the tears. She could not afford to think like that. It was only going to take a couple of days. That was all. 'I'll be back soon' she whispered to the figure watching the plane. When she got back Michael and Caleb could have the skull. It would be all theirs. Once they had hold of the skull again, they would be so taken with excitement about the possibilities it offered that Michael might find a way to put the incident behind them. At least that was how Laura reassured herself as the plane taxied towards the runway.

She couldn't bear to look at Michael anymore. She looked away, fastening her seat belt, and as she did so the details of her mission struck her with an alarming clarity of which she had previously been unaware. She was heading off to a remote jungle area of Central America in search of the rest of the prophecy stone, but she had no idea whether or not she would be able to find it. There were absolutely no guarantees that it would still be there.

After all, part of it had already found its way to her own office, via a modern-day pirate ship and the Customs Office. She was now counting on the fact that Luvantum's remoteness, its isolated position deep in the rainforest, away from any major roads, would mean that the rest of the stone would have escaped the looters. She was pinning all her hopes on this blind, and quite possibly unrealistic, assumption that the rest of the stone would still be in place.

As the plane took off down the runway bound for Guatemala City, the prospect that the rest of the stone might no longer remain intact began to lay heavy on Laura's mind. After all, how could she be so sure that what she had deciphered was really there, that it was really a message from Alice, and not just some wild phantom of her own imagination? Only time would tell. Until then, she would have to carry the crushing weight of the irreversible decision she had just made. She closed her eyes and fell into an exhausted sleep.

Chapter 46

'That Bitch! How could she steal my skull?' thought Caleb as he returned alone to his 25th floor penthouse apartment, following the evening's dramatic turn of events. He was far angrier than he had realised, angrier even than he had let Michael know. *'That woman needs to be taught a lesson. She needs to be put firmly back in her place.'* He poured himself a glass of Scotch. It was a single Malt, fifteen years in the making. He sat down on the dark brown leather sofa and looked out at the twinkling lights of the city, trying to calm himself down.

But as he swilled the amber liquid around the fine crystal glass and took a sip, he couldn't stop his mind from wandering back to his own short-lived marriage to Sonia, twelve years earlier. Caleb concluded, yet again, that *'wives are more trouble than they are worth.'* Sonia might have had the face, and the figure, that most men could only dream of, but she had a taste for shopping that made Imelda Marcos look prudent, and as for her demands for holidays, it had begun to compromise even his own commitment to his own company, his lifelong ambition of building the largest and most profitable crystal-based electronics company in the world.

Now he had Tanya things were less complicated. And that is the way he intended to keep them. She was still a slim, petite and attractive blonde. And although she had muttered occasionally about 'maybe moving in' and 'perhaps some sign of greater commitment', he was pretty sure she had got the message that work had to come first.

Michael should know better. Caleb sighed, for he already knew that although Michael was a dedicated, highly motivated professional, who showed occasional flashes of pure brilliance, when it came to his wife, it seemed he was little more than putty in her hands. *That woman is out of control and it's about time somebody reminded her who's boss!*

According to Michael, his wife, suffering from grief, had simply lost the plot and his main concern was for her safety. But Caleb wasn't so sure. For someone who was supposed to be in the grip of some sort of psychotic episode, she seemed to have a pretty clear idea of what she was doing and where she was going. In fact, he found himself wondering whether she wasn't perhaps working for some rival company. Whatever the case, she needed to be taught a lesson

Stealing the skull like that, from right in front of my own nose, what a humili-

ation! The skull had promised Nanon Systems so much. It looked set to be the jewel in the company's crown. Caleb couldn't believe it had gone. The very day that advanced, dedicated research into its applications was due to start. *Anything could happen to it out there in the jungle. It could get lost, it could get damaged or broken, somebody else could steal it and we would never have access to it ever again.* Caleb knew he had to get it back, and soon.

As he swilled another gulpful of whisky around like mouthwash he had an excellent idea. He hadn't spoken to General Jan Van Halmutt for ages. Not since the last time he had had a sticky problem that needed sorting, by somewhat less than conventional means.

As he picked up the phone he found himself thinking that, in retrospect, those days he spent back in the early seventies doing national service in the marines, when all around him were busy enjoying themselves taking drugs and indulging in 'free love', might just be about to pay off after all.

'Hi Jan, it's Caleb Price here. Sorry to bother you at this hour in the morning, but we've got a little problem that needs sorting...'

When Caleb had returned stateside after his year's national service and started to study the new subject of micro-electronics at Stamford MIT, Jan Van Halmutt stayed on and rose quite high up in the army before setting up his own company 'Van Halmutt Solutions'. With a client list that included most of the Western governments and large blue-chip companies in the world, Van Halmutt Solutions was now one of the most successful and discrete, clandestine mercenary operations on the American continent.

It didn't take long for Caleb to outline the situation. He told Van Halmutt exactly where he was sure Laura was going and agreed to email him a photo of her he could get from Michael or the museum the following day. By the time Caleb had finished Van Halmutt had only one final question;

'Exactly how far do you want us to go in order to successfully complete this mission?'

To which Caleb replied quite simply, 'Just get me the skull... whatever it takes!'

Now satisfied that he had done all he could, he calmly replaced the handset and poured himself another glass.

Chapter 47

December 14th 2012

'Por favour, quedense en sus asientos, y mantengan sus cinturones sujetados!'

'Stay in your seats! I repeat, please stay in your seats and keep your seat belts fastened!'

The captain's warning came over the crackling pa system. The little Cessna plane descended sharply, hitting against a cloud. The engines groaned noisily under the strain, before a gust of wind caught the tail and lifted it again. Laura clutched the skull in her lap. She had not been expecting this. The tiny aircraft was being tossed about in the storm, thrown recklessly around like a child's toy.

While Laura's flight to Guatemala City had arrived without problem, her connecting flight on to Luvantum was turning out to be a different story. What she hadn't known, prior to boarding, was that the aircraft would be caught in the tail end of a late-in-the-season hurricane that had blown in along the coast of Honduras and was now burning itself out over the Maya mountains, where she now flew. She wondered whether the pilot had anticipated it being this bad, or whether it had caught even him unprepared.

Rain lashed ferociously against the windows. Beneath the aircraft was a vast ocean of lush green rainforest, but in these weather conditions, all Laura could make out were the menacing grey outlines of jungle-clad peaks that seemed to grasp ever nearer to the tips of the plane's fragile little wings.

There were only seven other passengers on board, and they were unusually quiet. Even the air stewardess looked nervous. Having checked everyone's seatbelts were fastened, the stewardess took off her shoes and strapped herself into her rear-facing flip-seat behind the pilot's cabin. Laura closed her eyes and tried to calm herself.

Another gust of wind caught the plane, shunting it sideways. Laura thought of Michael. She knew he would be thinking she had behaved recklessly, taking the skull the way she had, but she felt she had no choice. What she had seen through the skull was remarkable. She could not ignore the possibility that it might really be a message from Alice.

The plane was suddenly lifted upwards. Laura felt her stomach lurch towards the ceiling, before the aircraft plummeted down again. The other passengers gasped. Laura had experienced turbulence many times before, but nothing of this magnitude, never anything quite as frightening as this.

Laura opened her eyes and looked to the air stewardess for reassurance, but even her face could scarcely conceal her fear. The stewardess glanced up to the heavens, before crossing herself, in the manner used by devout Catholics worldwide, when asking for God's protection.

Laura took refuge again in her own thoughts. It had been one thing to take the skull, unauthorised, just when Michael and Caleb needed it for their research. That had been bad enough for Michael to deal with, but now, her life was at risk. Laura tightened her grip on the skull as the engines roared. *If this plane goes down now, all of this will have been in vain. All my efforts will have been wasted.*

The stewardess was now adopting the 'brace' or 'crash' position, bent forward over her lap, with her arms cradling her head, forearms protecting her skull, as the whole fuselage began to shake. Another jolt and the oxygen masks fell free from their housings, dangling right in front of the passengers' fear-frozen faces.

The plane fell again. Suddenly, there was an almighty crash, and a 'crack' that sounded as if the aircraft were being wrenched asunder, torn in two with the impact of the plane abruptly hitting the ground, and continuing to bump, jolt and shudder as it sped down the hard dirt runway. The pilot was trying hard to stop it veering off course in the heavy wind and rain, as it finally came to rest just before the end of the tiny, jungle-clearing airstrip.

They had, miraculous though it appeared, finally landed. Several of the passengers burst into tears, others were clapping wildly. The atmosphere was palpable with relief, with a letting out of all the pent-up intensity of emotion that the passengers had just experienced, fearing that they were about to die, their bodies to be strewn across the jungle, never to see their loved ones again.

As Laura left the plane, she noticed that her knuckles, clasped around the skull in its rucksack, had become white from holding onto it so tightly. It had been quite a ride. She was glad when her feet felt the hard earth of the jungle airstrip underfoot. It was good to be on solid ground once again.

Between flights, back in Guatemala City, Laura had traded in the skull-case for a more practical rucksack. She had also exchanged her smart linen work suit and patent leather shoes for a pair of trainers, jeans, t-shirt, and a cheap plastic mac. Boy, was she glad she had. The rain was torrential.

The 'terminal building' at Santa Cruz airstrip, consisted of nothing more than a simple tin-roofed shack, with no walls, set amidst a vast expanse of untamed jungle. As she sheltered under its protection with the handful of other passengers, a battered old yellow school-bus bounced along the pot-holed single track 'road' towards them.

She hoped it was her escort, Dr Brown, but it had arrived to take the other passengers to the nearby 'town', though it was actually more of a village, of Santa Cruz.

Laura stayed put despite the driver's insistence that he took her to town also. The other passengers too seemed reluctant to leave her behind, such was the spirit of camaraderie that established itself in the aftermath of their troubled flight. They were all clearly concerned for her safety should she be stuck out in the jungle alone, especially after dark.

She watched the battered old bus bump back off down the track and disappear in a cloud of diesel smoke. Only then did she realise she was not entirely alone. A handful of rain-drenched, despondent local soldiers were sheltering under another tiny corrugated iron shack by the side of the track, smoking. Nobody else remained other than a scrawny pig and a couple of stray dogs.

Laura could scarcely believe this was where she had arranged to meet Dr Brown. He had agreed to get her to the Luvantum ruins by the end of the following day. The hastiness of her departure had left her ill-prepared. She had no map of the area and was entirely unsure exactly how they were supposed to get there. She hoped Dr Brown had not forgotten their appointment. She rummaged around for her new cell phone and tried to call him, but there was no signal.

It would be a long ten kilometre walk, especially in this weather, to the nearest settlement of Santa Cruz and, as the 'road' began at the airstrip, she could be sure there would be no-one passing who could offer her a lift. And even then she was assuming Dr Brown lived in Santa Cruz, but she didn't actually have any idea where he lived. There was nothing else for it but to wait. At least it was a relief no longer being on the aircraft.

As she waited she became aware of how small the airstrip clearing really was. Less than five metres from where she stood, dense jungle began. She could see giant buttress roots, the thick, knotted twist of tree trunks, branches stretching out high above, and the darkness of the forest beyond. It had been a long time since she had been in the jungle. She hadn't been back since she had been working on an archaeological dig in Southern Mexico and discovered she was pregnant with Alice.

Laura watched a tiny monkey loop through the upper branches of the trees. She could hear the whoop and shriek of jungle birds as they darted through the undergrowth. She couldn't wait to get going to Luvantum. She only hoped that Dr Brown would show up soon.

Then suddenly, as if from nowhere, a figure emerged from the jungle thicket. There must have been a track there that she could not see. It was a small, elderly Mayan man, dressed in a simple cotton shirt and white trousers. He wore a red patterned headscarf, and a red sash was tied around his waist. He was soaked through. The man stopped when he saw her and stared at her with an intensity that surprised her. His brow was furrowed as he approached. He shook his head. If this was someone who had come to give her a message about Dr Brown, his behaviour seemed a little odd.

'Are you with Dr Brown?' she enquired.

'Why did they send you?' he asked incredulous. 'Where is he?'

Laura was baffled. 'Who?'

'The one they call 'Ron',' the old man replied.

Laura wondered if there had been a mix-up over exactly which archaeologist Dr Brown had been expecting from the Smithton Geographic.

'You mean Ron Smith?' She had no idea how Dr Brown might have imagined it was Ron Smith who was coming, instead of her.

The old man was looking at her intently. 'He's dead, isn't he?'

'Yes,' she replied.

The old man seemed almost to stagger for a moment, as if he had become unsure of his footing. A look of utter devastation swept across his face. He stared blankly ahead, his eyes unfocused, and whispered,

'Then there is no hope, for any of us!'

Laura was about to ask what he meant when a deep booming voice began shouting in an American accent, 'Dr Shepherd! Hello! Dr Shepherd!'

She spun round to see a very overweight, bearded, middle-aged white man huffing and puffing down the track towards her. He was dressed in full cream traditional jungle-explorers uniform, complete with pith helmet, and sported a bright yellow plastic waterproof over his sodden wet jodhpurs, as he rode down the track towards her, on mule-back, shouting 'Hello!'

Behind him, a younger local man was pulling on the reins of two pack-mules, trying to coax them out from beneath their jungle cover. The group of soldiers nearby watched and laughed.

Reaching Laura, the man in the yellow waterproofs dismounted and held out a sweaty palm.

'Dr Shepherd, the name's 'Brown'.' Laura shook his hand, before he saluted 'At your service!'

'Nice to meet you. Please, do call me Laura.'

'Pleased to make your acquaintance Dr Shepherd,' he replied.

Laura turned back round to discover that the Mayan man she had been speaking to was gone. He had vanished as quickly as he had first appeared, and she found herself half wondering whether perhaps she had imagined him.

'Did you see...? Who was that?' she asked Dr Brown.

'Oh, his name's Hunab Ku,' he replied with a dismissive wave of his arm.

'So he's not with you?' she asked.

''Course not. And I wouldn't have much to do with him either if I was you.'

'Why not? Who is he?'

'Oh, he's the local shaman – medicine man, or witch doctor to you. 'Gives me the heeby-geebies,' he said as he checked the saddle strap on his mule for tightness. 'But don't worry, he's probably pretty harmless really.'

'It's OK, I wasn't worried,' said Laura as Brown clambered back onto his mule,

'But he just asked me about my dead colleague!'

'Doesn't surprise me!' shrugged Brown, 'They believe in talking to the dead around here, and as the shaman for these poor people,' he nodded towards his local guide, 'he's the expert in that area.'

'So has my former colleague, Ron Smith, been down here?' she asked.

'Been here two years, never seen him!' answered Brown.

'In that case I'd better find out how he knew him.' Laura made to follow after the old medicine man into the rainforest, but hesitated when she could see no obvious path and realised she didn't actually know which way he had gone.

'You go after him if you like,' said Dr Brown, 'but you'll never find him in there,' he indicated the depths of the jungle. 'In any case, we'd better get moving or we'll never get to the encampment before nightfall,' he added as the guide appeared alongside him with the other two mules.

The guide passed Laura the reigns of one of the animals. 'That looks heavy' he said, reaching for Laura's rucksack, 'Please, let me carry it for you' he offered.

'No. no… I can manage,' she replied, a touch hastily. She didn't want to risk anyone else handling the crystal skull.

The guide looked puzzled.

Laura took the reins of her mule, tied her rucksack to the coil of rope beneath its saddle, and climbed on, as she, Dr Brown and the guide set off into the sodden jungle on mule-back, with the guide hacking back leaves and fronds with his machete as they went.

As the mules made their way snail-like along the winding jungle path and the rain fell in steady sheets, Laura could not stop her thoughts from returning over and over again to the same question, of how this unassuming little old man, a total stranger in the middle of the rainforest, could possibly have known about, and been expecting to meet, her dead colleague, Ron Smith!? It just didn't seem to make any sense.

As they rode on in single file she realized too that she had never before left for a remote destination in quite such a rush and quite so ill-prepared. She had on her only the clothes she was wearing, a waterproof torch and a pen-knife she had purchased back in Guatemala City. She hadn't done any horse riding since she was a teenager, and she had certainly never before ridden on the back of a clumsy old mule.

Still, she was glad to be moving towards her goal even if the transport was a little slow and uncomfortable, and even if it was a little uncertain quite what she might find even once she reached her destination.

After a few minutes of trekking in silence, Dr Brown rode up alongside her.

'So what is it brings you out here at such short notice?' He raised his voice to be heard above the rain.

'I'm looking for the missing piece of a Mayan prophecy stone I've been decoding.' Laura was reluctant to reveal the full details of her mission, especially the slightly less than orthodox technique she had used to locate its whereabouts.

'So you have some of this stone already?'

'Yes, in my office.'

'And you think you're going to find the rest of it out here?'

Laura nodded.

Dr Brown took a sharp intake of breath and shook his head.

'You do realize you don't stand a hope in hell of finding the rest of this stone you're looking for intact?'

Laura looked at him askance.

'...What with all the earthquakes and erosion, not to mention looters over the years.' He shook his head again.

Laura didn't know what to say. This was all she needed to hear. That despite all her efforts, her risking her relationship with Michael, her effective demolition of her career, that there was no real chance of finding what she was looking for in any case.

Brown turned to his local guide. 'What do you think Carlos?' he yelled 'What are the chances of finding the remnants of some 'prophecy stone'', he said it almost with contempt, 'intact at Luvantum?'

Carlos stopped hacking, thought for a moment, and shrugged his shoulders before replying. 'It is difficult to say. It is very remote. We have only just started a proper, detailed mapping of the site. So we can't say for sure.'

Then he turned to Laura and added as tactfully as he could, 'Maybe you will be lucky. Maybe you will not.'

Laura felt filled with despair.

Chapter 48

Meanwhile, back at the jungle-clearing airstrip, a huge Chinook military helicopter descended in a storm of mechanical wind. Its giant rotating blades were almost large enough to slice a few more branches off the trees as it went.

As it touched down, a smartly dressed man, with reflective sunglasses and cropped blond hair stepped out onto the runway. He pulled the collar of his coat up as he surveyed the rain sodden scene. He took a final drag on his cigar, before he threw the butt down and ground it into the mud.

The four local soldiers were still standing around in their shack by the side of the runway, smoking, when he approached. The anonymous man showed them an emailed photograph of Laura on his mobile phone. The soldiers nodded enthusiastically, gabbling excitedly to each other in Spanish. They pointed to the jungle track where Laura and her companions had set off on mule-back earlier.

The 'man-in-black', Van Halmutt's Head of Command in Central America, handed the soldiers a wedge of cash. They shook hands on it immediately, before he climbed back into his helicopter and it took off again into the air, under a roar of spinning blades.

The soldiers threw their guns back over their shoulders and set off into the rainforest, hot on Laura's trail...

Chapter 49

Laura had forgotten how much she loved the jungle, even in the pouring rain, and quite how much she had missed it until now. But it was hard going in the oppressive heat, trying to keep the mules moving along in the right direction without losing their footing on the rough terrain, and bending to avoid low branches and long palm fronds that seemed determined to topple her from her saddle. And it didn't seem to Laura as though she and her party had got very far before Dr Brown announced that it was time to stop trekking and prepare a camp for the night.

Brown had hoped to get further, to get to the pre-prepared encampment near the main ridge that divided the Eastern and Western Maya Mountains, but the track was unusually overgrown, the rain and mud had slowed the mules' progress, and they would have to stop now and make preparations, before hunger and darkness overcame them.

Carlos seemed to have no end of energy. He stopped slicing through branches and turned his attentions, without rest, to getting a fire started, even though it looked to Laura as though there could be nothing left in the forest still dry enough to burn. Everything, literally everything, seemed sopping wet. Yet, in next to no time, Carlos had slung up a makeshift tarpaulin roof between the tree trunks. He then sliced open a strange-looking large jungle plant to reveal a strangely dry, inner core, and after a few strikes of his machete against the small 'fire-brick', or flint, he always carried with him, he was soon blowing gently on the natural kindling of the plants' dried-out 'hairs'. And it wasn't long before they were all boiling a tin kettle of tea and frying up some tortillas and beans on a small, but highly effective campfire.

Sitting around eating their dinner before erecting their tents for the night, Laura discovered that Dr Brown had chosen this remote posting because of his love of Mayan pottery. Apparently insights into the ancient Mayans' creation stories could sometimes be gleaned by piecing together tiny shards of their ancient broken ceramics some particularly good examples of which had been found I this area. Laura was about to ask Dr Brown whether any of these creation stories made mention of any crystal skull, but she bit her lip. She decided to keep all knowledge of the crystal skull to herself at this stage. After all, as far as she could tell, nobody else had any idea that her presence there had anything to do with the crystal skull. They probably had no idea that such an object even existed, let alone that she should be carrying it around in her rucksack, and her instincts told her it was probably safest to keep it that way.

As the conversation continued, it transpired that Carlos probably knew more about Luvantum than Dr Brown, and although his accent was thick, his English was excellent. He was currently studying for his PhD in Archaeology at the University of Tegucigalpa in Honduras. 'For his sins' he had actually chosen to do his PhD on 'the architecture of the ancient Mayan city of Luvantum'. He had chosen this city partly because its remoteness meant that very little proper archaeological work had ever been done on the site, even though it had originally been found way back in the 1930s. It seemed that very few archaeologists over the years had been prepared to make the long mule-back ride through the jungle to study a site that seemed to have 'no more treasures to offer' than a host of other archaeological sites that could be found just off the main east-west highway.

Laura asked if she could see a map of the site and Carlos pulled out a copy of his 'work in progress' – a very simple map of the Luvantum ruins which he had managed to have laminated on his last trip back to Tegucigalpa. Studying the map of the city, Laura recognised many of the features characteristic of Mayan cities all across their ancient territory; the houses, wells and pedestrian roads of the ordinary citizens all around the outside, and the main 'sacbes', or 'white roads' leading into the centre.

And in the centre of the city, the ball court, the royal palaces, the religious and academic buildings, and observatories where apprentices would study ancient codices, the movements of the planets and stars, and learn the mysterious workings of the ancient Mayan calendar.

In the very heart of the city she could see, the grand, paved, central plaza, flanked on either side by the palatial buildings of the highest ranking royals and astronomer-priests, and at either end of the plaza, the largest, most-towering stepped-pyramids on the site.

Laura knew that time was so important to the ancient Maya that in many ancient Central American cities there were two great central pyramids, built in such a way as to check and measure the workings of the calendar.

In most cases, the largest pyramid was aligned with the movements of the Sun, and from its temple one could easily mark, with phenomenal accuracy, the summer solstice, the winter solstice, and the spring and autumn equinoxes.

The other main temple-pyramid was usually smaller, aligned with the movements of the moon, and used to check the workings of the lunar calendar. In some cities, such as the great city of Teotihuacan, near Mexico City, these pyramids were actually referred to as the Pyramid of the Sun and the Pyramid of the Moon.

Often, other pyramids further out around the city were aligned with the movements of other significant heavenly bodies, such as the planet Venus, and the star-cluster, or constellation, known as 'the seven sisters' or the Pleiades. The position and orientation of these temple-pyramids would have been used to check the position of these planets and stars relative to the Earth.

So Laura recognised many of the features on the map in front of her, but she was puzzled by one thing, so she asked Carlos, 'I see you've managed to identify the pyramid of Venus, of the Pleiades, and the pyramid of the Sun and the Moon both at this end of the plaza here, but you don't seem to have labelled this, by far the largest pyramid, at the other end of the plaza here.'

'That's because we don't yet know what the largest pyramid at Luvantum was for,' replied Carlos. 'We don't know which heavenly body it was dedicated to. All we know is that the largest pyramid, at this end of the plaza here, is covered in stone carved images of the human skull.'

Laura was intrigued. Perhaps she was on the right trail after all.

But before she had a chance to ask any further questions, Dr Brown butted in, 'Then chances are it was used for human sacrifice!'

Chapter 50

Carlos' eyes turned to the sky. 'Dr Brown has a somewhat unsophisticated view of my ancestors,' he explained.

'But you do know what the Spanish conquistadors found back in 1520 when they entered the ancient Aztec city of Tenochtitlan, that is now Mexico City,' Brown continued regardless, 'They said that the main temple-pyramid in the heart of the city was used for human sacrifice. Apparently all around it the skulls of the victims were skewered onto wooden stakes and displayed in the main square as trophies of the great numbers killed. One of Cortez soldiers, a man named Bernal Diaz, tried to count how many skulls there were but lost count when he got past the 100,000 mark, all at varying stages of decomposition and decay.'

Carlos did not look happy, 'Yes, we all know the Spanish version of the history of our ancestors here in Central America. We know that the Spanish conquerors claimed that the Aztecs, and Maya too, were little more than blood-thirsty savages who sacrificed people by their hundreds of thousands.'

'That's right,' Brown continued to tell Laura, 'According to the original Spanish reports, the sacrificial victim was intoxicated by being forced to drink an alcoholic liquor, known as 'pulque'. They were then marched, hands bound behind their backs, up the steps to the top of the highest pyramid. There, in front of the temple, they were forced to lie backwards over a large, gently curved sacrificial stone, exposing their chest. The priest, reciting incantations to the gods, would then produce a sharp, black obsidian blade before plunging it into the victim's chest. And while the victim was still alive, they would tear out their still-beating heart and hold it aloft for all to see, before burning it as an offering, usually to the Sun God. Apparently the victim's body was then thrown down the pyramid steps where it was decapitated before being hacked into little pieces, and then eaten, by the eagerly awaiting crowd.'

'Blood-thirsty savages the lot of them!' he added with a wicked grin.

Carlos chose to ignore him and turned back to Laura. 'What has to be remembered is that these reports were written by an invading army, written by the same people who committed brutal genocide against my people. The Spanish conquistadors themselves are the ones who wiped out my ancestors in their hundreds of thousands, through murder, war, famine and disease, so their reports about my ancestors, the people they killed, may not be entirely accurate.'

'In fact, there may be very little, or no truth in these early Spanish reports at all. These reports may have been used simply to justify the atrocities the Spanish then committed against my people. After all, if one wanted to read an unbiased report about the nature of the Jewish people, one would hardly ask Adolf Hitler and his friends in the German SS, who murdered the Jewish people in their millions in the middle of last century, to write the report!'

'You may well have a point' said Laura. She'd never thought about it that way before.

'Huh. A point indeed!' huffed Brown, 'Then how do you explain all these images of human sacrifice we see in ancient Central American artworks?' he challenged Carlos.

'Most of these images actually date to a time *after* the Spanish conquest, or appear to be perhaps symbolic of the universality of human suffering. The handful of images of what looks like ritual human sacrifice we see in genuinely ancient Mayan artworks cannot be taken to mean that this was a regular and common practice, any more than we can conclude that we today are regularly crucifying people, every Sunday, simply because there is an image of a young man bleeding to death on a cross prominently displayed in every church, in every town, village and city in the modern Western world.'

Again Laura could see Carlos' argument, but Brown was not convinced. 'You're not telling me the Maya never sacrificed anyone?'

'No.' replied Carlos 'but it appears that human sacrifice was mostly a voluntary activity to the ancient Maya.'

'So that makes it all right then?' Brown interjected.

'..And it rarely involved actually taking a person's life. Normally only a minor amount of blood-letting was involved, and this was usually done through piercing one's own tongue, or penis, in order to encourage visions or other-worldly experiences.'

'Sound pretty primitive to me!' chimed Dr Brown, but Carlos ignored him. 'For example, at the ancient Mayan city of Yaxchilan there is a famous carved stone lintel which shows the ancient Mayan King called 'Jaguar Penis' performing a blood-letting act on his own unusually large member.'

'They sure knew how to have a good time!' smiled Dr Brown, while

Laura winced at the thought, though she had heard of this practice before.

'But it looks very unlikely' continued Carlos' that thousands of people really were sacrificed as the Spanish claimed. There is a growing body of evidence that this is in fact nonsense, nothing but propaganda perpetuated by an invading army of murderers.

'In fact,' he continued, 'My people now believe that most of these images of skulls you see on ancient temple-pyramids, such as this one here at Luvantum,' he said pointing at the map, 'have got nothing whatsoever to do with the so-called practice of human sacrifice, but are actually to do with the coded workings of the ancient Mayan calendar.'

Laura was fascinated. She had come here precisely to try to decipher a prophecy from this same ancient calendar.

'How do you mean?'

'Well, the only 'tzompantli', as these rows of human skulls were known, that we actually have concrete evidence of are the ones that still exist at famous Mayan cities such as Chichen Itza, and they are all carved in stone' explained Carlos.

'At Chichen Itza, for example, there is a huge 'tzompantli' of thousands of human skulls carved into a single solid block of stone, but this has got nothing to do with cutting off the heads of victims of sacrifice.'

'Instead, these rows of carved stone skulls are the way my ancestors marked the number of generations that had passed since the beginning of time,' Laura raised her eyebrows, 'or at least the number of generations which had passed since the beginning of the current world, or 'Sun' as they called it.'

Laura already knew about some of the workings of the ancient calendar but this was a new angle on it for her.

'You see, according to the ancient Maya, the world has been created and destroyed several times in the past, and we now live in the final world, or 'Sun'.'

Laura was familiar with this idea and knew that this theory actually finds some support in our own fossil records. The study of fossils by palaeontologists has shown that, ever since the Cambrian Era, the Earth has experienced several different periods during which life on Earth has grown, diversified, blossomed and flourished, only to be wiped out again during various sudden and distinct periods of mass extinction.

Laura also knew, for example, that according to the ancient Central

American records, the first world, or 'Sun', was 'ruled over by giants'. Many people now believe this was a reference to the era of the dinosaurs. According to the Maya this world was 'destroyed by fire from the sky' which may well be a description of the giant meteorite which hit the Earth some 65 Million years ago, and is now thought to have wiped out the dinosaurs.

This meteorite created what is known today as the Chicxulub crater in Southern Mexico. The impact of this meteorite was so great that it is thought to have thrown up a huge cloud of dust and debris that blocked out the Sun's rays and led to dramatic climate change, a global winter, which wiped out virtually all life on Earth. According to the Maya, the sun finally stopped shining, 'in the year known as 'thirteen''.

Indeed, according to the ancient Mayan calendar each of the previous worlds was destroyed by one catastrophic event or another, which ties in very closely with the fossil records, which show each historical period ending in an era of mass extinction. Laura even found herself wondering whether we might be entering just such a period now, as she thought about the rapid loss of hundreds, if not thousands, of different species which we have been seeing on this planet in recent years. So she listened intently as Carlos continued his enthusiastic explanation.

'According to the Mayan calendar the current world, or 'Sun' began on a day almost 5,200 years ago. And the Maya were very precise in their calculations and predictions. They liked to work things out right down to the day. So they gave an exact date for the beginning of the current world.'

'According to them, the current world or 'Sun' began on a day that translates into our calendar as precisely the 13th August in the year 3,114 BC.'

'And because this was the first day of the current world it was known to them as the day 'zero', in their 'Long Count calendar'.'

'It is known as the 'Long Count' simply because it is the longest of the Maya's most commonly used calendars. But it was actually based on the movements of the planet Venus, so it was sometimes referred to as the Venus calendar.'

'Now, according to this Venusian calendar,' Carlos continued, 'there was a day almost 5,200 years ago which marked the first day of the Long Count, or the beginning of the current world, or Sun, and the number of skulls on the tzompantli at Chichen Itza tells us how many generations had passed between that day and the day that the great city of Chichen Itza was founded.'

'You see, my ancestors sometimes used the stylised image of a human skull to represent the passing of 'a generation' in time. On average a generation lasted for about 52 of our solar years, and so, over time, the image of a stone carved skull came to represent a period of precisely 52 years.'

'So you can add together all the stone carved skulls on the 'tzompantli' at Chichen Itza, multiply each one by 52, and it will tell you exactly how many years had passed since the beginning of the Long Count calendar, since the 13th August 3114 BC, before the year the city of Chichen Itza was founded. In other words, the skulls can tell you exactly how many years had elapsed since the start of the Venusian calendar, exactly how many years had passed since the beginning of the current world, or 'Sun'.'

Laura was fascinated. She already knew about the Long Count calendar, but she had never thought about it as having any relation to skulls before. Representing time using the image of a human skull gave it a very human dimension. But what interested her most was what she might expect to find when she reached Luvantum.

'So you believe that even the skull images carved on the main temple-pyramid at Luvantum have got nothing to do with human sacrifice, but are instead related to the Maya's great 'cycles of time'?'

'That's right,' continued Carlos, 'I am sorry to disappoint you if you are one of those people who like the idea that my ancestors were nothing more than blood-thirsty savages,'

'On the contrary' said Laura as Carlos fired a disapproving glance at Dr Brown.

'..but we have excavated the ground around the pyramid and found no evidence of actual human skulls or bones. Like similar forensic studies at the foot of Mayan pyramids elsewhere – no evidence of actual human sacrifice.'

'In fact, most of the real skulls which we have discovered in ancient Mayan ruins, like the stone skulls, are nothing to do with human sacrifice either. They are instead the skulls of the Mayans own ancestors; relatives, parents, grandparents and loved ones. The Maya used to keep their skulls and bury them under their little thatched houses so as to keep their loved ones close by even after they had died. It is quite sad really and certainly nothing to do with sacrifice or trophies of war. Terrible things may of course have happened during periods of war, but then that is no different than today.'

'No. It is now becoming clear' said Carlos 'that very few skulls even in ancient Mayan artworks have got anything to do with human sacrifice. Instead these stone skull images appear to be symbolic of the 52 year period which was important in the ancient calendar system, symbolic of the number of generations which have passed since the beginning of 'Time'.

'And is there any evidence of skull imagery anywhere else on or inside the pyramid at Luvantum?' asked Laura.

'Yes, there is an altar adorned with a skull and a badly eroded doorway with a skull image carved at its centre at the entrance to a once secret chamber inside the heart of the pyramid, but we have no idea yet what any of it means, or what the chamber was used for. Perhaps you can help us answer this question?'

'Perhaps' said Laura. She was trying hard to conceal her excitement. It looked as though she was on the right track after all. She had a very good idea of what the skull imagery was related to and she wanted to ask Carlos more, but felt compelled to keep all knowledge of the crystal skull to herself, at least for now.

Laura was thinking to herself that if the main temple pyramid at Luvantum was carved with skulls, and skulls were now thought to be associated with marking the passage of time, then it made sense that this may well have been the temple pyramid in which Anna Crockett-Burrows found the crystal skull, the same temple-pyramid that contained the prophecy stone. This would be the place to look once they reached the site.

'I'm bushed,' said Dr Brown, who had remained un-characteristically silent throughout the latter part of the conversation, 'I think it's time for bed,'

As Laura and the others erected their tents for the night, she felt filled with excitement and anticipation. It looked as though she might be in with a chance of finding the missing hieroglyphs after all.

As she lay down on her makeshift pillow, a soggy towel wrapped in a plastic carrier bag, listening to the incredible sounds made by all the jungle animals that came alive after dark, her mind was buzzing with images of the mysterious archaeological site that now lay only one day ahead.

She felt once again the almost magical sense of delight she had felt in the past at the prospect of seeing a different Mayan city for the first time. Each city had its own beauty, its own atmosphere, its own unique features.

But this time she would be visiting not just as an interested archaeologist, but as someone who had a secret burning question that needed answering. What did the rest of the hieroglyphs say? What terrible event was due to happen in only one week's time? It seemed she might now be about to find out.

Chapter 51

December 15th 2012

The following morning they broke camp. Once again Laura tied her rucksack containing the crystal skull to the coil of rope beneath her saddle, hoping it would be safe there. At least it wouldn't be there too long, she told herself, buoyed by the knowledge that, all being well, they were due to reach their destination by the end of that same day.

It wasn't long after Laura's departure however that the soldiers discovered their abandoned campground. The soldiers were very excited when they stumbled upon the smouldering remains of her party's campfire, with the embers still warm from the night before. They were very pleased with themselves too that the damp and muddy conditions meant they had little problem in finding and following Laura and her companions' trail.

By midday, a few kilometres away, Brown and Laura were chatting about the mysterious origins of the ancient Maya, but they had to break off their conversation when they reached a fork in the path and had to decide which direction to take. Having taken the left fork, it wasn't long before they reached a large rock which was partially blocking the path ahead. Laura's mule took the lead and began to edge past the obstruction, when a deadly rattlesnake suddenly began to rattle its tail beneath the rock.

Startled by the sound, her mule reared up, braying loudly. Glimpsing the snake, the animal shied away backwards and stepped nervously to one side. As it did so, it did not see behind a thin row of shrubs, the cliff edge that bordered the path.

The animal began to slip off the edge of the cliff, its hooves scrabbling frantically as it tried to regain its footing. Loose rocks and stones tumbled over the side.

Laura grabbed the front of her saddle and held on tight. She stared down petrified as the debris appeared to fall in slow-motion before hitting the surface of the deep water far below with a splash.

Carlos intervened quickly, grabbing at the mule's reins just in time to help the frightened animal to regain its footing.

'That was close!' exclaimed Dr Brown. 'You wouldn't want to end up in there. If the fall didn't kill you the currents probably would,' he added helpfully.

Laura struggled to keep her terrified mule from galloping off back in the direction of the airstrip. Pulling sharply on the reins, she faced it squarely towards the rock that had concealed the snake. Her mule stood, shaking and snorting nervously.

Carlos dismounted and began hitting the ground by the rock with a large stick. He then led his nervous mule past the rock. Dr Brown followed Carlos' lead, his mule following carefully after his bulking form.

'I suggest you do likewise,' he advised Laura.

She dismounted and pulled on the animal's reins. At first her mule refused to budge. It stood ears flat against its neck unwilling to take a single step. Only when Carlos came back and got behind it waving his big stick did it reluctantly start moving. Then of course it broke into a canter, almost dragging Laura along on the ground behind it.

Once past the rock it stopped abruptly, and they all paused to look back at the precipice. Laura was chilled to see just how narrow her escape had been. She peered back through the trees to see that the cliff edge she had almost fallen from formed only a small part of the rim of a huge sink hole in the ground. It looked like a giant vertical-walled crater in the middle of the jungle floor.

'It's a 'cenote'', explained Dr Brown, 'an entrance to the underground river system. The ancient Maya believed caves like this to be doorways into the underworld. Diving in there was one of the initiation ceremonies for their medicine men. If a young apprentice could swim from one of these entrances to another they became a shaman.' He looked at Laura. 'Of course, the vast majority of them simply drowned.'

He turned away and got back on his mule.

'Dr Brown thinks of the ancient Maya only as primitive people,' said Carlos as he and Laura climbed back onto their mules and followed Dr Brown along the jungle track, 'He forgets that they built magnificent cities...'

'...Using only stone age technology!' chimed Dr Brown.

'OK, so they didn't have metal tools,' replied Carlos, 'but just look at what they did without them!'

Laura could tell that they actually both quite enjoyed this kind of banter.

'If the ancient Maya were so unsophisticated,' continued Carlos enthusi-astically, 'why is it that they had seventeen different interlocking calendars, while we only have one? That's seventeen different ways of calculating what day it is! And because each of those calendars was based on the actual movements of the planets and the stars throughout the universe, what day it was told them not only *when* the day was, but also *where* the earth was on that day relative to all those other planets and stars. They could even use the position and orientation of their temple-pyramids to check their calcu-lations and measure the position of all those seventeen different planets and stars relative to the Earth quite precisely. That doesn't sound much like a primitive people to me.'

'But they didn't even have telescopes,' offered Brown provocatively.

'Makes no difference' said Carlos 'They still understood 'the cycles of time', the cycles of all the different planets, like Venus. And the Venusian calendar, or Long Count, was highly complicated. Unlike our simple solar calendar, which simply measures how many days it takes for the Earth the orbit the Sun, or their simple lunar calendar, which measured how many days it takes the moon to orbit the Earth, their Long Count calendar didn't just measure the Venusian year. Their Long Count measured something much more interesting'

'It didn't just measure how long it takes for Venus and the Earth to effec-tively orbit one another. This is a process which takes on average 584 days, but it varies between 580 and 587. But their Long Count measured something far more interesting than this. The Maya were more interested in why the length of this cycle varies. They were more interested in the relationship between the axis of rotation of the planet Venus around the Sun relative to the Earth's axis of rotation around the Sun, a cycle which oscillates over a vast period of time.'

'They were interested in how long it takes for the Earth, the Sun and Venus all to return to the same position relative to each other. And this is a process that operates on a 5,200 year cycle, or as the Maya would say, this 'cycle of time' lasts exactly 1,366,560 days. And this is what gave them their Long Count calendar. They calculated and understood all this without the aid of modern telescopes. We really don't know how they did it.'

'Carlos is a specialist in Mayan astronomy and he won't hear a word spoken against them,' said Brown.

'So I'd noticed' answered Laura.

'In fact, Carlos has been studying the astronomy tower at Luvantum, and he has plans to try to restore it,' Brown explained.

'Yes, it is one of the finest of its kind in the ancient Mayan world,' said Carlos proudly. 'I've already done some preliminary excavation work around it and I've discovered lots of pieces of crystal,' he added.

Laura's ears pricked up.

'It seems that these pieces of crystal were used by the astronomer-priests in ancient times to help to clarify their vision. For example, when they looked up at the night sky, they believed that the crystal could help them to see the planets and stars more clearly.'

Incredible, thought Laura. She felt a sudden sense of vindication. She remembered how the crystal skull had enhanced her own vision of the hieroglyphs back in her office. And now it transpired that the ancient Maya themselves had used crystal to help enhance their vision.'

'In fact,' continued Carlos, 'it seems the ancient Maya believed crystal could help them see beyond the planets and stars themselves to the hidden dimensions of the heavens. And it was the workings of these dimensions, the hidden 'cycles of time' which were recorded in their calendar of all calendars, the sacred calendar, or 'tzolkin' as it was known.'

'As you probably know, experts have been puzzling over this sacred calendar for years, but we still do not understand it. Perhaps this is because it appears to be to do with another dimension, a 'parallel universe' if you like, which we mortals, we humble human beings going about our business on this small planet, simply cannot see. But the ancient ones it seems could see into it.'

What Carlos said offered Laura a glimmer of hope. She was still deeply unsettled by the fact that nobody else, neither Professor Lamb, nor Caleb, nor even Michael, had been able to see the hieroglyphs she had seen through the crystal skull in her office. They had all assumed that she was simply imagining things; that she was in the throes of some sort of mental breakdown, an idea which she herself found deeply disturbing, in case it were actually the case. But what Carlos was saying encouraged her. The ancient Maya themselves had apparently used crystal to try to see what could not normally be seen. So maybe she wasn't really going mad after all?

She was about to ask Carlos more about it, when Brown cut in.

'It sounds intriguing,' he said dismissively, 'but if we don't get to this archaeological site soon, we won't be able to see anything either!'

Brown was looking up at the sky. 'It's getting late Carlos. You'd better go ahead and get a fire started at the site before dark.'

'I will have coffee waiting for you,' grinned Carlos, 'Hasta luego!' He kicked his mule into a trot and rode on ahead.

Meanwhile, the four soldiers from the airstrip reached the same fork in the path that Laura and her companions had passed earlier. Unsure which direction to take, they stopped for a moment and rested their guns while one of them ventured ahead to investigate.

Taking the left fork he found a large rock partially blocking the path, and beside it something caught his eye. He noticed some hoof-marks in the mud at the edge of the rim of a cenote. He bent down to take a closer look. The markings were fresh. He peered over the cliff but there was no sign of any fallen mule or rider. Then he noticed the other hoof-marks, three sets of them, leading on beyond the large rock.

He whistled to his colleagues, pointing excitedly in the direction that Laura and her colleagues had left. His comrades threw their guns back over their shoulders, and they pressed on towards Luvantum, now in hot pursuit.

Chapter 52

As Brown and Laura rode on in silence, Laura noticed that the jungle around them seemed to have become even thicker. It was as though the further they got into the forest, the trees, not so easily accessible to loggers, had become larger, their branches seeming to reach right up to the sky itself. She had all but forgotten the awesome power of wild places such as this. The jungle reminded her how small and fragile she was. There was a rawness, a primordial power in these wild places that was both exhilarating and frightening. It was a place where nature reigned supreme. It reminded Laura of the respect human beings owed the natural world, whose forces, though easily overlooked, still determined the lives of everyone on the planet.

She found her thoughts turning again to the old man she had met at the airstrip. So he was a 'medicine man'. The idea intrigued her. She had never met such a person before, even on previous excavation trips to Central America. 'Dirt archaeologists' often seemed to have surprisingly little to do with the local people. She was struck by how unassuming he looked, how ordinary. It was hard to believe he was a man who would have known how to heal people. It seemed there might be more to him than met the eye. But what intrigued her most was what Dr Brown had said back at the airstrip.

'So what do you know about medicine men talking to the dead?' she called out to Dr Brown.

'Not a lot,' he replied.

'So what makes you think that man we met earlier was an expert?'

'Well, I would have told you it was all a load of nonsense, if it hadn't have been for that old boy.'

Laura looked questioningly at him.

''Told me my father was dead.' He looked intently at Laura. 'I was out here, had no way of knowing. 'Turned out to be true.' He looked away.

'I'm sorry to hear that,' said Laura.

''Happened eighteen months ago. He was 86 years old. Heart failure.'

Brown held out his palm and looked up at the sky. 'Hey, I think it's going to stop raining.' He rode on ahead.

Laura rode behind him, up a small ridge, in silence. Above them, the heavy monotone grey sky was beginning to break up as the rain began to ease and shards of sunlight were starting to penetrate the clouds.

'We're nearly there!' beamed Brown as they came over the brow of the hill, 'Take a look,' he said, passing Laura his binoculars.

At that moment, the forest was filled with the deep, booming sound of chopper blades, and Laura gasped in shock as a huge Chinook army helicopter reared up above the treetops right in front of them. It powerful searchlight pierced right through the jungle canopy, shining harsh shards of electric-blue into the forest, illuminating pockets of trees with its shadowy, artificial light.

Laura barely had time to register what was happening, when Carlos came galloping back towards them, shouting as he dismounted. 'Quick! Hide! They're looking for Dr Shepherd,'

'Shit!' whispered Laura, a she rushed to dismount, her eyes rapidly scanning the forest, looking for somewhere to hide.

'Here, behind these trees,' whispered Carlos, leading his mule just off the path, to behind a particularly thick cluster of trees.

Dr Brown sat stubbornly on his mule. 'What the hell's going on?' he demanded. 'You never told me you were a wanted criminal.'

'Please!' Laura begged, following Carlos, 'It's not how it looks. I can explain.' As she said it she began to wonder how on earth she could possibly even begin to explain quite how she had ended up in this situation.

'Yes, I think you'd better,' said Brown, petulantly, 'Endangering the whole party, putting all our lives at risk,' he muttered as he slid reluctantly off his mule, and joined Laura and Carlos hiding behind the huge buttress roots of the large cluster of silvery-grey tree trunks.

Hovering high above them now, like a mighty mechanical hawk, the helicopter's blades were whirring. The pilot and co-pilot were each scanning the rainforest below. Fortunately for Laura and her party, the foliage was so dense in this part of the forest that the pilots could see little beyond the thick greenery of the jungle canopy itself, over 200 feet above Laura and her companion's heads.

Behind the trees, Dr Brown cast a disapproving look at Laura. 'What did you do, rob a bank?'

'Of course not,' replied Laura, indignant. She was just about to try to explain herself when the whirl of helicopter blades suddenly got louder, as the aircraft circled lower, trying to catch a better angle between the trees.

The mules were getting tetchy, pulling nervously against their reins. Laura tried hard to calm them, but to no avail. Suddenly the sound of chopper blades became a thunderous roar, as a second huge troop-carrying helicopter swooped past overhead, before coming in to land at the ancient ruined city, that lay in the valley immediately beyond.

Laura's mule panicked. Its eyes flashed white with fear. She tried desperately to restrain it, but its reins were wrenched right out of her hands as it bolted. She just managed to grab hold of her rucksack, and the coil of rope by which it had been hooked over the front of her saddle, as the animal took off at great speed into the jungle, back in the direction of the airstrip. The other mules too stirred restlessly, pulling constantly against their reins, refusing to settle.

'We've got to get out of here!' Dr Brown panicked, climbing back onto his mule.

Carlos climbed onto the other remaining animal and held out an arm to let Laura get on behind him. 'Come on!' he said.

'I can't,' replied Laura, staying put and throwing her rucksack back over her shoulder, 'I have to find that stone!'

Brown and Carlos both stared at her for a moment, as if she were crazy. Laura had a terrible feeling of *déjà vu*, but her mind was made up.

'Well, not with our help you don't!' exclaimed Brown, turning his mule to leave, 'Come on, Carlos!'

Carlos restrained his animal long enough to give Laura one last chance to change her mind and get on. But Laura just looked at him, her mouth half-open, unable to explain her decision, before Carlos gave up and allowed his animal to turn and leave.

'No! Please! Wait!' Laura yelled after Brown as he began to ride off.

'You stay here if you like, Dr Shepherd, but you're on your own,' Brown shouted back to Laura as he disappeared into the jungle.

Carlos glanced back over his shoulder, concerned, as he too rode off and vanished into the forest.

Laura suddenly felt very abandoned and alone.

Chapter 53

Laura tried to cheer herself with the thought that at least she was very nearly at Luvantum, and the ever-present helicopter thankfully seemed to have gone, at least for the time being. Perhaps this way, without Dr Brown, Carlos and the mules, she would be less conspicuous and there would be less chance of her getting caught? Maybe now she would be able to find the missing piece of hieroglyph stone after all? At least that's what she told herself as she scrambled and crawled her way through the undergrowth, trying to get beyond the ridge, in the hope of being able to see what lay ahead in the valley beyond.

Eventually she found a spot beyond the ridge where the ground began to slope down into the valley ahead, and she discovered another good hiding place behind some trees. She still had Dr Brown's binoculars with her, so she raised them to her eyes and peered through a distant gap between the trees.

What she saw then took her breath away. For right there in front of her, encircled on all sides by steep jungle-clad hills, was one of the most magnificent sights she had ever seen. A vast ruined city of temples, palaces, plazas and mounds, even great limestone pyramids rising right up above the treetops, and all bathed in the most beautiful golden evening sunlight.

But there was only one small problem. The whole place, the ancient Mayan city of Luvantum that she had risked so much to get to, was absolutely crawling with soldiers, all looking for her. There appeared to her to be literally hundreds of them, all carrying machine guns, and overhead several more troop-carrying helicopters were circling, waiting their turn to land.

Laura was horrified, so much so she almost dropped her binoculars. Here she was at last, only a few hundred yards from her goal, but it was absolutely impossible to access. Her shock soon began to turn to despair. What was she going to do? How could she possibly get anywhere near the site – let alone into the sacred chamber inside the very heart of the main pyramid?

She slumped to the ground defeated, when she thought she heard a distinct rustling sound coming from some nearby bushes. She spun round. There was no sign of anyone. So she edged her way carefully round to the other side of the tree. She held her breath. She was sure she could hear soldiers in the distance shouting orders in Spanish.

She heard the rustling again. Alarmingly, it still seemed to be coming from behind her. *'Have I been surrounded already?' she wondered.* She heard the cracking of a branch immediately behind. As quietly as she could, she began to pull her pen-knife slowly from her pocket, and was just about to turn around and take a look, when a giant male hand clamped itself across her mouth and nose, her pen-knife arm was twisted behind her back, and she was violently man-handled to the ground.

Terrified, Laura began kicking and struggling against them, elbowing them in the ribs and kicking them in the shins.

'Ah, stop! It's me!' an exasperated male voice whispered. His Guatemalan accent was unmistakeable. Laura recognised his voice immediately. It was Carlos. She stopped struggling.

'What the hell?' whispered Laura as he released her and rubbed his shins where she had kicked him.

'They would have seen you' said Carlos, pointing in the direction of the soldiers' voices which sounded as though they were getting nearer.

'Sorry'

'We can't stay here,' whispered Carlos, 'Follow me!'

On her hands and knees Laura followed Carlos as he crawled through the undergrowth and it wasn't long before she found herself clambering into the entrance of a small cave that was hidden amongst thick vegetation.

Once safely inside, they peered out beyond the rim of the cave to see Dr Brown in the distance being frog-marched straight towards them. Behind him, Laura recognised one of the four soldiers from the airstrip. He was prodding Dr Brown forwards with a gun barrel in the small of his back, and shouting out orders at him in Spanish – 'Anda, cabron!' ('Keep moving, you old fool!').

His comrades meanwhile were fanning out amidst the trees, guns at the ready, and all heading in Laura and Carlos' direction. Laura realized it was these soldiers she had heard earlier barking orders at Dr Brown in Spanish. Initially he had protested his innocence, but now, terrified of what they might do to him, he was just trying to give them what they wanted – 'Come out, Dr Shepherd! Give yourself up! You've got nowhere to go!' he shouted.

'Damn!' whispered Laura, as she ducked back into the cave. This was it. They would find her now. She didn't like to think what might happen to her when they did. One thing was certain, she would never find the prophecy stone. Now, when she was so close to what she had come here for.

She looked around the cave in desperation, looking for somewhere better to hide. But its walls were smooth. In any case, she was sure they would soon find her even if she could find a suitable crack or cranny big enough to squeeze into.

But as her eyes adjusted to the gloom, she could see further into the back of the cave, and she realized that the cave had two chambers, front and rear. She scrambled through to the back of the cave, where she could see a narrow pin-hole shaft of daylight shining through from a tiny hole in the ceiling.

As her eyes followed the shaft of light down to the ground, she was surprised to discover that the rear of the cave was partially filled with water, some thirty of forty feet below the ledge on which she now stood. The back of the cave was in fact a 'cenote', an entrance to the underground river system, similar in principal to the large sink-hole in the ground she had almost fallen into earlier.

She gazed at the deep water far below, before turning to Carlos. 'Where does this lead?' she asked.

'Nobody knows,' said Carlos, 'Though some say it comes out underneath one of the pyramids.

'Another way in!' exclaimed Laura. 'Are you sure?'

'They say the ancients built the pyramid on top of the largest chamber, or cenote, as they considered it the most sacred – the main entrance to the underworld. But nobody knows for certain,' replied Carlos.

Laura thought about it a moment. That made sense, she thought. For she already knew that one of the most famous pyramids in Central America, the great Temple of Kukulkan (or El Castillo as the Spanish called it) at the ancient Mayan city of Chichen Itza on the Yucatan Peninsula in Southern Mexico, had originally been built right on top of what had been the main water well, or cenote, right in the very heart of the ancient city.

Some had speculated that this was to provide water to nourish the soul of the deity to whom the temple was dedicated. In Chichen Itza's case this was the great god of all of Central America – the rainbow-coloured flying feathered serpent known to the Maya as Kukulkan. To the later Aztecs this god was known as Quetzalcoatl. Though perhaps, Laura wondered, the pyramid at Chichen Itza was so positioned to allow the god Kukulkan to access the underworld.

And here at Luvantum, perhaps the idea had been to bury or hide the crystal skull in its secret chamber inside the main pyramid, right on top of the main cenote – right at the main entrance to the underworld – in order to somehow banish the skull to the underworld, traditionally the world of the dead in Mayan mythology.

So maybe what Carlos said was true – that the main pyramid at Luvantum was built on top of the main cenote, the largest chamber of the underground river system. But Laura was hardly in a position to write a thesis on it right now, particularly as, outside the cave, she could hear the soldiers getting closer.

There was only one way to find out. Laura removed her rucksack and began stripping off her shirt.

'What are you doing?' Carlos could hardly believe what he was seeing.

'I'm going in there,' came Laura's matter-of-fact reply, 'You coming?' She started to remove her trainers.

'Are you crazy?' exclaimed Carlos.

Probably, Laura thought to herself. But she had come this far and wasn't about to give up now. 'I'll take my chances,' she said.

'But nobody's ever come back out of this one alive!' explained Carlos.

'Are you coming or not?' insisted Laura, ignoring his caution and turning the question back on him.

'I'd rather face the soldiers,' he replied.

'Then give me a hand with this.' Laura passed him the length of rope from her rucksack and pulled out a large, waterproof flashlight. While she tested the flashlight, Carlos neatly coiled the rope before passing it back to Laura, who tied it to her belt.

'You be careful down there,' he offered gently, 'after all this rain the water level starts rising and there will not be many places to stop for air.'

'Thanks for the encouragement!' said Laura. Though she was trying to make light of her predicament, her eyes belied her nerves.

She checked her rucksack straps were on properly, flicked on her torch, took a deep breath, raised her arms above her head, and dived down into the deep water below.

'And watch out for strong currents!' Carlos' voice tailed off like a strangled cry, for Laura could not hear him, as she hit the surface of the water with a splash.

Chapter 54

Don't panic! Whatever you do don't panic! Laura attempted to calm herself. She tried hard to remember all the scuba-diving training she had had all those years ago, when she was still a young archaeology post-grad in her prime at Yale.

She had originally learned to dive precisely because the cenotes in this part of the world had historically yielded up so many secrets, so many ancient Mayan treasures. Like the ancient funerary vase she herself had discovered on a cave-dive near the ancient Mayan city of Coba in the Central Yucatan. A photo of this find still graced her office wall back at the Smithton Geographic museum.

But all the training she had had now seemed such a long time ago, dreamlike, almost irrelevant, like a whole other lifetime away. She could hardly remember any of it now that she suddenly found herself in the cold, dark waters of what she worried might turn out to be her own underwater tomb.

But she couldn't help noticing that the water around her, lit by the narrow pin-hole shaft of light that shone through the ceiling of the cave, was a beautiful turquoise colour. The light penetrated deep down into the otherwise darkened waters in which she now found herself immersed. Although her torch was on, she felt somehow guided by this narrow turquoise column of water that extended deep down into the abyss below.

The water became colder and her ears began to hurt as she swam down to the bottom of the beautiful sunlight-shaft-lit pool. Down and down she went until only her torchlight illuminated the silvery-white backs of ghostly pale fish as they darted out of her way.

At the base of the plunge pool the fish took refuge behind huge stalactites and stalagmites that guarded the entrance to a long, dark underwater passageway that led off to one side, away from the main body of the pool.

Laura felt as if she had entered another world, a world of beautiful but somehow menacing huge limestone rock formations. Many of the stalactites and stalagmites were several metres wide and tens of metres high. Some of them stretched right from the very bottom of the pool to the top of the vast cathedral-like underwater cavern in which she now found herself floating, like a weightless astronaut gazing upon some new found planet comprised only of transparent creatures and various undulating shades of grey.

As the translucent fish darted down the tunnel and hid behind giant fingers of rock, Laura felt almost as if the fish were showing her the way, as she followed them deeper and deeper into the huge underground passageway encrusted with limestone rock formations of all kinds of shapes and sizes.

Laura was unaware of the gentle underwater current that was actually carrying both she and the fish further into the enormous waterlogged tunnel. Glancing back, she tried not to panic when she saw the narrow shaft of light in the cenote plunge pool gently disappearing out of sight as she was carried off round a smoothly curved corner of the underground passageway.

Meanwhile above the water level, back in the cenote chamber, just as Laura's torchlight disappeared out of sight beneath the waters below, Carlos turned round to see three of the soldiers appearing just inside the cave entrance. Their guns were cocked and at the ready. They spotted him almost immediately. Without arguing, Carlos put his hands above his head, and gave himself up.

Chapter 55

Down in the long, dark underwater passageway below, Laura was fast running out of time. She was getting desperately short of air. She had hoped she would have found somewhere by now, somewhere to stop for breath, but unfortunately this had not been the case.

She knew from her cave-diving training that you should never free-dive for longer than half of what you know your own lung capacity can withstand. And she knew that back in the peak of her prime she could last just under two minutes underwater, and she was now fast approaching the one minute underwater mark!

Her plan had been to turn round and start swimming back if she had not found a breathing opportunity by this point in time. But that plan was not allowing for the fact that she was now being pulled along by a very gentle, but firm and steady current. Given this current, she was now beginning to get extremely worried that she had effectively miscalculated her options and had not left enough time to get back. Even if she turned around now she would probably not be able to make it back to the cenote plunge pool.

It seemed she had little choice but to press on in the hope of finding a breathing opportunity further on down the tunnel. She swam as close as she could to the ceiling of the passageway desperately searching for somewhere, anywhere that air might have become trapped. But it was to no avail.

She started panicking, now absolutely desperate for air, the muscles in her legs beginning to cramp, her chest feeling like it was about to collapse, to cave in on itself in excruciating pain, when she finally found it.

Just in the nick of time she discovered a small crevice in the ceiling of the tunnel, a small air-pocket in the rock just above water level. It was what cave divers call a 'pop-up', a place where a few litres of old air had become trapped when the cave system itself had originally become flooded with water.

There wasn't much to it. It couldn't have been much bigger than a motorbike crash helmet, but Laura thrust her head right into it and gasped in. Though it was old, stale air, to Laura's heaving lungs it tasted sweeter than the finest nectar. She breathed in as deeply as she could, her heart still hammering in her chest.

Her lack of judgment frightened her. She didn't know what she was thinking of swimming so far, trapped underground, without having any idea where her next opportunity for air might be. But she had been lucky. She gulped in the precious oxygen, knowing she had to calm herself in order to reach her optimum ability to swim on, an ability on which her life now depended.

As she breathed in again, she suddenly became aware that the water level was slowly rising. She had only been able to fit her head and neck into the crevice to start with, but now only her head was above water level and the water was rising still further with each and every moment that passed. It had crept up her neck and was now fast approaching her mouth. Any second now she was going to have to go back under again.

The question was whether she should attempt to swim back to the cenote, or press on. But she had only just made it from the cenote to here in the first place, and that was with the help of a strong current which, if she were to swim back, would be working against her. So, even if she did attempt to swim back there would be very little chance of her making it all the way back out again alive.

But to press on...

She dunked her head back under the water. The dark passageway ahead stretched on before her, way beyond the end of her torch beam. For all she knew it might stretch on forever, without any opportunity for air, never mind the opportunity to re-emerge above ground level. It seemed she had very little hope either way. How could she have been so foolish? It seemed that in her haste to find the prophecy stone, she had lost all sensible judgement.

But as she turned her torch beam away, something caught her eye. She could not be entirely sure, but she thought she glimpsed a tiny glimmer of light in the distance, coming perhaps from the far end of the tunnel?

But it was hard to tell. It might have been simply some strange reflection of her own torchlight. She had already learned all those years ago when she was doing her pot-hole diver training, that sometimes very strange optical effects could occur underwater, especially when free-swimming through underground caves, under stress. Apparently it was quite possible in these circumstances to see the light, when in fact there was none there. What she had seen might actually be nothing more than a deadly mirage, luring her onwards towards her death.

But she had no time to double-check. With the water level steadily rising, this was her last chance to get any air. But as she raised her head back into the 'pop-up' the crown of her skull struck the roof of the crevice before even her nose was clear of the water. Now only with her head bent right back and her nose and mouth pressed right up against the ceiling of the air-pocket was she able to breathe. In a few seconds time she would have no choice but to go back under and either attempt to swim back to the cenote, or take what was probably the even more dangerous option of pressing onwards in search of the next opportunity for air.

Her position in the 'pop-up' was fast becoming untenable. So, after one last desperate breath, she dived back under, and swam on. Whether she was being lured by an entirely imaginary light-source, Laura could not be sure. *'Perhaps I've just got a death wish?'* she wondered. But sheer desperation drove her onwards. She wanted to live. She wanted to see Michael again. Thinking of him helped her swim faster. It helped her press on.

On and on she swam. She was looking for the light at the end of the tunnel, but it seemed there was none. The dark passageway seemed to stretch forever, snaking first to the left and then to the right, but still no sign of any light-source, or any opportunity for air. And it wasn't long before Laura found herself once again running perilously short of breath.

She could feel a terrible, deadly fatigue setting in to all the muscles in her body. The crystal skull, in its rucksack on her back, which she had previously hardly noticed, now began to feel like a lead weight. Each kick of her legs, each stroke she made with her arms, to try to push herself through the water, took energy she simply no longer had. The awful cramping pain returned to her limbs as the oxygen was rapidly depleted from her system and paralysis began to set in.

The pain was becoming almost unbearable as the passageway snaked back again to the left. Laura felt she could not last a moment longer, when suddenly she saw a glimmering light ahead. She was absolutely sure of it.

As she drifted nearer, however, she realised it was not actually a light she had seen, but it was the next best thing. Her torch beam was reflecting back off a flat surface above. It was a vast ceiling of water not far ahead. It could mean only one thing. No rock surface could possibly be that flat, smooth and silvery. It had to be the interface between dark water below, and precious, life-giving air above!

Still not entirely convinced that what she was seeing was real, and not just some surreal pre-death illusion, she summoned the last of her strength and pushed herself through the water towards it. Suddenly her head broke right through the surface of the water. It was for real!

In a moment of unimaginable joy, she choked in the damp, dusky air, coughing and spluttering and, inside, crying tears of relief. She felt ecstatic as she filled her lungs, drinking in the life-sustaining oxygen. She had never been so grateful for air before.

Using all her fragile strength, she grabbed onto a rock by the water's edge, and dragged her tired body out of the water onto a nearby ledge, where she lay puffing and panting.

As she regained her breath, she shone her torch around her, slowly taking in her new surroundings. To her surprise, she now found herself lying beside a small lake hidden inside a vast, cathedral-like, underground cavern in the rock.

Chapter 56

The cavern was quite magnificent, like a huge underground dome, its ceiling dripping with thousands of small, sparkling quartz stalactites. But as Laura lay there thanking god for her luck, and admiring the beauty of her new environment, she could feel her sense of relief quickly turning to one of panic. *How the hell am I going to get out of here?*

She couldn't possibly fight her way back against the now strong currents, and heaven knew if there was any other way out. Laura wondered if perhaps there were some other small fissures in the rock below water level, but by the looks of things all the water in the underground river was just piling itself up inside this beautiful cavern. The surface of the lake appeared to have risen a couple of inches just in the time it had taken her to establish where she was. What was she going to do?

She couldn't bear the thought of going back underwater, so she shone her torch up at the ceiling, hoping there might be some small nook or cranny, some potential route out of this watery tomb. Straining her eyes to see, she thought she could discern something that looked like a small opening right at the very apex of the vast domed ceiling of the cave. But she could not be entirely sure, especially from this angle. She was going to have to get nearer.

So she climbed back into the cold water and shone her torch back up at the ceiling from immediately below. From this angle it looked distinctly like some sort of vertical shaft, perhaps man-made, cut into the rock at the highest point of the roof of the cavern. Immediately beside it was an unusually shaped rock, or perhaps it too was a man-made feature, like a small stalagmite protruding right into the opening, just inside the entrance to the shaft.

There appeared to be only one course of action.

Holding her flashlight now between her teeth, and treading water, Laura untied the length of rope from her belt. Remembering her pot-holing training, she coiled the rope and tied it onto a lasso shape as best she knew how, and threw the looped end up towards the apex of the ceiling. It took her several throws, but she eventually managed to hook it over the irregularly shaped stalagmite.

She tugged at it to test its strength and then began the extremely difficult task of pulling herself up the rope. Thanks to her training, she knew how to 'tie' her thighs into the rope as she went, but even so it took every ounce of energy she had left, as she pulled herself, inch by painful inch, up towards the ceiling.

She was soon tiring dangerously. Her treacherous underwater journey had already sapped her strength and the arduous climb now drained her energies even further. She dragged herself slowly upwards, conscious that in her exhausted state, she could all too easily let go and fall back down into the waters below. She slowed almost to a halt, her tired muscles and tendons straining with fatigue. *I have to do this for Alice*, she told herself, urging her tired body onwards.

Finally, she reached the apex of the giant ceiling, where she was able to grab onto the unusually shaped stalagmite and pull herself up. She managed to gain a footing just inside the entrance to the narrow, vertical passageway.

But just as Laura pulled herself further into the shaft, her rucksack caught at its entrance, and she realised she could not fit through with the rucksack still on her back. Hooking one elbow round the stalagmite, she was able to take the rucksack off, tie it to one end of the length of rope and tie the other end around her waist. She was then able to edge her way slowly up the narrow vertical shaft the only way possible, by pushing both her arms and legs outwards against its smooth walls, with the heavy rucksack now swinging from the umbilical cord of rope beneath her.

She didn't get very far however, before she discovered a large slab of stone blocking the passageway. Using all the strength she had left in her legs to wedge herself into the narrow shaft, she pushed with all her might against it, but it did not move. *This is it*, she thought, *I've come all this way for nothing, just to die inside this underground tomb.*

She steadied herself in her precarious position within the shaft and gritted her teeth. *You can't give in now*, she told herself. *Let's give it just one more try.* She redoubled her efforts and, to her surprise, this time the slab of stone began to move, quite easily, and she was able to push it to one side, right out of her way!

As she pushed herself past it, she was no longer restricted by the walls of the narrow shaft, and instead found herself emerging into a dark and cavernous space. The slab was clearly some sort of stone man-hole cover, over an opening in its floor.

She pulled her body clear of the shaft, and collapsed onto the floor by its side, where she lay exhausted by her efforts. She could have stayed there all night, were it not for her burning desire to know where she was, and whether or not she could get out of there.

Recovering her breath, she managed to manoeuvre herself into a sitting position, with her legs still dangling in the shaft. She was still disorientated, trying to work out where she was. She grabbed her torch back from between her teeth and shone it into the dark. She could scarcely believe what she saw lit up by her powerful flashlight beam.

For this was not just some dark, empty space. This was clearly some sort of man-made chamber or tomb. Laura shone her flashlight across the perfectly formed mosaic of paving stones that made up the floor to see that the walls were lined with delicately carved stone images of human skulls, row upon row of them.

This had to be the place, but she needed to be sure. So she shone her torch beam down to the end of the chamber and, sure enough, there it was, just as Anna had described it. A beautifully carved stone altar, its walls adorned with the image of a skull. Laura was stunned with amazement, as it dawned on her that somehow, against all the odds, she had made it.

This was it. The very place where, a lifetime ago, in a very different world, a young, innocent woman, an explorer's daughter, had braved the crumbling pyramid exterior, to discover hidden within its dark recesses, an object of transcendent beauty, a jewel on which no price could be laid; the solid quartz crystal skull.

Here she was at last, right inside the sacred skull chamber, inside the very heart of the great pyramid of Luvantum, exactly the place where Anna Crockett-Burrows had originally discovered the crystal skull.

She could hardly believe it. Carlos was right. The underground river system did lead right into the heart of the main pyramid, the very place she had been trying so hard to reach. She almost wept. She was so overcome with relief and joy.

Chapter 57

Laura was blissfully unaware, however, of the danger that lurked outside. Just beyond the walls of the chamber, outside the great temple-pyramid in which she now found herself, over two hundred troops had been ordered to explore the archaeological site, and they were busy doing so with an enthusiasm that surprised even their own commander.

Searching every outlying building, every creeper-covered jumble of stones, every fallen tree and crumbling wall, they searched. Their mission: to find the fugitive, Laura Shepherd, and to protect and preserve the crystal skull.

Maybe it was the unusual, slightly unorthodox nature of the mission that inspired them, or perhaps simply the fact that there was a woman involved. Whatever it was, something had led the men to show greater diligence in their efforts than usual.

As the shadows lengthened and the day began to draw towards a close, Commander Ochoa made a decision. Tonight, they would not break to camp. He would keep the troops on site, keep them vigilant and alert. After all, two of the fugitive's accomplices had already been caught within a few hundred yards of the city walls.

But the place was now surrounded. They had sealed off every track that led to the site, and a soldier had been posted every twenty yards around the perimeter. The commander knew that Laura was out there somewhere, in that jungle. And it was likely, given her general craftiness and unbalanced mental state, that she would try, under cover of dark, to enter the city. And when she did, they would be waiting for her.

And so it was that, just beyond the chamber where Laura now sat, a small unit of soldiers, on the lookout for her, began to climb up the pyramid steps, immediately outside.

Chapter 58

Back inside the pyramid, the question for Laura was whether or not the chamber she had just discovered still contained what she had come all this way to find.

Laura's hands were trembling as she turned her torch to look at the other end of the tomb. This is what she had travelled so far for, risked so much for. She could hardly bear to look, lest it had been removed, or somehow destroyed. But as she raised her beam up from the floor, there it was. The vast circular chunk of limestone, lit up in all its intricately carved glory. The magnificent prophecy stone doorway that had stood there for millennia was lying open on its giant hinges, exactly the way it appeared in Anna Crockett-Burrows photograph.

Laura was astonished. She simply could not believe her luck. She had finally found what she had been searching for. And apart from the chunk of stone she already knew was missing and some severe water erosion which she had been expecting, the stone appeared to have survived otherwise intact. She was delighted.

Meanwhile, however, back outside the pyramid, the group of soldiers arrived at the top of the pyramid steps. As darkness fell and the moon rose in the sky, they entered the little temple at the pyramid's summit. This was to be their post for the night.

The temple had seen little in the way of renovation since Frederick Crocket-Burrows and his team discovered the site nearly a hundred years before. The original creepers, now dead from machete wounds, still clung to the walls obscuring many of the inscriptions that had once adorned this sacred space.

As they looked around the temple, their torches illuminating what remained of the ancient writings , one of the older soldiers confirmed what all of the others were thinking 'Ella no esta' ('She's not here'). Weary from the steep climb, he let out a sigh and sat down on the jaguar stone figurine that served surprisingly well as a comfortable stool. He lit up a cigarette. His colleagues sat down next to him and joined in the impromptu cigarette break.

But one particularly keen young soldier, got up, torch in hand and wandered into the back of the temple. He couldn't understand why his colleagues were content to just sit about when they'd had a task assigned to them. This was his big chance. He wanted to be the one to find the stolen jewel. He'd been at the airstrip when the man had arrived in the helicopter and he knew that the skull's rightful owners were prepared to pay handsomely for its return.

He shone his flashlight down the wooden ladder that led down through the large hole in the floor of the temple to the bare chamber below. This was the chamber into which the young Anna Crockett-Burrows had tumbled on the fateful day that she had found the crystal skull.

'Me voy abajo a ver' ('I'm going down here to take a look') he said as he descended the steep ladder and took a deep breath before entering the once secret passageway that led deep down inside the heart of the pyramid.

Back inside the chamber, Laura turned round to retrieve the crystal skull, which was still dangling in its rucksack beneath her. When she pulled on the rope she felt some resistance, so she tugged harder. As she did so, she heard a ripping sound. She peered down into the shaft to see that the cheap rucksack had ripped along a seam, where it had snagged on a stalactite, and the skull was now visibly protruding from the sack, balanced precariously right on the edge of the torn fabric. One false move, one careless manoeuvre, would send the skull tumbling into the cenote below. She would probably never see it again.

This was all she needed. Without the skull her mission would be finished. She would not be able to translate the remaining hieroglyphs. She could not afford to lose it now.

As she began pulling the bag slowly towards her, the skull swung back and forth across the dark water, like a giant pendulum, marking out the passage of time. She waited until the bag stopped swinging, and then pulled cautiously on the rope, inching the torn rucksack slowly back up through the shaft towards her.

Finally she was able to grab the bag and catch the skull just moments before it would have fallen.

Greatly relieved, she unhitched the rope and untied the skull from the remains of the rucksack. As she did so, she thought she heard a noise, coming from somewhere above. Pausing for a moment with the skull in her hands, she listened intently. She could hear nothing. Thinking she had imagined it, she set off towards the far end of the chamber with the skull.

As she did so, she glimpsed the ornately carved stone altar at the near end of the chamber, through the transparent prism of the skull. She was almost tempted to take the skull and place it right there on the altar where it had originally come from, and wait for the glorious morning light to enter the spirit shaft behind it, and strike it, filling the chamber with light, just as Anna Crockett-Burrows had described in her journal. But there was no time for such luxuries. She had some hieroglyphs to translate.

So she turned and carried the skull carefully down to the other end of the chamber, towards the ancient prophecy stone doorway that lay open on its stone hinges, guarding the entrance to the tomb from the passageway and 'secret stairway' beyond.

The stone doorway looked magnificent, even by the light of her simple torch. As Laura stood before it, admiring its beauty, she was filled with a sense of reverence. For this was the stone that had led her here, that she had come so far for, that she had risked so much for. And now here it was right in front of her as plain as day.

She reached out for it as if mesmerised, unable to believe her good fortune. It was as though she felt compelled to check that she wasn't just imagining it, that this wasn't just a figment of her imagination, a desperate illusion, some fantastical hallucination.

Her fingers touched one of the beautifully ornate

hieroglyphs that decorated the face of the huge, circular slab of stone. The old limestone felt surprisingly cold to the touch, and rougher than she expected, but as her fingers gently traced the contours of the glyph, she found herself reassured.

She recognised the distinctive style of the glyphs and could clearly make out the now familiar outline of the missing chunk of stone as the piece still lying on her desk back at the Smithton Geographic museum. This was definitely it. She had come to the right place. The stone she had been so desperately searching for. She had found it at last.

The question was of course, what did it say?

The moment had come for Laura to find out.

Chapter 59

This was the moment Laura had been waiting for, longing for. This would be her moment of reckoning. Now she would finally discover whether she had really been called here by Alice, whether she was here to fulfil an important mission, or whether she was here because she had got things terribly, terribly wrong.

Laura looked at the painstakingly etched symbols before her, words carved deep into stone. Each shape, each line, each groove, each contour made by hands that worked day after day, using hard stone against hard stone to bring forth meaning.

The question was, did this stone speak merely of the lineage of kings that had governed the ancient lands of the Maya, or did it speak with a message about our future? That was what Laura was here to find out.

She stepped back to try to take in the whole stone, marvelling at its exquisite workmanship. But there was a problem.

Although the stone looked spectacular, magnificent, over the years it had clearly suffered considerable water erosion damage to many of the hieroglyphs.

Just as Laura had originally suspected, she was going to need the help of the crystal skull if she was going to even try to translate them. Without the skull, she wouldn't have a clue what most of the hieroglyphs said. They were simply too eroded to read.

Laura's hands began trembling involuntarily as she lifted up the skull to begin her decoding work. But just as she held the skull up in front of her eyes to look at the first inscription through it, she thought she heard something. She wondered whether her ears, rather than her eyes, were playing tricks on her. But as it continued, she realised that the sound she was hearing was for real. The noise was unmistakeable.

It was the sound of heavy boots coming down the once secret stairway just outside the chamber. It sounded as if they were coming straight towards her. She turned off her torch. She could hear the footsteps echoing down the stairwell and along the short passageway just outside. Somebody was heading her way, getting ever closer to where she was standing, in front of the open chamber door.

So before Laura had had a chance to translate even a single hieroglyph, she had to find somewhere to hide – and fast!

The young soldier entered the chamber, torch in hand and machine-gun at the ready. He wasn't going to take any chances.

He wanted to be the one to find Laura, the 'mad gringa woman'.

He knew she could be armed, he knew she could be dangerous.

But if he could be the one to catch her, it would help enormously with his promotion prospects, not to mention how helpful the reward money would be to his poor family back in 'el barrio', the corrugated iron shanty town just outside Guatemala City. It would change his life, and that of his extended family, completely, forever!

He took a few paces into the chamber and looked around.

But there was no sign of Laura anywhere.

Never mind, he thought to himself, he knew it had been a long shot in the first instance, but he was curious to have a look at this old place in any case.

He threw his gun back over his shoulder and wandered over to take a closer look at the intriguing carved stone doorway that lay open on its hinges right beside him. Curious, he went over and stood in front of it.

He ended up standing on exactly the same spot that Laura had been standing on only moments before, admiring, by the light of his torch, precisely the same hieroglyphs.

He stopped to light up a cigarette, before returning his attention to the glyphs. As he exhaled his cigarette smoke wafted gently away on the stale chamber air.

It took Laura all her efforts to stop her exhausted lungs from choking on his cigarette smoke as it tried to drift up her nostrils.

She was standing stock still, frozen with fear, trying to hold her breath, just on the other side of the door.

She was hiding immediately on the other side of it from the young soldier.

After a few moments, the soldier turned and wandered off further into the chamber. Laura could hear his heavy footsteps pacing the floor and then suddenly coming to a halt. She wondered what was happening.

The soldier had stopped abruptly and was now looking down at the ground. He couldn't quite make out what it was he saw lying there on the floor beneath his feet. So he bent down and picked it up. It was a length of rope and a dripping wet rucksack, lying there torn and empty beside what appeared to be some sort of open man-hole in the middle of the chamber floor.

After a moment's thought, *'Que pasa?'* (*'What the hell's been going on here?)* he pulled the machine-gun from his shoulder and shone both his torch and the laser-viewfinder of his gun down into the man-hole, as he started shouting for assistance from his comrades, 'Vene! Vite! ('Come! Quick!').

Laura was petrified. She could not imagine how on earth she was going to get out of this terrifying situation.

'Vene! Vite!' the young soldier shouted again.

Then, realising that none of his colleagues could hear him, he turned around, gun still at the ready, and headed straight towards the door. He dashed right past it and out of the chamber, with Laura's rucksack tucked under his arm, shouting excitedly as he ran back up the stairs to get the other soldiers.

The moment he disappeared, Laura emerged from behind the doorway and switched on her torch. She held the skull up in front of the hieroglyphs and began scanning them as quickly as she could in an attempt to translate them.

She didn't know exactly how long she had, but it would be only minutes at the very most before the young soldier returned with his comrades.

She already knew what the missing piece of the hieroglyph stone said, as she had translated it earlier in her office at the museum.

The prophecy began, *'It is written in the cycles of time that at sunset on the day 13 Baktun, 0 Katun, 0 Tun, and 0 Kin...'*. But she was now here to translate the rest.

She went to the next glyph in the sequence. This was one of the glyphs that was most eroded and that she could not possibly decipher without the aid of the skull. As she held the skull up close to it and looked through it hard, she hoped the skull would not let her down.

'Damn it!' she cursed. Her hands were shaking uncontrollably. They were shaking so much that despite gazing intently though the skull, she found it almost impossible to focus properly on the image of the hieroglyph beyond.

She held the skull up again, but still it was no good. Unless she could hold the skull steady it wasn't going to work. She knew she had to calm herself. She took a deep breath and leaned forward, resting both elbows on the prophecy stone, to try to give herself more stability.

Now as she looked though the crystal skull the eroded image

of the hieroglyph became startlingly clear, just as had happened back in her office. Immediately she recognised the circular form of the Mayan glyph that meant 'All', or rather 'All the…'. This was followed by the hieroglyph that represented 'children'. So the first two glyphs together read, 'All the children…'.

The next hieroglyph looked distinctly like the rays of the sun, so the sentence translated literally meant 'All the children of the sun…' However, to the ancient Maya the rays of the sun were often also used as a symbol of the future. So a better translation was probably, 'All the children of the future…'.

So the whole stone she had translated so far read, *'It is written in the cycles of time that at sunset on the day 13 Baktun, O Katun, 0 Tun, and 0 Kin (in other words, the 21st December 2012)… all the children of the future.…'*

But she couldn't quite make out the last glyph as her hands were still shaking so much, and suddenly even more than before, as she heard the distinctive sound of the soldier's footsteps coming back down the stairs.

She would have to work quickly. The footsteps were getting closer. It would be only a matter of moments before the soldier would reach the bottom of the steps and catch her. If she couldn't translate the final glyph, none of it would make any sense. She simply had to stay and try to decipher it.

Breathing deeply, she redoubled her efforts to calm herself and steady her nerves. As she did so her hands stopped shaking quite so much and the final glyph came properly into view.

At first she couldn't quite believe it. *I must be mistaken*, she thought. This was not what she wanted to see. But the hieroglyph was unmistakeable. She would have recognised it anywhere. It was one of the first glyphs she had ever learnt; the toothless jaw, the hollow eye sockets, and the wicked grin. It was an image of one of the gods of the ancient Mayan pantheon. His name was Cimi, or Mictlantecutli, - the great Lord of Death.

The way the hieroglyph was carved showed him scouring the earth for victims, searching for the flesh and bones of those he wanted to consume.

Laura reeled back in shock. *No, it can't be,* she thought, She looked again. There was absolutely no question about it. Ths last sequence of glyphs read,

'...all the children of the future... will be consumed by the Great God of Death.'

In other words, the whole of the stone was carved with a terrible prediction about the future, which when simply translated into our language said:

'It is written in the cycles of time that... at sunset on the 21st December 2012... all the children of the future... will die!'

Chapter 60

Laura was absolutely horrified, but she had no time to think any further about it. For at that moment the young soldier reappeared at the foot of the stairs. Seeing Laura he pointed his machine gun straight at her and shouted,

'Alto! Manos arriba!' ('Stop! And put your hands above your head!')

Laura turned to him and froze. She could hear the frenzied shouts of the other soldiers and the echo of their heavy boots coming down the stairs behind him, as they marched down the secret stairway, all rushing to assist their comrade.

This was it. They had finally caught her. She had no idea how she was going to get out of this one. *What am I going to do?*

But Laura hadn't risked so much, and come all this way, just to end up languishing in some Central American jail while all hell let loose around her, or worse still, she found herself thinking, just to die at the hands of some inexperienced, trigger-happy, young soldier.

That's when she had an idea. She glanced at the man-hole still lying open in the middle of the chamber floor, and back at the young soldier. She couldn't help making the tiniest of starts towards it, then hesitated, unsure whether or not she could make it.

'No mueve!' ('Stand still!') demanded the young man, then he looked down at the skull in Laura's hands. He seemed to be momentarily distracted by the fact that the crystal skull suddenly appeared to him to glow blood-red in the dark, lit up by the refracted light of his rifle's target-finding laser beam. Noticing this, Laura took her chance and suddenly made a mad dash for the man-hole.

The young soldier opened fire.

It felt to Laura as if everything had gone into slow-motion as his machine-gun blazed a trail of hard metal bullets immediately behind her fleeing heels. The bullets left behind what looked like a series of hammer-holes as they smashed into the ancient paving stones and ricocheted off in almost every direction. Laura sprinted across the chamber as fast as her legs could carry her, but the bullets were fast catching up with her. As she neared the man-hole she realised she had no choice but to dive for it.

Without further thought, she launched herself head-first into the air. Forming a dive position, she extended both arms above her head, clutching the crystal skull between the palms of her hands as she did so. Suddenly, she felt the shocking impact of one of the bullets striking the skull, just as it passed across her chest. As it ricocheted back off it, she was conscious of the fact that it would have penetrated her heart, had the skull not been there to protect her. It would almost certainly have killed her had she not lifted up the skull the moment she did.

Seconds later, another bullet sliced through her upper left arm. She felt the searing pain of it entering her flesh, then only numbness as it tore right through to the other side and out again, leaving a deep gash, as she continued to stretch her arms out into a full dive position.

Suddenly Laura disappeared, skull and head-first, down into the man-hole, with hundreds of machine-gun bullets firing after her, as what seemed like a whole army of soldiers now entered the chamber and opened fire on her. She was fortunate not to bash into the sides of the shaft or crash into the protruding stalagmite, as she completed her amazing, death-defying dive and plunged into the deep water in the cavern far below with an almighty splash.

A hail of bullets rained down after her, piercing and bubbling into the water all around. She could see them lit up in the dark by a multitude of rifle laser-search beams, as she swam down to the bottom of the now swirling pool.

Her wound bled clouds of red into the water, while she tried in vain to swim back towards the underwater passageway from which she came. But with one arm now out of action and the other clutching the skull, she was unable to fight against the rain-swelled currents. Instead, she was pulled in the opposite direction, towards a dark and narrow underwater passageway on the other side of the cavern from which she had come.

The young soldier jumped in after Laura and began swimming under-water towards her, taking aim at her with his machine-gun as best he could amidst the maelstrom. And then, all of a sudden, he and Laura each got sucked into separate underground passageways deep beneath the surface of the pool.

Laura found herself swept violently down the long, dark tunnel, rolling and tumbling underwater, as she was dragged and bashed against the sides. It took her all her energy to hold onto the skull as she was swept helplessly along. On and on the tunnel stretched, the fierce, relentless current pulling her ever on.

There was no opportunity for air, none whatsoever at all. Her chest felt as if it were about to burst and she could last no longer. It wasn't long before she opened her mouth to breathe in, and she began inhaling giant mouthfuls of water, drinking into her lungs her own demise.

Laura knew she was drowning, but she could not fight against it. And after a few moments of struggling for survival, she found herself, surprisingly rapidly, just giving in to it and accepting her fate. She felt unexpectedly philosophical about it. *This is it*, she thought with detachment. It was almost as if she were watching herself from outside.

She realised that all her life she had lived with the unanswered question of how she was going to die, and where. But now she knew. This was going to be how she died. She was going to drown, right here in this underground passageway, this tomb. This was how her life was going to end.

She felt her grip on the crystal skull slacken. It slipped from her fingers. And that was the last thing she knew, as she took her final breath.

Chapter 61

December 16th 2012

The next thing Laura knew she could hear a strange noise. It began softly, at first no louder than a whisper, but then grew in intensity, louder and louder, until it seemed to echo all around her. It was an eerie sound, like the sound of someone whispering or chanting in some strange foreign tongue;

'Oxlahun baktun, mi katun, mi tun, mi kin.'

It was hauntingly familiar. Laura had a vague sense that she had heard it somewhere before, although she wasn't sure quite where.

But when she opened her eyes all she could see were billowing white clouds in front of her face. She couldn't focus properly. The soft clouds seemed to surround her, enveloping her, flowing over her, and moving past her, forming a thick dense mist, a fog, through which she could see nothing. It was impossible to tell where she was. She had no memory whatsoever of how she had got here.

What happened? Where am I? she wondered.

She closed her eyes and opened them again and felt as if she were floating outside her own body, as if she were looking down at herself from above. Through a small gap in the clouds, she thought she could see herself lying on her back, naked except for a thin white cotton sheet that had been pulled up over her body. Her face was ghostly pale.

Am I dead?

Panic suddenly gripped her at the thought. The idea that her life might already be over filled her with desperation and sorrow. The thought that she would never see Michael again was more than she could bear. It felt too much for her when she had lost so much already. She bit back the tears that threatened to pour forth.

No, this can't be real. This can't be the end, she decided. She was filled with an overwhelming sense that there was more she had to do, more she had to accomplish. She couldn't die now when so much seemed unfinished. But the precise details of what seemed hazy in her mind, they were unclear to her, as if the fog that surrounded her had somehow penetrated her brain, making clarity impossible.

Trying to work out where she was, she struggled to get up, when she became aware of a pain, a terrible searing pain shooting through her arm, and bringing her attention back to the present with a lacerating intensity. This was real, it had to be. There was nothing celestial about pain like this. *No dead person could possibly feel this much pain. I must be alive!* She felt strangely relieved, reassured even by the feel of the hard rock beneath her back.

The source of the agony was the wound in her arm where, the night before, a machine gun bullet had grazed right through her flesh. Wanting to examine it, to see what was wrong, she tried to move, but she was so battered and bruised her body hurt all over. The effort was too much and she was left only with the pain as she spiraled back off into a fitful sleep.

How long she lay there drifting in and out of consciousness, trying to work out what was happening to her, she did not know. She felt as if she were stuck in same strange limbo.

Eventually the noise brought her back once more. It was a strange sound piercing through the foggy depths of her consciousness. It slipped through the layers of unreality that seemed to surround her and penetrated her awareness. She lay trying to make sense of it.

'Oxlahun baktun, mi katun, mi tun, mi kin.'

She realized it was the same strange noise she had heard back in her office, the sound that had terrified her when she had heard it before in the museum, the same sound she had heard the night Ron died. It was the eerie sound of a voice gently whispering or chanting. Only now it seemed to be coming from very close at hand.

Laura gazed into the dense fog as the rhythm of the sounds washed over her and gradually the mist began to clear. She could just to make out what looked like rough limestone walls above and around her. As the clouds parted she realized they were in fact plumes of smoke, and that she was actually lying on her back looking up at the ceiling of a dimly lit cave, surrounded by dark recesses and hollows.

Shapes began to emerge, shadowy at first, then gradually coming into focus. With a start, she recognized the crude, horrifying outlines of human skulls. She glimpsed one, then another, then another. The white clouds slowly dissipated to reveal that all around her were human skulls, row upon row of them. There were literally hundreds of them. She realized she was in a smoke filled cave that had been decorated with real human skulls, jam packed into every hollow and recess.

What is this place, and what on earth am I doing here?

The chanting was overwhelming now, filling her head, leaving no room for her thoughts. She tried to sit up, but her head was dizzy and the room seemed to spin like some bizarre fairground ride, skulls grinning at her from every angle. As she reached out an arm to steady herself, a ferocious pain gripped her so hard that she collapsed back onto the bed.

As she lay there, breathing heavily, an odour stung her nostrils. It was an unfamiliar smell, deep, woody, and strangely sweet. Staring up through the fog, she realized the clouds of smoke were coming from the burning of incense.

It was actually the warm fragrant essence of 'copal', the tree resin the Maya traditionally burned in their rituals to cleanse spaces and people and welcome the sacred. Laura had seen depictions of this stuff often enough on ancient Mayan pottery, the curling serpent's tails of smoke, to work out what it was.

Turning her head towards the source of the chanting, and peering through the smoke, she caught a glimpse of the mottled pelt of a jaguar. Its black and gold spots swayed before her very eyes.

But how could this be? How could the jaguar, this king of the rainforest, possibly be in this cave with me?

Here was an animal, so rarely seen, that stalked the jungle only at night with a roar so terrifying that it sent fear into the heart of every creature that lived there. It just didn't seem to make any sense. Surely her mind was playing tricks on her.

It must be a dream, a hallucination, or some drug induced vision. She dismissed the idea. But looking again she was convinced she saw it move. She saw its coat so rich and beautiful rippling across its firm shoulders. Yet as Laura continued to stare at the wild animal before her, the familiar shape of a man emerged.

Chapter 62

He was a Mayan man and would have been classified as an 'elder' in the tradition of the Maya, which was any person who lived beyond fifty two years. But the truth was he could have been any age between that and eighty. A jaguar pelt lay around his shoulders and his head was adorned with a headdress of brightly coloured feathers.

He came nearer and held a terracotta bowl to Laura's lips. As Laura drank of the strange and bitter potion, she gazed into his dark eyes. He looked back into her eyes with a frightening intensity. For a moment she felt as if he was seeing everything there was to her, as if he could see right into her very soul. He took away the bowl and disappeared into the shroud of incense smoke.

It must have been some time later that Laura made out the outline of his head and shoulders as he knelt a short distance away with his back to her. She realized it was from him that the chanting sound was coming. She tried to call out to this stranger, but the words would not form, her body was too weary. Too tired to speak, Laura lay there just watching him.

The smell of the incense and the sound of the chanting were strangely hypnotic in their effect. As the strange words ebbed and flowed, Laura found the fear and anxiety that had first gripped her were now gone.

Without even realising it they had been companions of old, those anxieties that had pushed her constantly to reaffirm her identity, to lay claim to who she was, to stake out her territory. Laura Shepherd, the good daughter, the bright schoolgirl, the brilliant archaeologist, the loving wife, mother, and now this.

Lying half naked, injured and alone, save for this stranger, she knew not where she was or how she had got there. She was nobody, nowhere, unsure if she was dead or alive, caught simply in the sounds that were pouring forth, deep and primordial, sounds that seemed to echo from a different age, a different space, sounds that seemed to reach beyond everyday human experience to touch something deeper, something more ancient and intangible.

The next time Laura opened her eyes, the smoke had cleared and the pain in her arm had almost gone. Nonetheless it took a great effort of will to prop herself up on her good elbow and take in her surroundings.

The cave in which she now found herself was almost circular in shape and about the size of a small sitting room. The only source of light came from the many candles burning on the far side of the cave, though most were obscured by the man who was seated in front of them.

Of slight build, he knelt on the floor at the entrance to one of the small recesses. His head was bowed and he was whispering and chanting in Mayan. Bunches of flowers lay before him, their lush tropical colours illuminated in the candlelight. It looked as if he were kneeling before some sort of shrine or altar. Perhaps he was praying or meditating, thought Laura.

Watching him, Laura had the strange feeling that she already knew him, but she could not be sure. So many details of her life had become hazy.

'What happened? Where am I?' she finally mustered the strength to ask.

The shadowy figure fell silent and turned towards her.

'I found you in the river. You are lucky to be alive. Now you must rest and recover.'

He turned back towards the altar.

The underground river system Laura had dived into the night before actually emerged above ground level less than a quarter of a mile away from where she had fallen unconscious, when her head had struck a rock in the underwater passageway. The river emerged as a small waterfall half way up a low limestone cliff beneath which was a plunge pool frequently used as a fresh-water spring by the local villagers. It was here that this small shadowy figure had found Laura floating face up, unconscious but still breathing, before dragging her into the cave to recover.

'What happened to my arm?'

'They shot at you. The wound is not deep. It will heal.'

It made no sense to her. Her mind was blank, unable to recall the events he described. She seemed to have no memory at all. 'Who shot me?'

The man rose wearily, with the air of someone who carried the weight of the world upon his jaguar-pelted shoulders. 'As the ancient city is suddenly full of mercenaries, I assume it was one of them.'

Then, handing her a white cotton shift, he informed her, 'Your clothes are still drying outside. Put this on.' He turned away while she began to pull it on. As she did so, she examined the area of her arm that had been wounded the night before and found it had been dressed and bandaged.

'You sorted my arm out. Thank you.'

There was something familiar about this stranger, an inescapable sense that their paths had already crossed. Never before had she seen a Mayan man dressed in such a ceremonial style and yet he spoke English as if he had used the language a great deal. This was unusual amongst those who still embraced traditional ways.

'I'm sure I've met you somewhere before,' said Laura.

He did not answer her, but instead began scraping seeds from a pod on a smooth rock that served very well as a table, its surface a clutter of pots and bowls, bottles of liquid, bunches of plants, bark and seeds.

Suddenly Laura recognised him. 'That's it!' She struggled to sit up, trying to ignore the pain in her arm. 'You were at the airstrip. You asked me about Ron.' She recalled the drenched figure that had appeared mysteriously from the rainforest when she had first arrived. 'Dr Brown said you are a shaman.'

He looked up sharply. 'Nobody calls me that.'

'Why not?'

He returned his attention to the seeds. 'I am simply a healer. No more than that.'

He put the seeds into a bowl of liquid. 'My name is Hunab Ku,' he said without looking up.

'I'm Laura Shepherd, an archaeologist from the Smithton Geographic.'

He placed some charcoal into a shell, reached for a candle and lit the charcoal.

'…What's wrong with being called a shaman?'

Laura knew that shamans had an important role to play in the culture of both the ancient and contemporary Maya. They traditionally combined the roles of both priest and healer. Shamans were regarded as being in possession of special sacred knowledge and, as far as Laura was aware, they had always been deeply respected by their fellow tribes-people.

Hunab Ku sighed. 'Nobody wants to be a shaman any more.'

He took a handful of dark resin crystals and shook them onto the coals.

'To be a shaman is to walk between this world and the next. It means to travel to the edge of everything you know, and when you stand at the edge of reality you see things that other people can't, and that can be hard to live with.'

The dark coals of charcoal began to flare red with heat.

'Where you come from many of those we would call shamans are labeled as mad, and are locked up.' He blew on the coals.

As Laura watched him, it all started to come back to her, what had happened. The events that had led her here began to clarify in her mind. For this was the same man who'd asked her about her colleague Ron Smith and had been devastated at the news of his demise.

'So Dr Ron Smith was a friend of yours?' she asked.

'No. I never met him.'

This puzzled Laura. *Why wasn't he telling the truth about Ron?* He had responded to the news of Ron's death only as you would expect a friend to react. Laura had hoped this man might have been able to help her piece together the role Ron had played in the events with which she had become involved.

'But you were so upset at the news of his death.' Something else the shaman had said at the jungle airstrip also bothered her. 'And when you asked me about Ron Smith you said that without him, there was no hope for any of us. What did you mean? I don't understand.'

The Mayan man's eyes held hers in a piercing glare.

'Did you not read the prophecy stone?'

Suddenly, the floodgates of Laura's mind opened completely. *Of course, the horrendous prophecy stone, with its terrifying prediction about the future. How could I forget?*

'Oh my God, yes! The children of the future... They're all going to die. We've got to do something. We've got to save them!'

The full urgency of her mission returned to Laura as the fog that had engulfed her consciousness suddenly dissipated. She tried to get up.

'What are you doing?' the Mayan shaman glared at her.

'I need to find out what's going to happen.'

'Only the ones on the other side know that.' Incense billowed in front of Hunab Ku and for a moment his face was obscured from her vision.

But Laura had no time to wait around for someone who spoke in riddles. She struggled to get up again.

'I need to get back inside that pyramid and see if there are any more hieroglyphs.' The urgency sounded in her voice.

'You can never go back there,' the shaman said firmly, 'The place is crawling with soldiers, all looking for you.'

'But something terrible is going to happen, and I need to find out what.'

It was only then that she realised she did not have the crystal skull with her. She knew that without it she would not be able to translate any more hieroglyphs, but she hadn't seen it since she nearly drowned in the underground river.

'Oh my God! Where is it?'

She started panicking, looking around desperately for her precious crystal skull.

'Is this what you're looking for?'

Hunab Ku stepped aside to reveal the crystal skull gleaming on the altar, sat on a blood-red cloth and lit by the flickering light of more than fifty candles. It glinted and gleaned, and seemed almost to grin before her. It was surrounded by small earthenware bowls each filled with a different substance; salt, copper, chocolate, crystals of copal. Laura presumed these were offerings to the spirits and the ancestors. She had seen such scenes painted on the fire-red terracotta pots produced by the ancient Maya.

Alongside the crystal skull, the hollowed eyes of real skulls gazed back at her, surrounded by flowers. This object that had so filled her with fear now looked magnificent, with a beauty so rare and fragile it almost took her breath away. It appeared almost as if it were shining with a bright and luminous inner light in the darkened recess of the cave.

'I found it in the river, near you,' Hunab Ku explained.

'Thank God!' cried Laura, as she staggered over to it. Never before had she been so pleased to see the crystal skull.

Yet as she bent down to pick it up she paused. Though she needed the skull to translate the hieroglyphs, it seemed almost sacrilegious to take it from this place. She felt an overwhelming sense that this was where it belonged. Not in some museum, locked inside a glass case, to be viewed only with academic detachment or cool, professional interest. Or worse still, subject to the giggles of schoolchildren, the object purely of spectacle and horror. It was here that such an object belonged, deep within this dark container of the earth, in this place where it was treasured and revered.

And as Laura lifted it from the altar she felt as if a spell had been broken, as if some deep and magical process had been interrupted or cut short.

The skull weighed heavy in Laura's arms as she staggered towards the cave exit. Each step was a trial to her. Outside, the great expanse of night sky beckoned her to leave the confines of the cave and continue her journey, her quest to find the answers, but her body resisted. Slumping back against the cave entrance, she waited breathlessly for her energy to return.

There was a small clearing outside the cave, in the centre of which was a pile of ashes, a place where fires were burned. Dark forest surrounded the cave, more than that she could not see.

The skull pressed down on Laura's lap, heavy as a rock. There was no strength left in her and there was no way that she could make it back to the pyramid in her current condition. Her hands were barely able to contain the skull. She could feel it beginning to slip through her fingers.

'You realise the answers you seek are not inside that pyramid?' The shaman said softly.

She looked up in surprise. She had not realized he had left the cave, but there he was, standing by her side.

'All that is written on that stone, came first from this skull.' He gently lifted the crystal skull from her.

Laura was puzzled. 'What do you mean?'

'To your people this is just an object, but for my people this skull is many, many things. You cannot even begin to understand how important it is to us.'

He took the skull back into the cave, placed it on the altar and dropped down to his knees in front of it. He closed his eyes, and began chanting again in Mayan.

The reverential atmosphere made Laura feel awkward, as if she were intruding on a private moment. She didn't know what to do. There was no way that she could make it back to Luvantum, but she was desperate to know more about the terrible prophecy she had just read on the hieroglyph stone doorway and its connection with the crystal skull.

What did the shaman mean when he said that the information on the prophecy stone came first from the crystal skull? How could that be? She wanted to ask him, but now didn't seem like an appropriate moment to do so. So instead she sank down onto the hard stone floor before the altar and waited.

It seemed her instincts had been right on first meeting this man, when she had been torn between pursuing him into the jungle and her equally strong desire to find the prophecy stone. It seemed he had knowledge that she urgently needed. Someone at last who might be able to help her get to the bottom of this mystery of the hieroglyphs, their message, and what could be done about them.

But why was he being so cryptic, and why had he said there was no hope without Ron? What did he mean?

Stone skulls, hewn in weathered limestone, looked down on Laura from the ceiling. Clouds of incense curled, snake-like, up from the floor. Oblivious to her presence, the shaman sat motionless before the altar. Laura couldn't wait for him to stop whispering and praying.

In the candlelight, the shaman's face looked pebble smooth, the creases, his careworn expression gone, transported into a silent reverie of peace, he began chanting,

'Oxlahun baktun, mi katun, mi tun, mi kin.' He repeated the words over and over, louder and louder, until they echoed around the chamber, as if he no longer chanted alone but in unison, united with a thousand other voices.

Outside, daylight began to fade. In the distance came the intermittent roar of the howler monkey, the chatter of a thousand animal voices, and soon night-time was upon them. Still Laura waited, as thirst gripped her throat and tiredness clawed at her limbs.

Eventually, Hunab Ku got up and lit a small lamp. He hesitated in front of the rock that served as a table before picking up a bottle of whisky and exiting the cave. Laura followed him as he walked across to a pool of water hidden amidst some nearby rocks. The waters gleamed black and gold in the lamplight as he set down the lantern. He scooped some water up into a bowl and drank it. He turned to Laura and offered her a drink. She drank the cool, fresh liquid down as if her life depended on it. The shaman turned to look at the stars twinkling above his head in the broad swathe of the Milky Way, before Laura broke the silence.

'What is it you keep chanting?'

'I am praying for assistance from the spirits and ancestors' he said, 'We will need their help on a particular day in the not too distant future.'

'Of course, that's it!' Laura had a sudden realisation, 'You've been chanting a day name, a date. It's the day 'Oxlahun baktun, mi katun, mi tun, mi kin' in the ancient Mayan calendar. It's the day 'thirteen baktuns, zero katuns, zero tuns and zero kins', in the Long Count. The day thirteen, zero, zero, zero, zero. It translates into our calendar as 21st December 2012 – only five days away.'

'You know your Venus Long Count dates. I am impressed.'

'Now it makes sense, now I understand what you've been chanting.' Laura was excited by her breakthrough in understanding. 'So what's going to happen then?'

'That is sacred knowledge,' replied the shaman, 'That is not something we discuss with anyone who happens to be passing.' He looked at her coolly.

'Look, it's not as if I'm here by accident.' Laura asserted herself. 'I'm here because I came to read the prophecy stone. I'm here because the crystal skull guided me here. I know that something terrible is going to happen in less than one week's time. I know that all the children of the future are going to die, and I need to know how. I need to know so that I can try to save them.'

'It is not just the children,' replied the shaman solemnly, 'To the ancient ones who carved that stone, we are all 'the children of the future'. We are all going to die in only five days' time, and nobody can save us.'

'Why? What's going to happen?' asked Laura.

'As I said, only the ones on the other side know that,' he replied cryptically.

'What do you mean?'

'You would not understand even if I were to tell you.'

Laura felt strangely reminded of Anna Crockett-Burrows' words when she had first gone to see her.

She tried another tack.

'Then tell me about the skull. What did you mean when you said that everything that is written on that stone came first from this skull?'

'Then you have not heard the legend of the crystal skulls?'

'Would I be asking you if I had?' answered Laura.

The Mayan shaman looked straight at her, starlight reflected in his dark eyes. 'Much of our wisdom has been hidden in legends. There are some truths that are too powerful for most people to understand and these truths have to be protected. That is why they are disguised as legends, so that only those who seek will truly hear.'

'So what does the legend of the crystal skull say?'

The shaman turned and took some small logs from a storage pile beside the cave entrance. He kneeled to lay a fire and lit it. As the fire crackled into life, he sat down on a large log beside it.

'I have never spoken to anyone outside my tribe about the crystal skulls before,' he commented.

'You mean there is more than one of them?' asked Laura, sitting down beside him.

Hunab Ku drew a deep breath. Fixing his eyes on Laura, he began to speak.

Chapter 63

'According to the legends of my people there exist thirteen skulls, the same size and shape as human skulls, but made of solid crystal. Sometimes my people call them the talking or singing skulls. These skulls were said to have been gifted to our earliest ancestors, way back in the mists of time. They are said to be a source of great knowledge, wisdom and power. It is said that if one knows how to use them, how to access their secrets, they can allow you to see deep into the past, and predict the future.'

Laura listened enrapt.

'The legend also prophesied that one day, at a time of great crisis for humanity, all of these crystal skulls would be rediscovered, for the knowledge and wisdom they contain is vital to the very survival of the human race. '

'But the legend also warned that mankind must first be suitably prepared, sufficiently evolved both morally and spiritually, because in the wrong hands the power of the skulls can be greatly abused.'

'So there is more than one of them?'

'According to the legend yes, but my people were entrusted with this one. The one the woman named Anna Crockett-Burrows found.'

'So you know about Anna?'

'Of course,' he replied as if it should have been obvious to Laura.

'So what did you mean when you said that everything that is written on the prophecy stone came first from the crystal skull?'

The shaman stared deeply into the burning embers, as he began to roll the crystal skull around in his hands.

'This skull is one of the talking skulls of legend. It first appeared to my people a long, long time ago. You see all the skulls inside the cave there?'

Laura remembered the row upon row of real human skulls lined up in the recesses all around the cave.

'...That is how many generations have passed since my ancestors first found this crystal skull. And ever since then my ancestors have been the guardians of the skull, and they have kept it secret now from the outside world for centuries.'

'Why all the secrecy?' asked Laura.

'Because all those many years ago,' replied the shaman, 'the wise ones amongst us learned how to go inside the skull and unlock its secrets. They learned how to go inside it and talk with the dead. The skull spoke to them. It gave them a message from those on the other side. It gave them the prophecy, which they carved in stone as a warning to the people of today. It spoke of a time of great crisis for all of humanity. It spoke of a world gone mad, of a world without hope, where the fires of destruction would reign.'

The flames the shaman was looking at so intensely began to spit and crackle as if they were punctuating his words.

'You mean December 21st 2012?' asked Laura.

'It is that day.' He nodded. 'That is when the crisis will reach its climax.'

Grave faced, he continued. 'But really this time of great crisis has already begun.'

Laura did not understand.

'You see, the problem really began up here.' He patted his own skull. 'It began with a way of thinking that started a long time ago. It is a way of thinking that your ancestors first brought to these shores over five hundred years ago. When the European conquerors arrived in this world this began a very dark time for all the native peoples of this Earth, a time known to my people as the Vale of Tears.'

'This is a time which the prophecy said would last over five hundred years. It is a time when the thinking of the people of this Earth has been dominated by what my ancestors called 'the mind of separation'.'

Laura was intrigued.

'The European conquerors brought with them not only trinkets and treasures from your world, they brought also disease and destruction, for they brought with them greed. They spoke of God as they wielded the sword, because it wasn't God they were really interested in but gold.'

'You see, there was a problem with the way these people thought. They brought with them this wrong way of thinking about the world and their place in it. They brought with them what my people call 'the mind of separation', a way of thinking where each person sees themselves as separate from everyone else and everything else around them. And now most people in the world think this way too. And because of this wrong way of thinking we behave now in ways which threaten all life on this Earth'

'Back then they thought we were stupid because we chose to live close to the land, as our ancestors in their wisdom had taught us. We chose to live simply, taking care of our children and taking care of our Mother, the Earth, who feeds and clothes us all. And we kept going through centuries of torture, through the destruction of our homes, our beliefs, and even our own families as many of them 'disappeared' at the hands of the military, only to end their days in mass graves, some here as recently as 1993.'

'We thought they had taken everything, over five hundred years ago, but now they have come again to take away the forests themselves. They have come to take away our friends the trees, 'the standing people' who have provided us with food and shelter and even the air we have breathed since the beginning of life itself. They have come now to rape and plunder the land for money, for timber mostly to rot in their back gardens, or grow food to feed their cattle, and to suck out the dark lifeblood from the earth's veins, for fuel to feed their cars and aeroplanes. They have come now to destroy this whole planet simply to fill all our lives with things we don't need.'

'You see, it is our whole way of thinking now that is wrong. We no longer see the sacred connection between ourselves and all other beings. The sacred bond between us has been broken. We have forgotten, as my people say, that we are all brothers and sisters, we are them, and they are us. And they have forgotten that when they destroy us and our homes, when they destroy the forests, they also destroy themselves, they destroy the very air that we breathe, for we are all one being.'

'This is why my ancestors said it would all end in 2012. Because the sacred balance of the earth has been broken and we now face nothing but the fires of destruction, which will rein down on us soon for all the ways that the people of this planet have not respected our Mother, the Earth.'

Chapter 64

Laura was speechless; momentarily unable to take in the gravity of his words, unable to comprehend that our everyday way of thinking and living could effectively be threatening the future of all life on Earth. The idea chilled her to the core. She felt numb with shock.

She stared at the crystal skull as the enormity of what she had just been told began to sink in. It felt to her that her whole world had just been blown apart, as if everything she had ever learned or believed had been suddenly and mercilessly ripped away from her.

Her mind began to race through all the possible ways the world might end. Perhaps it might end because of some huge celestial event, some dangerous planetary alignment, or some comet or meteorite that threatened to impact the Earth, something that would appear suddenly and about which we could do nothing.

Or was it possible that the earth might flip on its axis, irreversibly and suddenly altering the climate all across the globe? Perhaps 21st December marked the beginning of a whole series of devastating environmental catastrophes, earthquakes, tsunamis, tornadoes and hurricanes, ripping across the planet with such ferocity until not one single person remained.

And then of course there was the deadly nuclear arsenal that had been built up all over the globe in the name of defence. It now took only one trigger happy individual to plunge the citizens of the globe into a deadly nuclear holocaust that would destroy all life on Earth. All the myriad of life on our planet, the trees, the plants, the animals, the fish in the rivers and seas, all scorched to ash, all destroyed. It was a terrible thought, depressing even beyond words.

There were so many different ways in which the world might end. But what seemed most shocking about what the shaman was saying was the idea that the threat to humanity had come from humanity itself, from a simple corruption of our own way of thinking and behaving. But surely our 'way of thinking' wasn't really so bad, Laura wondered.

'What makes you say this problem began in my world?'

'It is to do with this wrong way of thinking that my ancestors have called 'the mind of separation'' the shaman replied. 'Believe me. I have seen it for myself. New Mexico, Los Angeles and New York; I have lived in them all. Many of my people have to go there for work. Wetbacks you call us. I went as part of my training, to help me to understand 'the mind of the West', so that I would know it for myself.'

'Whereas in my world I was the spiritual leader of my people, in your world I was nothing, nobody. I spent many years in your world and I got to know 'the mind of separation' very well, the loneliness, the isolation. I got to know it so well, it almost killed me. Like many others it led me to this stuff,' he said holding up the bottle of whisky, 'almost finished me off'.

'Like many of your people, I worked so hard for many, many years for such little reward.' He shook his head. 'Offices, shops, businesses, I cleaned them all. Some people saw me as little more than dirt as I scrubbed their floors and made their toilets clean. My job was to clean up the mess. And, believe me, it got to me to see what a mess your world was in.'

'So many people in your world have lost all sense of connection with each other, with their fellow human beings, with the animals and plants, and all of nature, and for many, even any sense of connection with their own families.'

''The world of separation,' is what my ancestors called it. They said there would come a time when people would forget their connection with each other, and with all the other creatures on this earth. That there would come a time when people would no longer see the sacred threads that bind us all together as one.'

'The prophecy of the crystal skull said that one day mankind would forget his connection with all other beings on this Earth. It said that when that happened, all the children of the future would die.'

The shaman lifted the bottle of whisky to his lips and took a swig.

As Laura stared at the fire, in that dark night, she felt with every bone in her body that what the shaman said was true. She realised that the world she lived in had somehow evolved into a way of being that was no longer healthy, a way of living that had lost its bearing, its direction, and its focus. She lived in world that had lost all sense of what was right and what was wrong. She realised that we as a society had somehow lost our connection not only with each other, but also with the sacred, with the reverent, with the holy, with the overall life force that surely existed in all things.

As the shaman said, we had lost our sense of ourselves as part of a sacred web of life that included all other people and beings on the planet. The way we now lived our lives, our disregard for the sacred balance of life, meant that a threat to the wellbeing of the planet was imminent, it was no longer a question of whether life on this earth would end, it was now simply a question of when.

And the prophesy stone had answered that question. The date had been set, December 21st 2012, now only five day's away.

So it was our own thinking that had led to the problems we faced, thought Laura. Whether it was the gold our ancestors craved or the other symbols of wealth that we sought today, big money, big houses, big cars. It was this that had upset the sacred balance of life, had cut us off from an awareness of all things and their connections to each other and to us. It was a problem with our consciousness, with our minds that had manifest in our world. Our minds had become polluted with at worst greed, and at best ignorance and it was this that was destroying our world, and what destroyed our world, destroyed us in the process.

Laura found herself wondering whether even if she were able to stop the events that were about to unfold, the deep and terrible malaise that had occupied the consciousness of humankind meant that it would not be long before another threat appeared to annihilate the human species.

No wonder the shaman in his despair had turned to drink. What else could be done?

A hopeless-ness came over Laura. A despair so heavy she was unable to move, as if the collective sins of the human race were crushing her. The sacred balance of the earth had been destroyed. It was a horrifying thought.

All those thousands of years of human endeavor, the cultural achievements of all those civilizations throughout history and across the globe, all architecture, all music and dance, poetry and drama, all science, all our grand theories and designs, and artworks of great beauty. They would all amount to nothing in the end.

And all of those people who had lived humble lives, quietly going about their own business, harming nobody and taking nothing of the earth's resources other than what they needed simply to stay alive. All of their lives, and those of their beautiful children and grandchildren, too would soon end.

What Laura now found extraordinary was that she had not realised any of this before. That she had been going about her everyday life, going to work, eating, drinking, being with Michael, without any awareness of the insidious threat that lurked behind the calm exterior of her existence, the devastation that stalked her, that threatened everything she knew.

It suddenly struck her as ironic that Michael had been so concerned recently for her safety. He had absolutely no idea of the horror that lay in store for us all. But now, if what the shaman said was true, she, her beloved Michael, and everyone she knew, would soon be no more.

She looked at the shaman. He was busy pressing the bottle of whisky to his lips. Had it really come to this? She couldn't stand it any longer. She couldn't bear the thought that she and the shaman were just sat around quietly discussing the end of the world, while he slowly tried to drink himself to death. The hopelessness was just too much for her.

'But we've got to do something to try to stop it,' she said, getting up with a start.

'It is too late,' the shaman replied. 'The prophecy said that the problem would occur in your world, but there would be little my people could do about it, unless we could find the one - the one from your world who could stop the terrible events that are now about to unfold.'

'Then there *is* hope!' exclaimed Laura. 'We just have to find that person.'

'I'm afraid not.' He shook his head. That one was Ron.'

'You mean Ron Smith?' Laura was mystified as the shaman took a crumpled letter from his leather pouch and passed it to her.

Chapter 65

Laura was deeply puzzled as she carefully opened up the letter and began to read it, intrigued. The letter said:

'Dear Hunab Ku, son of Hunab Ka,
As my eyes no longer work I am dictating this letter to you through my good friend Maria Castro who has been my loyal servant these last thirty years.

I am writing to you now as priestess of the Uxlahan Maya, keeper of the sacred skull. I have taken care of the skull in accordance with the teachings of the ancient ones that have been passed down through the lineage of your forefathers.

I believe I have honoured your ancestors' teachings and have now done all that was required of me, in accordance with the ancient legend and with all that has been detailed on the prophesy stone.

I was given the responsibility of taking care of the crystal skull until the time it would be needed to help repair, heal and restore the Earth, at the time when our Mother Earth would be in her greatest crisis.

I have followed the instructions given to me by your father to ensure that the skull would be connected with the one we have all been waiting for.

The task bestowed upon me was to keep the skull secret and safe until 'the time was right', until I was able to find the one who could save us, and now I have found him.

That one is Dr. Ron Smith, Mayan expert at the Smithton Geographic museum.

His initiation has already begun and he is very excited at the prospect of traveling to Guatemala to continue his training with you.

The time has come now for the skull to leave me. It can be no other way. My work at last is done. The task assigned to me this lifetime is complete, as I prepare now to join with the spirits and the ancestors once again.

Yours sincerely,
Signed Maria Castro
on behalf of Anna Crockett-Burrows.'

'It's from Anna Crockett-Burrows!' Laura said in amazement, looking back up at the Mayan shaman. 'I don't understand.'

'It was her job to find the one.' He replied in a matter-of-fact tone. 'That is why my father taught her and let her keep the skull. We waited all these years, waited for her to find him. But the years went by and we began to despair. We had not heard anything from Anna. We thought that perhaps she had taken ill, or died, or simply forgotten her mission.'

'That was the main reason I went to your world, to see if I could find her, to remind her of her life's purpose, the duty she had sworn to carry out; to find the one who could save us. But I could not find Anna, so I returned to these lands in deepest fear for the future.'

'And then only two week's ago, she wrote to say she had finally found him. She was going to send him here so I could teach him how to go inside the skull and talk with the dead. Anna, you see, could only just manage to do this herself, but she was not experienced enough to teach others to do this. That was to be my task.'

'But now he is dead all is lost.'

He crunched the letter up into a tight ball and threw it on the fire. Laura watched silently as it was consumed by the flames.

He stumbled back towards the cave, grabbed another bottle of whisky from his pile of things, and began to knock it back.

Laura was stunned and confused. She wondered if perhaps she had been hearing things. She found it hard to believe that the future of the world could possibly have depended on her colleague Ron Smith. The very notion that the future of the planet could really have rested on his small, unassuming and portly middle-aged shoulders seemed somehow preposterous. But the shaman was clearly devastated by the news of Ron's demise.

She recalled the moment when she had first watched the skull roll out of Ron's deadened fingers. She had been horrified. But she had no idea of the real horror with which the skull was connected, the momentous and terrible events that it would portend. She had no knowledge then of its significance in the history of our planet. Back then it had been purely an object of fear. How naïve she had been, how small her world had been.

She'd had no idea then of course that the fate of all humanity rested on that one human life, that one frail strand of nature, gossamer fine, like a seed carried by the winds of fate. It was positively terrifying to think the future of our whole species could possibly have rested on that one chance connection between Anna Crockett-Burrows and Ron Smith, ordinary, likeable Ron quietly going about his daily tasks, while our whole future depended on his survival. And now he was gone.

All those years Ron Smith had survived, had cheated death. All those years he and his wife had lived not knowing of the important task assigned to him, and then to die just before he had accomplished that task. It was all too tragic for words.

Laura began to wonder what had gone wrong. *Why had Ron Smith died when so much depended on him? Why had he not done what he was supposed to do? Had Ron perhaps tried to abuse the power of the skull? Was that why he was unable to complete his task? Or is it possible there was some foul play involved? Had someone somewhere not wanted Ron Smith to succeed?*

She turned to question Hunab Ku, but he was gone. The log he had sat on was no longer occupied. She looked around but there was no sign of him, he had vanished. She waited a few moments by the fireside, but he did not return, before she wandered back into the cave.

There, by the light of the candles, she found him. He had changed into a pair of old jeans and a T-shirt which read 'I love Guatemala'. On his feet he wore a pair of trainers that had seen better days. He was rummaging clumsily amongst the bottles and potions on his makeshift table. A glass jar fell over, the liquid it had contained dripped onto the floor.

'What are you doing?' she asked.

'What can I do? Ron is dead!' He was busy fumbling around looking for another drink. He found a small bottle of cane liquor, 'This I kept for the spirits,' he said holding the bottle up. 'But they won't be needing it any more'. He began to knock it back.

'But we've got to do something to avert this catastrophe.' Laura's voice was edged with desperation.

'It is too late. All is lost.' His tone was hopeless, as he took another swig. 'The end is now upon us.'

Laura was devastated. What was she going to do? She couldn't just sit around and let it happen. She wasn't going to see her precious Michael and everyone she knew just die without trying to do something about it.

She gazed at the crystal skull now sat back on the altar. The shaman had said that there was only one hope for humanity and that was the crystal skull. Only the crystal skull, with Ron's help, could save us all. If only she knew how.

She ran her fingers over the smooth crystal surface of the skull and as she did so slowly an idea began forming in her mind.

In a sudden flash of inspiration that cut through all the layers of fear that surrounded her, all the terror and despair she carried about the future, it became clear to her. If Ron was no longer there to play his part, to 'go inside the skull' and receive sacred knowledge from 'those on the other side', then maybe the shaman could do it. That was it. He had the expertise. He knew how to 'go inside the skull'. He knew how to 'talk with the spirits and the ancestors'. Surely he could do it. He just needed to be persuaded.

She turned to the shaman, with a determined look.

'Maybe you can do it? Maybe you can access the information? Maybe you can 'go inside the skull' and 'talk to those on the other side'. Maybe you can talk with the dead? If Ron isn't here to do it then maybe you can?'

'It is not to be,' replied the shaman, 'All night I have tried but the skull will not speak to me. The prophecy said, only the one who can stop it will be able to access this knowledge and now he's dead the future is set in stone.'

Laura was shocked. 'But that's what my daughter said. She gave me a message through the skull. That's why I'm here. That's why I came to read the stone.'

'Your daughter is dead?'

Laura nodded. 'I'm afraid I was unable to save her.'

She looked deep in thought, before she had another idea.

'But if only I could speak to her,' she continued, 'maybe she could help us.' Laura was beginning to sound quite desperate. 'Maybe she knows what's going to happen. You said you were going to teach Ron how to 'go inside the skull'. Well maybe now you can teach me?' she pleaded.

'It would be no use. Only Ron could have saved us.' The Mayan shaman picked up the skull and began wrapping it between two jaguar skins, just as the ancient Maya would have done. In this way they created what was called a 'sacred bundle', wrapping up their most precious objects for trans-portation. He made to leave the cave.

'Are you telling me my daughter's message was in vain?' Laura was staring to get angry with him, 'That even though I did listen the future is still 'set in stone'?'

The shaman just looked at her in silence

'Please! I may not have been able to save her, but maybe there's still time to save the other children.'

'There would be no point. The prophecy said only the one whose face was on the skull could save us.'

He tried to exit the cave with the skull, but Laura blocked his exit. 'Is that it? You know that something absolutely terrible is about to happen and yet you're prepared to just stand by and let it, without even trying to change things, just because you believe you can't.'

The shaman just walked straight past her and exited the cave.

She ran after him, shouting, 'That has to be one of the worst crimes a human being can commit. Sometimes we have to accept that we can't change things, but right now, we need to believe that we can.'

'Give me the skull!' She grabbed the sacred bundle from him. 'If you won't help me, I'll work out how to do it myself.'

Chapter 66

Outside the cave, the campfire had burned down low, and only embers remained. Laura sat down beside it and started to un-wrap the skull from its sacred bundle.

The shaman shook his head. 'I don't believe you have any idea what you're getting yourself into. Entering the skull can be very dangerous.'

'Well we're all going to die in five day's time in any case, so what have I got to lose?'

The shaman came and stood over her. 'Tell me. How did your friend Ron die?'

'Nobody knows. I just found him clutching the crystal skull.'

'It is as I feared,' said Hunab Ku, 'Ron tried to access the skull before he knew how, before he had been shown the proper way, and if you do the same you too will die. So if you want me to teach you,' he sat down beside her, 'you will have to listen, and listen carefully. For you will need to put your heart, your soul, the very essence of your being inside the skull, and if you do this the wrong way, you will never come back.'

'Like Ron?' asked Laura.

'Exactly!' the shaman nodded. 'He was not ready. He did not understand. It is not difficult to get inside the skull, but it is much harder to get back out again. For once you put your consciousness inside the skull, you will enter another world.'

'You mean like another planet?' Laura didn't understand quite what he meant.

'No. I mean another realm that exists alongside our own, an equally real but invisible world, a place where the souls of the departed live on. For this skull inhabits a place in this world and in the next. It dwells in the veil between the worlds. It is a doorway into another dimension, between the world of the living and the world of the dead'.

Laura was reminded of what Anna Crockett-Burrows had first said to her about the crystal skull what now seemed like a whole lifetime ago.

'Know what Ron did not,' cautioned the Mayan shaman, 'Once you enter that other world, for more than a few moments, you may find you want to stay there forever. For you will meet again with those who have gone before, and you may find that your love for them is so strong, that you forget your love for those in this world. Your desire to be with them can be so overwhelming, that it may draw your entire being right through to the other side, from which there can be no return.'

'So that's what happened to Ron, when he came back into contact with his wife Lillian.' Laura found herself thinking out loud. 'And that's why he seemed so happy the last few times I saw him, because he had found a way to be reunited with her inside the crystal skull'.

'That's right,' said Hunab Ku. 'His love for her was so strong that he forgot his love for this world. So before you go inside the skull you must remind yourself of your love for all other beings in this world.'

'What do you mean, my love for all other beings?'

She did not understand.

'It is far too dangerous to begin with the skull itself...' the shaman said as much to himself as to Laura. He looked around, got up and walked over to a nearby bush, plucked the bud of a frangipane flower from it, and returned to sit down again cross-legged by the fire. 'Watch!'

The Mayan shaman cupped the bud between the palm of his hands, closed his eyes, and an air of serene concentration slowly came across his face.

Just as Laura was beginning to think that he was simply meditating and that nothing was going to happen, he sighed with satisfied relief and opened his palms slowly. Laura was amazed to see that the bud in his palms had now opened into a beautiful pink frangipane flower in full bloom!

He looked her straight in the eye. 'Now you try!'

Laura wasn't sure quite where to begin, so he passed her another bud from the same bush. She copied all his actions. She sat cross-legged, closed her eyes and concentrated hard, for several minutes. But when she opened her palms the bud had not changed one little bit. In fact, looking down at it closely she wondered whether it might even have withered a bit, due to the heat of her hand.

'It is just as I thought,' said the shaman. 'You have forgotten your love for this world. You think you are separate from that little plant?'

Laura nodded.

'You think you are separate from everything around you, don't you?'

'Of course!' she replied.

'It is a common mistake made by people in your culture, but you are wrong,' he said firmly. 'You do not see that you and that bud are one.'

Laura looked at him puzzled. She had heard what he had said earlier about how everything was connected but still couldn't quite get her head around the idea in practice.

'Like so many today, you have forgotten that you are a part of all that is. This thinking is exactly what I meant when I told you about 'the mind of separation'. But before you put your consciousness, your soul inside the skull, you must remind yourself of your oneness with all other beings in this world. Though you can no longer see it, we are all, each and every one of us, connected by a thin thread that binds us.'

Laura wasn't sure she understood.

'More than this. All things are alive with the same spirit, with the sacred consciousness of creation.'

'What, even this lump of rock?' Her tone was skeptical as she indicated one of the stones that surrounded the fire-pit.

'I am not asking you to believe me. Your eyes are not yet open, but what I say is true. All things, however large or small, even what you call atoms, are alive with this same spirit. It is a powerful force. For it is love. And whether or not you believe it, it is this force that binds us all together and holds everything in this universe together as one.'

Laura still wasn't entirely convinced.

'And if you do not understand this before you go inside the skull,' he continued, 'then heaven help you, for you will never get out alive. If you go inside the skull thinking with this mind of separation, forgetting your connection to all that is here in this world, then your soul will be sucked right through to the other side, you will enter a coma, and in time you will die. Now try again!'

Laura closed her eyes and tried again. 'And this time really feel your love for this world, your oneness with the universe. Your love for that tree over there...' Suddenly there was a croaking sound. The shaman laughed, 'yes, even for that little creature.' It was the sound of a tree frog high up in the tree. 'Feel the warm glow of knowing that you are a part of everything around you. Now put the feeling into that little bud.'

Laura frowned.

'It is you and you are it. As my people say, 'I am another you, you are another me.' Now say that to the little plant in your hand.'

'I am another you...' Laura began.

'No. Not out loud.' The shaman interrupted her. 'Say it inside. Feel it here...' He touched her forehead gently, 'and here...' He placed the palm of his hand over her heart. 'Feel the love. We are all one being. What is in you is in everything. It is inside that tiny plant in your hand. It is inside each and every one of us.'

Laura tried several more times, while he talked her through it. But no matter how hard she tried she didn't seem to be getting anywhere. All night long she tried but she just couldn't seem to crack it.

Chapter 67

December 17th 2012

The first pale strands of dawn appeared, and golden sunlight began to illuminate the tops of the trees above Laura's head. She had to give it one more try; one last attempt. Cupping her hands and closing her eyes, she sat immobile. When she opened her palms two hours later the delicate petals of the flower in her hand had begun to stretch outwards very slightly, as the bud had finally half-bloomed in her hand.

'Am I ready?' she asked, eagerly showing the shaman the bloom.

The shaman looked at her gravely. 'You are no more ready than Ron Smith was. But we have no more time, it is now or never,' he said.

He led her back inside the safety of the cave, where she sat down cross-legged on the goatskin in front of the altar. He lit some incense and circled the smoldering mass around her.

'Is there anyone you want me to contact if you are not able to make it back?' he asked solemnly, whilst rummaging around on his table of herbs.

His words brought home to Laura the reality of the risk she was taking, the gravity of the situation she was in, by even so much as attempting to 'project her consciousness inside the skull'.

Finally locating an old worn down pencil and a scrap of scruffy paper, the shaman handed them to her.

'I would like you to contact my husband Michael.' She scribbled down her address and Michael's phone number.

Hunab Ku replaced each of the burned down candles on the altar with new ones. As she watched him remove the pools of hardened wax, she was almost tempted to tell him that on further consideration she had changed her mind. Trying to project her consciousness inside the skull was probably a bad idea. She wasn't properly trained and they had better just forget it. She couldn't bear the prospect of never seeing Michael again. The thought was unbearable.

Her hand reached up to touch the little silver heart-shaped locket she wore around her neck. What was she going to do?

The shaman had finished preparing the altar, it was ablaze with fresh candles and he was staring at her.

'Are you ready?' he asked.

The crystal skull gleamed on the altar before her. As she gazed at it she realized this was not an object of fear as she had first thought, but of hope. In this skull lay our salvation. For it had apparently been gifted to our ancestors in order to help us in our hour of greatest need. The idea was that the right person could somehow 'go inside it' and talk with the dead to find out how to save humanity from imminent destruction.

Admittedly she, Laura Shepherd, wasn't quite the right person. It was supposed to have been Ron Smith that was going inside it. But then whatever information Ron was going to get, it would have to be something he could actually do something about, otherwise what would have been the point in the Maya protecting the crystal skull all these years. So, Laura reckoned, if Ron could have got the information and averted imminent disaster, then why couldn't she? Besides which, there didn't appear to be any other options left. It was the only way to save the planet. She knew she had to do it, even if it cost her life.

'I am waiting for your answer,' the shaman asked and she realised she had been lost in her thoughts.

There was one thing she had to do first. She unfastened the heart-shaped locket she wore around her neck. 'If you ever meet Michael,' she said, 'Can you give him this and tell him that I will always love him.'

'I will tell him' said the shaman as he took the locket and folded it into his small leather purse. 'And don't forget, you must remember your connection with all beings on this earth' he added 'and if you do not do this before you go inside the skull, then you will never get out alive.'

A serpent of smoke rose up from the burning incense on the floor and began to curl around her.

'If you go inside the skull thinking you are separate from the rest of creation, then your soul will be sucked right through to the other side, you will enter a coma, and in time you will die.'

'And remember it is not really your body that is travelling inside the skull, although it may feel like all of you that is going in there. It is in fact only your consciousness, your mind, and your soul, that will travel inside the skull.'

'Now it is time,' he said, as Laura tried to make herself comfortable.

'We begin with the chant, so that the spirits know what we are asking of them, and on what date we will need their help.' Laura listened as he said the words softly in Mayan and then repeated them quietly to herself.

The shaman lifted the skull from the altar, passing it through the smoky incense, and gave it to her. Laura placed the skull in her lap and rested her hands on its cool surface while she repeated the chant,

'Oxlahun baktun, mi katun, mi tun, mi kin'.

These were the same words that she had heard in the museum that terrible night she had found Ron dead, slumped over his desk as the crystal skull rolled out of his hands. It was a sobering thought. Ron had gone where she was about to go and had not returned.

Still, even if she were about to meet the same deadly fate as Ron, she had to go on. There was too much at stake now to turn back.

She straightened her back, closed her eyes, and continued chanting.

Again and again, she repeated the sacred words. After a while she felt herself begin to relax and lose herself in the sound of the chant. On and on it went, until she was barely aware of the cave, the skull, the altar or the shaman.

He touched her gently on the shoulder.

'Now it is time for the most difficult task of all. In order to project your consciousness inside the skull you must now remind yourself of your love for someone on the other side, whilst still remembering your love for all those and everything in this world.'

The first part of the instruction was easy. For how could she ever forget Alice?

'You need to think of your daughter,' said the shaman. He saw the sadness on her face. 'I know it hurts, but if you can reach beyond the pain, you will find the love you felt for her, so much love; love that you still feel. Take your time.'

She thought of Alice. It took some effort to put the traumatic memory of Alice's last days out of her mind. But then she started to remember the good times. The trip they had made to the zoo on Alice's fourth Birthday. Alice had been enchanted with the monkeys. Laura remembered the strawberry ice cream she had dropped on the ground and the tears that had followed and the cuddle that helped to restore everything again. More memories came flooding back to her and with them a warm feeling, like a glow inside.

'Now you need to connect with her inside the skull,' said the shaman.

Eyes still closed, Laura took a deep breath. She then lifted the skull slowly up and placed it gently against her forehead, trying hard also to remember her connection with everything around her.

Suddenly, it felt as if her head was smashing against the skull. She wanted to pull the skull way from her, to wrench it off, and throw it to the ground, but a huge force seemed to be propelling her against it, so strongly that she was completely unable to resist its pull. Her head felt as if it were crashing into a solid wall and at the same time there was an intense ringing in her ears, so loud that it seemed to reverberate throughout her whole body.

The noise was unbearable. She wanted to scream. It seemed inconceivable that she might survive it. She realised she wasn't going to make it, whatever had gone wrong for Ron was going wrong for her too. Perhaps the shaman was right. She had still not been trained properly and now she faced a nightmare death. Any moment her skull would explode with the force, any moment the bone would be crushed or shattered into a million pieces.

I've reached the end. This is it. I must be dying. It felt as if her skull simply could not take any more of the pressure to which it was being subjected. Then an incredible blank-ness overtook her mind, as a steady darkness obliterated all her thoughts.

Suddenly there came the oddest of sensations. There was water all around her. As if she had landed from a great dive into a very large pool of dark water. One minute her head had been pressing hard against the crystal skull and now, all of a sudden she was lying spread-eagled, face down, in what felt like warm water.

What's happening to me? Am I still in the watercourse that runs under Luvantum? Did I die back then in that underground river system? Am I dying now?

She held her breath. She desperately, urgently, needed air. Trying to breathe, she tried swimming up to the surface, but her head bashed into something. There was no way of getting out of the water. Her lungs were bursting. She could hold on no longer, she had to breathe in. The end she feared was upon her, there was no choice but to inhale. Anticipating the burning sensation that came when water was inhaled, she drew a breath and waited, waited for the moment when her beating heart would beat no longer.

But it never came. It didn't happen. She was underwater, but was entirely able to breathe. The relief was delightful, as she drew in one breath after another.

Laughing, she opened her eyes again and suddenly found herself floating around in an ocean of iridescent blue, swimming and breathing underwater like a fish. It was as if one minute Laura had been outside the skull looking in to its glassy, watery-looking interior, and the next thing she knew she was actually inside it looking back out, as if she were suddenly inside some huge glass-walled pool. It was as if one minute she were a giant holding the skull in her hands, and the next moment she was tiny, floating around inside the huge skull, almost as if she were suddenly floating around inside some sort of enormous gold-fish bowl.

She realised she had finally succeeded in 'projecting her consciousness inside the skull'.

Outside the skull, through its exterior walls that looked like thickly distorting glass, she was sure she could see her body collapsing into a heap on the floor in front of the altar. She could see, as if in a dream, the shaman pick up the skull and place it back on the altar, while her body lay there in a heap on the floor. But she didn't care.

Here inside the skull it was like another world, a beautiful world, filled with radiant light, like some strange kind of cross between a tropical underwater paradise and outer-space. Thousands of beautiful crystal bubbles surrounded her, shimmering blue, silver and gold. She reached out to touch them and found them soft and springy. She could squash them almost flat and then let them spring back into shape. Grabbing several of them, she could shape them into one big large bubble and then they would separate back out into individual bubbles again. It was fascinating and delightful, just like being a child again and discovering the world for the very first time; the joy of not knowing all the rules by which things work, and experimenting with the environment.

As she played with the bubbles, lining them up and juggling with them, she thought about how much Alice would have enjoyed playing with her like this.

Laura was just beginning to get used to this strange new environment, learning how to 'swim' around and play in it, when she noticed a long, dark tunnel inside the skull. It stretched into the distance. She was surprised she had not noticed it before. It was quite awesome to behold, like some of the beautiful photos of distant star clusters and galaxies taken by the Hubble space telescope. It was big enough to 'swim' down and looked as though it might stretch on for all infinity. It looked as one might perhaps imagine a tunnel through time and space.

Laura swam just inside the tunnel entrance. Its walls had a soft, fluid look to them as if perhaps they had been painted in multi-coloured water paint. Laura wanted to touch the walls but when she 'swam' towards them, she was unable to reach them. They receded from her touch. No matter how hard she tried, they were constantly beyond her reach, like the end of a rainbow.

She noticed that the far end of the tunnel was illuminated by a soft light. She 'stood' for a moment transfixed by the way it shone through the darkness, seeming almost to ripple gently across the walls of the tunnel towards her. In some way she could not define, it felt as if the light was calling her towards it.

She began to swim down the tunnel, as the light beckoned her ever on. As she got nearer, the intensity of the light increased. And as she got further into the tunnel, she seemed to travel faster, accelerating towards the light as it glowed before her. Then, as she drew nearer towards the end, she began to slow down as she approached closer and closer to the light that was pure, bright and strong.

As she came to a halt at the end of the tunnel, she realised there was something between her and the light, like some sort of doorway made out of frosted glass, or perhaps it was pure quartz? Its beauty was breathtaking. Contained within it were layers of sumptuous colour, soft rainbow coloured light, shot through with fine threads of silver and gold. The colours appeared to be naturally occurring and were woven into the very fabric of the crystal, forming combinations of light and texture so magnif-icent she felt she could have stayed there forever, totally absorbed just looking at them.

As she raised her eyes again and looked through the door, she felt as if her heart would burst at the sheer beauty that lay before her. She felt as if she was standing on the very edge of infinity, with an inconceivably vast space immediately beyond. There was darkness and there was light. She had the sensation of floating above the clouds, and she could see more clouds of white and all the different colours floating in the distance. She felt as if she were looking at the whole universe, at a hundred thousand stars that had all exploded sending forth a blaze of light and colour in every direction.

Although she didn't know it, Laura was in fact looking through the doorway between the different dimensions, standing in front of the thin veil that separates the worlds, standing at the very threshold between life and death.

And just as she was thinking that nothing could be more amazing than what she was looking at now, she caught sight of something that lay ahead of her beyond the doorway, something that dazzled her, that took her breath away. It was the most incredible light she had ever seen, a shimmering orb of golden-white light, mesmerizing and enchanting. So beautiful, so stunning, she began to wonder if perhaps she was gazing upon an Angel.

But as she watched a small figure emerge from the centre of this shimmering golden orb, her heart missed a beat. She realised she was mistaken. For this was no unknown angelic stranger. It was in fact something far more incredible. And this time she knew she had not got it wrong. For the figure she saw emerging from, and backlit by, this iridescent golden-white light was in fact Alice. She had finally found her beautiful little girl.

She recognised her big blue eyes, her straw blonde hair, even the tiny birth mark above her happily smiling lips. This was her precious baby, her beloved daughter, the radiant, transcendent, glorious light that was her lost child.

Laura's heart wanted to sing with joy as she gazed upon this most beautiful of all sights.

'Alice,' she whispered.

Tears formed in Laura's eyes and one of them fell onto the crystal surface beneath her. As it did so, strange and beautiful music echoed all around her. Another tear fell, and another, and with each tear came the same beautiful sound.

Laura realised she had been waiting for this moment for what seemed like a lifetime. Without conscious awareness, she had been waiting for the years, hours, minutes and seconds to pass until Time could bring her to this place.

She realised there had been a constant yearning within her, buried deep like a seed that lay dormant, curled within her as if sleeping, waiting for the spring. It was a seed that now watered, stretched up and grew out of the darkness, unfurled and bloomed. It was a desperate longing she could no longer deny, a longing to be with her daughter once again, to embrace her, to hold her tenderly in her arms. She wanted to join with the light and lose herself in the joy of finding her again.

Compelled to get her, she tried to move forwards, calling out:

'Alice!'

This time Alice heard her, and turned towards Laura with a big grin. She held her arms out towards her as if waiting for a hug, and cried:

'Mummy!'

At that moment, a loud click, harsh and mechanical, entered Laura's awareness; a sound that had no place amidst such beauty and magnificence. It was a noise, ugly and brutal, that crashed into, collided with all that she saw and felt and reverberated with a hideous, soul freezing intensity. In an instant, before she understood what was happening, she was wrenched backwards at tremendous speed. She was dragged, twisting and contorting, back into the dark tunnel as if pulled by a mighty tornado. Even the flesh on her face puckered away from her skull under the strength of the force that now sucked her.

'No!' she screamed at the unrelenting, terrible and ferocious force as she was tossed and thrown back down the tunnel like a rag doll. Wrenched through the darkness, she was powerless to resist the force that dragged her, that tore her from this divine place. Her heart felt as if it were being torn in two, snapped in half like a twig in a hurricane. She felt broken with the excruciating agony of having to leave the light behind, of being dragged from such glory.

There was a pain in her forehead, a dull metallic pain, as if some object were boring into the surface of her skull. She opened her eyes to see the steel barrel of a gun, held against her temple. She was lying on the hard stone floor of Hunab Ku's cave, in front of the altar, exactly where she had been before she entered the crystal skull. A man had his knee against her shoulder; she could feel his crushing weight forcing her down against the ground.

Golden beads of incense lay scattered across the floor. The flowers from the altar lay strewn all around her, trampled and crushed. And an ancient human skull lay broken like an egg shell beside her.

She tried to get up.

'No Mueve!' ('Don't move') shouted the soldier.

She tried to turn her head, looking for the crystal skull, for the reassurance of its presence.

Suddenly she felt a searing pain as the barrel of the gun was smashed against her cheek.

'Move again, and I will kill you!' the man shouted at Laura in Spanish.

The soldiers, Caleb's men, had finally caught her.

Desperately, her eyes sought out the altar. It had been ransacked. There was no sign of Hunab Ku anywhere. And the crystal skull was gone.

Chapter 68

December 18th 2012

Caleb Price looked around the crowded conference hall. He felt a warm glow of satisfaction. His new eight thousand dollar suit was a little warm under the lights, but there was nothing he loved more than a crowd of his people, namely scientists, engineers and share-holders gathered to hear how his company was going to be making waves. How they were going to be hitting the big time.

'Imagine another world,' he began, 'so close you can almost touch it, only a hair's breadth away, and yet totally invisible. Now imagine that inside that world anything is possible, and everything you ever dreamed of could be yours.'

He stared out at the sea of grey suits and white lab-coats gathered before him in the plush, post-modern Millenium Conference Centre. The crowd was already in the palm of his hand.

'For millennia, this other world, this other dimension, remained solely the talk of psychics, mystics, sages, yes even lunatics. Then quantum physics suggested that some sort of parallel universe might just be possible. Well I am here now, as a scientist, to tell you that this other world, this other dimension, this parallel universe, call it what you will, it really does exist, and we here at Nanon Systems now hold the key to unlocking its secrets.'

'For I am here now to tell you about one of the greatest discoveries mankind has ever made, a discovery more profound than harnessing the forces of electro-magnetism, a discovery more powerful than the splitting of the atom. Hell, what I am about to tell you could make the splitting of the atom look like the invention of the firecracker! For I am here to tell you about something far, far more powerful. I am here to tell you that Space is no longer the final frontier. The final frontier now, my friends, is Time!'

Caleb's voice rose to a crescendo, echoing out across the vast auditorium. The crowd sat and listened enraptured.

'What we know about this other world, this other dimension is that Time and Space, as we know them, do not exist there. So we can break all the laws of physics that apply in our simple physical world. Without these old-fashioned restrictions of fixed time and space, all kinds of opportunities are opened up to us, including the possibility of Time Travel!'

'You see, without the limitations of fixed space and time, we could use this other dimension to travel, quite effortlessly, to other places, yes, even to other times in our universe. If only we knew how to access it.'

On a large screen behind him images appeared to illustrate his points.

'Quantum physicists have been searching for this doorway into the other dimension for decades. And as some of you already know, we here at Nanon systems have even built this special underground test facility,' he said as he pulled up an image of it onto the giant screen behind him, 'deep under the desert of New Mexico, specifically dedicated to finding a way to access this other world and unlock its secrets.'

'This Z-lab has been kept secret from the outside world for decades, whilst we have struggled to overcome the limitations of space and of time. Our quest has been to open up a 'wormhole', a doorway in the fabric of space-time. Because if we could open up a 'wormhole', a doorway between our dimension and this other world, we could use this parallel universe as a kind of 'time-tunnel'- a short cut to the future!'

'So far in the Z-lab we have tried all different kinds of techniques, from particle accelerators to gravitational densifiers. And we have tried all different kinds of materials, from tungsten to diamonds, to ultra-plastics.' He held up examples of these materials before throwing them down. 'But so far all our efforts have failed. None of these materials has proven suffi- ciently flexible to open up a space between its atoms whilst still maintaining strength enough to withstand the intense heat and pressure this process creates.'

'But now, we finally have the answer. Thanks to a chance finding by our new Head of Research, Dr. Michael Greenstone here,' Caleb indicated Michael sat on the stage alongside him, and Michael gave a slightly embar- rassed nod to the audience, 'we now have the right material for the task. We have finally found the key we need to unlock that doorway, we have finally found the key to unlock the secrets of the future!'

Caleb marched over to a plinth positioned in the centre of the stage and covered in a black velvet cloth. He pulled away the cloth to reveal the crystal skull - massive multiple images of which were simultaneously projected onto the giant screen behind him and onto several other monitor screens positioned around the vast conference hall, above the gasping heads of the horrified audience.

'Now this may not look to you or me like the technology of tomorrow but, believe it not, ladies and gentlemen, this crystal skull that you see before you, is actually a unique variable density portal. Dr Greenstone's brilliant research and equations have shown that, with enough electrical and laser energy applied, this crystal skull can actually open up a 'wormhole' - a doorway in the very fabric of time-space, that can allow us to access that elusive other dimension and enter the 'time-tunnel' that has been the Holy Grail of quantum physics for years.'

'And now is the time to test it - in our own dedicated test facility, the Z-lab.'

The audience were silent with awe.

'If this experiment works my good friends, just think of the possibilities; not only time travel, but cheap transportation and clean energy generation, not to mention various defense applications. The list of possibilities is almost limitless.'

'We could even use the skull to find out information from the future. Though if this experiment works you won't need a time-tunnel to tell you what your shares in this company are going to be worth even by this time next week!' Everyone in the audience laughed appreciatively.

'We could use the crystal skull to send materials backwards or forwards in time. Take nuclear waste, for example, problem solved! We could simply send it back, shall we say 65 Million years? Hell, the dinosaurs died out anyway didn't they?'

Everyone laughed again.

'But seriously,' continued Caleb, 'all the problems of the world, all the problems of the future, will become a thing of the past. For what you see here before you ladies and gentlemen,' he held the skull up high above his head for all to see, '*is* the future. Not just the future of Nanon Systems, but the future of humanity. It is ours now for the taking.'

'This is what we've been working towards for years, and I'd like to thank you all in advance for your help in making it a reality. For helping us here at Nanon Systems to 'Create the Future - Today!''. His speech reached its climax as he bellowed out the company's slogan.

There was a loud round of enthusiastic applause that rapidly turned into a standing ovation, as everyone in the auditorium rose to their feet, impressed.

In the foyer, after the speech, Caleb grabbed a glass of champagne as the waiters circulated with silver trays laden with drink. There was an excited buzz in the air as people talked about the skull and the possibilities it opened up.

Michael stood near the door wanting to leave; to go home and speak to nobody, but he knew he couldn't do that. He just wasn't in the mood for all this. It didn't help, not having Laura there by his side. The eminent Michael Greenstone and his wife; she should have been with him on such a momentous occasion, at such a high point, the very pinnacle of his career.

He had to speak to Caleb urgently. It was going to be difficult now that so many people were gathering round his boss, congratulating him.

Michael sighed, *What's wrong with me? I should be feeling great.* His work had never before been the point of such interest, such intense excitement. Here he was on the brink of accessing other worlds, something he and other scientists could only have dreamed of only days before. Here he was holding the key to a parallel universe, and yet he didn't feel like celebrating. Instead, he just felt anxious. It would be better when he'd spoken to Caleb.

'Hey. Michael! Come over here!' Caleb's voice boomed as he beckoned to Michael. Caleb had been joined by Sylvie, his latest girlfriend who was half-naked in a plunge-necked, split-sided red silk dress.

'Congratulations, master of the universe!' Sylvie enthused to Michael.

'Have a glass!' urged Caleb, slapping Michael on the back, as the waiter held out a tray of drinks before him.

'No, it's OK thanks!' replied Michael.

'Let your hair down a bit,' encouraged Caleb.

'I want to keep my head clear'

'Why's that?'

'I need to have a word with you about something, in private.'

'Not about your wife I hope,' whispered Caleb.

'No' said Michael. But before he had time to say more they were surrounded by well-wishers. The accolades continued for the rest of the evening and by the time it came to take the elevator down to the car park they had each shaken hundreds of congratulatory hands.

Michael didn't want to dent Caleb's ebullient mood but he knew it couldn't wait. He chose his moment carefully. When they were just reaching the underground car park, he reminded Caleb that he needed to ask him something. Reluctantly, Caleb asked Sylvie to go ahead and wait in the car so they could speak in private. Michael waited till the car door slammed shut. He glanced around nervously to double-check there was no one else around listening. He took a deep breath, knowing that Caleb wasn't going to be happy with what he had to say, but he knew it had to be said. He couldn't allow the situation to continue as it was. The sooner Caleb knew the better. It simply couldn't wait any longer.

'Caleb, because the crystal skull went er.. missing for a while, its put me a bit behind schedule and I think it's a little hasty to press ahead with the actual experiment, before I've had a chance to double-check my equations on the crystal skull itself, now that we've got it back in our possession.'

'Nonsense, Michael!' replied Caleb 'You worry too much. He slapped him on the shoulder. 'Let the guys further down the line do the double-checking. We've got a really tight deadline on this now.'

Caleb headed off to his car. He turned and called back to Michael 'Give yourself a break Michael. You've got more than enough to worry about in the form of your good lady wife.'

Maybe Caleb was right, thought Michael as he got into his car. Perhaps his concern for Laura and what now lay in store for her was making him worry too much about other things as well. Still, at least he and Caleb had worked out a plan to help her, although he wasn't sure that was how she would see it.

He'd booked an appointment to see her later that evening. He'd have to let her know then what they had in mind. He had a terrible feeling she wasn't going to like it, but it wasn't as though he had a lot of choice.

Chapter 69

The expression on Laura's face, as she stared at the grey wall of the police cell that surrounded her, was one of radiant joy. To her, there were no hard steel bars restraining her, no heavy sentence awaiting her, there was only profound peace. Her mind was totally occupied with what she had seen inside the skull, filled with the wonderful memory which she was now reliving.

She hugged her knees and smiled to herself. She couldn't wait until Michael got there and she could share the news with him, to let him in on her glorious secret; Alice was alive and well in the other world inside the skull, and more beautiful and radiant than he could ever imagine.

Michael entered the police precinct and glanced around uneasily. He waited in front of the beaten old wooden reception area, where a thin young policewoman, was having a long telephone conversation with a member of the public about police procedure. He stared at the row of faces on the hastily photocopied 'wanted poster' stuck to the front desk, half expecting Laura's face to appear. He was like a fish out of water. He had never seen a police cell before, or ever expected to see one, especially not to visit his own wife; the beautiful, and once eminent and professional Dr Shepherd, who was now no better than a common criminal. His cheeks burned with shame at the thought.

As he waited to be shown down to the cells, he wondered what had got into her. What had Laura been thinking, or maybe she hadn't been thinking at all. That was the problem, ever since she had come into contact with the skull she just hadn't been thinking straight. The stress of finding Ron dead was surely part of it. But it wasn't enough to explain why she seemed to have abandoned all reason. They had found her in a cave. He knew that much. One of the natives had the crystal skull rigged up on some sort of altar and he had been chanting and waving herbs around while Laura lay on the floor at his feet. God knows what they had been doing, it was all very weird.

But they had got her back that was the main thing. Caleb's friends in the military had managed to by-pass all the usual extradition procedures, but on arrival on US soil she had to be handed over to the authorities, and she was now under arrest in police custody, pending charges being brought against her for theft.

The humiliation of it all was almost unbearable to Michael, but he was grateful she was safe. At least she was back in one piece.

He glanced at his watch. He was on time for his appointment. The policewoman was still on the phone so it was a stocky middle aged cop with heavy bags under his eyes that led him down to the detention centre, situated at the rear of the building. They walked along the corridor, past rows of cells until the officer nodded towards the one occupied by Laura. The heavy metal security door echoed behind him, as the officer slammed and locked it, leaving Michael alone with his wife.

There she was, sitting on the low metal framed bed, hugging her knees. She was staring at the wall completely oblivious to the sounds of keys and the noise of the other prisoners. Michael was overwhelmed with relief at the sight of her, even though her face was bruised, streaked with dirt and her blonde hair was disheveled, it was still his Laura, the woman he loved, despite his anger at the way she had behaved.

Laura was smiling to herself, lost in some silent, private moment of reverie, when she noticed him. She leapt off the bed and rushed up to the bars of her cell.

'Michael, I'm so glad to see you!' He'd expected her to be crushed, defeated by all that had happened to her, but her face had a gentle softness to it and her eyes shone radiant with a joy he'd not expected to see - it threw him.

He greeted her less warmly. 'You had me worried sick, Laura. What the hell do you think you were doing?' he asked sternly. She was still smiling.

'I saw her, Michael. I saw her!'

'What are you talking about?' He'd expected her to be suffering from some kind of remorse or regret about what had happened. He realised that's what he had wanted; some sort of recognition that what she had done was out of order, an aberration. That it was quite plainly wrong to have stolen the skull and gone off with it the way she had. Yet here she was still in some cloud cuckoo land.

'The Mayan shaman, Hunab Ku, he showed me how to project my consciousness inside the skull and I saw her Michael' continued Laura.

She reached her hands through the bars to touch his. 'I saw Alice! She looked so beautiful.'

Michael shook his head in despair. 'Dear God Laura! What's happened to you?'

Laura didn't seem to notice the sound of the security door opening and closing as Michael looked away for a moment.

'You don't believe me, do you?' she said.

'I don't believe you have any idea how embarrassing this whole thing's been for *me*.' Laura looked quizzically at him. '...You, my wife, facing criminal charges for theft.' His hands were gripping the steel bars that stood between them.

'I'm sorry, Michael, but I had no choice... I had to find out Alice's message.'

'Jesus Laura!... This is hopeless.'

There was something odd about the way Michael was behaving, thought Laura. He'd turned his face away from her again, almost as if he were addressing someone else, off to one side, hidden from view of her cell. It was a little disconcerting, but she continued nonetheless.

'But I read the Prophecy Stone Michael. Something terrible's going to happen in only three days time and I need to find out what...'

'I just can't get through to you can I?' he said.

Her attempts to explain what had happened had fallen on deaf ears. Michael could not understand what she was saying.

'I need to see the skull again. I need to speak to Alice.'

'Just listen to yourself Laura! Do you have any idea how this sounds?' She paused, unnerved by the incomprehension and frustration in his voice. Michael was right in front of her, yet she felt further away from him than she had ever done before, as if they both suddenly occupied a different universe, a million light years from each other.

'Please, Michael. I need to see the skull', her fingers sought his, 'just one more time.'

He held firmly onto the bars.

'Do you seriously think you're going to be allowed anywhere near that thing, after what happened last time?'

A silence hung between them.

'I swear to you, Michael, this time I won't even touch it. I know it sounds crazy, but please, just trust me on this one.' Her eyes were imploring him, begging him to understand.

'Laura, you need help,' he said kindly.

'Exactly, you've got to get me the skull.'

'That's not the kind of help I mean.'

'So what do you mean?' She was puzzled.

'Look, it's possible that Caleb will agree to drop the charges.'

'That's great!'

'But there's one condition...'

She looked at him with a frown.

'...that you agree to undergo a full psychiatric evaluation and treatment at the Warnburton Secure Unit.'

'What!? That's ridiculous! There's nothing wrong with me!' Laura could scarcely believe what she was hearing.

'That's not how it looks from here,' said Michael turning to the side again.

Laura was stunned into silence.

'...I've spoken to a psychiatrist, his name's Dr Bacher, and he thinks that your ...'illusions' may be due to unresolved grief over Alice, brought on by finding Ron...'

'It was your idea wasn't it?' said Laura.

There was a pause.

'Look, it really is for the best,' Michael insisted. 'It's for your own good. I'm trying to help you.'

'Help me!? You're trying to incarcerate me!'

'Laura, we really don't have any choice. If you don't agree to this Caleb wants to put you in jail!'

'But I've got to find out what's going to happen. I've got to stop it!'

'In the Warnburton, they'll only keep you in for about three months or so.'

'Three months!' exclaimed Laura, 'We've only got three days!'

'With a prison sentence, you could be looking at a lot longer...' Michael trailed off as he saw the anger flare across her face.

'Just because I see things a bit differently from you, just because I've had my eyes opened, you think I've gone mad.' She was furious now, 'Wake up Michael - It's our world that's gone mad, not me! The children of the future, they're all going to die! And we've got to save them! You've got to get me out of here. I have to get back inside the skull!' Michael watched as she paced the cell, like a caged animal, 'I have to speak to Alice!' she shouted.

'See, this is exactly what I mean.' Michael was talking to someone who appeared to have been eavesdropping on their conversation from out of

Laura's sight, off to one side from her police cell. She looked puzzled as a small, balding, middle-aged man stepped forward into her line of vision. In his mid-fifties, he wore thick framed glasses and an ill-fitting but expensive suit over a dark red polo-neck jumper.

'Laura, this is Dr. Bacher,' said Michael, in a totally matter of fact tone.

Laura was horrified.

'Hi Laura!' said Dr Bacher enthusiastically.

'Dr Bacher is from the Warnburton Secure Unit,' he added.

'Michael, how could you do this to me?' She stared at him incredulous.

He stepped back away from Laura's cell, looking guilty.

'Michael, come back!' She called after him as he asked to be let out of the detention centre.

'Michael!' 'After all we've been through together.'

Then she noticed Dr Bacher. He was smiling at her inanely.

'Laura, we just need to have a little chat about how you've been doing,' he said. 'It sounds to me as though you may have been having some...how shall we say? ...unusual experiences.'

'Look, I'm perfectly normal. Leave me alone.'

'Laura. Is it normal to see things other people know aren't there?' he enquired.

Laura had had enough. It was bad enough being betrayed by the man she loved, but now here was this obsequious little man asking her stupid questions.

'Don't patronize me, you fool!' she shouted, enraged. She regretted it as soon as she'd said it, but it was too late.

Bacher stood silently for a moment as his jaw dropped. Then it closed resolutely.

'Very well!' His tone was one of menace. 'Let's play it your way.' He turned stiffly and stormed off out of the cells.

Chapter 70

December 19th 2012

The Warnburton Secure Unit was housed in an ugly, imposing neo-Victorian building on a barren island in the East River, overlooking a stretch of inner city water known, somewhat appropriately, as Hell Gate.

Laura had heard of this place. It was notorious for its use of ECT, otherwise known as electroconvulsive therapy, a controversial type of psychiatric treatment which had become popular during the 1950's. This type of 'therapy' involved tying a patient down with leather straps around their wrists and ankles, attaching electrodes to either side of their forehead, and then delivering a massive electric shock to their brain, a process usually accompanied by a series of involuntary convulsions or fits. 'A little shocking perhaps' Dr Bacher always liked to joke, but the technique appeared to be effective in treating a whole range of mental disorders, from extreme depression and anxiety to psychosis.

The treatment had however begun to fade a little in popularity when it transpired that the electric shocks had to be delivered regularly in order to be effective, often leaving the patients as little more than human vegetables in the process. Unwanted side-effects also included bone dislocation and fractures as well as heart seizures sometimes occurring during administration of the procedure. Indeed a number of studies showed that a significant number of patients had 'terminally negative results'. In other words, they either died or committed suicide during the course of treatment.

As a result, the technique was now used in most psychiatric institutions only as a treatment of last resort. Dr Bacher, Director of the Warnburton Secure Unit, however, remained a big fan of the procedure.

Though blindfolded and straight-jacketed on arrival at the unit, Laura still recognised the distinctive smell of hospital disinfectant, designed somewhat unsuccessfully to cover up the smell of patients' urine. Less familiar to her were the screams, yells and mad ranting of the other inmates as she was led past the wards and down the white corridor towards her cell.

'Here, this should help you calm down a bit,' said Dr Bacher, removing Laura's blindfold and holding her arm out for the large nurse now standing over her with a syringe. The nurse promptly plunged the needle beneath her skin and injected something that made her head swirl almost immediately. The two orderlies opened the door and deposited Laura somewhat unceremoniously into her new room before the door banged shut and locked behind her.

By the time the sedative had worn off she realised where she was. Laura's eyes wove their way along the neat squares of padding that, brick-like, made up the walls of her cell. There were no windows, nothing to show that any life existed beyond these four walls. She knew she should not have spoken her mind quite so vocally earlier, and now look where it had landed her. She glanced around at the thick, oppressive walls of the padded cell in which she now found herself trapped, and hoped Dr Bacher wasn't one to bear a grudge for too long.

Already she was half bored to death with the oppressive regularity of the solid grey seams of off-white, wipe-down plastic. She could only imagine the horrors, the terrifying states experienced by those who had been encased in this room before her. And now here she was, faced with the prospect of 21st December looming before her, while she was imprisoned in this monstrous hell-hole, unable to do anything about it.

Michael said she would be in there at least three months. The thought of being there even as much as three days was absolutely unbearable, and she didn't even have three more days before the events of December 21st would be upon her. Not only that, she still didn't know exactly what was going to happen then. She'd been so close to Alice, so close to finding out what was going to happen and now this. How was she ever going to get anywhere near the skull again? How was she ever going to speak to Alice?

She sighed. There was nothing else she could do but wait, while time ticked away and brought everyone closer to the end. All she could do was wait until she had her assessment with Dr Bacher, scheduled for later that day, and hope that she could find some way of getting him to see sense. Ironically, he was now her only hope.

Dr Bacher had categorically denied Michael access visits for the first month of her incarceration. The doctor had claimed that visitors were 'a distraction and would lead to an over excitation of the patient'. If only he knew! One month's time! The man had no idea that there would never even be a next week. If she couldn't get out of this place, the world would end and she would never see Michael ever again.

Desperately, she wrestled within the confines of her straightjacket, but it held her resolutely in check. She wiggled her toes, the only part of her that still felt free. If only she could explain things to Dr Bacher. If she could get through to him then she might just get him to appreciate the gravity of the situation they all faced.

A noise penetrated the oppressive silence inside the padded cell. A key moved in the lock and the door swung open. As it did so Laura heard the horrendous cries of one of the other inmates.

'Help!' a woman was shouting, 'He's going to kill me. Help!' she shrieked again. Dr Bacher stood before her, ignoring the cries from down the corridor. Two male nurses loitered behind him.

'What's going on?' asked Laura puzzled by the commotion.

'I'm here for your little assessment,' said Dr Bacher, 'Oh, that?' he said seeing Laura's puzzled expression, 'In her mind, poor Mary Macanaly gets stabbed to death at least five times a day.' He chuckled to himself.

God, thought Laura, *how did I ever end up in this nuthouse?*

One of the male nurses was stood in the door frame, leaning against it.

'We're here if you need us,' he reminded Dr Bacher. Built like a house, the man looked able to deal single-handedly with any patient, however challenging their behaviour.

'Yes, thank you. I'll only need about fifteen minutes,' replied Bacher.

God, all Laura had was fifteen minutes to try to talk her way out of this place.

The psychiatrist entered the padded cell, whilst the orderlies waited outside. The door slammed firmly shut behind him.

Bacher hovered near the entrance to the cell, rocking a little on his heels. After the sobering, solitary time she had had so far in the Warnburton, with only sound-proof cushioned walls for company, she was almost glad to see him. He was after all her only contact with the outside world, now that he had denied her all other visitors.

'Hi Laura, so have you calmed down a bit now?' he enquired, in his usual fake-friendly casual tone.

'Yes. Thank you.' Laura was now on her best behaviour. This was her one chance, however remote, to try to turn things around, to try to get Bacher on her side, to try to get him to begin to see things as they really were. So she was going to give him everything he wanted. She was going to tell him everything she knew.

'Now, where were we?' he continued. 'That's right!' he said looking at his notes. 'I understand that you have been seeing things that other people have not been so fortunate to see?'

'Yes, that's right,' she began and realised that sounded as if she were insane. The problem was where to begin, she only had fifteen, no less now, fourteen minutes to explain the whole thing.

As she tried to work out where to start Bacher began prompting her from his notes of what Michael had already told him,

'Let me see, now. There was the incident in your office with the stone carving, no before that you reported to your Doctor that you had been hearing things. Then when you saw your husband after your trip into the jungle you told him that you had seen your daughter, now how did all that come about?'

'It's not easy to explain,' replied Laura trying hard to work out how best to put it all, 'but I think I've stumbled on something important. You see, most people have closed their minds to any reality beyond this one. They think this is all there is. They don't realize there's a whole other world out there.'

'When you say another world, what exactly do you mean?' Laura wasn't sure whether he was genuinely trying to understand where she was coming from of just humouring her, but she had no choice but to give him the benefit of the doubt.

'I mean the dimension the souls of the dead go to. Nobody ever really dies, you see, we just go to another place. That's what I've been trying to tell Michael, but he doesn't understand. Our daughter, Alice, she isn't really dead and gone, she's just in another realm, and she's been trying to communicate with me through the skull' she added.

Oh dear, it was all coming out wrong, her explanation. She was under such pressure it was hard to put it all into words.

'So you say your daughter's been trying to communicate with you through the skull,' he said, 'now why would she want to do that?'

'I think she's like... a messenger.'

'A messenger? For who? For what?' he asked.

'For all the loved ones on the other side.'

Bacher looked puzzled.

'The dead can see everything that goes on in our world. And because there is no time in their dimension they can even see what lies ahead in our future. But they are powerless to intervene directly. Like the Mayan shaman, Hunab Ku said, they looked on helpless when they saw, thousands of years ago, that we would destroy our world. That's why they sent the crystal skull. So they could communicate with us in our hour of need. That's why they sent my daughter, Alice. She came to try and warn us.'

Now let me get this straight,' said Bacher. 'You believe that your dead daughter can talk to you through the skull, and that she has been sent by all the other dead people to try to save us from some sort of impending ...Armaggedon.'

'That's right...' replied Laura.

Dr Bacher nodded and rubbed his chin. 'Mmm, interesting...'

'...But I don't know exactly how it's going to happen,' continued Laura, 'That's why I need to speak to her. That's why I need to see the skull again. I need to speak to Alice.'

'That would help would it?' enquired Bacher.

'Yes. If I could only see her, just one last time, it could change every-thing.'

Chapter 71

The orderlies closed Laura's cell door firmly behind Bacher as he finished his assessment. He came out into the corridor talking to himself excitedly, as he scribbled into his little notepad, 'Fascinating, the fantasy about helping other children, a direct result of her inability to save her own child. The whole delusion designed to alleviate the pain of her loss.'

Michael was waiting in the reception area of the Warnburton. He'd buzzed the 'welcome' button when he arrived, but no one had come to greet him. Glancing round the lobby, he noticed there were still some original features of the old house, the mosaic of tiles on the floor, the solid oak staircase. But all the separate areas of the building had now been sealed off with reinforced glass security doors sporting coded alarms for access and entry. He hated Dr Bacher's ruling that he couldn't see Laura. He'd come out here anyway. He wanted to discuss his wife's future with Bacher as soon as he had finished his initial assessment.

The empty reception desk boasted leaflets about the Warnburton, showing a soft-focused photograph of a group of inmates smiling at the camera on the lawn outside, shot during midsummer. He took one and began reading.

Michael swiftly returned the leaflet to its stand. No wonder he didn't like the place, it specialised in ECT. Well, the Warnburton had been Caleb's choice and as Nanon was fitting the bill for Laura's 'rehabilitation', and Michael needed to be on his best behaviour at work, given Laura's transgression, he wasn't in a position to argue. Even more reason he needed to be at the unit now, so that he could be fully involved in Laura's treatment. Whatever happened, he didn't want to see her subjected to ECT. The prospect was brutal beyond words.

What Laura needed, he felt, was someone who could gently help her to see reason again. She'd been in such a fragile state since finding Ron, she needed very kind treatment. He wasn't sure if the Warnburton was the place to offer it. Simply talking it through with a therapist would probably be best. At worst, some medication to help with the illusions she'd been having.

His thoughts were interrupted by a severe looking middle aged woman who punched in the door code and let him enter. She looked him up and down disparagingly, as if she had better things to do than deal with the relatives of the insane.

Michael had already arranged his appointment directly with Dr Bacher. The nurse led him through a few security doors and down several gloomy corridors until they found him. He had just finished his initial assessment with Laura when they ran into him.

'Hello' he greeted Michael with a broad grin and nodded to the two orderlies, that they would no longer be needed.

'Well,' said Michael 'Do you think you can help her?'

'I think there's only one way to get her to see sense' began Dr Bacher. 'Let's go and discuss it in my office.'

Chapter 72

The Warnburton diagnostic area had been converted out of the former gun room of the old house, which had now been divided into two separate rooms. All the external windows had been bricked up and the walls painted a neat, clinical and uniform white. From inside the diagnostic room, one whole wall appeared to be covered in a large mirror that ran along the entire length of the room.

Hidden behind this mirror, which was actually a large sheet of reinforced one-way glass, was the observation room, a smaller space, in which the psychiatric staff were able to observe and monitor the behaviour of patients in the main room, whilst remaining completely hidden from the patient's view.

As well as a DVD recorder, several CCTV monitor screens, a telephone and a PC, the observation room also contained a row of comfortable office chairs, on which sat Dr Bacher, Michael and Caleb Price.

'I'm still not sure this is such a good idea,' said Caleb.

Caleb's body-guard stood at the back of the room with his arms folded, while Bacher continued his explanation,

'But it could be vital to my diagnosis. You see, the problem is that for Laura the skull has become a symbolic representation of her dead daughter. Watching her interact with it may be the only way for me to make an accurate assessment. It could help clarify whether she is purely delusional, perhaps also manic, or possibly even borderline psychotic.'

It made Michael wince to hear Bacher talking about his wife in this way. But there was nothing he could do, particularly if he wanted her home again soon. Whatever his own reservations about Bacher's plan, it had to be better than the prospect of Laura going to jail. And at least Bacher was being thorough enough to go through this process of properly investigating Laura's mental state, rather than going straight to his favourite form of therapy, ECT, without any further questions.

The last thing Michael wanted was Laura subjected to that, which was why he'd helped persuade Caleb to go along with Bacher's plan in the first place. And if he hadn't been working so hard, putting in sixteen hour days at Nanon and making such good progress on his research into the skull, he probably never would have won Caleb round. Admittedly, it was probably his offer to Caleb that if he did him this favour he might accept a lower percentage profit share on the crystal skull technology he was developing that had eventually twisted Caleb's arm. With Michael now even more indebted to him than ever, Caleb had reluctantly agreed to it.

'OK. Whatever! Just get on with it,' was what Caleb said now, lolling back in his chair, as if he were waiting for a show to begin.

Bacher's plan was two-fold; not only was he convinced that seeing Laura with the skull was an essential diagnostic tool but he also believed that it would also serve therapeutically as a profound means of 'reality testing' for Laura. When her wishes were granted, and she finally came into contact with the crystal skull, she would have to face the fact that the skull was no such thing as 'a doorway into another dimension'. This would help to 'normalize' her expectations and bring her back to a more rational and sensible model from which to make sense of reality, one that didn't include meetings with dead children!

Bacher's explanation had made perfect sense to Michael at the time. Letting Laura see the skull might help bring her back to normal. But now he wasn't so sure. Perhaps he had been motivated simply by his desire to see Laura again, and he knew if he set up her interaction with the skull he'd get to see her. He leaned forward and peered through the one way glass. Now he was here, he was beginning to have grave doubts about the whole situation.

He watched five psychiatric nurses, including an alarmingly large one, enter the diagnostic room. In the centre of the room, raised up on a chair and placed on a white pillow embossed with the letters 'Property of the Warnburton Clinic', was the crystal skull. Under the harsh strip lighting the skull looked a palid, ugly yellow.

Michael watched as Laura was brought into the room by two Nanon security guards, one on either side. He caught sight of her face, pale and anxious, close up from one of the four hidden cameras situated in the diagnostic area. He thought it would be reassuring to see her, but the sight of her straight-jacketed, arms forced flat and immobile against her body made him start.

Instinctively, his fingers raised to touch the one way glass that separated them. He wanted to tap on the glass to let her know he was there, with her, supporting her, but of course he knew he shouldn't. Laura wasn't supposed to know that anyone else was there watching.

Once she was inside the room, and the door locked firmly behind her, one of the orderlies began to remove her straightjacket. In its place, Nanon's Head of Security held her hands behind her back and snapped a pair of handcuffs onto her wrists - one of Caleb's conditions if Laura was to be allowed anywhere near the skull. He then took a black cloth out of his pocket. It was a blindfold - another security condition to prevent Laura trying to escape with the skull. The guard placed the blindfold over Laura's eyes then raised a hand, indicating they were about to proceed.

Michael, Bacher and Caleb peered through the one-way glass of the observation room window to see the Nanon security guards, at each elbow, leading Laura forwards, hands cuffed behind her back, towards the skull. The nurses waited silently by the door. The security guards were dressed in black, and as they led Laura over to kneel down in front of the crystal skull, they suddenly looked, to Michael, like her executioners. Michael's breath clouded the observation room glass in front of him.

'Sit down,' said Caleb, 'Relax'.

Michael reluctantly took a seat.

Over the audio-monitor they could hear Laura asking her jailors 'Please, just a last few moments alone with it?'

'I should be in there with her!' said Michael, starting to get up.

Bacher raised his hand 'Please, no.' he said firmly. 'We need to see how she interacts with it alone.'

'Hey, I thought we'd agreed...' said Caleb sitting upright in his chair.

'Look,' said Bacher, holding up the fingers of two hands to indicate the number of personnel they had at the ready. 'There are seven people in that room. We can have them all waiting immediately outside a locked door for her.'

Caleb got up and walked over to the observation window and slowly surveyed the scene.

'Caleb' continued Bacher, 'The woman is blindfolded and handcuffed. I can personally guarantee security will not be an issue. What harm could it do?' he asked.

The clock on the observation room wall ticked away the minutes noisily.

Caleb pressed his intercom to communicate with the guards, 'Alright, ...but only one minute!' He said begrudgingly.

The Nanon guards took a few paces back, before exiting the room with the nursing staff, leaving Laura alone with the skull.

From the observation room they all watched tensely as Laura sat cross-legged before the skull. The sight of Laura blindfolded was so strange, so disturbing that Michael could hardly bear to look at her, it was making him unbelievably tense. He looked down and noticed that he was gripping the arms of his chair so hard that his fingers were white. He let go. He had to calm himself down. It was only a psychology experiment, one designed with the express purpose of helping his wife. What could possibly go wrong? He took a deep breath.

He glanced at his wife. She was sat with her spine very straight and he could see that she was breathing deeply. She looked very still and peaceful, it was not what he'd expected at all. No doubt the tears and histrionics would come soon.

Caleb was tapping his foot restlessly. Michael wished he'd stop. No one else seemed to notice. They were all waiting for Laura's moment of realization, one that would, in theory be coming soon. It might happen in a few moments, or it could take as long as a couple of hours, but sooner or later Laura would have to confront the fact that there was no reality beyond this one.

When Alice failed to materialise, to appear in the room, or whatever else it was that Laura thought would happen once she was in the presence of the skull, her delusional world view would be seriously challenged. And it was a given that this process would upset her, Bacher had explained that, but it was a small price to pay for getting her on the mend again, thought Michael.

Bacher would then make his diagnosis, they would return the skull to the lab and he would be able to get on with his research knowing that Laura had a proper diagnosis, a treatment plan and possibly even a provisional date for her release, he hoped. That was what Michael wanted to know, that he was getting his Laura back again. So why couldn't he shake the terrible feeling of dread that was lodged in his gut? Particularly when the anxiety that had marked her face earlier, when she had walked in the room, was disappearing before his own eyes.

He wondered what was going on inside her head, what she was thinking about as he watched the remaining tension slip from her face and a serene expression appear. It would be over soon, he knew that.

Her lips began to move, it was inaudible at first and then, the words got louder. Laura began to chant, slowly at first, saying the words softly to herself;

'Oxlahun baktun, mi katun, mi tun, mi kin'.

Bacher took a pen from his pocket and scribbled a note to himself.

'What's she saying?' Caleb asked Bacher.

'Shssh!' whispered Bacher, staring intensely at Laura.

The chanting continued. 'Oxlahun baktun, mi katun, mi tun, mi kin', again and again, getting gradually louder and louder.

They all watched on tenterhooks as Laura's chant grew louder still. Then suddenly she leant forward and rested her forehead against the forehead of the skull.

Inside the observation room, Caleb leapt to his feet.

'What's she doing?' he exclaimed, 'Get her off it. She's not to touch it.' Furiously, he went to press his intercom to communicate with the guards.

Bacher touched his arm, 'Please, this is crucial, Please! Wait!'

Caleb's finger hovered over the button, while Bacher continued in a low voice.

'Don't worry, Nurse Simms is on standby with a shot of sedative? She's ready and waiting. We have pharmaceutical backup, should the patient..' he glanced at Michael, 'er, Laura become highly disturbed.'

Caleb stopped pressing. 'OK' he said firmly, 'She's got one more minute, and not a second longer'.

Tension crackled in the air as they watched Laura from behind the glass, her forehead pressed firmly against the skull.

Then suddenly, Laura's body went limp, and she collapsed into a heap on the floor.

Chapter 73

There was a moment of stunned silence as everyone tried to take in what had just happened.

'It must just be part of her psychosis,' begun Dr Bacher, but Michael was on his feet immediately, rushing to the observation room door. But it had been locked, to keep out any wandering patients. He hammered on it, horrified.

'Let me out of here!' he shouted as he stared at his wife's slumped body. 'Do something. Help her! Help her!' he yelled.

'I'm sorry' began Dr Bacher.

'Just get the door open!' shouted Michael. Bacher was fumbling with the keys in what seemed like the hour it took him to open the door. Flying out of the observation room and along the corridor, an orderly had just unlocked the diagnostic room. Michael burst through the door and ran over to help Laura. Pushing aside the gawking guards, he took Laura's dead weight in his arms and shook her to try to bring her round.

'Wake up! Laura! Wake up!' he shouted, but she did not respond.

He checked her pulse, but he could feel none.

As Bacher and Caleb came through the door, he cried out, 'Call an ambulance! Somebody please! Call an ambulance!'

His words seemed to echo around the whole of the Warnburton as he started desperately trying to resuscitate her. As he began clumsily administering the kiss of life, he felt sick. His mind became a blur of swirling images, as if he were watching the whole thing in a film, played in fast-forwards, happening to someone else.

The next thing he knew, he was in the back of an ambulance, siren blaring overhead. He was leaning over Laura. Her face looked deathly pale.

He pleaded 'Speak to me, Laura! Please, speak to me!' But there was no reply.

A paramedic appeared at his side and placed a bag and mask over Laura's nose and mouth to try to administer some air. He began pumping vigorously on the respirator, before turning to his colleague, with a worried tone,

'I'm getting resistance. Quick! Give me suction!'

The paramedic removed the bag and mask, and as his colleague passed him the suction device, Michael' mind flashed back to two years earlier, leaning over Alice as she too was rushed to hospital unconscious, in the back of an ambulance.

But back then, Laura was by his side, while he watched four year old Alice, the colour drained from her cheeks, as the paramedic forced a suction tube down her little windpipe, to try to remove the blockage. Michael was holding Alice's hand, trying to reassure her,

'It's OK Alice, you're going to be alright.'

But she hadn't been alright. Moments later the paramedic had turned to his colleague and whispered,

'It's no good. I can't get it out. She needs surgery.'

He couldn't bear to think about it. He had lost his beautiful little Alice, but he wasn't going to lose Laura, she was going to be alright, she had to be. He wanted to grab her, to hold her, to tell that she would make it, but the paramedics were still hovering around her checking, monitoring, making sure the oxygen was being pumped into her system.

Minutes later the ambulance arrived, lights flashing in the dark, at the hospital's accident and emergency entrance.

A team of medics rushed out to meet it as the paramedic shouted,

'Quick! Get her to resus.'

Laura's trolley burst through the double doors of the A & E entrance, as the team wheeled Laura's stretcher into the hospital, with the paramedic still trying to pump oxygen into the airway tube inserted down Laura's throat. Michael ran after the octopus of emergency medical staff and equipment now crowded round Laura's gurney, his face a frozen mask of incomprehension and fear.

Laura's trolley finally came to a halt in the resus. room. The doctor in charge tore open Laura's clean white Warnburton-issued smock, while the nurses frantically attached ECG electrodes to her chest, and the OP tube down her throat was replaced with one attached to an automatic ventilator, as Laura was quickly wired up to a full life-support machine.

A senior nurse tried to lead Michael outside the curtained area; 'Sorry sir, it doesn't help us to do our job if you're standing there. Please wait outside.'

Michael refused to leave, 'She's my wife for Christ's sake' he answered angrily.

'Please, just for a few moments,' she requested

Michael could only just glimpse Laura through the sea of busy people around her.

'I'll have to call security,' the senior nurse said firmly, trying to pull the blue plastic curtain around him.

But Michael didn't hear her, didn't register her at all. He was in such a state of shock as he gazed at his wife.

'Sir!' the senior nurse raised her voice. 'I will have to call security!'

At that moment a terrible high-pitched beeping sound began to emanate from the oscilloscope, and everyone turned round to look at the heart monitor. Now even Michael could see that Laura's heart trace was beginning to go haywire across the screen.

One of the medics shouted, 'She's arresting!' and another immediately began to perform manual CPR, pressing the full weight of his body down onto Laura's chest with his arms outstretched, palms crossed and elbows locked, trying to administer chest compressions. Another medic began to inject a shot of adrenalin into the vein on the back of Laura's hand and the heart monitor began to beep with some semblance of normality once again.

One of the medics exclaimed, 'Thank god, she's stabilizing!'

Michael had never felt so relieved in his life.

He sat next to Laura, holding her hand as she lay motionless on the gurney on which she had arrived. Only a thin curtain separated her from all the others who had been admitted to A&E and were also awaiting treatment. He sat there numb with shock, unable to believe that things could have gone so dreadfully wrong. Here was Laura, his beautiful wife lying half-dead, unconscious in hospital.

He kept expecting a doctor to arrive, to unhook all the wires that were attached to her and say 'That's it. It's alright, she can go now,' and Laura would smile and get up and say 'Let's go home, Michael' like it had all been a bad dream, a terrible nightmare from which they would soon wake safely. But this nightmare was for real.

Chapter 74

It must have been nearly an hour later before a couple of hospital porters arrived and wheeled Laura's body on her trolley down the corridor to Diagnostics.

Dr Panish, a short man on an internship from Pakistan, greeted Michael then followed Laura into the MRI suite. As Michael caught Dr Panish's eye he saw a look of sympathy in the man's face, and knew that it wasn't over yet.

'We are preparing for an MRI scan, you've heard of those?' said Dr Panish. His manner was calm, devoid of emotion.

'Yes' mumbled Michael.

'Magnetic Resonance Imaging. Using magnetic force rather than X-ray to build up a picture of the brain. It is standard procedure when we have a case like this. I just need to know if your wife is pregnant?'

'No' replied Michael tonelessly.

'I also need to check if she has a pacemaker or any metal anywhere in her body. If she has, then an MRI scan would be very dangerous, the magnetic force will disrupt any metal which could cause brain damage or serious injury'.

'No' Michael answered again.

'You can wait in the observation room,' said Dr Panish. Michael felt a stab of painful guilt. An observation room – that was the last place he wanted to be. Christ, if he hadn't agreed to the psychiatrist Dr Bacher's insane plan for 'observation' in the first place then he wouldn't be here now. If they hadn't put Laura together with the skull, none of this would have happened.

Reluctantly, he entered the glass-walled observation room, the diagnostic area adjacent to the hospital's brain scanning room.

He watched in silence as Laura's pale comatose body, covered in a long white sheet, was placed on a special couch. At the press of a switch, Laura's couch wheeled silently forward. As it moved into place, Laura's head and shoulders disappeared inside the enormous MRI scanning machine. It looked strangely similar to a very large, white washing machine. There was a loud noise as the machine started up.

Michael waited inside the observation room, staring blankly at the grey screens of a bank of TV monitors.

A gently rotating 3-D image of Laura's skull appeared on one of the screens. He was looking at his wife's brain. Her brain was highlighted as a series of colourful cross-sections, of the kind expected in a child's anatomy text book.

'There's colour ...activity, that's good, isn't it?' asked Michael.

Dr Panish was examining the images carefully. Panish didn't look away from the screens. 'There are signs that the brain is carrying out some of its most basic activities, but we need to wait'.

As Michael looked at the amorphous areas of blue, green and yellow on the screen, it struck him as weird that he could see what was going on inside Laura's brain, but it told him nothing about what had been happening for her personally. How little he really understood about Laura, and the way she had been acting recently. It struck him how little it was possible to truly know another person, even if you share a life with them. For Laura had changed in a way he could never have foreseen. She saw the world now in a way that was so alien to him. How that had happened, he couldn't understand. But that was the least of his worries right now.

The consultant examined the images that had been printed out by the scanner. Michael studied his face, looking for some sign that would help him understand what was going on, but there was none.

Dr Panish pursed his lips, and turned to Michael.

'I'm sorry, Dr Greenstone. We've run every test we can think of, but we still don't know what's wrong with her.'

'Surely there must something you can do?' Michael's anxiety was obvious.

The consultant shook his head. 'We're doing everything we can, but it's very difficult to know how to treat her condition unless we know what caused it. You say she just touched her forehead on some sort of... skull, and then collapsed into a coma?'

'That's right,' replied Michael, 'a crystal skull.'

Dr Panish looked confused. He'd obviously never heard of a crystal skull before.

'She had this idea she could somehow project her consciousness inside it,' continued Michael. The consultant raised his eyebrows. 'She met this medicine man who...' Michael was stunned into silence by a sudden realization.

He turned to look at Laura whose body was slowly being wheeled out of the machine.

'Look after her,' he nodded towards Laura, 'I'll be right back!' he added, without finishing his explanation. He turned, dashed out the door and ran off down the hospital corridor, leaving the consultant wondering what the hell was going on.

Chapter 75

Jumping out of the cab, Michael trudged through the grey half-melted snow then sprinted up the steps to the red brick apartment block. He scarcely noticed the concierge waving him a happy 'Hello!' before he dashed up the stairs to the apartment he shared with Laura.

He burst into the gloomy hallway, and rushed over to the bureau behind the front door, where Laura kept most of her paperwork. He began frantically rummaging through its drawers, trying to find the one where she kept her work-related documents. He wasn't sure where her staff handbook would be. He had seen it in here once before, but now it could be just about anywhere.

He was in luck. Laura had recently been issued with a new copy and it was sitting near the top of the second bottom drawer. Grabbing it from the drawer, he flicked hurriedly through its pages. There were a couple of loose scraps of paper, late entries or something Laura had added by hand, which he ignored, and carried on looking until he found the right page.

It was the one that read, 'Smithton Geographic Institute – Field Offices'

He scanned down the page to the entry named 'Central America - Maya Mountains - Area Office – Dr Brown' and a phone number.

He pulled out his mobile phone and dialled quickly.

'Pick up! Please pick up!' he willed Dr Brown as the phone rang. He was praying that Brown would be there, that he wasn't off in the jungle on some expedition or another, without his phone. He was counting on Dr Brown, hoping against hope that this guy knew how to find the shaman character. And hoping that this shaman character might be able to shed some light on what had happened to Laura, something that could help the medics, some clue that would help them bring her back.

The idea of depending on some illiterate, uneducated subsistence farmer from some Central American backwater, a man who probably didn't even speak a word of Spanish, let alone English, made very little sense, he knew. But it was just that he was so utterly helpless he didn't know what else to do.

After a few rings Michael's heart sank as he heard the unwelcome sound of Dr Brown's outgoing message. He had got through only to his answering system. He really needed to speak to him direct. Frustrated, he left his message after the tone,

'Dr Brown. It's Michael Greenstone here, Dr Laura Shepherd's husband. I need your help. Something terrible has happened. Laura's in a coma in Eastside Hospital, it's critical. The hospital can't help her. But there's a medicine man in Luvantum. He got her into this mess and I need you to get hold of him. I need to speak to him urgently. Please, it's an emergency. Call me back on this number as soon as you can.'

He put Laura's staff pocket-handbook away in his jacket pocket and slumped into the antique arm chair by the side of the desk, in despair. All he could do now was to wait for Dr Brown to call, and hope he'd call soon. He tapped his phone nervously between his fingers, willing it to ring. He didn't like waiting, hated it in fact. He liked to be doing, sorting things out, making things happen, he always had. Waiting was one of the hardest things for him.

He glanced around the empty apartment; there was so much of Laura, here in this place. The turquoise chair he was sat on, that she had found in an antique market, the colour subtly blending with the blue and gold prints they had hanging there in the hallway, elegant and understated. She'd chosen them with her artist's eye for how things should go together, in this home they had made together. Her absence from this place felt like a terrible, bottomless abyss that he was now falling into.

Looking up, he noticed on the top of the bureau a photo of the three of them; himself, Laura and Alice. It was framed in pale driftwood. He'd walked past this picture everyday barely seeing it. He reached out and picked it up. They were on a family holiday together, on the big expanse of white sandy beach at Long Island. It was a little early in the season and there was a fresh breeze, so they'd put their cardigans on. They'd just been building a huge sandcastle, Alice and he, while Laura collected shells and seaweed to decorate it with. They looked so relaxed and happy, as they'd watched the waves of the sea come swirling in.

He remembered how they'd laughed as the surging white foam smashed against the sand structure they had built, tearing down the fortress they had created, until it was as if their castle had never been. Their smiles were so innocent of the fate that awaited them, so unknowing of the tragedy that lay less than a year ahead, a tragedy that would tear Alice from them, that would destroy Laura's sanity, and now threatened to end her life. A sob rose in Michael's throat. He gulped it down. He could not afford to fall apart. He had to believe that Laura was going to be OK. He simply could not countenance the alternative. It was just too awful, too bleak.

He was putting the photograph back in its place on top of the bureau, when he noticed something unusual lying on the door mat, just beneath the letterbox, behind the front door. He was used to clearing away the pile of junk mail that appeared beneath the letterbox on an almost daily basis, the detritus of printed leaflets advertising the latest take away joint or taxi service that had set up in the vicinity. But this was different; it looked like an A4 laminated photograph. Surely the local take-away joints had not got that elaborate in their marketing efforts?

Curious, Michael went over and picked it up. As he stared at it, trying to absorb what he was looking at, he staggered backwards with shock, the image slipping from his fingers as he collapsed back into the chair. Scrabbling for the image again, he stared at it gasping. It was a life-size, close-up image of Laura's face, as pale and lifeless as a ghost.

He could not comprehend how he could be staring at an image of his wife, and in such a state. Her eyes were closed, and the colour was drained from her whitened cheeks. She looked like a corpse.

What's going on? Is this some kind of hate mail? he wondered. Yet who would do this to him? Who would send him a picture of his wife, looking dead? He could not imagine anyone so sick, so disturbed as to do such a thing.

After his shock had subsided, he looked again. There was something even odder about the photo. Whoever had taken it had clearly doctored the photograph, changing her hair. For this was not Laura's fine golden blonde hair, with a central parting. The photograph showed dark hair, swept back severely from her face in quite a different style than she ever wore. Her eyebrows too were much darker.

He flipped the photograph over. The back of the photo was stamped, 'NYPD - Homicide Department'. And beneath that a handwritten note read, 'Call me.'

It was signed 'Detective Frank Dominguez' and a phone number.

Michael used the landline, he didn't want to risk Dr Brown ringing back and not catching him. Dominguez answered almost immediately.

'What is this?' Michael asked angrily, 'Don't you realize, Laura's in a coma! She could die any moment! I could lose her. And you're sending me this! Is this some kind of sick joke? Where the hell did you get this from?'

There was a pause before the detective on the other end of the phone answered in a matter-of-fact tone, 'I think you'd better come down here and take a look for yourself.'

Michael put down the phone, now even more bemused than he was before. He had never expected to hear from Detective Dominguez ever again. Christ, the guy hadn't even shown the slightest bit of interest in the fact that Anna Crockett-Burrows had been involved in Ron Smith's death and clearly posed a threat to Laura. When they'd reported the threat to him, they'd got about as much of a response from Dominguez as they would have expected if they were reporting that someone had stolen a dollar from Laura's pocket. And now here was Dominguez calling him down to the precinct to discuss this bizarre photograph.

Michael held the photograph out at a distance, as if it were somehow contaminated. What was going on? Had something terrible happened to Laura in the short time it had taken for him to get from her bedside to the apartment? It seemed unlikely, but he could think of no other explanation. He put in a call to the hospital to try to check Laura's condition but he got stuck in an automated voicemail loop.

He checked his watch. A round trip to the police precinct would only take about forty minutes and he would be back by Laura's side within the hour, assuming of course she was still there. He set off without further delay and drove downtown to the Police Precinct.

The last time he'd spoken to Detective Dominguez' had been to report the horrific clay effigies he had stumbled upon in Anna Crockett-Burrows' basement. He shuddered as he remembered Laura's face, looking like a death mask impaled on a skewer. He only hoped that what he had seen that day had not been prophetic. But as he looked at the photograph now in his hand, of Laura's face, still and lifeless, he began to wonder whether perhaps it might have been.

Ever since he had lost Alice he had not been able to stop himself worrying about Laura, always fearing that somehow her life also was under threat, that some unnamed tragedy was stalking her, waiting for its chance to snatch her from him too. Losing Alice had exposed the sometimes terrible, random and tragic nature of life to him, a truth that most people avoided for as long as they could, until it struck them. But it had struck Michael already. He clutched the bizarre photograph. He couldn't allow anything so terrible to happen to him again.

Minutes later, he drew up outside Precinct Thirteen. As he entered the building, he wondered exactly how Dominguez was going to explain the disturbing image of Laura he was holding. He couldn't imagine what kind of explanation there could possibly be.

Inside the foyer, Detective Dominguez greeted him with an air of deep sympathy, before leading him through the back of the building to the forensic laboratory. There, manning the controls in front of a bank of computer screens, was a skinny-looking forensic scientist with short curly hair and thick rimmed glasses. Dominguez introduced him as Sandy Stanter.

Sandy was the systems development manager for the 'missing persons' software the forensic department had pioneered. Whenever a skull was found, Sandy was involved in creating facial reconstructions of the victim, not just for NYPD but for other departments across the USA. Michael watched in stunned silence as Sandy explained what they were looking at on the computer screens in front of them.

'You see, this is the software we normally use in homicide or missing persons cases to try to identify unknown individuals when all that is left of them is their skull. The guys here originally took this 3-D scan of the crystal skull pretty much for fun when we had it here just after Dr Ron Smith's death.'

On the screen Michael watched a 3-D computer graphic image of the crystal skull rotating slowly in front of him. As Sandy spoke, the computer began a process of 3-D forensic reconstruction of the person's face that best fitted this particular skull. It built up on top of the skull in layers the muscles, tendons, ligaments, nerves, blood vessels, cartilage for the nose, eyeballs, and other soft and fatty tissues such as lips, and finally skin, necessary to present a likeness of the original face on the crystal skull.

As the computer continued its work a face gradually began to appear on the screen. Michael watched in horror as the face that began slowly to emerge right in front of his eyes was Laura's. It was the same haunting 'death-mask' image of Laura's face that he had just seen in the mysterious and disturbing photograph.

Chapter 76

'I don't believe it!' Michael gasped. But there was no mistaking it was Laura's face on the crystal skull on the screen in front of him.

'No kidding!' said Detective Dominguez, his hands buried deep in his pockets, 'One of the strangest things I've ever seen'.

'But how?' asked an incredulous Michael.

'You've got me on that one,' replied Dominguez. 'We'd like to have asked the old lady, Miss Anna Crockett-Burrows, more about it. But I'm afraid she died before we had a chance to speak to her, so we questioned that woman who worked for her, you know that woman from Mexico, her maid,' he continued with his somewhat faltering explanation. 'All she knew was that the old lady had her taking photos and then making clay heads of the people she asked her to photograph, because she said she was trying to find 'the one'. Apparently the old lady, Miss Crockett-Burrows', life mission was to find 'the one whose face was on the skull'.' He sniffed. 'Sounds crazy I know, but we thought we'd better check out her story and, what do you know...Looks like your wife's the one she was looking for.'

At that moment, Michael's cell-phone rang. His heart leapt as he answered it.

'Hello, Dr Brown...' he began, but it wasn't Doctor Brown who was calling.

'Dr Lievervitz?' he replied in response to the female voice on the other end of the line. 'I was expecting Dr Brown to call... So you're not in Guatemala..?' his voice trailed off. It was taking a few moments for what Michael was hearing to sink in. 'From Eastside Hospital?'

A doctor from Laura's hospital was on the other end of the line. 'You'd better come quick. Your wife's deteriorating.'

Chapter 77

Michael arrived at Laura's bedside in the intensive care ward just in time to see Laura's heart-trace flat-lining across the ECG monitor screen. It was accompanied by a dreadful emergency droning noise. The doctor shouted, 'Quick! She's flat-lining!' and the team of medics rushed to apply a cardiac defibrillator to her chest.

As Michael stared at the defibrillator, his mind began to spin. He'd seen this equipment before. They'd used an identical defibrillator on Alice's little chest only two years previously. His thoughts were interrupted by a deep thudding sound, as they delivered the first of a series of electric shocks, and Laura's body convulsed violently. Another thud and Michael was transported back in time once again to Alice's bedside, as they'd tried to electronically kick-start her little heart back into beating.

Another thud and Laura convulsed violently, before the doctor exclaimed, 'She's stabilising!'

Michael watched in relief as Laura's heart-trace began to return to normal.

I'm so sorry Laura! He bitterly regretted having made the trip to see Detective Dominguez. What had he been thinking, with Laura in such a critical condition? *I'm here now, Laura, my love. I'm here by your side.*

The doctor in charge was silent as he examined Laura's chart. Michael knew the situation. Laura was in a very bad way and yet none of the medics could work out what was wrong with her. None of them had any idea what had brought her to this point. There was absolutely no history of medical problems in her family; no history of heart disease or strokes, and none of the tests were showing up any underlying problems with her brain, her lungs, her heart, or her chest, and yet the medics were in a constant battle just to keep her alive. It was all so weird, so inexplicable, and Michael was becoming increasingly disturbed.

'What's happening?' he asked.

'There is no change, I'm afraid,' replied the doctor.

Michael was beginning to feel he just couldn't take any more; the waiting, the uncertainty, the terrible feeling that he was losing her. He pleaded with the doctor, 'Please! You've got to get her back!'

'I'm sorry Dr Greenstone, but we've done everything we can,' came the reply. The doctor was holding one of Laura's eyelids open, shining a light pen into her eye, but her pupil did not contract. 'We just can't get her to respond. I'm afraid there's really nothing more we can do.'

All Michael could do was sit by her side and wait. He sat there, in numb silence, looking at his wife. She was still breathing, but that was all. She lay there surrounded by medical equipment, cocooned in a deathly silence. The only noise was the sound of the various electronic machines which supported and monitored her vital systems. Michael had been here before and it terrified him what would happen next. He and Laura had been through it all with Alice.

Things had been so similar then. Alice's heart-trace had stabilized. It had been an unimaginable relief. Back to a normal heart trace; they'd thought they were winning then, that they'd turned a corner, that their beautiful little daughter would be OK. They'd sat there, feeling that it was all going to be fine, that it would all work out and that they would soon be returning home.

Michael couldn't quite remember when it was that they'd been told. Was it several days later, or was it only a few hours, before the doctor explained? Before those words fell on them like an axe destroying everything, just then, when things had started to look so good, when it was all going to be OK.

He could remember the paediatrician. She had been kind, yes and gentle in her manner, but the words she'd spoken were the cruelest words he'd ever heard. Words that he had hoped blindly, like any parent, never to hear.

'We've removed the obstruction, and we've managed to assist her heartbeat and breathing so Alice has now stabilized. But I'm very sorry to say that...' there was deep concern in her voice as she paused, 'she was in a coma, oxygen deprived for so long that... I'm afraid she has suffered irreparable brain damage. Alice will never return to full consciousness. She can only exist now in a vegetative state, totally dependent on the life-support machine even for her most basic functions, entirely dependent on the hospital's technology to survive.'

She paused again, and coughed. 'Of course we can keep her alive indefinitely but she will never recover. It's up to you. What do you want us to do?'

It was the hardest decision they had ever made. The most painful decision any human being ever has to make is deciding whether their precious child should live or die. It is a decision that goes beyond what human beings are capable of sensibly deciding. It was several agonizing weeks later before they made their choice.

Then they'd watched in agony, as the medics began slowly to disconnect Alice form her life-support machine, one piece of technology at a time. Laura held her daughter close to her chest, while Michael embraced them both, with one arm gently stroking Alice's back while she died. For the last time, they gazed at Alice's little face; her soft pink cheeks, her eyes already closed as quietly, oh so quietly she took her last few breaths, in their arms. Michael felt her little hand in his as it slipped slowly out of his gentle grasp.

Chapter 78

Michael now held Laura's limp hand lovingly in his own as he sat in the depths of despair by her bedside. He lifted her hand to his lips and kissed it tenderly.

'Laura my love, can you hear me?' he asked.

Somewhere along the line he'd heard how important it was to speak to a person who had lost consciousness, to treat them as if they were still fully there, as if they knew what was happening, just in case they could actually hear. He had also heard that you should remind them about the details of their life and their plans for the future, and talk to them as if they were about to recover, in the hope that it might actually encourage them to do so.

So, for what seemed like hours, Michael sat holding Laura's hand and talking softly to her about their life together and their hopes and dreams for the future, like the idea they had shared about one day moving to a big house in the countryside, even though it was beginning to look increasingly unlikely that they would ever have any such future together.

At one point, overcome with emotion, Michael hurried to the hospital shop to buy himself the coffee he needed to steady his nerves and stay awake by Laura's side. Whilst there he noticed a small bunch of pale pink frangipane flowers – Laura's favourites. He bought them and returned to her side, where he arranged them very neatly into the little glass jar on the bedside cabinet, still talking gently to her.

Yet as Michael spoke, he found himself wondering whether the apparent benefits of such communication, might have more to do with helping the surviving family members come to terms with the gradual loss of their loved one, than with helping the person in the coma to come round.

Perhaps it was simply the medics' way of giving the distressed relatives something to do, something positive to focus on, rather than actually helping the patient themselves. If only it made a real difference, if only she could hear him. Yet if she could, there was certainly no sign of it.

Michael pleaded with his wife, whispering desperately in her ear. 'Come back, Laura. Please! I love you.'

But she made no response. Not even the flicker of an eyelid, or the twitch of one of her fingers in his own. Nothing.

Instead she just lay there, her face a ghostly pallor, and her hand so horribly limp, devoid of all energy and life.

And yet, Michael couldn't help noticing, she looked surprisingly serene, contented even, almost as if she had a frozen half-smile on her face. He did not understand.

Of course, what Michael did not know, what he did not realize as he sat by her bed in Eastside Hospital, with his wife in this undiagnosed and yet critical condition, was the extraordinary fact that Laura's consciousness was actually no longer residing in her body.

Chapter 79

What Michael did not understand was that Laura had been instructed in secret knowledge by the Mayan shaman. He had taught her what shamans the world over have known for millennia; that it is possible for human consciousness to travel to other places right outside the human body, and, if done correctly, to return in one piece. And Laura had been prepared by Hunab Ku, although by no means adequately, to experience this tantalizing, but extremely dangerous truth.

Laura had wanted to explain all this to Michael earlier but simply hadn't had the chance to do so as he, along with everyone else, seemed to be convinced that she had taken leave of her senses.

Nobody it seemed could understand that what she was trying to do was actually very noble and selfless. That she was trying to do something that would save all their lives, as well as her own. That she was actually attempting to access sacred, secret information which could help avert imminent catastrophe. But she knew all too well how that would sound; confirmation no doubt, to Dr Bacher that she was well and truly insane.

And so, unbeknown to Michael, although Laura's body lay there, like a ghost, before his very eyes, her consciousness, the very essence of her being, was, quite literally, in another world.

You see, what Michael did not realize was that when Laura had pressed her forehead up against the crystal skull when she was still under observation back in the Warnburton Secure Unit, she had actually succeeded in projecting her consciousness into another realm, into another dimension, just as the Mayan shaman had taught her. And so Laura's consciousness, her whole sense of self, and therefore her awareness of the world, was no longer located inside her body, as was normally the case, but was instead located inside the crystal skull.

As a result Laura's un-conscious body had collapsed into a heap on the floor of the Warnburton, although Laura – or at least her consciousness - remained quite unaware of this fact. Indeed Laura remained blissfully unaware of the fact that her body meanwhile was being rushed to hospital in an ambulance. She was completely unaware that to anyone in the outside world she was in a deep coma.

For what Laura was experiencing was not what was happening to her body, but instead what was happening to her consciousness, the essence of her being. And this consciousness, and therefore her awareness of the world, now resided deep inside the crystal skull.

Having undergone few of the punishing rigors or discipline of a proper shaman's training, however, Laura had little understanding of how fragile the connection between human consciousness and the human body can be – a connection so tenuous, so easily broken. And once the link between one's consciousness and one's body is severed, or broken, one's consciousness can no longer return to the body. If this happens, as the Mayan shaman warned, if the person's consciousness can no longer return to their body, eventually the abandoned body will wither and die, and that person will be no more.

But Laura had forgotten about the dangers the shaman had warned her about, in her desperation to contact Alice through the skull. So all the while that to the outside world Laura appeared to be in a coma, all the while her body was rushed to hospital, the medics tried to revive her, and Michael waited anxiously by her side, she was completely oblivious to these traumatic events.

For the only experience Laura now had was not the experience of being inside her own body, but only the experience of being inside the other world inside the crystal skull, wherever the crystal skull happened to be at the time.

Back in the Warnburton Secure Unit, with all eyes upon her, critical and dispassionate, as her psychological condition was assessed, Laura had been filled with anxiety lest the process she had been shown back in the cave under the auspices of the Mayan shaman, failed to work.

As she was led into that over-heated, over-staffed Diagnostic Room surrounded by those waiting to label her as unstable, delusional or psychotic, she had felt under incredible pressure. She feared she might not be able to make it into the appropriate mental state to make the transition. She found it difficult to 'remember her love for this world' or calm her mind enough to project her consciousness inside the skull.

But she thought of 'her love for someone on the other side' just as the shaman had taught her. Her thoughts of course turned to Alice. She remembered how, at the end of a long day, after a warm bath and short bedtime story, she would hold her in her arms. Her little body felt soft and sleepy as she tucked her up in bed. She remembered bidding Alice goodnight and kissing her gently on the forehead, before switching off the bedside light.

Laura chanted the shaman's mantra and felt her body relax as she leaned her forehead against the forehead of the crystal skull, and the next thing she knew was this terrible painful sensation in the middle of her forehead.

Although she had felt this once before, back in the darkness of the shaman's cave, she felt the full terror of it again, as if she were experiencing it for the first time, as if it were about to obliterate her completely.

She felt equally certain that she was about to die, as her normal state of consciousness began to ebb away. Her mind started to slow, and a creeping darkness slowly but steadily obliterated her thoughts, as her innermost consciousness finally made its transition right out of her body and into the crystal skull.

As a result the pain soon passed, the ringing sensation in her ears ceased, and suddenly to Laura it felt as if her whole body had just landed as if from a great dive into some sort of pool of water that was not water. She found herself floating around, weightless, in some place that was like a strange combination of underwater and outer-space. It was like floating underwater, but she was completely able to breathe, almost like floating on air, but it was a dark, vacuum-like, texture-less air that seemed to stretch on almost to infinity.

In the distance she thought she could see thousands of tiny glittering stars, and clouds of multi-coloured space dust, or perhaps they were whole galaxies, of the type normally only glimpsed through the Hubble space telescope. And further on into the distance still, although it appeared tantalizingly near, she was sure she could make out the familiar contours of the long, dark tunnel through time and space that she had traveled down before. It seemed to be beckoning her to continue her journey once again right to the very doorway between the worlds.

Laura was just about to set off for the tunnel, when she became aware of one of the strangest of paradoxes. Before her, was such infinity, it was as if she could see beyond the furthest reaches of the universe, and yet at the same time she felt somehow contained within this watery world, as if she were in but a tank full of water, not much bigger than a small swimming pool, and all around its edges she could just make out a thick layer of some sort of translucent material. This semi-transparent boundary seemed to separate Laura's inner watery world from something beyond, but what?

It was as if Laura were floating around in a giant tank full of water whose walls were made of some kind of thickly distorted Perspex or glass. It was almost as if she were floating around in some sort of giant goldfish bowl.

What was particularly intriguingly was that there appeared to be a whole other world beyond. But why did it all look so distorted? Laura swam towards the outer edge of the boundary to take a closer look.

As she did so, she was struck by the sight of a highly regular pattern in the transparent material that made up the outer edges of her watery world. Somewhere in front of her, the glassy material was shaped into two rows of grave-stone-like forms, each about half a metre tall.

On second thoughts, they weren't grave stones, but there was something strangely familiar about these shapes, their symmetry, the way they were arranged touching each other, side by side in two very neat rows, one above the other. Laura squinted and moved back a bit. That was it! Of course! They were in fact teeth. Or at least the giant sized images of teeth shaped into the transparent material ahead. But it was as if Laura was tiny in comparison to these enormous teeth, and as if she were seeing them from behind, from inside instead of outside the mouth.

She moved back a little further and looked a little higher to see what she now clearly recognized to be the contours of a fleshless nose and deep hollow eye sockets, all shaped into the thick semi-transparent material in front of her. Of course! Why hadn't she realized it before now? What she was seeing was the face on the crystal skull, as if she were tiny and seeing the features on the crystal skull from inside the skull itself. Laura was absolutely amazed. She, or at least her consciousness, her whole sense of herself, seemed to be floating around inside the crystal skull!

She could now clearly discern all the contours of the face on the crystal skull, and she could still just about make out a strangely distorted image of some sort of world beyond, some sort of world outside the crystal skull, but it was as if she were seeing it all through thickly distorted glass walls.

Intrigued, she moved closer to this glassy barrier, convinced there was something out there. She found that if she got really close and held stock still, she could actually see through this strangely distorting surface, right through this crystalline lens, to the world beyond. What she saw out there stunned her.

Peering beyond the face of the crystal skull, she could just make out that she was in a large room, a very odd room, in that it was pitch dark save for what appeared to be rays of infra-red or laser light that ran in a series of narrow beams across the floor. These pin-point rays of deepest red looked like sensor beams, of the kind used by museums and other institutions that housed items of great value. Such rays were used for monitoring an area, picking up on any sign of activity, and linked to sensory alarm systems to ensure the protection of valuable artifacts. This was a room where security issues were clearly paramount.

Just as Laura was trying to work out where it was and what object its owners were trying to protect, there was a loud click, and a glass-windowed security door on the far side of the room swung open. The red laser lighting switched off automatically as the strip lights flashed on.

Suddenly, someone was walking towards her, a person. It was one of the weirdest things imaginable. Here was Laura, looking out at the world from inside the crystal skull, watching a man heading straight towards her. He came right up close and peered in, as if he was looking straight at her. Christ, it was Caleb! She was looking at Caleb Price, Michael's boss, how could that be? And in close-up! She had never been that close to him, ever.

'Er, hello Caleb!' she said awkwardly.

'You are a beauty aren't you?' Caleb was looking right in at her.

Laura was shocked. 'I'm not your beauty,' she responded angrily. *How dare he?* 'What are you doing here anyway?' she asked, but he ignored her.

Instead he just gazed at her licking his lips and nodding to himself as he rubbed the bristles on his chin, 'We'll soon see what you're really made of.'

'Caleb!?' she exclaimed, but he turned away, showing no sign of having heard her.

'Caleb, I'm talking to you!' She raised her voice. He did not respond. 'Hey!' she shouted. She banged her fists on the skull's translucent exterior, but he did not notice. He obviously could neither see nor hear her and was already heading out of the room.

Laura was bemused. *Where the hell am I and what the hell is going on?*

But just before Caleb turned out the lights and reset the alarm, she realized where she was. She recognized some of the equipment on the clean, white surfaces that surrounded the room. They looked vaguely familiar. That's it! She was in Nanon Systems' Crystal Laboratory, where Michael had taken her only a few weeks earlier, and heaven only knew what had happened to her body?

Thinking back over things carefully she managed to piece together what had happened. She realized she must have managed to project her consciousness inside the crystal skull back in the Warnburton Secure Unit after all. That was why her consciousness, and her awareness of the world, was no longer located inside her own head, attached to her own body, as it normally seemed to be. But instead all her thoughts now appeared to be located 'inside the crystal skull', wherever the crystal skull happened to be at the time!

She realized that after the Warnburton, Caleb and his guards must have taken the crystal back to Nanon Systems offices, as that was where it could be kept under the tightest security, and nowhere more so than in the crystal laboratory, surrounded by its layers of security doors, and codes, and web of alarm systems.

That was it. That was why she, or at least her conscious awareness, appeared to be located inside the crystal skull, now right inside the very heart of Nanon systems office complex. Laura couldn't help chuckling to herself at the thought. After all of Caleb's efforts to keep her away from the crystal skull, all his high security measures, specially trained personnel, security codes, alarmed steel doors, barred windows and barricades, here she was now right inside the crystal skull, looking back at all the means Caleb had used to keep herself and others out of there. If only he knew!

She was tempted to keep staring out at the crystal laboratory to see if Michael might come in and try to examine the skull one more time. How strange it would be to be with him while he was at work and for him to have no knowledge of her presence. At least that's where Laura assumed Michael was and what might be about to happen next. But suddenly her attention was drawn back inside the skull, back to something else, something far, far more important.

She heard a voice calling in the distance, 'Mummy!' She could not be entirely sure, but it sounded like her little girl. She turned around to see, once again, the strange tunnel, like a passageway through time and space. It was like a circle of stars and galaxies, spiraling off and disappearing into the distance. And inside the tunnel there was a light, a soft light shining from the far end.

Laura felt compelled to swim down the tunnel towards it. It was a long swim, and the liquid around her felt like treacle, trying to drag her arms and legs back, but she knew, or at least she hoped, it would be worth it. As she moved nearer, the light seemed almost to ripple down the tunnel towards her. On and on she swam and as she got closer, the intensity of the light increased. Nearing the far end, the light became even brighter, until it was shining out pure and strong.

Laura's mind was clear and focused. Her life had led her to this place. This was her destiny. This was what she wanted. This was how it was going to be. This time she would be ready. This time she would be reunited with her daughter. This time nothing would stand in her way.

Chapter 80

Finally reaching the far end of the tunnel, Laura was dazzled by an explosion of light and sound and colour that spread out in almost every direction. She felt as if she were watching the birth of the stars and the planets, almost as if she were witnessing the very moment of the original creation of the universe, but it was as if she were seeing it all through some sort of crystal or lightly frosted glass, all shot through with wispy threads of silver and gold and all manner of rainbow colours. It was so magnificent she almost had to look away lest she be tempted to spend forever gazing on such beauty.

And then in the distance she glimpsed once again something even more beautiful. A shimmering orb of golden white light appeared and began floating gently towards her, radiating sparkling slivers of light all around.

Trembling, Laura moved gently towards it. This time, she knew who it was.

'Alice!' she cried out with joy.

Just then, a sudden and remorseless terror gripped her, as the memory of last time, when she had come so close to her little girl, so close and then she had been dragged away, propelled mercilessly back to the cold dark shaman's cave where the soldiers had been waiting for her, waiting to impound her.

'Alice!' she called again, anxious lest she be snatched away.

The golden light continued towards her. It opened up slowly and from its gleaming white interior emerged what looked like a small dark, figure, back-lit in the distance. Though it was in silhouette and appeared to be on the other side of some sort of frosted glass, Laura recognized it instantly. The figure opened its mouth and from its parted lips emerged the sweetest of sounds, the most magical word, that Laura had never expected to hear again.

'Mummy!' Alice's high-pitched voice cried back in excitement. It was indeed her little girl. It made Laura's heart ache to hear the innocent cadence of that little voice, its purity and sweetness. She was convinced it was the most beautiful sound she would ever hear.

That was why, to Michael, sitting watching over her in the normal world outside the skull, Laura's face now looked such a picture of contentment and peace. For this was the moment Laura had been waiting for, hoping for,

for what seemed like an eternity. Ever since Laura had heard that sweet little voice on her last visit inside the crystal skull, ever since she had seen her daughter's beautiful face, she had been yearning to hear her again, longing to see her, pining to hold her in her arms once more. And now here she was right in front of her, almost as plain as day, almost close enough to touch.

'Oh Alice, I've missed you so much,' Laura said as she got near enough to speak.

'I've missed you too mummy,' Alice replied in a very matter-of-fact tone, 'but I've got lots of friends here ... and grandma and grandpa,' she explained. 'They said I could come and see you if I promised to tell you to go back and talk to daddy.'

Getting nearer, Laura reached out instinctively to touch her daughter, but something was wrong. Her fingers bashed into something. She had come up against some sort of semi-visible membrane or barrier.

'What!?' she exclaimed.

Alice was so close now Laura could see her big blue eyes and straw blonde hair, her petite hands and feet, even the tiny birthmark on her upper lip. She was wearing the pale pink fairy dress and red shoes she had worn to her last birthday party. Here at last was Laura's precious baby, the radiant, transcendent and glorious light that was her lost child.

How Laura craved the small everyday tactile moments that came with having a young child, hugging one another, snuggling up together in bed. Here was Alice at last, and yet she couldn't even touch her.

Laura pushed against the barrier once again, and it stretched a little, but still stood between her and her beautiful little girl, who hovered within reach.

'I can't touch you, Alice!' She was horrified. Tears filled her eyes. Alice was right there, only a hair's breadth away, but whenever Laura tried to touch her, she was blocked by this strange, semi-translucent barrier that separated them and seemed to keep them forever apart.

Laura tried again. She pushed against the membrane with all her strength, but to no avail. She simply bounced right back off it. She was unable to get any closer to Alice, unable to hold her in her arms. She started to sob.

'Don't cry mummy,' Alice's said sadly, 'It's simply the veil between the worlds, the barrier between the world of the living and the world of the dead,' she added in her totally matter-of-fact tone.

Laura tried to rein in her emotions and wiped her eyes. She remembered that the Mayan shaman had mentioned 'the veil between the worlds', the thin membrane that separated 'this world from the next'.

Well, no 'membrane', no 'veil' was going to keep her from Alice.

She redoubled her efforts, using her whole body weight now against the semi-visible divide. She kicked hard with her legs to propel herself forward and pushed back against it. The strange frosted-looking membrane began to distort slightly under this renewed pressure, and it began to stretch almost like a piece of giant 'cling-film' being stretched around Laura's head and shoulders. But just as Laura tried to force her way through again, Alice shouted,

'No mummy! Please! Don't come any closer. You won't be able to go back.'

Laura stared at the beautiful shimmering form that was Alice. 'But I don't want to go back,' she replied wistfully.

Alice was insistent. 'But you must mummy, you must go back. Daddy and his friends are playing with toys that they don't understand and they will leave no world left for any of us. You must go back and stop them.'

'No my precious one,' replied Laura, 'Now I've found you again, I don't ever want to leave you.'

Chapter 81

December 20th 2012

Meanwhile back outside the skull, Michael was still sitting by Laura's bedside in the intensive care ward, sinking steadily deeper into the depths of despair. He stared at the array of electronic machinery that surrounded her, that she now depended on to stay alive. The sound of the air being periodically forced into her lungs and then deflating and the constant beeping of the heart monitor un-nerved him. He had been so terrified that something might happen to Laura, that he might lose her. How much he had wanted everything to be OK, for their lives to be livable again, and now it had come to this.

He cradled his head in his hands, and sobbed, 'Laura! Please! Don't leave me! Come back!'

He reached a hand out to gently move aside a thin strand of hair that had fallen across Laura's face, and as he did so he noticed the bunch of frangipane flowers he had bought her earlier, sitting on the bedside cabinet behind her. It pained him now to see them. He had always been so bad at remembering to buy Laura flowers, but these were her favourites, their delicate pink petals concealing their beautiful, warm, golden centres.

He was struck by the sudden and terrifying realization that Laura might never see them. Already the edges of the petals were beginning to look bruised and lack-lustre in the heat of the hospital room. The flowers were starting to wither. And beyond them, on the monitor screen, Laura's heartbeat was beginning to falter.

Through his tears, Michael dove a hand into his jacket pocket and pulled out Laura's staff address book. He gave Dr Brown one last call on his mobile phone. Once again he got Dr Brown's answer-machine. Unable to believe his bad luck, he left another even more desperate message:

'Dr Brown! Please! I'm losing her. You've got to get hold of that medicine man.'

As Michael was putting the address book away again, a slip of paper fell out of it and landed on the side of the bed, just by Laura's hand. Noticing some type of cryptic formula scrawled on it in her handwriting, Michael picked it up.

It was the slip of paper Laura wrote earlier in the crematorium chapel when Anna Crockett-Burrows had 'channelled' the message of the crystal skull for her, just after Ron's funeral. Puzzled, Michael read the formula to himself:

'SK x MC2 = -1, not 0.' He read it again, 'SK times MC squared equals minus one, not zero.' And then it read 'You will die, daddy will die, all will die.'

Michael's puzzled look suddenly turned to one of horror, and panic.

'Oh my God!!' he said out loud. He recognized the formula.

He fumbled immediately for his cell-phone and dialed quickly;

'I need to speak to Caleb!' he half-shouted down the phone.

The secretary on the other end explained the situation.

'I don't care if he's in an important meeting, this is urgent!' Michael yelled.

But Haley, Caleb's personal assistant, wasn't about to interrupt her boss. She outlined the situation in more detail.

'An hour's too long, I need to speak to him immediately!' Michael demanded.

But the secretary on the other end had obviously had enough of Michael's 'abusive behaviour' and hung up the phone.

'Damn!' Michael grimaced. He slammed away his cell-phone and got up quickly to leave.

He leaned over his wife and whispered in her ear.

'Laura, I love you. But you must wait for me. Please, I have to do this.'

He kissed her gently on the forehead, then dashed out the door.

Chapter 82

Caleb Price took a deep breath and felt his chest expand. He was feeling magnificent, filled with energy and enthusiasm at the prospect of what he was about to discuss with fellow members of the 'Z-panel'. He was stood at the front in Nanon Systems Boardroom. Situated on the second floor of Nanon Systems office building, it was a large room, dominated by a huge circular walnut table, and straight-backed leather chairs, just comfortable enough for lengthy meetings, they added an old-fashioned element to the stark simplicity he normally favoured. A silver metallic cloth over the table concealed details of Caleb's plan.

He glanced around the room, his eyes alighting on the two photographs that adorned the pale cream walls. One showed himself accepting, on behalf of Nanon Systems, the National Science Award three years previously and the other showed Caleb gracing the front page of the 'The Economist' magazine. With this latest project, he soon planned to have another addition to this, his own personal Hall of Fame. He made a final, quick visual check to make sure everything was in order, before he began his presentation. As planned, the large plasma screen, that covered almost the whole wall behind him, displayed an image of the crystal skull rotating on a plinth, behind what looked like some sort of reinforced glass screen.

It was moments like these that made Caleb Price feel truly alive. For this was the work he was born to do, pushing back the frontiers of science and making masses of money in the process. It was gratifying work of the highest order.

He began, 'We are gathered here today for me to fill you in on a major experiment we now have planned'. He glanced around the room. These were his own people, the chosen few, all men, he found women too tiresome. For these men in grey suits and white lab-coats were the esteemed members of the Z-panel, all consummate professionals, the best scientific and technical advisors Caleb could find, who had been brought on board to help fine tune the details of his upcoming big experiment.

Amongst the panel there were some raised eyebrows and quizzical expressions. Many were surprised to hear of this latest enterprise. Caleb had kept it under wraps from most of them until now, informing and involving only a few of the most core staff before today. He had clearly put some of their noses out of joint in the process, but this was the way Caleb often operated. 'Divide and rule' was one of his favourite mottos. It was also one of the ways he'd always ensured that things got done quickly, and he had a reputation to maintain as someone whose company could get things done fast. Besides which it also had the added bonus of making sure there was little chance of word leaking out to his competitors, who would no doubt soon be scrambling onto his patch to try to catch up.

On this occasion, however, he was pretty confident that his main competitor hadn't even come close to thinking about what he was planning to do now. At least not as far as he could glean from his latest employee, Gerry Maddox, recently poached from Ambient, Nanons' lead rival in the crystal technology field. Maddox was carefully studying the documents that had been laid out for the team. The guy was a little over-serious, a little too nerdy, but he was good at what he did. In fact, Michael had better watch out, thought Caleb. Maddox was only 26, but had already won the 'Young Scientist of the Year Award'. He was potentially Head of Applied Research material, particularly as he didn't come with any of the complications of a difficult wife, like Michael.

Caleb glanced at the screen behind him, at the image of the crystal skull spinning around silently on its rotating plinth. It really was something. There was no way on earth his competitors could have discovered anything like it.

'The experiment we have planned, gentlemen, is going to blow your beautiful minds!' exclaimed Caleb, ever the showman, as he pulled aside the metallic fabric from the smooth shiny wooden surface of the boardroom table to reveal a 3-Dimensional scale model of the layout of an underground test facility or laboratory.

'For those of you who don't already know, this is a scale model of our prized 'Z-lab facility', our latest state-of-the-art experimental centre, our secret quantum physics laboratory, buried deep beneath the deserts in New Mexico,' he declared proudly, 'and this will be the centre of our research into the crystal skull'.

Members of the panel looked with interest at the model as Caleb continued, gathering pace, 'In essence, we plan to use the crystal skull to open up a 'wormhole' in the time-space continuum, which will enable us to fire a sub-atomic particle, fired from this laser machine here, right into the future…'

Caleb pointed to the various parts of the scale model to illustrate his points, and just as he reached the crescendo of his explanation, the boardroom door burst open and Michael stormed into the room. Dazed and unshaven, he looked like a man possessed.

Caleb turned to Michael, completely un-phased by his unplanned interruption, 'Michael, so glad you could join us.' He welcomed him warmly, before enquiring, 'How's Laura? She must be doing well.'

But Michael ignored Caleb's question, 'You can't go ahead with the experiment!' There was a dreadful urgency to his voice. 'There's been a terrible mistake.'

Caleb frowned at him questioningly, 'What are you talking about?'

'The formula. I got it wrong!' explained Michael. 'I'm sorry'.

'What!?' exclaimed Caleb. He could scarcely believe his ears. How could Michael let him down like this? He'd already spent millions of dollars making all the necessary preparations, based on Michael's equations, and the experiment on which he was staking not only his own personal reputation, but his whole company's future was about to go ahead.

'I made a mistake.' Michael confirmed simply. 'I'm very, very sorry.'

This was the last thing Caleb Price wanted to hear, he had a very low tolerance for mistakes. He sat stunned as Michael continued his explanation,

'SK times MC squared equals minus one, not zero. That means if we send even one tiny particle into the other dimension it will take every other particle with it, creating a black hole of anti-matter that will suck in everything else around it, destroying the very fabric of time-space.'

'You've got to be kidding me Michael.' replied Caleb, but Michael's face made it clear that he wasn't. 'It's not like you to get an equation wrong,' continued Caleb, 'Where did you get this information?'

'It was a message from…' he paused,

'From who?' Caleb prompted

'…from my daughter.' Michael looked shocked by his own words.

'I thought she was dead?' said Caleb.

'She is, but she gave Laura the correct formula.' Michael blurted out, before he'd had time to stop himself.

Caleb stared at him. 'Dear God, Michael. I think the strain's been getting too much for you.'

He turned back to address the other members of the Z-panel, raising his voice' 'For those of you who don't know,' he looked around at the sea of faces, 'Michael's wife, Laura, was undergoing psychiatric evaluation before she ended up in a coma.'

He paused and turned back to Michael.

'I think that's all we need to know about your new formula, Michael,' he added quietly.

Michael stood there in stunned silence. I should never have mentioned Laura to Caleb, he thought. He realized he'd blown it. He never meant to tell Caleb about Laura's note, let alone that it was from Alice. It was just that he was under so much stress, knowing that every second he was there in the boardroom, he wasn't with Laura. Trying to get the message across to them, while his wife was in the intensive care unit fighting for her life, was horrendous.

And the fact was, it wasn't working, they weren't getting the message at all. He looked at their faces; some were embarrassed, others were re-arranging papers, while others simply looked at Michael with pity in their eyes. All they saw was a man who was under too much pressure and had lost it, a man who, following this outburst, was no doubt without much of a future at Nanon.

Caleb turned back to the panel, 'Now, as I was saying, we've made good time and pretty much have everything in place, so we're all ready for the experiment to go ahead as planned, tomorrow.'

'Tomorrow!?' Michael interrupted him,

'Yes. Tomorrow' said Caleb impatiently.

The colour drained from Michael's face. 'But that's December 21st!'

'Yeah! So?' replied Caleb.

'At what time?'

'4:30' Caleb replied, bemused.

'But that's sunset at this time of year!' Michael gripped hold of the walnut table to steady himself. He was horrified.

'Makes no difference, it's all underground,' replied Caleb, nonchalantly.

'Oh no! You've got to cancel it, postpone it, delay it, anything!'

Caleb was even more puzzled. 'We can't change the date now, Michael. I've got a meeting with the President and the Chiefs of Staff. The President wants to announce the results of the experiment in time for Christmas.'

Caleb clearly expected the results of this experiment to be so significant, so earth-shattering, so revolutionary that he'd even taken the unprece-dented step of informing the President about his plans. The President himself had apparently now taken a keen interest in what was happening with the crystal skull. Although still officially secret, this interest no doubt explained the newspaper headline now sat on the table in front of Caleb outlining Nanon Systems' recently soaring share price. Michael was going to have a hell of a job getting Caleb to change his mind. It would be even harder than he originally thought.

'But Caleb,' insisted Michael, 'I got it wrong. I saw only what I wanted to see and it was a mistake. Remember what the skull printed out?' He was referring to the cryptic code the skull had printed out in his early experiments. 'I thought it was a tertiary code, but it isn't. It's a warning...'

'What are you talking about?' exclaimed Caleb.

'The skull gave us the date...' Michael began, when Caleb interrupted him.

'Michael, we really can't have you disturbing proceedings like this.'

But Michael ignored him and marched over to the flip chart behind Caleb, at the end of the boardroom table. Grabbing a black marker pen he began scrawling large digits across it.

The digits read,

'122120121221201212212012122120121221221221201212212012', just as the crystal skull had printed out earlier when a laser was fired through it.

'Think about it,' said Michael, 'one, two' he added a full stop after the first two digits, 'two, one' he added another full-stop after the next two digits, 'two, zero, one, two' he added a final full-stop. 'It's a date...'

He pointed to the date now clearly displayed on the flip-chart, which read,

'12.21.2012'.

'It's the date December 21st 2012!'

Chapter 83

'Don't tell me, that's another message you got from the dead.' Caleb was as cutting as he was dismissive.

'No, it's from the ancient Maya,' replied Michael. He was beginning to sound to everyone else in the room as if he was even more confused than ever. 'That's when they said the world was going to end.'

'Oh really?' said Caleb, in an even more sarcastic tone than before.

'Laura didn't know how it was going to happen, but now I know,' continued Michael. 'It's because of the experiment!'

'Security! We have a disturbance on 2B.' Caleb had pressed his intercom and was now communicating with the guards.

'No wait!' Michael shouted in desperation; then tried to sound a bit more calm as he realized he was in danger of losing his audience. 'You have to understand, everything is connected. It's something we all need to realize, that everything is connected to everything else. Like you, I couldn't see it before, but now I do. What this equation shows,' he held up the slip of paper that had fallen out of Laura's address book, 'is that the particles are not separate from each other. Once you see it, it's so obvious. But until then you will never understand how the world, the universe really works.'

'What happens is that where one particle goes, the others follow, because they are all connected one to another, just like you and I, though it is something we all tend to forget. And where the particles go, we go too – because we are all, each and every one of us, connected to those tiny little particles too. What this means is that if you send even just one tiny sub-atomic particle into the other dimension, you will send every person in this room, in this city, on this planet, into a black-hole, a vortex of oblivion.'

Two Nanon security guards appeared in the doorway behind him.

'Can't you see?' continued Michael oblivious to their presence. 'You're about to rip a hole in the structure that holds our world in place. You'll destroy the very fabric of the universe!'

He looked around at the Z-Panel. It suddenly struck him as a terrible irony. These people were so knowledgeable in their areas of expertise, and yet so ignorant of the truth. He realized that the normal rules of physics, by which they all lived, worked and breathed, could not explain it to them. The normal rules of physics hadn't got there yet, they simply hadn't yet worked it out. Something that Michael now saw as so blindingly obvious, was now falling on deaf ears. For these people still understood the world according to a dualistic model of physics. A model that saw every person and every object as separate from each other, a model, thought Michael, that was now dangerously out of date.

It horrified him that here were these men, all leaders in their respective fields, and yet they were completely unaware that they were now involved in planning what was going to be a momentous and catastrophic mistake, an experiment that would inevitably turn out to be a terrible suicide mission for everyone involved.

'Please, just give me time to explain it to you, before you make this disastrous mistake' Michael pleaded, but the guards grabbed him from behind by both arms and started dragging him out of the boardroom.

'No! We'll all die! Please! You've got to listen to me...!' he shouted as the two security officers manhandled him out into the corridor.

'My apologies gentlemen,' an embarrassed Caleb tried to explain to the shocked members of the Z-panel, 'Dr Greenstone's been under a lot of pressure recently. Now if we could get back to our plans for the experiment'

Chapter 84

Outside the boardroom, Michael was frantic. He struggled to break free as the guards began to march him off down the corridor. 'Please, let me go, I've got to get them to stop!' They hadn't got very far however when they met one of the office catering staff coming the other way, trundling a coffee cart intended for Caleb and his guests in the boardroom. They were just beginning to negotiate their way around this obstruction, when one of the guard's beepers went off. Whilst he was temporarily distracted by answering his beeper and the other guard was preoccupied with negotiating his way around the trolley, Michael seized the opportunity and managed to break free of their grasp.

He grabbed the coffee cart and thrust it between himself and his captors, sending a stream of hot black coffee spilling towards them, and a stack of delicate white crockery smashing to the floor all around, then ran off as fast as he could down the corridor.

'We've a security breach on level two' the security guard spoke into his beeper as he set off after Michael, limping from where the cart had caught his shin. The other security guard ran in the opposite direction, to set off the alarm system.

In the board room Caleb was continuing unabated with his plans, as he outlined the experimental design; 'Subjecting the skull to monumental amounts of power will lead to the necessary reduction in structural density, a change necessary for us to gain entry into the parallel universe'.

But he was soon interrupted as the peace of the entire building was shattered by the penetrating wail of the security alarm.

'But don't let that alarm you!' he joked. 'Just give me a minute, gentlemen.'

He opened his laptop and called up the building's CCTV camera system on his computer, just in time to see Michael running down a long corridor, towards the crystal laboratory. Michael knew this was where Caleb would be keeping the crystal skull, under lock and key. If only he could get there in time.

The emergency wall lights were flashing all around as Michael arrived at the end of the long corridor. He could see, through the thick window of the reinforced glass security door, the crystal skull sitting on its plinth in the centre of the lab.

He pushed against the door, but it was locked. So he inserted his staff ID card into the slot on the door's electronic security access system.

Meanwhile in the boardroom, Caleb typed quickly into his laptop computer.

Almost immediately he accessed a file that read, 'Personnel'.

He pulled down a document, complete with a colour photo, a mug-shot entitled,

'Dr Michael Greenstone'.

Back in the corridor outside the crystal laboratory, Michael punched his PIN number into the keypad on the lab door's security system. He glanced back over his shoulder to see a group of security officers appearing at the far end of the corridor. He looked around him. There was nowhere to hide.

In the boardroom, Caleb pulled down a menu on his computer, which read, 'Security Access Codes'. Quickly, he typed in a few commands.

In the corridor, Michael stared intently at the digital display on the security door.

It read, 'Processing'.

Behind him the security guards were getting closer.

'Come on, come on!' he muttered as he waited for his card to finish processing.

It seemed to take forever before the red lettering of the digital display flashed up, 'Access Denied', only moments before the team of security officers caught up with him. They surrounded and captured him.

Chapter 85

Minutes later Michael was rough-handled back into the boardroom. He'd have thanked God, if he was religious, for here was another chance to talk to Caleb and the team and try to get them to see sense.

But Caleb now stood alone on the far side of the table. He had asked his esteemed guests politely to give him a few minutes alone with Michael.

His bulking frame looked bigger than ever. Backlit by the blank white plasma screen, it cast a foreboding shadow into the room before him.

'Now, Michael, you know how important it is to the success of this experiment that we have everybody fully on board...' he began.

'Yes, of course,' Michael agreed. 'We all need to take a long cool look at the problem, and then we might be able to see that this sort of experiment really isn't the answer.'

'Michael I don't think you understand me.'

'But Caleb, can't you see, our whole world view is dangerously flawed. This type of technology isn't the answer. Like you, I thought it was, but it's actually just leading us further down the road towards self-destruction.'

'I'm sorry Michael, but we can't afford to have any loose cannons on this one,'

'Please Caleb, I'm begging you, don't go ahead with the experiment. It's absolute madness...'

'I hate to have to do this to you Michael,' Caleb continued, 'but I'm afraid we're going to have to relieve you of your position.' He nodded to the guards.

Before Michael even had a chance to object he was dragged back out of the room and off down the corridor towards the lifts. There he was stripped of his ID card and pass before being marched across the entrance foyer and somewhat unceremoniously thrown out of the front doors onto the pavement. There he stumbled to the ground under the force of the guards' ejection from the building.

He lay on the tarmac for a brief moment, examining his scuffed palms. He couldn't believe what had just happened. He'd gone in there in good faith to try to stop the experiment, and now not only had he been thrown out of the building but he'd lost his job in the process. The job he loved, that was his life-line, the work that gave his life shape and purpose, was now gone. And all because he'd found a fatal flaw in his own formula, and had shared that knowledge with his boss. All he was trying to do was save people. Could that be so terribly wrong? How could it be that he had ended up here, on the pavement?

He glanced back at the building. Staff who had been going about their normal duties were now looking on, gazing at the spectacle of Dr Greenstone, lying on the tarmac, having suffered such a humiliating exit.

Picking himself up, he tried phoning Caleb, but he was on answerphone, no doubt anticipating Michael's calls. His secretary too was unavailable.

'Shit!' Michael muttered to himself

He tried to get back into the building again, but the doors were all locked.

He began hammering his fists on the locked glass doors into the foyer.

'Please you've got to let me in!' he begged through the glass with the security guards. 'We've got to stop the experiment!' he shouted.

But they were impervious to his pleading, unable even to hear him through the reinforced glass walls that surrounded the reception area. Instead they just smiled awkwardly and joked with each other about his misfortune. One of the guards behind the security console picked up his phone and placed an earnest call.

Several other members of staff now gathered in the foyer and stared, puzzled at the bizarre sight of this desperate man hammering away on the doors, shouting inaudibly at the top of his lungs, as a police car pulled up slowly behind him.

And before he knew it, Michael was confronted by the sight of a giant, six and a half foot tall, grotesquely fat police officer standing on the pavement, with his hands on his hips, before him. Despite Michael's objections, the officer gave him a final ultimatum,

'I don't give a monkey's what they're going to do, if you don't leave this site immediately, I'll arrest you for obstruction.'

The cop stood there staring at Michael, a cold hard look in his eyes. 'I'm warning you... Mr former big-shot scientist, I said leave this instant. And if I catch you on these premises ever again you'll be arrested immediately for trespass.'

Michael glanced back at the stark, dark chrome and glass edifice of the Nanon Systems building behind him. He had little choice but to leave. There was no way he was going to get back in there now. He thought about all the hard work he had done in that building, all his research, even the work he had done with the crystal skull. It was history now, there could be no going back.

He pulled his collar up against the cold winter air, returned to his car, under the constant, watchful eye of the gross police officer, and drove back to the hospital.

Chapter 86

Michael returned to Laura's bedside now even more despondent than ever. Laura just lay there, her condition unchanged. He stroked her cheek, and thought about everything he had lost. He'd lost Alice, he'd lost his job, and Laura could go at any moment. He only wished he'd listened to what she had tried to explain to him earlier. And now here she was completely unable to communicate anything.

He took her hand. He'd been so convinced of her insanity when she'd told him about the prophecy; 'All the children of the future will die!' The words now sent a shiver down his spine as he remembered the conversation they had had back in the police cell.

God how it pained him, if only he'd listened to her. But all that stuff about talking to Alice, he just couldn't handle it at the time. He really was convinced that Laura had lost the plot. And he'd been so caught up in his own research into the crystal skull, he really was angry that she had taken the skull off to Central America with her. But now he understood. She'd needed the skull to translate the prophecy, the prophecy which might have helped to stave off destruction. But now nobody would listen to him, now, when the threat was so imminent, so deadly.

'I'm sorry Laura, I didn't listen. Now they won't listen. I'm so, so sorry.'

Michael lowered his head in shame, as he sat by Laura's bedside and sank deeper and deeper into an ocean of despair. He held her limp hand in his own, his eyes scanning her face for any sign of life. He had reached the lowest point in his life, and yet he was completely unable to share it with the woman he loved, unable to find solace in his wife's arms, or comfort in her words. Laura was totally oblivious to everything. Michael had to fight the temptation to grab hold of her and shake her, and say 'Wake up Laura! We have to get out of this nightmare we've found ourselves in.'

Beyond her helpless body, he could see the hospital window. Through its dull metal frame was an empty sky on which the heavy, dark clouds of night were beginning to descend. It seemed that only seconds ago it had been morning, and now the light had drained from the heavens, and the day was ending. The stark red digits on the electronic clock beside Laura's bed read four thirty five pm. Michael fought hard to hold back a sob that rose in his throat.

'No!' he shouted 'No!'

The senior nurse appeared at the doorway.

'Are you OK?'

But Michael was too numb to answer.

The nurse glanced around nervously. 'Please sir, this is a hospital. Your wife has not got any worse.'

When Michael failed to respond, the nurse walked off. He barely registered her presence. All he could think of was that in less than twenty four hours, everything would be gone, Laura's life, his own life, everything he saw, touched and felt would be no more. Everything, and everyone, he knew would be consumed in the final maelstrom.

There was no future for anyone. All was finished. There was no hope. There was nothing more he could do than wait. It would be a truly agonizing wait until the end, knowing what nobody else knew, although maybe it was better that they didn't, that within 24 hours there would be no tomorrow.

'Wake up!' he wanted to shout at the world. 'This is the end. Don't you know this is the fucking end! There will be no tomorrow! Don't any of you get that?!'

But what would be the point? Who would believe him? It would simply be one guaranteed way to get him quickly evicted from the building, and deny him his last few, precious hours with Laura.

Suddenly, Michael was seized with bitterness at the thought that Laura was already half-way there, half way to death, little more than a corpse already. And very soon he would be joining her. He couldn't take anymore. He cradled his head in his hands, and broke down in tears, sobbing uncontrollably under the crushing weight of his own despair.

At that moment an old, dark, wrinkled hand appeared gently on his shoulder. He turned round to see who it was. Michael could scarcely believe his eyes.

Standing behind him was a little old, dark-skinned man, dressed in jeans, jacket and an apple green T-shirt sporting the logo, 'I love Guatemala'.

'I got your message. ...from Dr Brown,' he said softly.

It took Michael a moment to realize who it was.

'My name is Hunab Ku,' he said holding out his other hand.

It was the Mayan shaman. Although Michael had been trying to get hold of him, he had to be the last person he actually expected to see standing now by Laura's bedside in hospital in New York.

Michael grabbed his hand with both of his own and shook it enthusiastically. 'Thank God you're here!' he exclaimed, wiping a fresh tear from his eye. He kept holding the shamans hand and shaking it, 'Thank you, thank you so much for coming.'

But his face fell again as he turned his attention back to Laura, 'Please! You've got to help her!'

The shaman looked gravely at Laura in her inert, lifeless state. He walked slowly around the bed, assessing her condition. He leaned forward and put the palm of his hand on Laura's forehead.

'It is as I feared,' he said, 'Her love for someone else, someone on the other side, is so strong that she has forgotten her love for this world.' Michael looked at him, perplexed. 'Her consciousness is now trapped inside the crystal skull.'

'What do you mean?' exclaimed Michael

'Consciousness is the only thing that can travel between the dimensions,' explained the shaman 'the only thing that can travel between the worlds.'

'You've got to get her back!' Michael pleaded.

'I'm afraid there is nothing I can do.' The shaman replied quietly.

Michael looked at him in anguish, he'd pinned his hopes on this man helping him and now he was telling him he couldn't do anything.

'But there must be something.' Michael sounded desperate.

The shaman put his fingers to his lips as if to silence him. 'I will try' he said. He walked around Laura's bed. He walked around several times, looking deep in thought, examining her carefully from all angles. Then he stopped. He'd caught sight of something that was sat on Laura's bedside cabinet, beneath the small vase of withering flowers. It was the disturbing photo of Laura's pale, lifeless face that the police detective had given Michael earlier that evening, just before he had been called back to the hospital. It was still lying on the bedside cabinet where Michael had dropped it earlier, alongside the withering flowers.

The shaman reached over and picked it up.

'What's this?' he asked.

'Oh that.' Michael replied solemnly, 'It's a reconstruction of the face on the crystal skull.'

The shaman's face lit up. 'Then there is hope!'

Michael looked mystified.

'Ron wasn't the one!' The shaman was animated with glee.

'What are you talking about?' Michael stared at the shaman's beaming face wondering whether the old man had taken leave of his senses.

'The prophecy said only the one whose face is one the skull could save us.' The shaman's voice was filled with excitement. 'That one is Laura!' he exclaimed.

'But can't you see, she's dying!?' Michael was beginning to get angry.

'Nothing I can do will save her' replied the shaman. 'She needs to be reminded of her love for this world.

And the only person who can do that is you.' Michael looked taken aback. 'You need to go in there and get her back.'

'But how?' Michael was confused.

'Where's the skull?' the shaman asked.

'It's at Nanon Systems' Crystal Laboratory'. Michael replied before looking at his watch. 'But it'll be leaving for the Z-lab around now.'

'Then that's where we're going!' the shaman declared.

'But we'll never get in there,' cautioned Michael.

'Then we must stop it before it gets there!' the shaman replied, making to leave, 'Come on!'

'But what about Laura?' Michael looked at her lying white as a sheet and unconscious on the bed.

'That's who we're going to get!' the shaman exclaimed.

'But...' Michael had no idea what he meant.

'And bring those flowers!' the shaman shouted as he flew out of the room.

Michael hesitated a moment, then grabbed the bunch of withering frangipane flowers, bewildered. He kissed Laura lovingly on the forehead, whispered, 'Hang on in there. I love you!', and followed the shaman out the door.

Chapter 87

They drove to Nanon Systems' stark modern office building on the outskirts of the city as fast as Michael's sleek silver Audi would carry them, and pulled up on the service road just outside the car park.

There they tried to remain inconspicuous, despite the fact that a couple of weary-looking workmen had just been commissioned to work through the night, erecting some new railings around the once open science park, as an added security precaution, an extra line of defence around the site. Michael sighed. There could be no stopping Caleb's increasingly elaborate attempts to protect the crystal skull.

Though they were technically outside the site, they had found a spot where they could get a pretty good view of the foyer, despite the fact that there was a small landscaped hillock between themselves and the office block itself - a hillock which thankfully afforded them some protection from the roving eye of the buildings' security cameras.

Michael sat furtively in the driver's seat, spying on the foyer. He stayed down low, completely unable to keep his eyes off the building, and half-expecting to be caught at any moment. He was, after all, dangerously close to trespassing on the 'scene of his crime' the police had already warned him from returning to.

Meanwhile the shaman was sat in the passenger seat beside him, scolding him, 'You *must* give this your full attention.'

Michael frowned at the wilting bunch of frangipane flowers in his hand. He was having a hard time getting his head around everything the shaman had been trying to tell him.

'Try again!' the shaman insisted.

'I don't think we've got time for this.' Michael was getting impatient. He still couldn't understand why he was being asked to feel a connection with a bunch of flowers.

'If you do not master this you too will enter a coma and die! Now, close your eyes, breathe deeply, and remember your connection to everyone and everything else around you,' the shaman continued.

'OK' said Michael and closed his eyes.

'The flowers will help to remind you of your connection, your love for all other things in this world. Now, try to put all the love you feel inside you into those flowers.'

But one of Michael's eyes could not help sneaking open as he tried to spy on Nanon Systems' foyer. He appeared only to be paying lip service to his mentor.

The shaman was insistent, 'Please you must learn to do this properly before you project your consciousness inside the skull.'

'I just don't get how you think it's possible for me to project my consciousness, my whole experience of the world, my whole sense of myself, into some... lump of rock!'

The shaman raised his eyebrows.

'Look, no offence, but I'm a rational person and I just like things to make sense' continued Michael.

'It does make sense, and it is possible. But before it can happen, you need to believe it is possible,' the shaman explained.

'But I'm not sure that I do believe it.'

'Then you had better talk yourself into it, persuade yourself that it is true, that it is possible. Now try again!' the shaman commanded.

Michael tried to get himself more comfortable.

'I'm not sure I can do this.'

Laura had been such a willing student, thought the shaman, but trying to get Michael to master the art of realizing his connection to all other things before projecting his consciousness inside the skull, was proving to be a bit more challenging.

'But you have to be able to, if you want to save your wife, yourself, and every other person on this planet.'

Michael fell silent. It was a sobering thought.

'It is only your own mind,' said Hunab Ku, 'It is making it like you are trying to roll a very big stone... How do you say? ...a boulder, up a very steep hill, but it doesn't have to be that way. It is only the resistance of your own mind to new ideas, new ways of seeing things.'

It was true. Michael had been experiencing an incredible amount of resistance to everything the shaman had been saying. It was all so alien to him.

'Here, this may help you to stay focused, to remember the purpose of your mission,' Hunab Ku said as he reached into his pocket. He opened the palm of Michael's hand and gently placed in it a small silver-heart shaped locket.

'That's Laura's!' exclaimed Michael, sadly.

It was the locket Laura had given to Hunab Ku back in his cave, just before she had first attempted to access the crystal skull.

'She told me she wanted you to have it, if she didn't make it back.'

There was a pause before he added gently. 'It looks like she didn't make it, so it's yours.'

Michael cradled the little silver-heart shaped locket in his hands and sighed a deep sigh. Finally, he closed his eyes properly and began to breathe deeply.

But at that very moment, the shaman caught sight of something, just out of the corner of his eye.

'Oh dear!' he said, and Michael's eyes sprung open, just in time to see a high security van, escorted by two police vehicles, pulling up outside the entrance to Nanon Systems' offices.

'Shit!' Michael exclaimed. This was the moment he had hoped would never happen.

Chapter 88

He and the shaman watched as two armed security men got out of the van, went round the back, opened the rear doors and took something out. As they marched up to the revolving glass doors of the building Michael could see they were carrying an empty 12" square, glass and metal, carry-case.

A third security man waited in the driver's seat of the van and the police stayed in their vehicles as the two uniformed guards entered the foyer. Through the chrome and glass doors Michael could see the guards being searched and having their ID cards checked by front desk security.

Then Caleb Price appeared in the foyer, surrounded by a whole group of Nanon security guards. He was cradling the crystal skull in his arms. It was very Caleb to want to do the handover himself, thought Michael, making sure that nothing would get in the way of his plans. The guards from the van remained for a while in the foyer being briefed by Nanon's head of security.

Meanwhile, outside the building, the driver of the security van was busy tucking into a doughnut, when suddenly, as if from nowhere, the Mayan shaman appeared in the car park right in front of him.

'Please! I beg you. For the sake of yourself and all the children of the future, don't take the skull!' the shaman shouted.

The driver, who had been quietly enjoying his snack, was stunned to see this elderly Central American man suddenly admonishing him. And he was even more surprised when the old man got down on his hands and knees on the tarmac right in front of the vehicle and started pleading and praying in Mayan.

Michael was almost as surprised as the driver of the van. He had been so busy wondering what the hell to do that he hadn't even noticed the shaman slipping quietly out of his own vehicle.

The driver started shouting at Hunab Ku, 'What do you think you're doing, old man!' and the police officers climbed out of their vehicles. The big fat officer said to his skinny counterpart, 'Come on, let's move this old drunk on,' as they approached the Mayan shaman with caution, thumbs to the guns in their holsters, just in case of further trouble.

Meanwhile the two security guards in the foyer signed for the crystal skull and Caleb helped them to lock it carefully away inside its futuristic new hi-tech carry-case.

Further out around the perimeter of the site, the workmen, who had been busy welding together the different parts of the new security fence, stopped to watch all the commotion. Whilst they were temporarily distracted from their task, Michael, thinking quickly, stole off with one of their tool-bags, the one containing the portable mini blow-torch. He threw it over his shoulder then sneaked across the car park, hiding amongst the various parked vehicles as he went.

He knew he only had a few minutes before the workmen would raise the alarm, and if he was seen, he would be in deep trouble. He realized the security briefing in the foyer must have ended because the two security guards, accompanied by four of Nanon's guards, were about to leave the building.

'Oh shit!' he thought as he ducked back down again amongst the few remaining cars and made his way as quickly as possible towards the security van.

Meanwhile the police had reached the front of the security van, where they were being confronted by the Mayan shaman,

'Please! You must not let them go ahead with this experiment or the world will end!' he ranted.

'What you talking about?' the fat cop replied.

'The prophecies of our people, the ancient prophecies said that the world will end on 21st December 2012. That day is tomorrow. The world will end tomorrow and it is all because of what you people are about to carry in this van.'

'Get out of here, you crazy old fool,' said the cop.

'If you take the skull, they will carry out this experiment and the world will be destroyed, at sunset, tomorrow! Please it is written in the cycles of time!'

'Come on old man, the world ain't gonna end, at least not on my shift!' he laughed, turning to his colleague. 'Beside which I'll tell you what time it is. It's time to be moving along now. These people have a job to do, so you best be moving on…'

While the police were still round the front of the security van, like the driver, totally preoccupied with the Mayan shaman, Michael meanwhile was able to climb right under the van, unnoticed – just.

For at that moment, the other two security guards returned from the foyer carrying the crystal skull in its new hi-tech carry-case. Michael could see their boots as they began to load the crystal skull into the back of the van above him. He lay there on his back, holding his breath, sandwiched between the tarmac and the bottom of the vehicle.

The four Nanon guards stood watch. Their head of security called to the police officers, 'Do you need any help there?'

'No, he's just a harmless old fool,' the smaller officer shouted back.

But the police were fast running out of patience with Hunab Ku.

'Look, I don't care if the world's going to end, but I do care if you don't get out of here. Come on, move along now or we'll have to arrest you,' Michael heard the big cop threatening.

'Please you must not take the skull or they will destroy the structure of the universe!' the shaman pleaded.

'OK that's enough! Come on Jake' the officer said to his colleague and Michael watched Hunab Ku's feet getting dragged across the pavement. The shaman was still protesting as they forcibly removed him from in front of the vehicle.

'Please, you don't understand what you're doing....' he insisted.

Michael heard the heavy thump of the doors as the guards finished loading the crystal skull into the back of the van above him. They locked the doors and climbed back into the front of the vehicle. He fumbled around the underside of the van, searching urgently for something to hang on to.

The engine started and began to rev. Quickly, Michael strapped his trouser belt around the exhaust pipe and held on tight to the chassis, as the security van began to pull off out of the car park, accompanied by its police escort.

The van drove fast through the busy suburban streets, while Michael clung for dear life to the underside of the vehicle. Cold, dirty water from the melted snow sprayed up at him from the thick tyres, while he hung suspended underneath, as the van began to accelerate past other vehicles.

He could see the surface of the road skimming past just below his cheekbone and he could feel the buckle on his belt straining under his weight. He looked at it, praying it would hold out, when all of a sudden the leather ripped from one eyelet to the next, and he felt his whole body drop dangerously nearer to the ground, as the tarmac skimmed past still faster and now even nearer to his face.

His heart hammered in his chest. This was it, he was going to die on this freezing wet highway, dragged along under the van, and no doubt driven over by the following line of traffic. His body would be nothing more than a pulp. He should have stayed with Laura rather than taking such a stupid risk. Any moment now and it would all have been for nothing in any case.

He clung on to the underside of the van for what felt like an eternity, praying that his belt would not tear any further and that the cramping muscles in his fingers and arms wouldn't give out completely, as the van and its escort pelted along the freeway.

Chapter 89

Michael was so relieved when the vehicle finally began to slow down. He had no idea where it was going as it pulled off the highway and ground to a halt in front of some security gates. All Michael could see was their boots as a group of soldiers checked the drivers' papers and did a quick visual inspection of the vehicle, before lifting the barriers and waving it through the entrance to what was clearly a military airbase.

There seemed to be soldiers every where, providing security cover as the vehicle made its way towards the runway. Michael was fortunate not to be spotted as the security van drove up a low-sided ramp and right into the cargo hold of a large bomber aircraft.

As Michael stayed there clinging to the underside of the van, his belt finally gave way completely and he fell to the floor with a gentle thud, just as the driver and guards climbed out of the van. One of the guards turned around, wondering if he had heard something.

'What was that noise?'

Michael lay there stock still, holding his breath. He was about to be discovered.

'Don't worry, it's just the sound of the engines starting' replied the driver. He slammed the door of the cab shut and he and his colleagues exited the hold.

They climbed into the plane's passenger area, the ramp closed and the plane taxied towards the runway and took off.

Inside the cargo hold, Michael looked around from his cramped space beneath the van to make sure the coast was clear. Then he unhitched the portable mini-blow-torch from around his shoulders. He set the gas switch to 'on' and fired up the ignition. The blow torch burst into flame, a searing hot pale blue conical flame, which he directed at the underside of the security van above him.

He held up his forearm to protect his eyes from the sparks which flew towards his face, and held the flame steady until the metal began to bubble and melt.

Then he began to move the torch slowly in a sweeping circular direction. He had to stop several times and wipe the sweat from his brow when the heat became too intense to bear, but when he had finished, he had burned a complete circle into the bottom of the vehicle – a circle a little wider than his own shoulders.

He pushed hard against the circle and it suddenly gave way, collapsing into the van's interior with the sound of metal chanking against metal. He stopped and held still, hoping nobody in the passenger area had been able to hear it above the sound of the planes gently humming engines. After a few moments he breathed again, pretty sure the coast was clear. Then he climbed carefully through the hole he had made in the base of the vehicle, and into the back of the security van.

It was too dark to see much inside the back of the van, so he switched the blow torch on low, and there it was right in front of him. Illuminated blue by the light of his torch, it looked almost luminous amidst the darkness of the van's interior. It seemed for a moment as if he were staring at the moon or some distant planet.

As his eyes fell on it he felt a sense of awe and wonder. He gazed at it enrapt, as if for the first time, suddenly acutely aware of its terrible power. For here it was now, right in front of him, the crystal skull that had come to mean so much to him. He had never thought about it this way before, but it struck him now like an icy bolt from the blue, a bolt that he felt like a sudden stab right into his heart.

For this crystal skull had the power over life and death, the power to make or break his own future, for this crystal skull had the power over his beloved Laura. It was the vital key to her future. In fact, it was the vital key to the whole world's future. And it sat before him now, on a gently raised plinth, encased only in a thin layer of glass.

Michael's hands began to tremble as he reached out for it. He grabbed the skull-case by the handle and lifted it upwards, but it would not move.

He redoubled his efforts and tried again, pulling it harder, but still it would not budge. He put his whole body weight into it and tried to pull it free from its plinth but it was no good.

'Damn!' Michael grimaced.

The transparent skull-case had been bolted into place.

It was to be expected really, he thought. Caleb wouldn't have wanted to take any risks with the skull-case coming loose and getting damaged in transit.

So, he tried opening the latch but it was locked. Using the gun of the blow-torch for leverage he tried to prise it open but it was securely fastened, so he tried to smash the glass. He took off his jacket and covered the glass, to deaden the noise, then lifted the circle of heavy metal he had just cut from the floor high above his head and dropped it down on top of it. The metal circle just bounced off the glass with a 'clang!'

Michael paused, anxious about the noise he had just made. From beyond the van he heard the door into the passenger section of the plane open. *Shit! They must have heard it,* he thought. He ducked down out of sight and waited, his heart pounding. He heard the sound of footsteps and was pretty sure he could see the shadow of someone peering through the little window on the side of the vehicle into the back of the van. But the crystal skull appeared totally unharmed. Then a few minutes later the passenger section door closed again.

Michael began to breathe. He wouldn't be trying that again. In any case, the glass was way too hard, and thick. *It must be bullet proof,* he deduced.

So he tried blow-torching his way through the lock. Sweat poured from his brow as he worked, and the metal glowed white hot in the flames, but still the lock remained solid.

Then he attempted to torch the whole thing free from its bolts. But it was all to no avail. *The lock and bolts must all be made of tungsten,* he concluded.

Finally, he pointed the blow torch at the fabric of the case itself. Holding the torch steady in his tired hands he fired ceaselessly at the glass, but it refused either to shatter or melt. It remained stubbornly intact. As he suspected, it was not only bullet-proof, but flame-proof.

Michael felt the plane lurch as it began its descent towards its destination.

He slumped down next to the skull, exhausted by his efforts. He'd have to give up on his attempts to release the skull. It was hopeless. There was no way the skull could be moved. His plan to release it and find some means of escape wasn't working, and he was fast running out of options.

As a shard of light penetrated the hold, Michael looked at his watch. It was 7.30 am on December 21st 2012.

Chapter 90

December 21st 2012

Michael's heart sank. It was already dawn on the day of the experiment and his plane was well on its way to 'Los Ammuno', a high security military airbase in the middle of the New Mexico desert, and the last stopping off point before the skull's ultimate destination, 'The Z-lab', Nanon systems own underground test facility, one of the most staunchly guarded and secret locations on the planet.

Michael was probably only minutes away from being discovered at the air base. He had at best an hour before they reached the lab and the van doors would be opened.

The plane touched down and as it pulled to a halt at the end of the runway Michael could hear the guards as they returned to the hold and climbed back into the front of the security van. He crawled quickly to the area immediately behind their cab and pinned himself to the interior wall. Just in time! The driver started the engine and glanced back over his shoulder, through the little window at the rear of his cab, to check that the crystal skull was still alright in the back. Michael hid down out of sight, immediately behind the driver.

Under tight security, the van reversed back down the low-sided ramp off the plane and across the runway. It was joined now by a military vehicle escort and accompanied by a police helicopter circling overhead as it left the base and the whole convoy drove off across the desert, headed towards the top secret underground 'Z-lab' facility.

Although Michael couldn't see it, the above ground section of the lab was just visible in the distance from the aerial perspective of the police helicopter. It lay only a few miles away beyond a low ridge of mountains.

From the outside the facility looked deceptively unassuming, like the notorious 'Area 51', a simple collection of non-descript aircraft-hangar-type buildings in the middle of the desert. But the huge perimeter fence, complete with CCTV cameras, guard dogs, and constant armed patrol suggested there was more to the site than might at first appear. The whole complex was further surrounded by a ring of low-lying mountains, and the only means of access to the top-secret, high-security base was via a road tunnel through these hills.

All of Michael's attempts to release the crystal skull had been futile. In less than thirty minutes' time the convoy would be arriving at the underground complex. Then he would be finished.

He could hear the sound of rock music blasting out of the driver's cab of the van as it drove across the desert. The security guards had put on the radio. Their task almost accomplished, they were beginning to relax and were now cheerily singing along, hopelessly out of tune. Though Michael normally enjoyed a bit of prog rock, he felt a bitter stab of irony as he realized what they were singing.

It was rock band REM's famous tune 'It's The End of The World, as We Know It'.

He shook his head sadly. If only they knew. This would be the last time these guys would ever sing along casually to the radio, the last time they would ever let their hair down on a mission almost complete. By the end of this very day they would be decimated, their bodies crushed and destroyed as they were sucked through the coming black hole into total annihilation.

Michael was the only one who understood the irony of the situation, as he stayed down out of sight in the back of the van. But he almost wished he could trade places with the guards and be in a place where he was blissfully unaware of what the future had in store. He wished that he too could sing along loudly, out of tune, and in ignorance, without any concept of the terrible fate that lay ahead, without any knowledge of the approaching apocalypse.

How could I have got it so terribly wrong? He berated himself. He'd been so convinced that the only thing that could come out of his research into the crystal skull would be beneficial, that it would help humanity to push back the frontiers of time and space. It was such a wonderful and exciting idea. But he realized he'd simply been seduced by this scientific concept, completely unable to see that tampering with the very fabric that structured our lives, Space and Time, could possibly be so dangerous.

All he'd been able to see were the wonderful possibilities, the formulas, and the theories, and not the cold hard reality that what he was proposing was potentially far more destructive than anything he could ever have imagined.

Suddenly he felt filled with rage. He wanted to smash the crystal skull, to shatter it into a thousand tiny little pieces. He wished that he'd never seen it. Just look where it had led him, led everyone. It was about to destroy everything and everyone he ever knew. And it was all, his fault. He buried his head in his hands. Oh how he wished he'd never set eyes on that skull, ever.

He sat there for a moment, not knowing what to do, before he decided that what the Mayan shaman had suggested was probably the only option left open to him. Even if he could hardly get his head around what Hunab Ku had been trying to tell him, he ought really to give it a try. He owed it to Laura, and to everyone else, at least to do that.

He knelt down in front of the transparent skull-case, closed his eyes, breathed deeply and leant forward to let his forehead rest gently against the glass, just as Laura had done with the crystal skull in the Warburton Secure Unit. There he remained for a few minutes, his head pressed against the glass, as he tried to 'project his consciousness inside the skull'.

Outside, the convoy entered a long tunnel through the mountains, and the interior of the van was plunged into darkness. But apart from that, inside the back of the van, nothing happened. Michael quickly began to get frustrated.

'Come on, come on!' he whispered to himself, impatient at how long the process seemed to be taking.

He was trying hard to project his consciousness inside the skull, just as the shaman had attempted to teach him, but it seemed that nothing he did made even the slightest bit of difference.

He redoubled his efforts, trying to think of those damned flowers, and frowning intently as he pressed his forehead even harder against the glass case. But still nothing happened.

Back outside, the convoy emerged from the far end of the tunnel. It had traveled under the ring of mountains that protected the Z-lab. Less than a quarter of a mile further along the road it pulled to a halt in front of some security gates. As Michael peered out of the side window of the van his anxiety levels rose.

They had reached the entrance to the secret underground research facility, the security checkpoint where the narrow road met the vast perimeter fence.

At regular intervals all along the perimeter fence armed sentries were standing. The guards on the gate began checking the driver's papers and quizzing the driver about the nature of his mission. Michael was finding it impossible now to concentrate on projecting his consciousness inside the crystal skull. He pressed himself up against the rear of the driver's cab and listened intently. He heard the guards ask the driver of the van and his colleagues to get out of the vehicle.

He froze, and waited, like a man condemned, certain this was a sign that they wanted to search the van. Dear God, if they searched the vehicle now his whereabouts would certainly be discovered and that would be it. Game over!

What on earth would he say? How could he possibly explain himself? There wasn't a word he could utter that would get him past those security gates now.

As he strained to hear what was happening, the guards on the gate began to body search the driver and his cohorts. The chief guard then stepped up to the van and shone his powerful flashlight through the narrow side window into the back of the vehicle to verify that they were carrying the payload they claimed.

Michael stayed down low, staring at the rear doors of the van. Any moment now those doors would swing open, he would be discovered and it would all be over.

He felt his heart hammering in his chest as he waited for the combination lock to click and whir and the doors to fly open. All hell would surely be let loose then. He would be in deep trouble. God knows what the penalty might be for what he had just done, attempting to hijack the crystal skull on its way to Caleb's big experiment. He didn't like to imagine.

Worse still, he would never see his beloved Laura again and the whole world would be lost forever, stupidly and needlessly destroyed, in the name of scientific progress. It was a very bleak prospect indeed.

Michael closed his eyes hard and, for the first time in his life, found himself praying, 'Please, I've got to get to Laura, I've got to stop what's going on here'.

At that moment he was stunned to hear the Chief Guard stamping the driver's papers and returning them, confirming that everything appeared to be in order. The driver and his colleagues climbed back into their cab, the barricade was raised, and the guards on the gate waved the whole convoy through as they drove on, right into the Z-lab compound.

Even at this hour in the morning the place was buzzing with activity. Peering over the driver's shoulder, Michael could see scientists in white lab-coats scurrying around with their clipboards in hand, technicians in orange jackets and safety helmets inspecting various bits of machinery, and all around them, posted at strategic locations all around the site there were armed men in black uniforms, some of them driving around in Humvees and Jeeps. He also noticed a handful of oil tankers parked by a docking point near the centre of the base.

The van drove up to an enormous domed building at the centre of the compound on the side of which was a large doorway protected by a security grille. On provision of the correct, properly stamped papers the grille was raised and the van was allowed to drive right into the heart of the building. It looked like some kind of futuristic factory or power station. Everywhere Michael looked there were huge electrical generators, enormous metal pipes carrying fuel and thick plastic cables carrying electricity. Precisely what each cable, pipe or piece of machinery did was not entirely obvious even to Michael's highly trained eye, but there was clearly a heavily industrialized electricity generating process involved.

The van was directed by the guards along the concrete access corridor between the giant pipes, fans and generators towards what looked like a large cage in the centre of the facility. As the vehicle drove into place between its metal bars, Michael realised it was actually an oversized elevator, like the type found in a modern-day coal-mine, designed to allow vehicular access to the underground section of the Z-lab complex below.

As the resident guards closed the cage doors, with a loud clunk, and the elevator began its slow descent to the lower levels, Michael was struck by the terrifying realization that only a few brief minutes from now, the van would reach the lower level, the centre of the Z-lab, and he would finally be discovered. That would be it. Any attempt to bring Laura back or to stop the experiment would be over. His time was up. It was too late. The future was now set in stone. There was nothing more he could do than sit there and wait to be discovered.

He slumped back against the wall, and as the lift continued its slow, steady descent, he put his hands in his pockets, and gave up the ghost. Suddenly he became aware of a small object inside his pocket. He had been so preoccupied he hadn't even noticed that he had put his jacket back on, let alone that his hands should have crept inside its pockets.

But it was almost as if the object had nudged his hand. He pulled his hand back out and opened his palm. He felt a deep sense of sadness at what he saw. It was Laura's little silver heart-shaped locket. The one he had bought for her, that she always wore around her neck, to remind her of Alice. She had never been separated from that locket until the day she had given it to the Mayan shaman to pass on to Michael in the event that she didn't make it back from inside the skull.

He opened it up to see the tiny faded photograph Laura kept inside it of himself, Laura and Alice all smiling happily on their last holiday together on the beach.

They had all been together as a family then, but first Alice, and then Laura, were both gone from him. But he was happy to have this small reminder of them, this small part of the world that had been so personal to Laura was with him now.

Overwhelmed with sadness, he sighed a deep and sorrowful sigh, and then, almost involuntarily, his fingers closed around the locket and he lifted it to his lips and kissed it, through his own gently clenched fist. He felt a shiver run down the back of his spine as he turned back to look at the crystal skull, still sitting before him in its bullet-proof glass and tungsten case.

As he stared at the crystal skull, something within him shifted. The anger and resentment he had felt towards it were gone and he no longer felt filled with a desperate sense of urgency. There was nothing more he could do now than look deeply into the skull's crystalline interior, at the beautiful inclusions and soft bubbles that seemed to glitter before him like tiny stars in a distant solar system.

His breathing was more relaxed and deeper now as he gently rested his forehead against the skull-case once again. He whispered 'Laura! I love you!' and as the elevator continued its slow but steady descent, his body suddenly collapsed into a heap on the floor, as he finally succeeded in projecting his consciousness deep inside the crystal skull.

Chapter 91

Michael, of course, had no idea at first what was happening, no understanding of the concept that his consciousness, his mind, had been separated from his body. Instead, it felt to him as if he had just taken a deep dive into some strange sort of pool filled with something like a cross between water and air, as his consciousness, in a form that looked and felt to him like his whole body, appeared with a silent splash inside the ethereal world inside the crystal skull.

After a few moments of panicking that he might drown, Michael quickly realized he could not only float, but also breathe in his new-found environment, the watery, space-like, 'other world' inside the crystal skull. He soon learned that he could 'swim' around quite comfortably like a weightless astronaut, exploring a whole new dimension of time and space. As he learned to relax and slowed down his movements, he found himself in awe of his new surroundings.

It was a world where it seemed as if outer space and underwater had somehow merged. Distant galaxies appeared to be only an arm's length away, but as he reached out, he discovered he could not actually touch them. They defied the tips of his fingers, just as colourful fish defy the touch of the scuba-diver as they float around them in coral seas. Michael was fascinated, mesmerized. As far as he was concerned, he was dreaming, a beautiful dream, from which he had no desire to wake up.

Then he noticed that further out, around the perimeter of his new found world, he could see something, almost like another world beyond, but it was as if he were seeing it through a distorting lens. He swam to the exterior where he could just make out what looked like the back of the security van, but it was as if he was looking at it from underwater or through a thick layer of undulating glass.

He recognized the circle of metal he had cut from the base of the van, and there was something else lying on the floor beside it. It was an arm, an immobile one. Someone was lying motionless on the floor of the van, apparently in some kind of trouble. Whoever it was, they liked the same kind of expensive jackets as he did, and, as if that wasn't enough of a coincidence, they were wearing the same watch as his own. His eyes quickly traced the length of the arm up to its torso.

But nothing had prepared him for what he saw next, the jolt of horror he felt as he recognized the body, as it suddenly dawned on him that the man lying there crumpled and unconscious in front of him was himself.

He realized, with a start, that what he must be seeing was the real world still going on outside the crystal skull. That just as the shaman had said was possible, his mind had become separated from his body, and his consciousness, his whole sense of himself, was now located inside the crystal skull, and that what he was now looking at was clearly his own unconscious body now lying there inert and lifeless on the floor of the van beyond.

Michael was still in the process of trying to come to terms with this shocking realization, when he became aware of a swirling pattern in the 'heavens' around him. He turned round to see what looked like a vortex of galaxies spiraling off into the centre of his new-found world, creating what looked like a passageway, a tunnel through time and space.

He found himself drawn closer to peer inside it, and there in the distance, at the far end of the tunnel he could see a light gently glowing. This was where he needed to go. He knew it instinctively. He could feel the pull of the light, beckoning him forth. As he got nearer toward the end of the tunnel the light became stronger, until he was almost blinded by its brilliance. It looked so beautiful, he felt as if he were witnessing the very birth of the cosmos itself.

And there in the distance, beyond the tunnel's end, he could see Laura, floating around with her back to him. Her long blonde locks were flowing softly, waving back and forth around her head as if they were being pulled to and fro by some gentle, almost imperceptible breeze, ocean current, or waves.

He cried out 'Laura!' and began swimming down the tunnel towards her, unsure whether or not to believe what he saw, doubting it, fearing it might just be his imagination or some cruel trick of the light. For the last time he had seen her she had been lying comatose in a hospital bed, on the verge of death, her face pale and ghostly, all the gentle, animating life force that made her his Laura gone.

As he approached Laura spun around slowly and held her arms out to greet him. Michael pulled her close as they engaged in a beautiful, loving, swirling, swimming embrace. He held her tight. It was a moment of unimaginable ecstasy. To finally be reunited with the one he loved was more than he had ever dared to hope for. In her hospital bed, her life run by machines, Laura had been but a shadow of her former self, barely recognizable. And yet here she was, his beautiful wife, real, complete and whole, smiling at him, her eyes dancing with joy and her face more radiant than he had seen it in years. He closed his eyes, willing the moment to last forever, to be all there was for all eternity, his lovely Laura back with him, in his arms, where she belonged.

When Michael eventually opened his eyes, and they adjusted to the bright light, he saw something that had until now been hidden from view behind Laura.

For a moment he was completely stunned. Nothing he had ever dreamed of could have prepared him for this. It was completely beyond all comprehension.

'Alice!' he gasped, for there was no doubt in his mind, just as there had been none in Laura's, that the magnificent, shimmering being of light, only a short distance away from him now, was his beautiful daughter.

It was a moment that he had never thought he could experience, a moment that belonged beyond the realm of imagination, beyond even the wildest fantasy. For what he was experiencing now had simply never figured anywhere in his understanding of how the world worked.

'Is this real?' He wondered, not even realizing that he had said it out loud.

'Yes it's real,' replied Laura, with a beaming smile.

Michael's face lit up still further. His eyes glowed with pleasure as he drank in the sight of his beautiful little girl. He never thought it possible. He had been convinced she was gone forever. But now here she was right in front of him, almost as clear as the day.

'Alice! My little one!' he whispered and reached out to touch her, but his fingers bashed into something that he had not noticed until now.

He so desperately wanted to reach her, to hold her in his arms once more, but he was prevented from doing so by a strange semi-visible membrane that came between him and his daughter. It looked like a thin layer of flexible plastic or lightly frosted glass. It was the thin membrane that separated their two different worlds, the barrier between the world of the living and the world of the dead.

Chapter 92

Meanwhile, back outside the skull, the security van arrived at the bottom of the vehicle elevator. The giant lift had reached the underground section of the Z-lab. The cage doors opened and the van drove slowly on along the service corridor and right into the very the heart of the underground complex. There it pulled to a halt just outside the main door into the Central Chamber.

Caleb Price, who had traveled to the site separately, in the luxury of his own private Lear Jet and limo, came out of the Control Room to meet the security van. A small party of scientists and technicians gathered around him and watched.

They waited patiently as the van's driver and guards came round to the rear of the vehicle and proceeded to spend a full two minutes de-activating the alarm system and entering the correct numbers into the digital combination lock. The lock whirred and clicked and the small crowd looked on eagerly as the guards finally opened the back doors of the van.

Craning their necks to peer into the back of the vehicle, they were shocked at what they saw inside. The crystal skull was still there, bolted safely into place on its plinth inside its custom-built bullet-proof glass and tungsten case, but beneath it lay a body, a middle-aged man's body, crumpled in a heap on the floor.

'What the hell?' exclaimed the driver, and as the crowd gasped, he leapt into the back of the van and turned the body over. 'He's alive!' he yelled.

Caleb was stunned to see that it was Michael who lay unconscious on the floor of the van, beneath the transparent skull-case.

'Quick! Call security!' one of the lab-coats shouted,

To which Caleb replied, 'We already got security!' he glowered at the van driver, 'Call the medics!'

Within minutes, a couple of medics arrived. They carefully lifted Michael's limp, comatose body out of the back of the van and carried it into a nearby store room, accompanied by two of the security guards.

The medics took Michael's pulse, then slapped his face to try to bring him round. But it was to no avail. One of the security guards filled up a cleaner's bucket with cold water from the tap inside the store room and threw it in Michael's face. But still he did not respond.

Michael, meanwhile, was in another world, deep inside the crystal skull. He gazed longingly at Alice, on the other side of the invisible divide.

'Oh, Alice! My precious little angel! God I've missed you!'

'Me too, Daddy!' she replied. Michael laughed with joy at the sound of her beautiful little voice, before he frowned, 'But how can it be? I don't understand. I thought you were...'

''Dead?' It's OK Daddy, you can say it, you know.' Her tone was unflinching. 'Nobody ever really dies you see Daddy, we just go to another place, to live in another world than the one that you know.'

Michael just sighed and shook his head, 'I never ever thought...'

'It's fantastic isn't it, Michael?' said Laura turning to him, with a beaming smile across her face. 'And now you're here we can all be together, a family again.' She turned to Alice. 'We don't ever have to go back.'

But Alice shook her head sadly and said, 'Mummy, there's something I have to show you. And you too Daddy.' 'Come with me' she said 'I need to show you something.'

She turned and led the way, swimming off along her side of the membrane that separated their two worlds.

Michael took Laura's hand and they began to follow her, swimming along their side of the semi-visible divide, while Alice led them deeper and deeper inside the crystal skull.

'You see, your world and mine are both part of the same universe, like two sides of the same coin,' said Alice, 'And it is a very beautiful universe. Look!'

Suddenly it seemed to Michael and Laura as if they were surrounded by a hundred million twinkling stars. They were all around them, even beneath their feet, as if they were standing in space.

'Wow! Look at this!' Michael was awestruck. They could see distant galaxies glimmering like jewels, and stars exploding all around, sending streamers of brilliant multi-coloured light across the far horizon.

'I never thought I would ever see anything so beautiful' whispered Laura.

'This is your world, your universe,' said Alice, 'I am just helping you to see it properly again.'

And then, suddenly spinning through space beneath them, they saw a beautiful blue-green planet.

'I don't believe it, that's Earth!' gasped Michael. It took his breath away.

'But how?'

He looked at Laura. She hugged him and smiled. 'I.. I don't know,' she answered, marveling too at how they had suddenly found themselves gazing across the vast, impossibly beautiful vista that lay before them.

'Sometimes there is not a how or a why things happen that humans can understand,' said Alice.

'Like why you died?' asked Michael.

'That's right,' she replied.

A tear formed in Laura's eyes and trickled down her cheek. As it fell from her face it appeared to land on the Earth and suddenly the Earth itself looked momentarily like a huge tear drop that was falling through space.

'But why are you showing us all this?' Michael asked.

'Because I need you to understand that there is an invisible force that holds all this together,'

'What do you mean?'

'It is a very powerful force. It is the force that holds everything in the universe together in its place. It is what binds you and I together as one. It is even what holds atoms and sub-atomic particles together, although your scientists have not realized this yet. It is the force that holds everything in the universe together. And it is a very powerful force. It is what you and I would call 'love'.'

'I don't understand,' said Michael

'You and your scientists are not ready to understand this yet, but one day you will understand. Love is the force the holds everything in the universe together, even what you call atoms, neutrinos and quarks. Although you do not understand it yet, love is what holds you, and I, and all particles together.'

'Because all the particles love each other, if you send even one tiny particle into the other dimension all the other particles will follow, because they love each other so much. So if you try to pass anything, other than pure consciousness, through the membrane that separates the worlds you will rupture the fabric of the universe.'

'That's what I was trying to tell Caleb,' said Michael.

'I know,' said Alice.

'But I still don't get why you're showing us all this?' asked Laura.

The Earth spun before them, fragile and delicate, part of a vast universe, an ocean, of un-comparable beauty.

'I wanted you to understand what you might lose, mummy. I wanted to show you that you are part of something bigger, that this skull is part of something bigger, and everybody needs to know that. The universe is evolving. We are all evolving and our consciousness is part of that. Our consciousness needs to evolve now to a much higher level and this skull is part of that.'

'So what do you want us to do, my love?' asked Laura.

'This message I have for you, mummy, it needs to be shared, and it can only be shared if you can stop the experiment. Now that you are listening the future is no longer set in stone, but if you don't stop the experiment, there will be no future.'

'What experiment are you talking about my dear?' asked Laura. Alice seemed to be talking in riddles, and Laura had been in a coma now for so long she had never even heard of Caleb's big experiment.

Michael just shook his head. He didn't know where to begin his explanation.

'Come with me again Mummy and I will show you.' Alice turned full circle and began swimming quickly back again, back the way she had just come, back along her side of the membrane, towards the outer edges of the crystal skull.

'Come and see what they are doing mummy, and you too daddy. Come and see what they are doing to your beautiful planet, your universe, back in the real world outside this crystal skull.'

Michael and Laura swam after her as fast as they could along their side of the divide. Alice led them towards the outer edge of the crystal skull, to just inside its eye sockets, where, squinting to look outside, they could just make out what was going on in the real world outside the skull.

'Look!' exclaimed Alice, as they saw what looked to them like a giant pair of hands reaching towards them, as if they were seeing them through thickly distorted glass.

Outside the skull, Caleb was reaching for the crystal skull in its sealed glass case inside the back of the security van. It was his hands that Michael, Laura and Alice were seeing from their perspective inside the crystal skull. One of the guards assisted Caleb by unlocking the tungsten bolts that held the case firmly in place on its plinth. They then carried the case carefully out of the van and into the hi-tech Central Chamber at the heart of the underground complex.

In the centre of the Z-lab chamber was an enormous gyroscope-like construction. Its gleaming metallic arms reached out around the chamber like the tentacles of a giant octopus. It was approached by several raised metal walkways. Reaching the end of the main walkway, the guard undid the lock and Caleb lifted the skull gently out of its case. Assisted by several technicians, the crystal skull was then mounted into the centre of this strange gyroscope, where it was securely bolted into position, held in place by a number of spiral-wired electrodes.

Looking on at this from inside the skull, Alice tried to explain to her parents,

'You see, the two worlds are connected. What happens in your world affects our world as well. The physical world and the spirit world are like two sides of the same coin. The ancestors and the future generations that live in my world are deeply affected by what you do in your physical world.'

'But only pure consciousness can travel between the dimensions. If you send an actual particle of matter between the two dimensions, then you will destroy the fabric of your physical world. And because the two worlds are connected you will destroy the fabric of our world as well. The world of the living and the world of the dead will collide.'

'So if your people go ahead with this experiment, if they send a particle from your dimension into ours, from your physical world into our spiritual world. Then you will destroy both of our worlds. You will destroy not only the world of the living, but also the world of the dead, and of those who are yet to be born.'

'The ancestors did not raise you and give you life so that you could destroy your world. And the future generations, if you destroy your world, will no longer be born, so our world too will have no future any more. So if you destroy your world, our world too, it will die. And then none of us, neither the living, nor the dead, will exist anymore. It will be the end of you and me. It will be the end of everything.'

Michael and Laura listened, and gazed on in horror at what was going on in the physical world around them, outside the crystal skull.

Further out around the edge of the chamber, another group of technicians were wheeling huge laser-machines into place. They looked like massive hypodermic syringes, each surrounded by a giant electrical coil. Their angle of calibration was accurately adjusted, using remotely controlled hydraulics, so that their needle-like points were aimed directly at the crystal skull in the centre of the room.

A computer-synthesized voice announced over the pa system, 'Stand by to test lasers.' The scientists and technicians took refuge in the neighbouring control room, before a huge pulse of laser light was fired at the crystal skull, with a zap!

Inside the crystal skull, Michael, Laura and Alice were blasted back by its force, which penetrated the interior like a bolt of lightning from the blue.

Recovering his balance, Michael swam back towards the outer edge of the skull, shouting, 'No! Stop! You'll kill us all!', but nobody back in the real world could either hear or see him.

So he tried to get back out of the skull again, to try to stop the experiment. He swam right up to the outer edge of the skull and threw himself against the thick layer of 'distorting glass' that separated the inner world inside the skull, from the comparatively giant real world going on around it outside. But he ended up simply bashing his face, and indeed his whole body, against it. He tried again, hurling himself with all the force he could muster against it, but no matter what he did he still could not get past the solid transparent outer shell of the crystal skull.

'Daddy wait!' Alice tried to explain the situation to her father, 'You can't leave without mummy. Your love for her is too strong for you to go back alone.'

Michael and Alice both turned to look at Laura.

'Laura?' Michael asked. He wanted her to go back with him.

But Laura simply turned to Alice. 'Come with us, Alice' she begged.

'I'd really love to mummy,' she replied, 'But I can never come back to your world.'

At that, Laura broke down in tears. 'I'm so sorry, Alice. I'm so, so sorry,' she sobbed. She still blamed herself for Alice's death.

'Don't cry, Mummy' said Alice, 'It wasn't your fault. You did everything you could, and you too daddy,' she turned to him and back to Laura again. '...And now I need you to do everything you can again. Please mummy! You must go back and reverse the experiment, before it is too late.'

Michael had already resolved to do so. He reached his hand out towards Alice.

'Goodbye my love.'

She responded, gently pressing her little fingers into the palm of his hand from the other side of the invisible membrane.

'Goodbye daddy.'

Gazing into Alice's eyes, Laura reached both arms out as if to embrace her, placing both hands up against the invisible divide.

'I love you.'

Alice responded, softly pressing the palms of both little hands into hers from the other side.

'I love you too mummy.' She paused. 'But please, now you must go and save us all.'

Michael took Laura by the wrist and started to lead her gently back down the 'time-space tunnel' to try to exit the skull. All the while, Laura was looking back over her shoulder at Alice slowly waving goodbye.

Suddenly, Laura broke free, as if coming out of a trance, and swam back to Alice.

'But Alice, I'll never see you again.' She sounded forlorn.

'You will see me again, mummy.' answered Alice, in her usual solemn tone. 'You will see me in the first drop of dew that falls in the spring. You will see me in the butterfly as it opens its wings. And you will see me in the glimmer of sunlight that ripples across the grass and then loses itself in the twilight.'

A long tear trickled down Laura's cheek as Michael took her by the other hand and led her back down the tunnel, to just inside the skull's forehead.

This time, when Michael pressed his body weight against the outer edge of the crystal skull it was no longer like solid glass. Instead it began to bend outwards, like a giant sheet of stretchy transparent plastic, or cling-film, and, without too much effort, they both burst right through it.

Chapter 93

Back in the real world, Michael came to in the store room of the Z-lab. It took him a few moments to register where he was, lying on his back looking up at a low white ceiling. He had no recollection of how he'd ended up there.

A couple of medics were deep in conversation beside him. They didn't seem to have noticed that he'd come round. He tried to speak, to ask them where Laura was, but an oxygen mask had been placed over his face.

He tried to move before he felt the grip of metal on his wrists, as a pair of cuffs bit into his flesh. He realized his arms had been handcuffed behind his back. Any lingering sense of elation he had at his reunion with Laura and Alice was quickly replaced with anxiety about how he was going to get out of there.

The medics, meanwhile, were almost as mystified as Michael. Why should he suddenly have come round now, when they had originally applied the oxygen mask some minutes before?

But the security guards had quite a different set of questions on their minds.

'Now! You've got some explaining to do!' barked the chief guard, as he and his colleague dragged Michael to his feet and rough-handled him out of the room.

It was the buzz and hum of electronic monitoring equipment that Laura noticed first, before she opened her eyes to find herself lying in a hospital bed. She was baffled. *Where am I? What am I doing here?* She had absolutely no idea where she was or how she had got there. It was a total mystery. She was very confused.

There were wires and electrodes attached all over her, and respiratory equipment forcing her to breathe in and out. *My God what has happened to me?*

It was such a shock to find herself there. She had no idea there had been anything wrong with her. She wondered if perhaps she had been in some terrible accident and had lost her memory of what had happened.

Well that was certainly true, she had forgotten what had happened, a sort of temporary amnesia had indeed affected her. Yet, as she lifted her head off the pillow and scanned down her body, there didn't appear to be anything wrong, no arms or legs missing, and no apparent physical damage.

So what on Earth was she doing there?

A middle aged nurse appeared, ruddy faced and Irish, she began busily folding back the sheets on Laura's bed, making sure she wasn't getting bed sores. She did a start to see that Laura's eyes were wide open, amazed that she had suddenly come round from her chronic coma, and for no apparent reason.

'Where am I?' Laura asked the stunned looking nurse.

'Why, you're in East Side Hospital, in New York, where you've been for some time, my dear.' The nurse beamed at her, delighted she had finally come round.

What had happened was that Laura's consciousness had now been reunited with her body, and that body was still in hospital, in the intensive care ward, back in New York! But Laura still had no idea what was going on.

'Where's Michael?' she asked.

The nurse just shrugged her shoulders. She had no idea what Laura was talking about.

'Ah, you mean Dr Michael Odajee. He's in the office. I'll go and get him for you.' And she was off down the ward before Laura had a chance to correct her.

Laura wondered how long she'd been lying there. She looked at the digital clock by her bedside, which registered the time and the date in bright red digits.

The time read '10.30 am.' But it was the date on the clock that sent a bolt of shock through Laura's system and sent her pulse soaring, its rapid pace echoing back across the electronic monitoring screens.

It read '12.21.2012'

The end date! Laura realized, as it all came flooding back to her.

Oh my God, Michael! He's still in the Z-lab! She suddenly understood what must have happened to them both. That she and Michael had now been reunited with their bodies, and that Michael's body must still be in the Z-lab somewhere. At the same time, she felt the cold, horrifying realization that the experiment they needed to prevent was about to happen that very day, in only six hours' time, over two thousand miles away, beneath the deserts of Los Ammuno. But how on Earth was she going to get there? How was she going to save Michael and stop the experiment before it was too late?

There wasn't a moment to lose. Ripping the respiratory system from her face, she tore off the electrodes. As the monitoring equipment bleeped and flashed into emergency mode, she leapt out of bed and began rummaging through the drawers of her bedside cabinet, searching for her clothes and wallet.

There was next to nothing there, only a small plastic folder labeled 'Warnburton Secure Unit – Patient ID and Personal Effects'. She opened it up and poured its contents into the palm of her hand, recovering her passport and a handful of dollar bills. She closed her fist around them and dashed out the door.

The nurse was emerging into the corridor, accompanied by a tall, black doctor.

'Here's Dr Odajee!' she said in surprise as Laura ran right past them.

'Wait! We need to discuss your... progress.' The doctor tailed off as Laura disappeared down the corridor.

As she flew round the corner and into the next ward, Laura's eyes fell on the open-mouthed expression of a young woman sat upright in her bed watching Laura running through the ward in her hospital gown.

It occurred to Laura that she was probably still under the jurisdiction of the Warnburton Institute and that, technically, having emerged from her coma she was probably due back in their care. So she had better get as far away from the medics as possible, lest they return her to that nut-house.

But how the hell was she going to get out of that hospital without being formally discharged, especially when all she had to wear was a regulation hospital gown?

She marched over to the young woman, opened her bedside cabinet and said

'Look, they can give you my details, but I just need to borrow a few things.'

Laura then proceeded to help herself to a neat leather overnight bag.

'That's my stuff!' the woman protested.

'Yes I know and I'm very sorry, but I haven't got time to explain.'

'What are you doing?'

'Thank you!' said Laura, 'Thank-you so much!' She then ran quickly out of the ward with the bag, leaving the baffled young woman speechless.

As Laura disappeared round the corner however she could hear her shouting 'Nurse! Nurse! That woman just stole my things!'

Laura blushed furiously as she tore off down the corridor in search of the nearest opportunity to change clothes and get out of the hospital.

Chapter 94

Back in the Z-lab, the guards brought Michael into the Control Room where he was made to stand hand-cuffed in front of Caleb.

'Ah Michael!' Caleb turned his attention away from the observation window overlooking the Central Chamber, to look at him. 'So glad you could join us! You're just in time for the main event!' Caleb was clearly enjoying his own sense of irony and sarcasm.

'Caleb, please! We're not God! It's not safe to tamper with the fabric of space-time! You've got to stop the experiment...!'

Caleb indicated something to the guards, who quickly silenced Michael by applying thick electrical insulation tape across his mouth.

'That's better!' said Caleb, 'Now, as I was saying, we're just running through the final preparations so please, do, come and take a seat...'

He gestured to the guards to deposit Michael into the empty office chair alongside his own, where he would be forced to look out through the observation window at the preparations going on in the Central Chamber right in front of him.

The guards attached Michael's handcuffs to the arms of the chair as Caleb continued, 'Of course, all of this is really thanks to you, Michael. It's your baby, so to speak. So why don't you just sit back, relax, make yourself comfortable, and enjoy the show!'

Michael continued to struggle hard against his cuffs and gag.

Chapter 95

Later that day, an airport taxi pulled in to a scruffy, deserted-looking diner cum gas filling station on a lonely New Mexico hillside. The old sign outside read: 'Last Chance - Gas/Café'. A dry breeze blew clumps of tumble-weed that spun aimlessly along the dusty road.

Inside the taxi, the driver's eyes narrowed as he scrutinized his ride in the rear view mirror. He sucked his own teeth as he tried to explain the situation to her.

'No, I'm sorry, ma'am. This is as far as I can take you. It's a military exclusion zone beyond here.'

After a couple of attempts to persuade him to go further, including an offer of as many dollar bills as she had, which was derided as not even enough to have driven her to this god-forsaken spot, Laura gave up and got out of the cab.

The driver looked her up and down slowly as he chewed on his gum. 'I gotta admit though, mam, I was tempted!' he added, salacious but unhelpful.

Laura had to admit that the clothes she stole from the young woman in the hospital would not have been her first choice; a shocking pink mini-skirt, thigh-high stiletto boots and a t-shirt emblazoned with fluffy white kittens. Still, she never would have got this far in her regulation hospital gown.

She fished around in the pockets of her beaded buckskin jacket for the tip the driver demanded on top of the fare she had already paid, and handed it to him, before the dirty cab drove off, a cloud of dust following behind as it pulled away.

As the taxi disappeared, Laura looked out across the lonely desert, eyes half-closed against the burning sun. Overhead a couple of vultures were circling and in the distance beyond them she could see the above ground section of the Z-lab she had come so far to reach. Inside its high-security perimeter fence she could just make out a few military vehicles buzzing around patrolling the area and a number of oil tankers entering and leaving the compound. Two police helicopters were circling over the site, silhou-etted against the sky, like the vultures, waiting for their prey, as the sun began to sink lower.

Laura looked at her watch. It read 3pm.

'God Damn!' she said out loud.

She was so close to her destination, and yet so far. She had managed to grab a cab and fly out from New York to Albuquerque almost immediately, and once there she had even persuaded the last taxi in the rank to take her out to this remote area, all without any major difficulty. But it seems that was the easy bit. Now she was stymied. She looked down at her new white stiletto boots. How on earth was she going to get anywhere near the site, let alone inside the complex, especially when she was wearing these?

She was just trying to work out her options, and beginning to come to the conclusion that she didn't have any, when she heard the hiss and judder of brakes, as two huge oil tankers pulled into the filling station forecourt.

The tankers looked identical, each with the name and bright orange logo of the 'Global Oil' company painted on their sides. But they did not fill up with gas and instead parked away from the pumps. As their drivers got out of their rigs and headed for the diner, Laura overheard their conversation;

'Come on, Sam,' said the thinner of the two drivers, 'If we don't get this load to Los Ammuno before dark, we'll both be out of a job. An' all coz you can't go past lunchtime without filling up that big, fat gut of yours.'

To which Sam replied, 'Chill out Max. 'S' only 'bout three miles from here. This won't take more than a few minutes. An' a promise, a won't order any cherry pie.'

'OK, but mine's on you then!' said Max.

They strolled into the diner, but not without noticing Laura as they passed.

'Hey! What's a lovely lady like you doing in a place like this?' asked Sam with a big cheesy grin.

Laura just glared back at him before they went on inside. She'd always hated this kind of sexist remark.

She watched them through the window. They were the only customers in the cheerless joint. They sat down at one of the formica tables, placing their jackets over the backs of their chairs near the door.

Inside the diner, Max declared, 'I'm off to the John!' He got up and left to visit the restrooms. While he was away, Sam went up to the counter to order.

Seizing her opportunity, Laura sneaked quietly into the cafe, crouching down low beneath the level of the window. She hoped that nobody would notice her as the door creaked open. Fortunately the noise it made could not be heard above the Country and Western music playing loudly on the jukebox and the crash and bang of pots and pans in the kitchen.

She held her breath as she heard Sam calling into the back of the restaurant, before a tired looking woman in her mid thirties appeared, wiping her hands on her faded floral apron. Laura stayed down low and hoped that Sam would take his time, while she edged slowly closer towards his table.

'Well hello pretty lady!' Laura panicked before she realized it was just Sam trying his charms on the waitress. 'Now before I find out what you're doing later, I wonder if you wouldn't mind fetching me a little piece of cherry pie!?'

'One pie!' said the sullen waitress, marking it on his order and making it clear she didn't want the conversation to continue. Sam began to turn away.

'Damn!' thought Laura, she had almost reached Sam's table, but needed him to take longer if she wasn't to be spotted. Then he turned back to the waitress, 'And coffee. Make that two,' he added.

The waitress skulked back into the kitchen, and the minute she turned her back Laura reached over and grabbed Sam's jacket off the back of his chair, and crouched her way quickly back towards the door.

Sam didn't seem to notice her as he sat back down at the table with his back to her, but Laura had only just managed to edge the door open with one foot when she saw Max headed towards her on his way back from the toilet.

'You need to get that door fixed!' he said to the waitress who was starting to come out from behind the counter with the coffees, 'Blowing around in the wind like that.' He stopped to pick some music at the jukebox, and as soon as his eyes were averted Laura slunk quickly back out again, keeping down low as the door creaked noisily shut behind her.

She waited with baited breath, pressed against the wall outside the diner, hoping that nobody had decided to investigate the broken door any further. Luckily for her, Sam was happy eating and Max was now singing along as the jukebox blasted out his favourite tune, the famous rock song, 'It's the final countdown!'

The forecourt stretched out before her, with the oil tankers parked at the far side. Laura made her way over to them, hoping that she didn't draw too much attention to herself in her ridiculous outfit.

She sneaked round to the far side of the tankers and pulled out a set of keys from Sam's jacket pocket. Using the pair of pliers she found in the other pocket, she cut the air valve clean off one of the tyres on Max's rig as she passed.

Then she climbed into Sam's tanker cab. She turned the keys in the ignition. The engine revved. She slammed the truck into gear, and roared off as fast as she could, leaving thick clouds of dust trailing behind.

Meanwhile inside the diner, Sam was too busy scoffing his cherry pie to look out of the window and cheerily assumed it was someone else's truck he heard revving its engine. But Max, returning to his seat from the jukebox, noticed the oil tanker pulling away outside the window.

'Hey Sam!' he said, 'Isn't that your rig out there?'

Sam looked at the truck, then turned to the back of his chair to look for his jacket and keys, but they were gone.

'Holy shit!' he exclaimed, and ran out into the forecourt shouting, 'Hey, you! Come back! That's my rig! Come back here, Goddammit!'

'Don't worry Sam,' said Max, who had run out of the café behind him, 'We'll get 'em. Come on, hop in!' he indicated and they both climbed aboard his rig to chase after Laura, only to discover that one of his tyres had been deflated.

'They let my god dammed tyres down!'

So they didn't stand a hope in hell of catching up with her.

Instead, Max got on his CB radio and called the police. He knew he couldn't get a mobile signal in this area.

Inside Sam's cab, Laura shifted down a gear as she approached a junction in the road at the foot of the hill. There she joined a number of other 'Global Oil' tankers all heading out across the desert towards the Z-lab.

Max got through to a local policeman, who was sat in his patrol car, in a road siding, CB radio in hand, trying hard to hear Max due to poor reception.

'Did you say it was a 'Global Oil' tanker?' he asked.

'Yes, that's right.' Max confirmed.

The policeman sighed a deep sigh as several identical-looking 'Global Oil' tankers sped past in front of him.

Well that's just great! He thought to himself as he put on his siren and flashing lights and drove after them.

He radioed another of his colleagues for back up. His colleague was flying one of the police patrol helicopters when he got hold of him.

'What did you say the registration number was?' he shouted into his radio-set, and listened to the reply.

'OK, I'm onto it, Hank.' The policeman in the helicopter confirmed. From his aerial vantage point he had spotted a whole convoy of oil tankers driving out across the desert in the distance. He banked steeply to the right, in mid-flight, and headed after them.

Laura's tanker was about half way along the line of speeding vehicles. She was sweating profusely, due to a combination of heat and adrenalin, especially in the beaded buckskin jacket she was wearing, designed for colder climes. She could hardly believe that she had stolen a bag from a poor woman in a hospital bed, and now she had helped herself to an oil tanker! Still, the way she saw it, she didn't have a lot of choice.

At that moment she glanced in her left rear view mirror to see the police patrol car beginning to catch up with the convoy. The policeman was driving fast, closing in on the last tanker of the group.

Hearing the sound of chopper blades, she glanced nervously in her right rear view mirror to see the police helicopter coming in on the other side, swooping in low to try to read each vehicle's number plate.

Shit! They were onto her already.

The policeman in his patrol car, on the wrong side of the road, began to overtake each of the tankers one by one, as he too craned his neck trying to read each of their number plates. The convoy just kept going as he hadn't actually flagged any of them down and they were on a tight schedule.

Laura however started to panic as she realized that both the patrol car and the police helicopter were getting almost close enough to read her rear plate, when her tanker suddenly disappeared, along with the rest of the convoy, like a train, into the entrance to a deep tunnel under the mountainside.

The cop car slammed on its brakes just at the last moment, as the road narrowed at the tunnel entrance, and the helicopter pilot had to swerve in mid-air, to avoid crashing into the hillside. It was the entrance to the tunnel Michael had entered that morning, the tunnel through the mountains that led to the Z-lab beyond.

Chapter 96

Emerging from the far end of the tunnel, Laura pulled to a halt, as she took her place in the long line of oil tankers all waiting to get through the checkpoint in the perimeter fence, in order to get into the above-ground section of the complex.

She became increasingly anxious as her vehicle neared the front of the queue. The police car re-appeared at the back of the queue and started working its way along the line of vehicles, checking number plates, and all the while getting nearer to her position, and she could hear the police helicopter hovering menacingly overhead.

A team of guards on the gates was busy checking all the ID cards of the tanker drivers in front, inspecting their vehicles and noting down their number plates. Laura glanced around her cab wondering what to do, when it came to her.

A set of dirty overalls were lying behind the driver's seat. Quickly, she took off her beaded buckskin jacket and pulled them on. She then donned Sam's big jacket instead and put on his 'Global Oil' cap which was lying on the dashboard. Then she smeared her face with an oily rag she found lying on the floor, and popped the rag back inside Sam's thick pockets.

She was almost at the front of the queue when the chief guard was called back into the security booth by one of his juniors. 'It's the police!' shouted the junior guard, as he stood in the doorway holding out the CB mouthpiece.

Apparently the oil tankers were bunched too close together for the helicopter pilot to read their plates and the helicopter now had to return to base to refuel.

The chief guard grabbed the receiver as he entered the booth.

'Could you repeat that registration number?' he yelled, but all he could hear in response was the loud crackling of interference on the line. He held the handset away from his ear to protect his hearing.

Laura meanwhile had broken out in a cold sweat as she pulled up at the very front of the tanker queue. She wished she could cover up not only her face but also her number plate as the chief guard re-emerged from his booth.

'ID please!' he demanded, and Laura held out Sam's 'Global Oil' ID card, with her thumb placed carefully over the photo section.

'Closer please!' he barked and Laura held it out further but with her thumb still strategically placed over the photograph itself.

'I need to see the whole…' said the guard, when he was interrupted by his junior again.

'I'm sorry sir, but it's the big boss on the intercom. He wants to speak to you urgently.'

'Wait here!' the chief guard snapped at Laura and disappeared back into his booth, while one of his colleagues noted down the number on Laura's plates.

Inside the booth, the chief guard held the handset away from his ear again, as Caleb was shouting so loudly even Laura could hear him raging over the intercom; 'I don't give a damn if some idiot's tanker got stolen!' Caleb stormed. 'We ordered plenty of oil, just get it in here, and fast! Hadn't you noticed we've got a deadline to meet here!?'

The chief guard let out a deep sigh as he returned to Laura's tanker and just waved her through.

'Dock at Terminal A, over there.' He pointed her in the right direction. He'd had enough of Caleb's tantrum throwing and didn't give a damn anymore.

Chapter 97

Laura kept her great sigh of relief to herself as she drove on, right into the heart of the Z-lab compound. 'Oil Terminal A' was adjacent to the main domed building in the centre of the complex. Laura was just about to pull up and park at her allocated docking point, when she noticed that it was right beside the main entrance to this central building. Through the glass doors of the entrance she could see that the foyer beyond was manned by a single guard who was sitting behind a security console desk. He was protecting the entrance to some elevator doors just a little further inside the building.

Thinking quickly, Laura intentionally ground her gears and let her tanker shudder to a halt right in front of the entrance. She climbed out of her cab and strolled into the foyer, hoping nobody would notice her inappropriate footwear.

She approached the guard behind the console, and told him, in her best Southern drawl, 'Hey, my rig's broken down. Could you give me a hand to fix it?'

'Sorry lady. Not my job.' replied the guard, 'Ask one of the mechanics out there.' He indicated to the compound outside.

'But I know it's my transmission shaft gone again,' answered Laura, 'I'll need a spare part, and my mobile is out of juice. Could I use your phone to call for assistance?'

Laura was craning her neck as she leaned over his desk. She was trying to look at his bank of CCTV monitors - on one of which she saw Michael, gagged and handcuffed to his chair, with Caleb and his colleagues, down in the underground Control Room below. The guard was beginning to get a little suspicious of Laura's behaviour.

'No lady, you're not supposed to be in here' he said firmly, 'If you want a phone go back to the main entrance.'

Glancing back over her shoulder at the main entrance, Laura could see the cop car now arriving at the front of the tanker queue. She had to think fast.

'Gee, that's a long walk' she said, which it wasn't, '...and I'm desperate for the bathroom. Do you have a Ladies restroom in here I could use first?'

But the guard was having none of it. 'I already told you lady, you're not allowed in here. If you want the bathrooms they're right over there.' He pointed through the glass doors of the entrance to the far side of the compound, beyond her truck.

'Thanks!' *But no thanks,* thought Laura as she exited the foyer.

Back in the Z-lab compound Laura walked round to the far side of her truck, out of sight of the guard. As she made her way back to the driver's cab, her brow was furrowed. She was thinking hard, when she found a packet of cigarettes and a lighter in Sam's jacket pocket. She had an idea.

She looked around furtively to make sure nobody was looking, and pulled out the oily rag she had deposited in the other pocket earlier. Then she used Sam's powerful cigarette lighter to set fire to the rag, before throwing the burning fabric in through the open window of her tanker's cab where it landed on the driver's seat. Then she snuck back along the far side of her truck from the guard, to wait near the rear of the vehicle.

Moments later, the security guard, still sat behind his security console in the foyer, noticed flames leaping in the window of Laura's oil tanker cab, parked just outside his window.

'What the hell!' he exclaimed.

He got up and grabbed a fire extinguisher off the wall as he rushed outside to try to prevent a disaster. He pulled open the door of the cab and began trying to douse the flames, but the fresh gust of wind that then blew through the cab seemed only to make the flames burn higher.

Meanwhile, Laura sneaked back unnoticed into the foyer. She crept behind the guard's security console desk and began urgently scanning his monitor screens.

One of the screens displayed a wonderfully helpful plan view, and another a cross-section layout of the whole complex, both over and underground. Laura studied these maps carefully, taking in the layout of the elevator shafts in particular. She grabbed the security guard's ID swipe-card off the top of his desk, where he had carelessly left it in his hurry, and headed back out the door.

While the guard was still busy trying to extinguish the flames in her cab, she sneaked back, unnoticed, to the rear of her vehicle. There, she detached the tanker's large flexible dispatch hose and dragged it back into the foyer, where she carried it right over to the elevators.

The display panel between the two elevator doors showed that one of the lift carriages was down below and the other up top. Laura also noticed an emergency fire-hammer case mounted to the wall beside the elevator doors.

It read, 'In Case of Fire – Break Glass'

So she did just that. Padding her fist with the long sleeve of Sam's jacket, she smashed the glass and then, as the fire alarm began to go off, she used the fire-hammer to lever open one of the elevator doors – on the shaft where the lift carriage itself was still down below.

Then she opened the nozzle on the tanker's hose-pipe and, as it began to spill oil across the clean white lobby floor, she placed the pipe between the elevator's open doors. She then pulled away the fire-hammer so the elevator doors automatically closed around it, holding the hose-pipe firmly in place as it continued to discharge its oil down into the empty lift shaft.

Laura then used the security guard's stolen swipe-card to open the other elevator. She climbed in and pressed the button. The doors closed and the lift began to descend.

Meanwhile, out at the main entrance gates, the chief guard was just finishing his conversation with the policeman in the patrol car, whilst checking through his colleague's clipboard.

'I just let that one in!' he exclaimed in horror, and dashed into his booth to raise the security alarm, which joined in with the fire alarm, ringing out loud and clear across the whole complex.

Even inside Laura's elevator, the alarms were going off, the emergency wall lights began to flash, and the elevator's digital display lit up with the words,

'Fire!' alternating with 'Security Breach!'.

Meantime, in the compound just outside the entrance to the main building, the foyer guard had almost brought the fire in Laura's tanker cab under control, when the professional firefighters turned up. Only now did he turn around and notice the huge oil hose-pipe coming out of the rear of the tanker and snaking its way through the lobby to the elevator doors. He was absolutely horrified.

Minutes later, Laura's lift arrived at the bottom, and the elevator's electronic voice announced, 'Welcome to Level Z!'

The doors opened and Laura found herself confronted with a whole SWAT team of armed security officers. Dressed in black and sporting bullet-proof jackets and dark-visored safety helmets, they were standing or kneeling in position all around the elevator doors, and all pointing their machine guns straight at her!

The SWAT team leader shouted, 'You are under arrest! Step forward and put your hands on your head!'

Laura obeyed his command and came out quietly with her hands up, while another of the team came forward ready to put some handcuffs on her.

Meanwhile however, just a few yards away, one of the lab-coats who had arrived in front of the doors to other elevator, ready to evacuate the building, pressed the button to ascend. As the doors opened he heard the sound of a large drip. He looked inside the elevator, puzzled to see a couple of big drops of dark, gooey liquid landing on the floor inside the lift carriage.

Hearing this, Laura stepped back into her own elevator carriage. The SWAT team leader shouted 'Stay where you are!' and cocked his gun.

But Laura had stepped back just in time. For at that moment, the roof of the neighbouring lift carriage suddenly collapsed with an almighty crash, under the weight of the tons of gallons of oil piled up on top of it. And as the elevator doors opened completely, a huge torrent of thick, black oil came gushing out into the pristine white underground service corridor.

The SWAT team and lab-coats watched in horror as the huge tide of oil came gushing straight towards them. Some of them, as if by reflex, opened fire into the air, their bullets only just missing Laura, as every member of the team was swept off their feet and carried away down the various side corridors.

As soon as they were gone, Laura re-emerged from her lift carriage and began to wade her way through the oil towards the entrance to the Central Chamber, at the far end of the corridor. Its raised submarine-style pressure door lay temptingly ajar, with the crystal skull just visible in the distance beyond, mounted onto the huge gyroscope in the centre of the chamber.

Laura had finally made it! She'd actually reached the Central Chamber. Now all she had to do was get the skull.

Chapter 98

But just as Laura reached the door a familiar figure emerged out of the shadows before her. She had finally reached the centre of the Z-lab only to be confronted by Caleb, who stepped out of the Central Chamber right in front of her.

He had come to see what all the commotion was. Seeing Laura, he pulled out his gun and pointed it straight at her.

'Some people just don't get the message, do they?!' he snarled. 'Raise your hands. You can't stop the future now, Dr. Shepherd!'

Laura obeyed and put her hands on her head, as Caleb stepped forward into the oil-filled corridor. He looked down at his feet, which were now above their ankles in oil. Hearing a 'click', he looked back up at Laura, only to see that she was now holding Sam's powerful cigarette lighter ablaze in one hand above her head. She had adjusted the flame to full power and locked it off in the 'On' position.

Caleb looked down at his feet again now swilling around and soaking in the oil.

'You wouldn't!' He sounded a little nervous.

'What? You don't think I'm mad enough?!' scowled Laura. 'Release Michael! – and give me the skull!' she demanded.

Immediately beside Caleb were a few steps that led up to the adjoining Control Room, through the open glass door of which a couple of Caleb's security men had just appeared, coming to see what was going on. Caleb lowered his gun and nodded for them to do as Laura said.

The guards in the Control Room brought Michael out towards the door and were just beginning to release him from his cuffs, when one of the recovering SWAT team members came up behind Laura, just as Michael was being un-gagged.

'Laura!' Michael tried to warn her, but it was too late. The SWAT guy grabbed her, like a rugby tackler, and she watched, as if in slow-motion, as the flaming lighter flew from her fingers and began spinning through the air before it headed steadily downwards towards the oil-drenched floor.

Everybody's jaws dropped at the sight, and the thought of what lay in store.

Then, like a goal-keeper in action replay mode, desperate to save the match at any cost, the SWAT team member lunged forward again, throwing himself to the floor. He managed to catch the flaming lighter just before it landed in the oil.

Everyone, at least on Caleb's side, breathed a sigh of relief.

'Well done, young man, you saved the day!' Caleb congratulated the SWAT team member as he got up, sticky with oil, and handed him the lighter.

'The day isn't saved until you stop this experiment!' said Laura firmly.

'Why is it that you two are so determined to spoil the party?' replied Caleb, adopting the mock-weary tone of someone addressing small children.

'The police are on site,' offered Gerry Maddox, Caleb's new assistant, keenly. 'We can have them arrested immediately.'

'This one's due a lengthy spell in a psychiatric institution,' replied Caleb looking at Laura with contempt. 'Throw her on there, and arrange for the helicopter to take her back to the Warnburton Secure Unit as soon as possible!' he commanded despite Laura's protests.

The guards bound Laura's wrists and ankles with heavy-duty electrical insulation tape and threw her into the store room, where she landed heavily on the floor.

It was the same cleaner's store room where they had carried Michael earlier. Laura looked around the room as she struggled to break free from her bonds. She could see plenty of cleaning equipment, but there was obviously no way out, as she heard the guards lock the door firmly behind her, and she was plunged into darkness.

She writhed around helplessly on the floor, like a caterpillar inside a cocoon, but she could not escape her bindings. Try though she did, she was completely unable to break free.

Chapter 99

Caleb meanwhile turned to Michael. 'And as for you,' he was thinking, 'we'll hand you over to the police later, but you never know, you might just come in handy yet.'

Caleb was well aware of the fact that the whole experiment was really thanks to Michael's research and his expertise might still come in useful. Michael had been on the project from the start and if there were any technical hitches he might just be able to help solve them. Besides which, Caleb couldn't help admiring the guy for his sheer determination, if nothing else. 'In fact, I thought you might enjoy a front seat at the show!' he added.

He turned to the guards 'I want him ready before the final countdown!' Michael was re-cuffed and gagged and rough-handled back into the Control Room, where he was deposited back into his chair overlooking the Central Chamber.

With Michael and Laura both now safely recaptured, Caleb climbed back into the Control Room himself and went over to the p.a. system. 'False alarm everybody!' he announced to the whole complex. 'The fire and security breach are under control! That's the end of the emergency!'

Within moments, the alarm system stopped flashing and ringing.

Caleb looked around him, at the rows of scientists and technicians all sitting staring intently at the bank of monitoring screens in front of them, at the vast array of displays and switches on the main panel at the front, and the grand observation window overlooking the central chamber beyond.

He needed to calm himself, to get himself ready for the big adventure that lay ahead. People were counting on him, waiting for him to achieve what he had set out to do today, to push back the boundaries of knowledge, to explore the final frontiers of science and technology. Even the President himself was waiting on the other end of the secure, dedicated phone line now sat on the front desk, the hot line that had been set up especially so that the Commander in Chief could hear the outcome of the big experiment immediately it was complete.

He gazed through the observation window at the crystal skull mounted on the giant gyroscope and marveled at what he and his team had achieved, and with such speed. The mighty steel arms that spanned almost the entire width of the chamber interior, and encircled the skull, looked like the rings of planetary orbits, with the crystal skull itself like a gleaming star at the centre of the galaxy.

This image pleased Caleb. He'd always hankered after new worlds, and now he was about to explore one of his own, a whole new parallel dimension to the universe. It would be a discovery that would change the world even more than Columbus first finding the Americas, a discovery even more profound than mankind's first landing on the moon, for what he and his colleagues were about to do would change human history forever.

Caleb checked an 'oil gauge' display on the panel in front of him, which showed that the tanks were now 'full', and Gerry Maddox, his new Head of Research, came over and confirmed, 'Everything seems to be in order now, sir, and everybody's ready,' so statesman-like, Caleb continued his announcement over the p.a. system.

'It was a vision of a new world that built this great country, and a vision of a new world that is driving us to achieve what we are going to achieve today. If we all stand together we can do anything. So let's stand together.'

'We've got enough oil now. Our fuel cells are charged. We are ready and waiting, ready to begin this new adventure, ready to explore a whole new chapter in the history of this planet, ready to explore a whole new world.

'So stand-by everyone! We're going ahead as planned.'

He looked at his watch. 'Right on schedule. Start the countdown! The future of a whole new world begins today!'

An enormous digital clock inside the Control Room, and another inside the Central Chamber itself, displayed the countdown in large red digits, while a computer-generated voice announced to the whole complex,

'Countdown commencing! Ten minutes to zero-hour.'

Chapter 100

Inside the store room, Laura heard the terrifying announcement. This was it. The final countdown had begun. The end had come, just as predicted in the ancient Mayan calendar. The future was now set in stone.

After all Laura had done, after all the risks she had taken, to decode her daughter's message, to try to save the children of the future before it was too late. It had all come to nothing. Her days, and theirs, would soon end. Laura here alone, on the floor of a cleaners store room, only seconds away from the crystal skull.

The skull was now about to open up a hole in the fabric of space-time, through which the whole planet, the whole universe would be sucked, into a vortex of oblivion.

Inside the Control Room, Michael strained against the cuffs and gag in his chair, while Caleb caught sight of the mess of oil still swilling around in the service corridor outside, and barked at his staff, 'Now somebody get this place cleaned up!' He had to restore order quickly. He couldn't let what had just happened with those two renegades spoil his big day.

Caleb was gratified to see that, within minutes, a couple of Latin American contract cleaners had arrived in the corridor. Complete with their cleaning-equipment carts, they were soon hard at work trying to mop up the oil. One of them started mopping around the door into the store room where Laura was being held.

Inside the store room, Laura wondered what was happening. She could hear the slosh of a mop as the cleaner tried to remove the oil that filled the corridor just outside her door. She strained desperately against the masking tape that bound her, and tried crying out to them for help, but her shouts could not be heard above the sound of the huge generators, as they began firing up, getting ready to send their deadly electronic charge into the crystal skull.

I'm so sorry, Alice, she heard herself say. *I did try to stop the experiment. Believe me I tried, I tried my very best.* But it was no use now, it was over. There was nothing more she could do. She so wished Michael was with her, so that they could spend their last remaining moments on Earth together.

Outside the door, the cleaner had stopped working. A diminutive, elderly figure wearing regulation uniform of white overalls and matching company baseball cap, he seemed to go unnoticed by the team of technicians hurrying to take up their positions for the final countdown. When the cleaner was sure no-one was looking, he pulled out his bunch of keys, and started trying them in the lock.

The next thing Laura knew, the door flew open, the lights came on, and the cleaner stepped into the room. She wondered what on earth was going on as he came up behind her and began to cut her free. But her heart sang with joy as he rolled her over and she could see his face;

'Hunab Ku!' she cried with relief as she recognized the Mayan shaman! 'But how...?' Laura could scarcely believe her eyes as he rushed to untie her.

'Let's just say I have friends in low places.' Laura gave a quizzical frown. '...from a past life,' he added, smiling enigmatically.

In actual fact Hunab Ku had used most of his remaining life savings to fly down from New York to Albuquerque the night before, immediately after Michael's brave disappearance. There he had used his old contacts from his heady days as a contract cleaner, to get himself a new job on the contract for the Z-lab.

'Now hurry!' he whispered as he finally succeeded in cutting her free from her bonds.

At that moment, they heard Caleb's voice announcing over the p.a. system, 'Prepare to seal the chamber!'

Thanking the Mayan shaman profusely, Laura pulled off her high heels and crept back out into the service corridor, where she could see the last few remaining scientists and technicians now leaving the Central Chamber.

As the command team, a select group of scientific experts in white lab-coats, disappeared into the Control Room, Laura dashed down the corridor towards the submarine-style chamber door which was slowly beginning to close.

The team of technicians did not notice her as they were now behind the heavy door pushing it shut. She just managed to get inside before the door slammed-to immediately behind her, and the technicians sealed it shut for pressure, by spinning its huge metal wheel-lock into place.

As the lights above the door began to glow red, the computer-generated voice announced,

'Auto-lock system now engaged.

Commencing power generation and warming up lasers. All systems go. Stand by for final firing in precisely five minutes.'

Chapter 101

Inside the Control Room, Caleb sat down in the master chair, alongside Michael's, facing the chamber. *What a find that skull was. Now let's see what magic it can work for us.* He took a deep breath and sat back. 'Here goes – our doorway into the future!' he announced, his voice filled with excitement and anticipation.

The whole earth seemed to quake as the generators began to roar, and through the observation room window everyone could see the strange mirror-like liquid crystal lower floor of the Central Chamber start flickering with huge arcs of blue-white electric light, like giant forks of lightning spreading out across the surface of a vast underground lake.

Then the inner arm of the gyroscope-like contraption on which the crystal skull was mounted and bolted into place by sparking electrodes started to move, only slowly at first.

Everyone in the Control Room looked on amazed, and Michael aghast, as they saw Laura running across the raised central walkway towards the crystal skull, now lit up at the centre of the chamber on its gently rotating machine.

Michael managed to hook the gag he was wearing over the arm of his chair and pull it off. 'Get her out of there!' he screamed.

'It's too late,' replied Caleb, 'The computer's in control now. There's nothing we can do but stand by and watch.'

Michael gazed on horrified as Laura began to climb off the raised metal walkway onto the slowly moving gyroscope. As it turned her round and round, and even upside down, she started desperately trying to release the skull. But it was firmly bolted into place by the electrodes and she could not release it by hand.

She fumbled inside the large pockets of Sam's jacket and found the pair of pliers she had used earlier. Holding onto the rotating gyroscope now with one hand, she tried to unscrew the bolts with the pair of pliers in the other. But the jaws of the pliers would not open wide enough, and not even by hammering away at the electrodes was she able to release the skull from the grip of the machine.

Meanwhile, the second ring of the gyroscope began to move slowly, and the sleeve of Laura's jacket got caught between the machinery. She watched in horror as her hand was pulled closer and closer to being crushed to a pulp between the gently rotating arms of the machine, as she tried in vain to pull away.

She heard a high-pitched mechanical screeching sound and turned round to see the syringe-like points of the huge laser machines begin to extend and spin like giant dentist's drills, as the computer voice came in,

'Prepare for final test pulse!'

Laura leapt from the gyroscope, just in time! She heard a rip as the arm of Sam's jacket got left behind in the machinery, and she landed hard on the raised metal walkway only moments before the lasers fired a final test pulse at the skull.

There was a buzz and hum of static as the skull was illuminated by the surge of light and electricity passing through it, and the arm of Sam's jacket burst into flames, ignited by one of the mighty laser beams.

As the beams subsided, Laura got to her feet and clambered back onto the gyroscope, but it was beginning to spin faster and faster now, and she was soon flung violently from it, crash landing heavily against the walkway railings, on the far side of the chamber from the Control Room. The computer- generated voice came in again,

'Three minutes to full power generation.

Stand by to commence firing lasers at 25%'

In the Control Room, Michael was beside himself with fear.

'Where's the abort function?' he yelled.

'We didn't have time to install one,' said Caleb, 'The President wanted to make his announcement before Christmas,' he explained.

'I'm sorry, Michael. I really am.' He added quite genuinely.

Chapter 102

Inside the chamber the lasers began to fire with ever increasing frequency and intensity, and as the gyroscope accelerated, one of the scientists watching exclaimed, 'What the hell...?' as he gazed into the chamber.

Everyone in the Control Room turned to see that the crystal skull was starting to expand, its face beginning to distort, as if it were turning to liquid. Clambering to her feet, Laura turned round to see that a small black hole had started to appear inside it.

As the gyroscope spun faster, and the electrodes and lasers powered up even more, the skull continued to grow bigger. The black hole at its centre began to expand and the skull started to suck things towards it, as if some strange almost imperceptible whirlwind or twister had suddenly been unleashed inside the chamber.

Laura's hair began to get pulled towards the skull, and as she looked at it in disbelief, a pen got sucked right out of the top pocket of Sam's jacket she was wearing and started to orbit the skull in the middle of the vast chamber.

As she gazed on in amazement and horror, she herself began to get pulled across the walkway towards the skull, her cheeks beginning to distort slightly with the changing pressure in the room.

She grabbed onto the railing with one hand, to try to resist the pull of the skull, and as she did so, the pair of pliers she was holding got wrenched right out of her other hand and flew into the middle of the chamber, where they joined the pen, now circling round and round the enlarged skull.

Suddenly, a fire extinguisher, which was mounted to the chamber wall behind her, got pulled free from its housing by the powerful electro-magnetic force and increasingly strong wind. Hearing this, Laura turned around to see it flying straight towards her face.

She ducked out of the way only moments before she would have been de-capitated by it. The fire extinguisher flew over her head and whacked into one of the ever faster spinning arms of the gyroscope, bouncing off it before it began to ricochet wildly around the room.

The alarm system went off, the emergency wall lights began to flash, and the whole underground complex began to shake violently.

Back in the Control Room, Caleb was called over to the controls by one of the most senior scientists on the team. 'You need to take a look at this, sir.' His expression was grave as he pointed to a display which read,

'Safety Limits in Violation'.

'My God!' whispered Caleb. 'We're all doomed!' Michael and Laura were right after all. Something had gone seriously wrong. The experiment was fatally flawed, and they were all going to die.

Everyone in the Control Room was immobilized with shock as they stared through the observation window at the black hole now growing inside the crystal skull. The skull had become grossly enlarged, its features having taken on the appearance almost of molten wax. As the big, black hole inside it continued to grow, the eerie computer-voice announced,

'50% laser and electrode power generation.

Two minutes to full power.'

Chapter 103

Inside the chamber Laura was shouting desperately,

'Michael, what do I do?'

But Michael, who could just about still hear her over the intercom, just shook his head and whispered to himself in quiet despair, 'I don't know, Laura. I don't know.'

At that moment, the ricocheting fire extinguisher suddenly burst right through the Control Room window. It made a neat hole before it crashed into Michael's chair, sending him reeling across the room as it knocked him to the floor.

Seeing this, Laura screamed, 'Michael!' and rushed to his aid. But she had to struggle to hold on against the force of the ever-sucking wind, as she tried to make her way across one of the raised metal walkways around the skull.

She had to pass between the gyroscope and one of the firing laser machines to get to the Control Room, timing herself very carefully before dashing between the pulses of its beam.

But as she did so, a huge arc of electricity, buzzing loudly, suddenly rose up through the walkway grating from the electrically charged lower floor, like a massive spark from some giant Van Der Graaf Generator machine.

She dodged out of its way, but not before the side of her upper arm was severely singed by the mighty laser beam.

She reeled the other way, wincing with pain, and almost losing her grip on the railings, before proceeding now with great caution to avoid the giant arcs of electricity now beginning to rear up at random from the liquid crystal below.

She looked anxiously towards her destination.

Inside the Control Room, Michael was lying face down on the floor, still pinned to his chair. As he gradually recovered from the shock of having been thrown across the room, he began struggling to break free of his seat. And as he did so, something fell out of his pocket.

It was Laura's little silver heart-shaped locket. Pulled across the floor by the wind, its chain caught on the arm of his chair, and it lay there sparkling in the light, right in front of his face. Michael stopped to look at it. He could clearly make out the name engraved on it. It read simply, 'Alice'.

Michael had a moment of realization, before he struggled to get back up. Using all his might he strained to break free of the damaged office chair, and its arms finally came away in his cuffed hands.

Grabbing the locket, he staggered over to the p.a. system before anyone could stop him, and shouted to Laura in the Central Chamber, 'I've got it. We need to...'

But at that moment, the p.a. system cut out as its loudspeaker was ripped from the chamber wall by the swirling tornado.

'What?' Laura shouted. But she could not hear his reply from behind the 'bullet-holed' window, above the buzz of electricity and the raging winds.

So she struggled on across the walkway, which was now beginning to shake and judder in response to the swirling winds and the massive amount of power being generated beneath it.

She was finally getting close to the Control Room window, almost near enough to read Michael's lips, when the loudspeaker ricocheted off the gyroscope and slammed into the window right in front of her.

The window cracked into a pattern of tiny pieces so she could no longer see through it. But the force of the wind was now so strong that the window shattered and thousands of glittering shards of glass came flying straight towards her as they were sucked into the centre of the chamber.

Laura grabbed the flying speaker baffle and used it as a shield, just in time! It became embedded with hundreds of shards of glass, some of which protruded right through to her side of the shield.

And now everyone, even inside the Control Room, was having to hang onto whatever solid object they could find to avoid getting sucked into the chamber.

However, with the window now broken, Michael, holding on tight, managed to climb right through it onto the balcony overlooking the central chamber. He kept clinging to the railings as he struggled down the metal staircase to Laura's level.

But just as he reached the bottom of the steps, the upper section of the stairway started to come away from its bolts under the force of the now hurricane-strength winds. This upper section of stairway then collapsed right on top of him, trapping him underneath as it pinned him to the ground.

Finally reaching him, Laura tried unsuccessfully to release him.

'Remember what Alice said,' Michael spoke through gritted teeth as he grimaced in pain, 'We must reverse the experiment!' Laura looked baffled. 'We've got to reverse the circuit that leads to the electrodes!'

'But how?' asked Laura.

'The Control Panel. Over there!' Unable to point, Michael gestured with his shoulders to indicate something on the other side of the chamber.

Laura looked desperately around the chamber in the general direction indicated, when she noticed some thick cables leading to an enclosed metal switch box, mounted high up on the wall on the far side of the chamber. She could just make out the lettering on the box, which read 'Control Panel'.

It suddenly appeared to her as if it were hundreds of miles away, as the computer-generated voice announced,

'75% power generation.

One minute to full power.'

Chapter 104

'But Michael!' she said. She didn't want to abandon him, in this perilous state.

'Go, Laura! Go now!' he shouted and she began to dash back across the chamber.

But as she did so, the central walkway she was trying to run across began to withdraw slowly on its hydraulics, taking her further away from her destination, as the various sections of walkway all started to separate from each other and retract back into the walls.

She had to act fast before the walkways became fatally impossible to cross. She ran as quickly as she could, reaching the end of her section only to be faced with an ever-widening gap. She steadied herself and leapt across the gaping divide. Her heart skipped a beat as a huge arc of electricity rose up, and missed her only by inches.

She just made it to the other side, clinging desperately to the now flimsy-looking railings, when the section of walkway she left behind suddenly collapsed in the hurricane and plunged into the hell-fire below.

She pulled herself up and staggered on to the end of the next section. But just as she was preparing to make the next great leap, the largest outer ring of the gyroscope, which had remained stationary until the walkways had retracted out of its way, suddenly began to spin past right in front of her and she reared back to avoid being hit by it.

She just managed to maintain her footing, and was about to attempt the jump again, when the section of walkway in front of her, that she was about to leap onto, also fell away. She lost her balance and toppled off the edge, only just managing to hang on with one arm as she stared down into the abyss.

She was now dangling from the end of a lone island of collapsing walkway, when the hurricane force winds stepped up another notch and she suddenly found herself hanging horizontally, as the black hole inside the skull tried to pull her in by her feet.

She looked at the bolts that held the walkway in place. To her horror she could see that they were beginning to come lose. With all the shaking and vibration they had started to come away from the wall by a few inches. Then, all of a sudden, they came away completely.

Though it was for less than a second, it felt like an eternity, as Laura felt both she and the walkway to which she was clinging being sucked swiftly in towards the big, black hole and swirl of inner gyroscope blades at the centre of the chamber.

They flew through the air together, but only for a moment. Laura let go of the walkway and grabbed on to the large outer ring of the gyroscope as it spun back round, while the broken section of walkway she had been holding onto flew on in towards the black hole.

She now clung for dear life to the outer ring of the gyroscope as it spun around the chamber.

She flew past the Control Panel a couple of times, still trying to work out how to get to it.

Some distance below the panel was another section of retracted walkway on the far side of the chamber. Timing it very carefully, she waited for the outer ring to spin back round, then, just as she could see the walkway getting closer, she held her breath, gritted her teeth, and let go of the gyroscope – using its centrifugal force to counteract the centripetal pull of the skull.

She grabbed onto the walkway just in time, only moments before the piece of broken walkway she just let go of slammed into the outer ring of the gyroscope, and it snapped, creating a deadly sharp razor edge now spinning round the room.

Meanwhile, the piece of walkway to which she was now clinging, under her extra weight, began gradually un-retracting from its socket in the wall. As a result, Laura's legs started to dangle ever closer to the now sharp 'chopper blades' of the broken outer ring of the gyroscope as it spun past again and again, threatening to cut off her legs each time it spun past.

Using every muscle in her arms, she dragged herself further onto the walkway, seeming to get nowhere, like in a nightmare, where each time she pulled herself forward, the walkway itself got pulled just as far back towards the centre of the room, its near end getting repeatedly sliced shorter by the giant spinning blade.

Then, just as the outer blade of the gyroscope skimmed Laura's leg, drawing blood, the walkway finally reached its full extent, and stopped un-retracting.

Writhing in agony, with one leg now dripping blood, Laura fought the searing pain and dragged herself on. She just managed to reach out and grab onto the thick cables that lead to the Control Panel, running up the wall at the far end of the walkway, only a second before this remnant of walkway too came right off the wall noisily, and flew in to join all the other debris still orbiting the skull in the centre of the chamber.

Now hanging by her arms, Laura began to work her way slowly along the thick cables towards the Control Panel. As they bent and strained under her weight, and her feet dangled near to the spinning blade of the disintegrating gyroscope, she was still faced with the constant hazard of crashing and colliding objects going on all around.

She finally got right alongside the Control Panel, as the computer-generated voice announced,

'30 seconds to zero hour.'

Chapter 105

She reached for the switch box, but she could not remove its outer casing, at least not by hand. She turned around to seek advice from Michael, when a piece of flying glass skimmed by, grazing her cheek. Grimacing with pain, her grip on the cables slackened, but she managed to grab on again with the other hand, when she noticed the pair of pliers from Sam's jacket pocket still spinning round the room, flying past in an orbit nearby.

She reached out for the pliers the next time they came past, but she missed them. They flew right past her fingertips. So she had to start swinging herself on the straining cables to reach out further still. She waited for the pliers to return and swung out again. This time they landed with a painful whack, right into the palm of her hand.

Still hanging on against the howling wind, she used the pliers to unscrew the outer casing of the Control Panel, which promptly flew off, just missing her face, towards the black hole.

She stared into the switch box, gazing at all the various wires inside, completely confused, totally unable to figure out what she was supposed to do with all the mass of circuitry in front of her.

Michael shouted from the other side of the chamber,

'If you cut the red wire it will reverse the circuit, which will reverse the electrodes, and reverse the experiment.'

But Laura could barely hear him for the raging wind. She shouted back, 'What? Which one?'

Michael bellowed, 'Cut the red wire, not the green. If you cut the green one, the power will surge and the whole place'll blow!'

Laura looked at the wires again. Lit up by the flashing red emergency lights inside the chamber, it was absolutely impossible to tell the difference between the red wire and the green. She positioned the jaws of the wire-cutting pliers on either side of one of the wires.

She glanced at the countdown clock on the chamber wall which read, '00.00.05 seconds'.

She closed her eyes and gritted her teeth, whispering under her breath, 'Alice! Please! Help me!'

She was just beginning to close the jaws of the cutters around the wire, when, at the last moment, she hesitated and swiftly cut the other wire instead...

The clock stopped on the reading,
'00.00.01 seconds'.

Chapter 106

But it was OK. Nothing blew.

The whirlwind ceased immediately. All the debris that had been circling the skull crashed to the ground, as everything and everyone fell back to the floor, including the now normal-looking crystal skull. It had melted its bolts, the electrodes that had once held it in place, and now rolled off the gyroscope onto a piece of broken walkway below.

Greatly relieved, everyone clambered slowly to their feet amidst the devastated interior. Scientists and technicians dusted themselves down in the Control Room while Laura slid back down the wall cables and climbed across the debris in the chamber.

'Michael, are you OK?' she yelled.

She picked her way across the wreckage, through the jumble of collapsed walkways, the sheets of metal and sharp blades of the remains of the gyroscope, and picked up the crystal skull as she made her way back towards him.

She reached Michael to find he was still trapped under the collapsed staircase. She tried to move it but was unable to.

'We need help here!' she called out across the chamber.

'You did it, Laura!' said Michael, his face glowing with pride as she knelt down beside him.

'We did it, Michael,' she smiled 'I couldn't have done it without you.'

She reached through the metal bars of the stairway to stroke his face. But Michael was looking right past her, a deep frown engraved into his forehead.

'Oh my God!' he whispered.

'What is it?' Laura turned round to see that a small black hole was still there. In fact, it was still skull-shaped, but now hovering in the air at the centre of the ruined gyroscope, at exactly the same spot where the crystal skull had just been.

It appeared to be some sort of 'wormhole in space-time' and although it had stopped whirl-winding, it was still growing, at an accelerating pace.

'I don't believe it! The hole's still there!' said Michael aghast, 'Only now it's outside the skull.'

At that moment the shaman stepped up to the shattered Control Room window, having used his cleaner's keys to get into the room.

'You have simply reversed the process' he explained. 'Now it is a hole into the past, instead of the future.'

'But it's still growing!' Michael exclaimed.

'Laura,' the shaman continued, 'you must throw the skull into the black hole – back into the past, back to where it came from.'

Laura raised the crystal skull up high above her head and was just about to do as the shaman suggested, when she caught sight of something appearing inside it. It was only the most fleeting glimpse, the most momentary glance, but her face was unmistakable. It was Alice. Her little face looked just like Laura had seen inside the crystal skull back in her office all those weeks ago. Laura hesitated as she gazed at her beautiful little girl.

'But what about Alice? I'll never see her again' she protested.

'Laura, you must let go of it,' said the shaman firmly, 'You can't change the past, but you still have time to save the future.'

Laura just stood there for a moment, frozen in time, not knowing what to do for the best. She looked between the skull in her hand and the black hole which was continuing to grow bigger, beginning to 'warp-in' more and more of the chamber around it.

Michael shouted, 'Just do it, Laura! Quick, before we all get sucked in!'

Laura looked at the skull again to see that the image of Alice had now gone. It had vanished as quickly as it first appeared. Laura spun the skull back round in her hands to try to see her again, but it was to no avail, when she thought she heard Alice's little voice in her head. She was saying,

'You will see me again, mummy. You will see me in the first drop of dew that falls in the spring. You will see me in the butterfly as it opens its wings.'

A lone tear welled in the corner of Laura's eye.

She held the skull close to her chest, and whispered, 'Forgive me, Alice.'

She thought for one moment she heard Alice reply 'You must forgive yourself, mummy. You did everything you could,' but she wondered if perhaps she had imagined it.

'I will always love,' Laura said softly.

Michael shouted again, from his position still trapped beneath the broken stairway, 'For God's sake, Laura, just throw it, or we're all going to die!'

A single tear trickled slowly down the side of Laura's cheek, as she held the skull up between the palms of her hands and kissed it gently and lovingly on the forehead.

'Goodbye my love, Goodbye!' she whispered.

Then she lifted the skull slowly back over her shoulder and threw it, in one long smooth shot, right into the centre of the black hole.

Chapter 107

All of a sudden there was a huge flash of blinding white light, and a whooshing of wind, like a near-silent nuclear explosion. Everyone was thrown back to the floor by the force of the wind and it took some time for their vision to recover from the glare. But as the blurring of their retinas gradually faded and their sight returned to normal, they could see that the black hole had finally gone.

'Thank God it's all over!' Michael sighed.

Slowly recovering from the shock, everyone clambered to their feet once more. A drill sounded behind the locked chamber door before it was forced open by a group of engineers. Laura looked up. She was so grateful they were finally coming to release Michael that she expected to greet them almost with open arms, but instead her eyes were immediately drawn further down the service corridor behind them.

'Oh no!' she whispered in horror.

'What?' Michael turned round, straining his neck to see something terrifying hanging from the damaged suspended ceiling of the service corridor, beyond the chamber door.

It was a large live electrical cable which had been stretched by the force of the hurricane winds which had been sucking it by one end towards the Central Chamber, and had then torn shear, snapped completely when the engineers had forced the door open. As a result, it was now dangling down, sparking wildly, and thrashing around like a giant snake, just above the large pool of oil which was still lying on the service corridor floor.

The enormous weight of the giant cable was gradually pulling down more and more of the suspended ceiling, which was starting to collapse one sectional support at a time, as the cable dropped in stages, getting steadily nearer to the thick, black oil below.

It would be only a matter of minutes before the cable touched and ignited the oil.

'Help! Someone, please, we need help here!' Laura yelled in desperation.

'Quick! Everyone out before it blows!' Michael shouted, and all the scientists and technicians began to run for it, dodging their way past the trashing cable to try to get to the elevators beyond.

'Please Laura, go!' He yelled as the cable pulled down another section of ceiling.

'No Michael, I can't leave you here.'

'Please Laura. Get out of here while you still can!' He insisted.

'I'm not leaving you.'

'You must go!' he admonished her angrily. But she shook her head.

'Please someone help us!' she shouted.

They watched terrified as another sectional support collapsed.

'Help!' Laura hollered at the top of her lungs.

Tears began streaming down her face as the cable dropped steadily nearer to the oil below. She reached through the bars and held Michael's hand.

'I will stay with you to the end,' she said.

They both knew it would be only a matter of moments now before the cable touched and ignited the oil.

Suddenly, two pairs of boots appeared on the walkway beside them. The Mayan shaman and his fellow cleaner had come to lend a hand. Laura leapt to her feet and the three of them put their shoulders into it. Using all the strength they could muster they finally managed to lift the broken section of stairway clear and release Michael from his trap.

They dragged him to his feet.

'Now run! Before it blows!' he said, and they all scrabbled out of the chamber, ducked out of the way of the thrashing cable, and off down the corridor.

They were the last people to enter the already crowded lift, jamming themselves in like sardines in a tin.

Michael pressed the button to ascend, but the elevator was packed way beyond capacity and there was a groaning of cables as the lift carriage began a painfully slow climb. Terrified the lift would not make it, everyone hardly dared breathe. Laura gripped hold of Michael's hand, consumed with regret at the thought that filling the complex with oil had been a terrible, deadly mistake.

All ears were attuned to the inevitable sound they expected to hear from below. Everyone was waiting for that fatal moment when the cable now snaking down from the service corridor ceiling finally landed in the oil, for the deadly inferno that would ensue, for the terrible furnace that would race up the lift shaft and engulf them all. There was a deafening silence in the lift as the passengers all waited and prayed that the carriage would reach the top. You could have heard a pin drop as they all listened for the terrible whooshing sound that would indicate that the oil below had caught fire. It could only be moments away.

But instead they heard only the steady creaking of the elevator cables, and then the carriage shuddered and stopped. It had ground to a halt only half way up the shaft. Everyone took a deep breath, terror-struck at the prospect of the coming repercussions of what was happening below. And then a great sigh of relief as the carriage began to crawl back up the shaft again, but still it was traveling tortuously slowly. Each moment that passed seemed like an eternity as it continued to inch its way up the shaft towards its final destination.

The lift had almost reached the top, when suddenly the lights went out and the lift juddered to a halt again. It took a couple of moments for the implications to dawn even on Michael. A power failure could mean only one thing – a short circuit in the electricity supply. The cable below must have landed in the oil. And then everyone heard it, the explosive burst of the oil as it ignited below.

Chapter 108

They could hear the sound of the fire as it raged beneath, gathering strength and ripping its way through the underground complex. The only thing holding it back from traveling up the lift shaft was a couple of thin metal doors at the bottom that were now bound to be melting. But they were now so near the top daylight was just visible through the crack at the top of their own carriage doors. The upper half of the lift at least had to be above ground level. Michael pressed for the doors to open, but nothing happened. The doors of the lift were jammed.

There were whimpers of fear from within at the prospect that they were all going to be trapped there only to roast to death in the flames. Smoke was beginning to fill the carriage. Asthma sufferers were already coughing and wheezing. Then Michael noticed a fire hammer lying on the floor beneath his feet. It was still where Laura had dropped it earlier. The lift was now filled with thick black smoke and everyone was coughing. Michael squeezed down and picked up the fire hammer, then wedged it between the steel doors. Then as many people as could reach, pulled on the fire hammer, pitching their strength against the doors, which pulled slowly open on one side.

People climbed up and threw themselves out of the lift, tripping over one another as they raced to get out of the lobby. Holding the doors open, Michael and Laura were the last to leave. The lift began to shake violently as it was chased up the shaft by a giant ball of flames rising up from the inferno below.

As Michael and Laura finally let go of the hammer and flew across the lobby, the lift carriage was engulfed in flames, and the whole building that housed it began to catch fire.

Outside in the compound, fire was taking hold everywhere. It even appeared to be spreading towards the oil storage depot. They had to get out of there fast. As they dashed across the compound, it seemed to ignite all around them, as the massive fire raging below sought every route it could to the surface.

Michael's heart was pounding in his chest, his breath coming in gasps as he pushed himself forward, and Laura was temporarily oblivious to the pain in her leg as he helped to pull her along by his side. All they knew was they had to get out of that site before the oil storage depot caught fire.

They sprinted past the tanker with its burned out cab that Laura had started a fire in earlier, and ran past an office block which was now enveloped in flames. Past burning Jeeps and Humvees they went, desperate to get to safety before it was too late.

They could see the perimeter fence in the distance with its now defunct CCTV cameras, arc-lights and razor wire, and the abandoned checkpoint ahead. This was the only means of escape from the coming inferno and it was now within sight. If only they could get there.

They were almost within reach of the gates when there was a near-deafening roar and the oil storage depot burst into a massive fireball of explosions. The terrifying immensity of the blast threw them both sideways and they had to turn their hands and faces away lest the searing heat scorched off their skin.

But the adrenaline is his system drove Michael to his feet again, and he pulled Laura onwards, through the entrance gates, out of the compound and beyond.

They finally staggered to a halt, exhausted. Collapsing onto the desert road beyond the perimeter fence, they turned and gazed back at the whole complex, now engulfed in flames, against the darkening sky.

Regaining her breath, Laura said wistfully, 'The crystal skull. It's gone. I'll never see Alice again.'

Michael took her in his arms. He reached into his pocket and pulled out Laura's little silver heart-shaped locket. He opened it to reveal a photo of the three family members; himself, Laura and Alice all smiling happily on their last beach holiday together the summer before Alice died. It was the same photo Laura kept on her desk at home.

Closing it again, Michael placed the locket gently back around Laura's neck where it glinted in the golden evening light as they both turned away from the site to look at the sunset.

The sun had emerged from behind a cloud and its sinking rays were illuminating the landscape.

'Remember what she said,' Michael said gently.

As Laura noticed the effect of the sunlight on the softly blowing desert grass, she could have sworn she heard Alice's little voice in her head. She was saying,

'You will see me again, Mummy. You will see me in the first drop of dew that falls in the spring. You will see me in the butterfly as it opens its wings.

You will see me in the glimmer of sunlight that ripples across the grass and then loses itself in the twilight.'

They whispered simultaneously 'Alice!'

'It's beautiful' said Michael staring at the grass.

'Yes it is, isn't it?' answered Laura. She even managed a half smile before they turned to one another and kissed. Michael put his loving arms around Laura's shoulders and helped her to her feet. She needed his support now, with her limp.

Caleb lay on the ground nearby and watched them in silence. He saw them both now framed in silhouette as they staggered off into the sunset, with the last few rays of the sinking sun slowly disappearing beneath the horizon behind them.

THE END

Epilogue

As Michael and Laura made their way further along the desert road they came across the other scientists, technicians and staff who had fought their way out of the place that had once been the Z-lab. They stood scattered across the vast expanse of desert. Mute, they stared back at the site being consumed by flames against the blackened sky, before the noise of the roaring inferno was drowned out by the sirens of emergency vehicles as they began to appear on the scene.

Hunab Ku walked silently through the crowd towards Laura and Michael. He had a rucksack thrown over his shoulder, the same one he'd been carrying ever since he turned up unexpectedly at the hospital in New York.

'Come. It is time to go,' he said.

'Where?' asked Laura.

'It's not over yet,' he said, 'Follow me!'

Puzzled, they made their way over the rough desert ground, beyond the emergency vehicles, when Michael and Laura were approached by a tall, glamorous blonde woman, followed by a man in his forties, holding a professional video camera.

'Hi, I'm with Nat Morgan, NBC. We want to tell your story,' she began.

'That's all we need,' groaned Michael.

'But you must tell the world about the crystal skull,' said Hunab Ku. 'The time is right. The skull needs to be in the consciousness of all the peoples of this planet.

You can share with others all I have told you.'

Michael sighed. Laura touched his sleeve.

'No, it's important,' she said, 'I promised Richard Forbes, that we would tell the world about the origins of the crystal skull.'

'But who's going to believe us?' answered Michael. 'The skull's gone. It's in there,' he nodded towards the blazing inferno behind him.

A police chief came over and approached Michael. 'Michael Greenstone, right?'

'Yes.' Michael's heart almost missed a beat.

'And is that Laura Shepherd with you?'

'Er... yes.'

'Good! The press are going to need both of you to make a full statement. They want to know all about that crystal skull.'

Michael was speechless.

'We've set up a facility at the Last Chance Café. I'll drive you there.'

Behind one of the tables at the Café was sat Caleb Price. A few carefully placed drapes had transformed the café into a make-shift news studio.

'It's scientists like Michael Greenstone who make history.' Caleb Price was speaking to the cameras. 'It was his insight, his tenacity and determination against all the odds that meant that today we averted what would have been a global catastrophe.'

As Caleb's interview finished, he got up and shook Michael's hand, and then Laura's. 'I guess I owe you both an apology,' he said.

'Can we move things along?' Nat Morgan asked firmly. 'We want this on the 6 o/clock news'.

Laura and Michael sat down and a little make-up was applied to their exhausted, battle-worn faces, before Michael began.

'The crystal skull is an incredible object,' he said, 'one that challenges the rules by which we make sense of our world. Apart from anything else, it has shown us, with what went on at the Z-lab today, what can happen if you don't have a proper moral, spiritual framework for working with some of the most powerful forces in the universe. What can happen if you don't temper pure science with a bit of commonsense humanity...'

Hunab Ku passed his rucksack to Laura. She wondered what the hell he was doing, handing her a bag in the middle of a press conference. Obviously he had no idea that you didn't do things like that in these circumstances, she thought, about to put it discretely away. But glancing inside, she could hardly believe her eyes.

There inside the rucksack was the crystal skull...

...or rather *a* crystal skull.

She looked at it again. It didn't look quite right. She played it around inside the bag where only she could see it. It seemed to have changed slightly, very subtly.

She was puzzled. She looked at the shaman with a frown.

'I may have forgotten to tell you,' he whispered, 'that my people are the caretakers of one of the other crystal skulls too.'

Laura could scarcely believe her ears.

'In fact, we're going to need your help, to try to find out whose face is on it. So they can help to save us from the next catastrophe that comes to face this world.'

Laura shook her head, but she could hardly help herself from smiling, as she took to centre stage.

'When the crystal skull arrived in my office,' she began, 'I had no idea of what I was dealing with.' Laura opened the rucksack and lifted the new crystal skull onto the table, as Michael and everyone else in the room gasped in disbelief.

'But what we have here is an object that can help to unify the consciousness of humanity, that can help us to ascend to a higher level of functioning as a species. For this object can help to lift us beyond the shallow confines of our own individual lives, and see that we are all a part of something far, far greater than we ever realized before.'

'For this crystal skull can help us to see the connections between each other and between all things. It can help to fill our lives with the light of destiny, the light of knowledge of a deeper, more spiritual purpose that lies within each and every person on this planet.'

'But before I tell you how the crystal skull is here to change our consciousness, to 'change the mind of humanity', I'd like to start by telling you the story of the skull's discovery. Because although the crystal skull was discovered in an ancient Mayan tomb, there is strong evidence to suggest that it was actually created by a much older civilization, a more advanced civilization, a civilization that exists perhaps not even in this physical dimension of our own.'

'But whoever it was that created the crystal skull, they understood the incredible power of quartz crystal as a means of communication between the worlds. They understood that quartz crystal has the potential not only to transform this world technologically, and the power to transform the human race as a species. It has the power to transform each and every one of us as individuals too....'

THE BEGINNING

BOOKS

O is a symbol of the world, of oneness and unity. In different cultures it also means the "eye," symbolizing knowledge and insight. We aim to publish books that are accessible, constructive and that challenge accepted opinion, both that of academia and the "moral majority."

Our books are available in all good English language bookstores worldwide. If you don't see the book on the shelves ask the bookstore to order it for you, quoting the ISBN number and title. Alternatively you can order online (all major online retail sites carry our titles) or contact the distributor in the relevant country, listed on the copyright page.

See our website www.o-books.net for a full list of over 500 titles, growing by 100 a year.

And tune in to myspiritradio.com for our book review radio show, hosted by June-Elleni Laine, where you can listen to the authors discussing their books.

MySpiritRadio